"I couldn't sleep."

Harrison's voice was so low that at first Hannah thought she'd imagined it. But then he was standing there, on her porch.

"Me neither." She shook her head, rising to her feet, tipping her head back so that she could see his eyes. "I'm sorry about earlier. At the house, when I pushed. I was just trying..."

He shook his head, covering her lips with his finger.

"No more talk." Then he bent his head, replacing the finger with his mouth, his lips hard against hers, taking possession. Hannah's stomach lurched as he threaded his fingers through hers, her desire rising as their kiss intensified. She arched against him, wanting more, the thrust of his tongue against hers a promise of things to come.

He lifted his hands, carrying hers with them until her arms were over her head, his body pressing against hers, the bricks from her house cold against her back. His mouth moved, his tongue finding the soft whorl of her ear, and she shivered in response, tipping her head back as he trailed kisses down her neck to the hollow at the base of her throat.

She knew she should stop him, but she didn't want to pull away. The events of the past few days had taken more of a toll than she'd realized. Truth was, she just wanted to forget, to escape into the silent seduction of his kiss...

Raves for Dee Davis's A-Tac Series

DEEP DISCLOSURE

"The bullets are flying in this fast-paced, high-octane, romantic adventure. Don't miss *Deep Disclosure*—it's Dee Davis at her best!"

—Brenda Novak, *New York Times* bestselling author of *In Seconds*

"Davis creates a compelling, entertaining story line, action-packed and full of mystery, suspense, and an unlikely romance. Readers will not be able to put it down; this is a real page-turner."

—*RT Book Reviews*

"Dee Davis brings a pulse-pounding tale of romantic suspense in *Deep Disclosure*...This is the latest in Davis's series about hunky special operatives and the danger surrounding them, and they all continue to bring in the heat and the action."

—*Parkersburg News and Sentinel* (WV)

"*Deep Disclosure* is a fast-paced and taut suspense with passion and excitement all wrapped up into one neat package. The characters are dynamic, and the reader is able to become easily immersed in the story, even though it is the fifth book in the A-Tac Series...a great read!"

—RomRevToday.com

"5 stars! This series is chock full of adventure. I have to say that this one is the best so far. You will never guess who the villain is. This story will keep you on the edge of your seat . . . Ms. Davis brings two not too trusting souls together and shows them how to trust and what love is all about."
—NightOwlReviews.com

DESPERATE DEEDS

"Delightful . . . The perfect weekend or vacation read. The fast-paced story takes you through an intriguing game of cat and mouse as protagonists solve the crime, save the world, and, of course, fall in love."
—*RT Book Reviews*

"Five Stars, Top Pick! This series is fast-paced and action-packed. This book is a keeper. I, for one, cannot wait to see what Ms. Davis will bring us next."
—NightOwlReviews.com

"The characters were charming, the action fast-paced, and the romance hot. This is an author who knows how to pace a book and add conflict." —Bookpleasures.com

DANGEROUS DESIRES

"Rich in dialogue [with] a strong heroine and intricate plot. Full of twists, turns, and near-death encounters, readers will consume this quickly and want more."
—*RT Book Reviews*

"Danger, deception, and desire are the main literary ingredients in Davis's high-adrenaline, highly addictive novel of romantic suspense." —*Chicago Tribune*

"Dee Davis never fails to write exciting, sensuous stories featuring a diversity of strong flawed characters you empathize with. *Dangerous Desires'* pace is perfect, the dialogue clever, and the plotlines are surprising, captivating, and brilliant." —ReadertoReader.com

DARK DECEPTIONS

"High-stakes action and high-impact romance...Dee Davis leaves me breathless."

—Roxanne St. Claire, *New York Times* bestselling author

"Dee Davis always keeps me on edge from start to finish! I read this book in one sitting...a keeper!"

—FreshFiction.com

"Dee Davis sure knows how to nail a romantic suspense. Packed full of tension, action, and romance, this book is a page-turner from beginning to end."

—BookPleasures.com

"An exciting, fast-paced romantic suspense packed with action, adventure, and hot romantic chemistry."

—FictionVixen.com

DEADLY DANCE

ALSO BY DEE DAVIS

Dark Deceptions
Dangerous Desires
Desperate Deeds
Daring (novella)
Deep Disclosure

DEADLY DANCE

DEE DAVIS

FOREVER

NEW YORK BOSTON

Forever
Hachette Book Group
237 Park Avenue
New York, NY 10017

www.HachetteBookGroup.com

Printed in the United States of America

First Edition: April 2012

10 9 8 7 6 5 4 3 2 1

Forever is an imprint of Grand Central Publishing.
The Forever name and logo are trademarks of Hachette Book Group, Inc.

To my brother-in-law, John—the original inspiration for the A-Tac series. And to Harrison Blake, who refused to give up the idea of having his own book.

PROLOGUE

Sunderland College, NY

Sara Lauter looked up from the textbook she'd been reading. The English Industrial Revolution just wasn't holding her attention. Too many other things on her mind. She stretched and looked around the edge of her study carrel. The library was almost empty. Frowning, she checked her watch, surprised to see that it was so late. Almost midnight. The library would be closing in another couple of hours.

With a sigh, she closed the book and gathered her things. She had an early class tomorrow, and her professor wasn't one to tolerate tardiness. Not that Sara had any intention of being late. She'd just have to set an extra alarm. Her roommate was going to love her.

"Hey, babe? You ready to go?" she asked, smiling over at her boyfriend, Anthony Marcuso. He'd been buried in a midterm paper on Keynesian economics. Everyone said the new Econ prof was a major hard-ass. And if this paper was evidence, Sara was inclined to believe it. Tony was spending every spare moment on the thing.

"I can't," he shook his head, his gaze apologetic. "I've still got three sources to verify. And I'm having trouble with the Internet in the dorm. So I'm afraid I'm here for the duration. Paper's due at three tomorrow."

"All right," Sara nodded, reaching out to squeeze his hand. "I won't waste any more time talking. But I'm beat, and I've got an early class, so I'm heading out. Meet you for breakfast?"

"Definitely," he said. "And this weekend, we'll celebrate." He smiled up at her and as usual her heart melted. They hadn't been dating all that long, but somehow, she knew that this was different. Something worth hanging on to.

"I'll call you."

"You can't," she shook her head. "Remember?" She'd lost her cellphone. Left it God knows where, and she hadn't had the chance to replace it yet. "How about we just meet in front of the cafeteria at eight?"

"Perfect," he said, his concentration still on his paper as she bent to drop a kiss on his tousled head and then swung her book bag over her shoulder.

"All right then, I'll see you tomorrow."

She waved at a couple of friends as she headed upstairs to the library's entrance. Built into the side of a hill, most of the building was underground. Which was nice when it came to avoiding distractions. And also the terraced area outside the front doors was a favorite student hangout, with grass-covered hills on both sides making the perfect place to sit and watch passersby.

Outside, the night was crisp, the last remnants of autumn making her think of cider and pumpkins and flag football. Their dorm was currently in second place in the intercampus league. Not that anyone took it that seriously. She pulled her coat closer as she started up the stairs leading to the quad. Passing the Aaron Thomas Academic Center, she noted a light on in an upper-floor window, a professor or grad student working late no doubt. Most students didn't have after-hours access.

Other than the library, the campus was pretty deserted this time of night. Not that she minded. It was kind of nice to be alone with her thoughts. Although she wouldn't have minded if Tony had been along. She passed the Student Center, darkened like the rest of the buildings, and smiled as she thought about their first kiss. Right there under the hanging oak. So called, because legend had it that some revolutionary figure or other had died there. But in modern times, the arching branches were the perfect cover for a stolen kiss.

Despite the fact that most of the buildings were closed, the campus was still bathed in soft light, the fixtures mounted high in the trees. So the squirrels could study at night, was the standing joke. Primarily an insult from the state school across town. But Sara had always found it funny.

Behind her, the bushes rattled, and despite the fact that she had made this trek almost every night since coming to Sunderland, she sped up the pace, suddenly fighting the feeling that someone was following her. She glanced over her shoulder, then sped up even more, her gaze moving automatically to the nearest blue light.

The security station was at the far end of the cafeteria building, the opposite direction from her dorm, but she knew there was another one at the edge of Regan Hall. And besides, she was being silly. Nothing ever happened at Sunderland. It was one of the safest campuses in the state. Her mind was just playing tricks on her. As if to support the idea, the wind gusted, leaves swirling. She smiled to herself, turning the corner, the lights of Varsley Hall just ahead. There were three women's dorms. Varsley, Regan, and Gallant. It was kind of old-fashioned these days to have single-sex housing, but Sara had always liked it.

And besides, there were always ways of getting around the problem if the need arose. Again she smiled, her thoughts turning to Tony, and the endless possibilities their relationship presented. She'd even phoned her mother to tell her that she might have met "the one." A conversation that hadn't gone particularly well, her mother being convinced that marriage before thirty would be a mistake.

Not really a problem since Sara wasn't interested in marriage—but she *was* interested in Tony.

The sound of footsteps broke through her reverie, nervous energy pushing her to move even faster. It was probably just another student, but it was always best to be careful. Off to her left, she could see the shadowy outline of Regan and the faint glow of the blue light. Maybe a hundred feet.

She shot a glance behind her, but there was no one there, the empty sidewalk only serving to ratchet up her worry. Still, there was no point in panicking. She tightened her hold on the book bag, thinking that as weapons went, it probably wasn't lethal, but her biochem book was at least three inches thick.

She reached in her pocket for her keys, wishing she hadn't put off replacing the damn phone, but she hadn't wanted to tell her father. He sort of went ballistic when she lost things. Which, unfortunately, happened a lot. Anyway, she'd definitely take care of it tomorrow, first thing.

The night had grown eerily quiet, but she was only a short distance from the back porch of Regan now. Two minutes and she'd be safely inside. She pulled out her keys, relaxing a little, and then something hit her. Hard. The keys went flying, and a man's arm clamped around her shoulders, his gloved hand covering her mouth as she opened it to scream. Twisting and kicking, she tried to pull free, but he was strong, and a sickly sweet odor filled her nostrils, making her feel woozy.

Chloroform.

Panic crested, along with adrenaline, and she rammed her elbow into the side of her attacker, but he was too strong, and the drug was taking effect. She tried to hold her breath, but even that was too much effort. She felt her strength ebbing as her vision started to cloud, and her last thought was of Tony.

CHAPTER 1

Montreal, Canada

"You guys picking me up all right?" Hannah Marshall asked as she adjusted her short skirt, pulling it firmly down.

"Coming through loud and clear," her boss, Avery Solomon, replied, his voice crackling in her earpiece. "You all set?"

"Good as I'll ever be," Hannah said, sucking in a fortifying breath as she walked across the street toward the five-story office building where she'd arranged to meet Alain DuBois. It was a quarter past eleven, and the street was dark, the surrounding buildings shuttered for the night. The sole streetlamp flickered ominously, and Hannah couldn't help feeling as if she'd been dropped into the middle of a film noir set.

Avery was set up in the building just behind her with Simon Kincaid, A-Tac's newest member. Harrison Blake, the unit's computer guru, was in the adjacent building with Annie Brennon, A-Tac's sharpshooter.

Their target, DuBois, was a high-end antiques dealer who had recently been connected to the Consortium, a secretive arms cartel that was directly responsible for planting a nuclear bomb in lower Manhattan. They had also created a plan to infiltrate A-Tac that had ended with one of the team, Hannah's friend Jason Lawton, losing his life. Add to that the fact that the Consortium had attempted to take out Drake Flynn's wife and sister-in-law, and there was quite a score to settle, with DuBois being their only lead.

Unfortunately, up until now, A-Tac hadn't had any success running DuBois to ground, the man always one step ahead in the chase. So they'd concocted a scheme to pull him into their net. Something that DuBois wouldn't be able to resist. Hannah was posing as a woman who'd recently inherited a large collection of art, including a presumably "lost" painting by Claude Monet.

Le Jardin, reputed to have disappeared during the Second World War, had taken on cult-like status among collectors, experts split on whether the painting actually existed. And the chance to possess the elusive canvas had proved too much of a pull for DuBois, who, despite his desire to remain off the grid, had agreed to a meeting.

The painting Hannah had stowed in her portfolio was actually a forgery. But the artist was very good, an American living in Ireland with a talent for reproducing the masters. There was, of course, some risk that DuBois would connect Hannah with A-Tac, but since she was a background player most of the time, it had seemed worth taking the chance. And besides, in her high heels and designer suit, minus her trademark glasses and streaked hair, she wasn't certain she'd recognize herself.

"The place looks pretty deserted," she said, as she slowed, coming to a stop in the shadows just to the left of the building's front door. "Any sign of life inside?"

"Roger that," Harrison Blake replied. "I've got infrared up and running." Harrison was Jason's replacement. And although she'd never have thought she'd be able to accept anyone else in the position, she had to admit that Harrison was good. And more important, he'd proved himself loyal to the team. Truth was, she liked the man.

"Looks like there are three hot spots," he said. "One in a back office on the second floor. A second on the first floor near the lobby. It's moving, so I'm guessing it's probably the security guard. And the last hot spot is in the corner office on the fourth floor."

"The one where I'm supposed to be meeting DuBois," Hannah responded, stepping deeper into the shadows.

"Yes," Harrison acknowledged, his voice crackling with static. "Annie's in place, but the blinds are drawn, so we haven't been able to establish visual contact other than infrared."

"How about audio?" she asked. "Have you got confirmation that it's DuBois, Simon?"

"I do. There was a phone call about three minutes ago. Confirming an appointment tomorrow. It was definitely him." Simon had taken over as the team's communications officer. He was young, gung-ho, and disarmingly charming. But in truth, Hannah preferred her men a bit more cerebral and definitely more seasoned. Still, Simon's enthusiasm could be contagious.

"Look, if this is going to work," Harrison said, pulling her thoughts back to the task at hand, "you're going to have to get DuBois in front of the window."

"And we're certain Annie can make the shot, even with the blinds down and the window closed?" Hannah asked, even though they'd already discussed the logistics ad nauseam.

"It won't be a problem," Annie's voice assured her. "All I need is for you to get him in place. There'll be a shadow. And you'll give me voice confirmation that it's DuBois." The plan was to tranquilize him. Then Avery and company would move him to a secure location for interrogation. The key was not to tip their hand.

"Okay, people." Avery's voice rang out, his baritone as usual brooking no argument. "Enough talking. If Hannah is late DuBois is going to get suspicious. Or worse, he'll fly the coop."

Hannah nodded, straightened the skirt again, and walked over to the front entrance of the building. After studying a lighted keypad, she typed in the code DuBois had given her. There was a whirring sound followed by a click as the door in front of her unlocked. Feeling a bit like David heading into the lion's den, she pushed open the door and walked into the small lobby of the building.

"There's no one here," she whispered into her com-link. "I'm headed for the elevator."

"Copy that," Harrison said as she pressed the button and the doors slid open. "The guard's over in the next hallway."

"All right then." Avery's voice boomed over the com-link. "It's showtime."

The doors slid shut, and the little elevator lurched as it began the ascent to the fourth floor. A minute or so later and she was walking down the hallway toward the office at the end. Heart pounding, she knocked on the door, surprised when DuBois himself pulled it open.

He was a small man with graying hair, dressed in a tailored suit with a handkerchief tucked in the pocket. His gaze was wary, but there was also a spark of appreciation. Despite herself, Hannah smiled. Maybe the new look had been worth the effort after all.

"You must be Rebecca Andrews," DuBois said, extending his hand, exposing cuff links that were probably worth a year's salary.

"I am," she said, allowing her smile to broaden as she shook his hand. "I appreciate your meeting with me."

"You have the painting?" he asked, his eyes dropping to the portfolio.

"I do." She searched his face for some sign that he recognized her as A-Tac, but his gaze remained politely impersonal as he motioned her inside the office and then closed the door, gesturing to a table near the window.

"You can put it over there."

She placed the portfolio on the table, and after opening it, carefully removed the forged Monet, then stepped back to give him access. There wasn't any way to force him to align with the window, so instead she held her breath as he examined the little painting, praying he'd buy into it long enough to give her time to figure out how to manipulate him into place.

"You've had it authenticated?" he asked, pulling out a jeweler's loupe.

"Yes," she said, reaching back into the portfolio to produce the paperwork. "Charles Avignon. My attorney recommended him." She handed him the file.

"He's one of the best," DuBois agreed, placing the

papers on the table as he continued to examine the painting. "What about provenance?"

"Considering the painting's history, I'm afraid it isn't what it should be. I can prove that my grandfather bought the painting from a dealer in Lucerne in 1956. But there's nothing to attest to the fact that the dealer's acquisition was legitimate."

"That won't present a problem," DuBois said. "There are people who will pay most any price for the painting, with or without provenance. That is, of course, if it is in fact the missing Monet."

"If?" Hannah asked, holding her breath as he frowned down at the canvas.

"Yes," he said, "there are certain anomalies I wouldn't have expected."

"Now you're frightening me, Mr. DuBois." Hannah moved closer, patting the gun tucked into the holster on her thigh.

"I'm sorry." His smile didn't quite reach his eyes, but his tone seemed sincere and Hannah relaxed. "I'm probably just seeing things. The light here is not the best. I'll have to have it tested to be certain."

"I have no problem with that," Hannah said. "As long as you're discreet. I'm sure you can understand why I want to keep the painting off the radar. If it were to go public, then there would most definitely be questions. Questions my family would prefer to avoid."

"I assure you, Ms. Andrews," DuBois said, lowering the loupe, his gaze probing, "my reputation is built on discretion."

"Absolutely," she soothed, trying to figure out a way to get him in front of the window. Time was running out.

"That's why I chose you. Maybe you could show me these so-called anomalies?"

"Of course." His smile this time seemed genuine.

"Could we move into the light?" she asked, answering his smile and nodding at the fluorescent fixture on the ceiling in front of the window. "I'm afraid my untrained eyes need all the help they can get."

"That's totally understandable. It takes years to be able to identify a master." He picked up the painting and carried it over to where she was standing beneath the light. She made a play of looking at the painting as he explained the things that didn't conform with Monet's style.

Heart pounding, she shifted slightly, forcing him to turn his back to the window. "It's really amazing," she said, the words her cue to Annie. "It almost doesn't matter who painted it."

"Yes, well, I suppose in a perfect world that would be true. But in actuality—" DuBois's words were cut short as the window exploded, glass flying through the air like shrapnel. The man's eyes widened for a moment and then he fell to the floor as another volley of bullets strafed the walls.

"What the hell?" Hannah barked into the comlink, hitting the ground, glass cutting into her knees and palms as the gunfire continued.

"It's not us," Avery said, her earpiece crackling to life. "And those sure as hell aren't tranquilizers. The operation's been compromised. What about DuBois?"

"He's down." She twisted to reach over and check his pulse. "Damn it. He's dead." More shots rang out, and she ducked lower as a second wave of glass rained down on her.

"Hannah, get the hell out of there," Harrison's worried voice broke in. "Now."

"I'm working on it," she said, already crawling toward the door. "Have you still got visual on the building?"

"Hang on," he said, his worry carrying over the airwaves. "We're taking fire—" One minute Harrison was there and the next he was gone, her ear filled with the sound of static.

"Harrison?" she called, still inching forward, the glass cutting with every move. "Avery?" She was almost at the door. "Can anyone hear me?"

For a moment, silence stretched almost palpably, and then all hell broke loose again as the gunmen resumed their barrage. Hannah reached for the doorknob, ducking back down as the shooters ricocheted a bullet off it. After a silent count of three, she tried again, this time managing to get the damn thing open.

The hallway outside was quiet, and, fortunately, devoid of windows, but she still had to make her way out of the building. And if A-Tac was taking fire in both positions that meant there had to be more than one group of shooters and that she was well and truly pinned.

Wincing as she straightened, she started for the elevator and then stopped, switching directions as she heard the telltale ding at the end of the hall. Heading for the stairway now, she sprinted forward, her heels and tight skirt impeding her progress. Angrily, she grabbed the hem of the skirt, tearing straight upward until she'd created a slit that allowed her to move more easily.

Then she removed the heels. Christian somebody or other. Madeline and Alexis would have a fit if they knew that Hannah was ditching them. But they were miles away, and, at the moment, the shoes were anything but practical. So with a quick toss, she sent them flying back into the office as she passed, the leather exploding as the motion caused a renewed hail of bullets, red soles spinning as the pumps careened onto the floor.

At least they'd think she was still stuck in the office.

Behind her, she heard the doors to the elevator sliding open and just managed to duck into the stairwell before anyone could see. Painted submarine gray, the stairs were dimly lit, slowing her progress as she made her way down toward the third floor. But before she'd made it halfway, she heard a door below her open and the thud of feet on the stairs.

Damn it all to hell.

She'd have to go up. Risking precious seconds, she stopped to unholster her gun. Better to be ready in case there was a waiting party on the roof. "Anyone out there?" she whispered into the comlink as she took the stairs two at a time.

The silence was damning. Communications must be down. She gritted her teeth as she skidded to a stop, reaching out to grab the doorknob. No way was she going to consider the alternative.

At first, she thought the door was locked, but then it groaned and finally yielded, swinging open to reveal the inky night sky. The sound of footsteps behind her had grown louder. They were close, which meant her window of opportunity was closing. Even if she didn't accept the idea that something had happened to the rest of the team, she was astute enough to know that they weren't going to be able to help her.

She was on her own.

The night was chilly, a hint of winter in the air. She shivered, then moved cautiously across the shadowy rooftop, hoping to gain access to one of the adjacent buildings. But on the left there was a barbed-wire-topped wall, too high for her to scale, and to the right, a gap too wide to jump.

A quick tour of the perimeter proved equally fruitless. There wasn't a fire escape, and the drop down to the ground from both the front and the back would be suicidal. Across the street, she could see the flash of gunfire, which meant that at least for the moment, someone was still alive and kicking.

Clutching her gun, she moved back to the west side of the roof, scouring the windows of the building across the way to try to find some sign that Annie and Harrison were okay. There was no light at all, and as she strained into the silence, no sound of gunfire. Again she assessed her options, hoping that maybe she'd find something she'd missed.

"Hello?" she called into the transmitter. "Anyone there?"

She hadn't expected a response, so was surprised at the rush of disappointment that followed the silence. Behind her, the door to the stairway slammed open. She had company. Spinning around, she got off a couple of shots before diving to the floor of the rooftop, gravel adding new scrapes to her already shredded knees.

If she made it out of this alive, she was never wearing a skirt again. Ever.

She rolled over behind a ventilation cover, and after bracing herself on her elbows, lifted her gun to fire again. It was hard to see in the dark, but there were at least three men. All of them armed. And if there were more, it was possible they were circling around from the back.

If a solution didn't offer itself soon, she was screwed. After firing again in the direction of the advancing men, she popped up, risking exposure for another quick look around the rooftop. But nothing presented itself, and when a bullet whizzed past her ear, she hit the ground again, the masonry in front of her exploding as another round came too close for comfort.

She was trapped with no way out, but she'd damn sure take as many of them with her as possible. Resigned to her fate, she started to push to her feet, but just as she tensed her muscles, the comlink sprang to life.

"Hannah, you there?" It was Harrison, and nothing had ever sounded as good in all her life.

"I'm here," she whispered, "but I'm in a world of trouble. I've got approaching hostiles, limited ammo, and no obvious way out."

"We're on the roof of the building to the west."

"There's no way I can jump the gap," she said, popping up to fire, hoping to at least slow the advance.

"I've got a plan." He sounded so sure of himself, she actually felt a swell of hope. "Just get over here as fast as you can. Annie and I will give you cover."

"Copy that," she said, glancing behind her, trying to make him out in the gloom.

"On my count." Harrison replied, his confidence reassuring. "One . . . two . . . three."

A barrage of bullets rang out, but this time coming from behind her. The men in front slowed, one of them falling, and Hannah didn't wait to see more. Running full out, keeping as low as possible, she maneuvered herself across the roof, sliding to a stop when she reached the two-foot ledge that rimmed the building.

"You've got to be kidding."

Across the way, she could see Harrison, and at intervals, Annie, as she moved to get the best angle on each shot. Spanning the gap between the buildings was an old wooden ladder, the ends precariously planted on each building's edge.

"You can do this," Harrison's voice coaxed in her ear. "It'll be a piece of cake. Just like a—"

"Walk in the park?" Hannah finished for him. "You're out of your mind." She sucked in a breath and climbed up on the ledge. Behind her she could hear footsteps, and a bullet smashed into the masonry at her feet.

"Come on, Hannah. I've seen you deal with worse." Harrison held out a hand, and Hannah stepped onto the ladder, the wood bowing downward with her weight.

"Son of a bitch," she mumbled under her breath as she teetered five floors above the street. She took a hesitant step and then, eyes locked on Harrison and the safety of the other rooftop, she dashed across the groaning ladder. She'd almost made it to the other side when the ladder suddenly shimmied, and a low rumble behind her sent the hairs on her neck into the locked and upright position.

Then all hell broke loose, the office building exploding, the ensuing roar engulfing the night. Behind her, all she could see was a wave of fire coming right at her, and then suddenly the ladder dropped. Panic laced through her as she reached up to grab a rung, the still-cognizant part of her brain registering the fact that somehow the ladder was still attached to the other building.

It was only when she looked up that she realized it

was Harrison, holding the ladder in place through sheer strength of will. "Climb, Hannah," Harrison ordered, the words coming through gritted teeth.

Instinct kicked in, and she scrambled upward, his hand closing around her wrist when she reached the top. Annie appeared over the edge as well. She shot Hannah a quick reassuring look, then shifted her focus up again as a second explosion ripped through the night. Hannah could feel bits of the building as they cut through the fabric of her jacket and skirt.

"I'm going to drop the ladder now," Harrison was saying, his voice barely audible over the din, even with the comlink in her ear. "But you've got to let go first. Then I can pull you up. All right?"

Hannah nodded. The whole world seemed to be shaking with the fury of the blast, but even so, she could feel the ladder shimmying beneath her again. Her heart hammered so loudly it echoed through her head, threatening to swamp all rational thought.

But she'd be damned if she lost the battle now. So, summoning every ounce of willpower she could muster, she let go of the ladder. Harrison's grip tightened as he jerked her upward, the ladder spiraling downward toward the street. In one fluid motion, he pulled her up and over the building's edge to safety.

"You all right?" he asked, his eyes searching hers.

"I'm okay." She nodded, not quite believing the words. "I'm really okay."

"Then we need to get going," Harrison said, helping her to her feet, his arm strong around her waist when her knees threatened to buckle. "Annie?"

"We're safe," Annie said, lowering the rifle as she

waved toward the office building now completely engulfed in flames. "No one could have lived through that."

In the distance, Hannah heard the wail of sirens. "Avery and Simon?" she asked, still leaning against Harrison. "Are they . . ." she trailed off, unable to say the words.

"They're fine," Harrison assured her. "Both in one piece."

She nodded, relief making her giddy. "But I don't understand. Why would the Consortium destroy the building? Kill their own men?"

"Evidence," Annie said. "They wanted to erase any trace of what really happened here."

"DuBois's death?"

"And, conceivably, ours," Annie added, her tone grim. "The magnitude of the blasts and the resulting fire will destroy any chance we might have had to track the source. So it looks like they've won again."

"Except that we're still standing," Harrison said. "That's got to count for something."

CHAPTER 2

Sunderland College, NY

"It's important to understand that gender is different from sexuality," Hannah said, as her gaze swept across her students. "Sexuality concerns the physical and biological differences that distinguish men from women. Cultures construct differences in gender."

"Like in Afghanistan or Iraq?" Ginny Walker asked.

"Yes." Hannah smiled. "But even advanced cultures like ours define genders differently and as a result inequalities are created."

"Like the glass ceiling," Ginny said, rolling her eyes.

"Yeah, but thanks to women like Hillary Clinton, there are cracks," Mia Robertson said, her tone hopeful. Hannah never failed to be amazed by college kids and their idealism.

"Only cracks," Herb Jackson shrugged. "But thanks to Obama the ceiling stayed intact."

The girls turned to frown at Herb, while most of the guys smirked.

"I hardly think you can lay gender inequality at President Obama's feet," Hannah said, her gaze encompassing her students. "He had his own battles to fight. But I do think the 2008 election is a good jumping-off point for our discussion. That and the two essays you'll find in your syllabus." Everyone groaned, and Hannah suppressed a second smile. "Just read them. And we'll talk tomorrow. I think you'll find the material provocative. At least I hope so." She let her gaze settle on Herb. "Remember we're supposed to be one of the enlightened cultures."

The students pushed out of their seats, stuffing books into bags as they headed to their next class. Hannah closed the file holding her notes and blew out a long breath. Every muscle in her body ached. She'd explained away the cuts and bruises with a fall off her bike, determined not to miss a class. Still, the idea of a hot bath and a cold beer appealed on more levels than she cared to admit. But first she had a meeting with her TA and then a debrief with the team beneath the Aaron Thomas Academic Center.

Founded over fifteen years ago by the CIA, the American Tactical Intelligence Command used Sunderland College as a cover, its elite team trained both as academicians and as covert operatives. And quite fittingly, their headquarters were located in a secret command center beneath the building that shared their acronym.

Put simply, yesterday Hannah had been a superspy with the bruises to show for it, and today she was back to arguing with students over gender equality. The best of both worlds as it were. So much for professors who only teach.

Smiling, she walked out of the Fischer Building and

headed across the courtyard to the quad and the social sciences building at the far edge of the campus. The leaves were swirling in the wind, colors still brilliant but fading fast, the crisp smell of autumn filling the air. Hannah hoisted her messenger bag higher on her shoulder and nodded to passing students, her mind turning away from academia to espionage. Or rather the lack thereof.

The Consortium had managed to undermine A-Tac's efforts to uncover them yet again. DuBois was dead, and for all she knew, a bunch of innocents as well, although Harrison had indicated that the building had been more or less empty as she'd walked in. At least that was something. Still, it seemed it was always one step forward and two steps back, but her frantic expedition to the roof had only made her more determined to expose the Consortium and bring it down. For Jason.

She stopped for a moment at the foot of the curving steps that led up to the Snodgrass Building. Named for some forgotten donor, no one actually called it that. Instead, most referred to it as the social sciences building. The three-story brick building had been built in the mid-1800s. Its timeless beauty made it one of the centerpieces of the campus.

But for Hannah, it would always be the place where Emmett had died. She couldn't walk by his office without shuddering. Thinking of what he'd done to Jason—to all of them really. Betrayal was the worst human offense because it came at such high price. Trust broken, possibly forever.

She shook her head and headed up the steps and into the front hallway, angry at herself for letting her thoughts grow maudlin. Better to keep looking forward. Never back. She turned past the great staircase and headed for her office in the back of the building. There were larger offices both upstairs and toward the front, but she'd always preferred the quiet of the back rooms. Less traffic. More peace.

She turned the last corner, grateful to see light spilling into the hallway from her office, the evenings already grown short, and she welcomed the warmth as she walked through the doorway. Her assistant, Tina Richards, was engrossed in a large stack of test papers.

"How was class?" Tina asked, pushing back a strand of red hair as she looked up from her work.

"Split along gender lines as expected," Hannah laughed. "But that should lead to some vigorous discussion." She winced as she dropped her book bag.

"You all right?" Tina asked, her forehead wrinkling with concern. "I heard you had a run-in with your bike."

There was no such thing as a secret at Sunderland. Word traveled quickly. Hannah had always marveled that they'd been able to keep A-Tac so completely under wraps. Although there'd been a couple of close calls over the years.

"I'm fine," she shrugged, negating the gesture with another wince. "Or at least I will be. No real damage. Except maybe to my pride."

"Well, if it helps," Tina said, breaking into a smile, "I brought you some coffee. And not the sludge they serve over at the cafeteria either. This is the real thing. Java Joe's."

"A latte?" Hannah asked, already reaching for the large cup Tina was holding.

"Two shots with foam."

"You're a life saver." Hannah sank into her chair and took a sip, sighing as the warm toasty beverage slid down her throat. "Heaven in a cup. I've no idea what Jasmine's secret is. But she makes a damn good cup of coffee."

Jasmine Washington was a past student who'd never been able to bring herself to leave. So instead, she'd created Java Joe just at the edge of campus. And between her coffee and her scones, she'd changed Hannah's life, along with the rest of the Sunderland population's, for the better.

"I'll say. I can't tell you how many times I've started and ended a day with a caramel macchiato." Tina held up her cup in testament. "It's the only way to get through some of these tests."

"I'm sorry I had to leave them all to you. But I couldn't turn down the opportunity in Montreal."

"No worries. That's what you pay me the big bucks for," Tina said with a laugh.

"Well, maybe not the big bucks." Hannah smiled. "But at least enough for the coffees."

They both sat in silence for a moment, Tina finishing up the paper she'd been working on and Hannah just allowing herself to unwind. Teaching always left her keyed up, but considering that she'd almost taken a full-gainer off a five-story building less than twenty-four hours ago, she figured she deserved a moment to just "be."

"Actually," Tina said, pushing away the stack of papers, "there is something I wanted to talk to you about. It's probably nothing but..."

"What?" Hannah sat forward, her calm evaporating as something in Tina's voice set off inner alarms. "What is it?"

"It's a video I found on my phone. In my email account. It's kind of creepy." She picked up her cell and handed it to Hannah. "It's already cued up, just hit play."

Hannah hit the button, and at first it was almost impossible to make out anything, as the room was so sparsely lit. But after a moment, she began to make sense of the scene. A woman lay on a bed, struggling against the ropes that bound her arms to the headboard. Shadows obscured her face, making it impossible to ID her, but even without being able to fully see her, Hannah could sense her fear.

Seconds ticked by and then someone—a man—brandishing a knife walked into the room, and Hannah could almost feel the woman tensing. There was no sound, but it almost wasn't necessary, the man's actions screaming off the tiny screen, each cut more vile than the last. Bile rose in Hannah's throat, the horror threatening to engulf her. Forcing her finger to work, she hit stop, her attention jerking back to reality. To Tina.

"Who sent this to you?"

"I've no idea." Tina shook her head, eyes wide, clearly as revolted as Hannah had been. "It was just there in my email. At first I thought it was from Princeton. You remember I applied for the Ph.D. program there." She blew out a slow breath, clearly still shaken. "The header said it was from Anderson Wells. He's the recruiter that first talked to me about the program. I figured he had some news. But instead I found," she paused, looking down at the phone again, "*that.*"

"But you don't think it's from him."

"No way. He's a great guy. He'd never send me something like this."

"It's easy enough to hijack an email address." Harrison did it all the time.

"So do you think it's real?" Tina asked, her eyes still on the cell's screen. "I mean, maybe it's just for show." She actually sounded hopeful. "I've heard about people making movies like that."

"I don't know." Hannah shook her head, suppressing a shiver. "It certainly seemed real enough. Do you recognize the woman?"

"No. But then you can't really see her. Or the man. The whole thing is pretty grainy, and it's so dark. Maybe it got sent to me by mistake?"

"At this point, I don't think we can rule anything out. Have you shown anyone else?"

"No." Tina shook her head. "I thought about calling the police, but then I thought that if it was a fake, I'd be over-reacting. So I brought it to you."

"You did the right thing. I've got a friend, Harrison Blake—"

"The new head of the computer science department," Tina said. "I've got a class with him this semester. We all think he's dreamy."

Despite the seriousness of the moment, Hannah smiled. She had to admit Harrison did have a certain charm. "Well, more important, he's really good with things like this. He'll be able to tell us if it's real and quite possibly figure out where it originated."

"And if it's real?"

"Then we'll call in the authorities. But I want you to keep it on the down low for now. All right? If it comes out, you know it'll go viral. Which could be exactly what whoever sent this is hoping for."

Tina nodded, chewing her bottom lip, her eyes back on the phone. "So you'll take it? The phone, I mean?"

"If you can manage without it," Hannah tried for a smile, needing to lighten the mood.

"Yeah, at least for an hour or so." Tina grinned, the resilience of youth coming to her aid. "But after that, I don't know..." She shook her head, still smiling, then sobered. "Seriously, I need to know what this is. What it means. If someone's in trouble, we have to help."

"All things considered, you're looking pretty damn good today," Harrison said as he walked over to where Hannah was waiting for access to A-Tac's inner sanctum.

"I'll take that as a compliment, I think." Hannah smiled up at him as she turned the key to summon the elevator marked "professors only."

"Absolutely. I don't think I could have pulled off what you did and still have made my classes this morning."

"But you were there, too," she said as the elevator doors slid open and they stepped inside. "And you're obviously working today." She nodded at the briefcase he held in his hand.

"Just grading some papers. No classes until tomorrow. And besides, I didn't have to make my way out of a building full of hostiles wearing three-inch heels and a skirt slit to here." He grinned, motioning to his hip as he inserted a second key in the slot behind the Otis elevator sign.

"Well, for the record, I ditched the shoes, and the slit was self-inflicted." She shrugged. "It was the only way I could move in the damn thing."

"That's what's so great about you," he said, as the

elevator lurched downward. "Always resourceful. Got to love a woman who thinks on her feet."

"Two compliments in one day. A girl could get the wrong idea."

His smile turned a little wicked. "Well, they do say that once a person saves your life, you owe them."

Their gazes met as the elevator lurched to a stop, and just for a moment, she let herself get lost in his eyes. Tina was right. Harrison was hot. Tousled brown hair and the half stubble of a beard. Broad shoulders leading to what had to be an equally muscled chest. And judging from last night, arms that could not only pull a woman to safety but also...She shook her head, clearing her thoughts, grateful when the doors slid open.

She was already dealing with two jobs, which meant there wasn't time for anything else, and just because the rest of the team were acting like A-Tac was the latest incarnation of the Love Boat, it didn't mean she had to fall for all that nonsense. Hannah didn't do relationships. The risk of fallout was simply too great.

And besides, Harrison was her friend. He was joking around. Nothing more. She was the one with the runaway libido.

"You okay?" he asked, his hand warm against her shoulder.

"Yeah." She nodded, as she slapped her palm against Aaron Thomas's bust and a door in the far wall of the reception area slid open. "Just a little more out of it than I thought."

"A brush with death has a way of doing that." His gaze had turned somber. "If you need to talk, I'm here."

"Thanks. But I'm fine." Except for the part of her brain

that was still picturing him naked. "I do have something I want you to take a look at though." She reached into her bag for Tina's cellphone. "My grad student found this in her email," she said as they stopped just outside A-Tac's war room, the door leading to the elevator sliding closed behind them. "It's pretty gruesome stuff."

"Gruesome as in?"

"Torture. Murder. I don't know. I'm not even sure it's real. It could even be a student's project. A horror movie or something. But just in case it's not, I was hoping you could work your cyber mojo and figure out what's what. And maybe track down who sent it."

"I take it your student didn't recognize the sender?" he asked, taking the phone from her.

"Well, she did. Or at least she thought so. But she says the guy whose name was on the thing wouldn't have sent her something like this. He's a recruiter for a Ph.D. program she's interested in."

"Sometimes really frightening people hide under perfectly normal guises."

"You're preaching to the choir." Hannah nodded. "That's why I brought it to you. And I told Tina to keep it to herself until you had the chance to look at it."

"Did you tell her you were bringing it to me?"

"You *are* the head of the IT department. Seemed logical. Besides, she thinks you're dreamy."

"Smart girl," he said, his eyes crinkling as he smiled down at her. "Now if I can just convince her mentor."

Hannah's heart literally did a stutter step, and she ducked her head, making a play of adjusting her glasses. When the hell had she turned into a simpering coed?

"You guys going to stand here making eyes at each

other or do you want to maybe come inside and get this show on the road?" Simon's voice echoed in her ears, and Hannah felt her face go red.

Running a hand through her hair, she nodded and slipped past them both, taking a seat next to Annie, who was already at the war room conference table. Across from them sat Drake Flynn, the unit's extraction expert. He'd flown in just this morning from California.

"So how are the newlyweds?" Hannah asked, ignoring Harrison as he walked into the room with Simon. There was nothing to be embarrassed about. They'd just been kidding around, and she'd let her stupid pheromones get the better of her.

"I wouldn't really know," Drake was saying, blue eyes twinkling. "Except for meals and some long walks on the beach, they really haven't left their bedroom all that much."

Drake's brother Tucker and his new wife, Alexis, had rented a house in Laguna Beach for some much-needed downtime after Alexis's near miss with the Consortium. Drake and his wife, Madeline, had been visiting when the news about Alain DuBois had surfaced.

"Did Madeline come back with you?" Annie asked.

"No. I figured with the house under construction she's better off in California. And nocturnal activities notwithstanding, I think Tucker and Alexis are happy to have her there. Besides, she's been having a time with morning sickness so flying cross-country wasn't exactly on her top ten list of fun things to do."

"This too shall pass," Annie said with a shudder. "I thought I was never going to be able to eat again the first two months with Adam. But then I hit month three and started eating everything that wasn't nailed down. It's a wonder I didn't gain five hundred pounds."

"Well, I'll be happy when we get to that stage. Right now, she's pretty damn miserable."

Across the table, Simon cleared his throat, looking decidedly uncomfortable.

"Welcome to the new and improved A-Tac." Harrison laughed, making a face over the top of his laptop screen as he settled behind the computer. "Not exactly the kind of conversation you expected when you signed on, huh?"

"No worries," Annie said with a calculated smile. "We may talk domestic bliss, but as you saw in Montreal, we're more than capable of rising to a challenge."

"Which brings us to the case at hand," Avery said, cutting through the small talk as he walked to the front of the room. "I just got off the phone with Tyler, and it's just as we expected. The bomb site is practically clean." Tyler Hanson was the team's ordnance expert. She'd flown in to Montreal with Nash Brennon, A-Tac's second in command and Annie's husband, almost before the dust had begun to settle. Annie was heading back after the debrief to help them.

"So we've got nothing?" Simon asked, his impatience showing.

"I wouldn't say that. Tyler and Nash still have a long way to go with their investigation. And based on the coordination it took to instigate a blast that size while at the same time taking out DuBois, I think we can safely assume that the whole thing had to have been planned well in advance."

"Which means it was a set-up." Annie frowned. "They were trying to take us out along with DuBois."

"Whoever the hell these people are, they've definitely got a hard-on for A-Tac," Drake said, leaning forward so that his elbows rested on the table, his fingers steepled. "Hell, they can't seem to get enough of us."

"Maybe they're just trying to keep us occupied," Annie suggested. "I mean, the whole thing with Jason was just a ploy to keep us from the real threat—the bomb in Manhattan. Maybe this is the same kind of thing."

"They knew we were looking for DuBois," Hannah said, picking up the thread. "So why not just kill him outright? Why risk us getting to him first? There had to be another reason to pull us into it."

"Like maybe to wipe us out?" Simon queried, lips quirking.

"It wouldn't have been all of us," Harrison said, his eyes on his computer screen, as usual multi-tasking.

"Harrison's right," Drake agreed. "So while I'm fairly certain our deaths would have been icing on the cake, I still think there had to be something more."

"Hannah, you're the expert with intel. Are you seeing anything in the chatter to indicate that there's something else going on?" Avery asked.

"Nothing concrete, no." Hannah shook her head. "But that doesn't mean anything. The Consortium has made an art form out of staying under the radar."

"Well, we can't ignore the fact that they seem intent on taking us down," Annie said. "One way or the other."

"I think that's a given." Avery paused, his gaze encompassing them all. "But until we can identify these people, the only thing we can do is to monitor the situation, keep our eyes open, and hope that Tyler's investigation turns up a lead."

"And in the meantime?" Simon asked, clearly wanting more.

"It's business as usual. But make no mistake, we're going to run these people to ground, and we're going to eliminate them. After all, that's what we do best."

CHAPTER 3

"So I'm assuming you found something?" Hannah said as she walked into A-Tac's computer room.

"Sort of." Harrison shrugged, looking up from the computer where he and Avery were studying the video. Hannah had stopped in the doorway, confusion playing across her face. She was dressed in jeans and a T-shirt, her hair in more disarray than usual, her glasses glinting in the light. "Thanks for coming so quickly."

"I thought we'd agreed to keep this between us until we knew what was going on."

"We did," Harrison said, lifting a hand in apology, truly sorry to have broken her confidence, "but that was before Avery shared his news."

"There's been a potential complication," Avery said, swiveling his chair so that he was facing Hannah. "We've got a coed missing."

"Damn," Hannah said, crossing the room to take a seat beside Harrison. "Who is it?"

"A junior named Sara Lauter. History major." Avery nodded to Harrison, who pulled a picture up on the computer monitor mounted on the wall above his desk. The girl smiled out from the screen as if she had no cares in the world.

Memories surfaced, but Harrison pushed the thoughts aside. There was nothing yet to indicate that the girl and the video were related. Still, he couldn't control the wash of dread, and prayed it wasn't a premonition.

"I know her," Hannah said, pulling Harrison from his thoughts. "At least a little. She was in a seminar I taught last year on nineteenth-century political philosophy. If memory serves, she was the kind of person you want in class. Smart and studious. So how long has she been missing?"

"Not quite twenty-four hours. She was supposed to meet her boyfriend for breakfast and never showed." Avery sat back, looking up at the screen. "College policy states that we wait forty-eight hours before launching an investigation, but under the circumstances, it seemed prudent to at least consider the possibility that the video is tied in to her disappearance."

"It's an awful thought," Hannah sighed, "but I don't see how we can avoid it."

"I knew you'd agree," Harrison said with a somber nod. "That's why when Avery told me about the missing girl, I figured bringing him into the loop was essential." Actually, he'd had an uncanny sense of déjà vu, but he wasn't ready to share that with the team yet. Not even Hannah, who'd been his right hand since coming on board with A-Tac.

"So have you found anything?" she asked, eyes

narrowing as she studied him. "You look like you're holding something back."

"I'm not. I swear," he said, shaken by the fact that she'd nearly read his mind. "This kind of thing is tricky. I've tried to trace the email and all I've been able to do is verify that it wasn't sent from Princeton. Avery's got Simon tracking down the dude who supposedly sent it to your TA, but I'm pretty sure he'll just corroborate what we already know."

"What about authenticity? Have you been able to verify that the mpeg wasn't just a prank?" she asked.

"I haven't been able to prove it technically, but I sent it to a friend of mine who used to be a profiler with the FBI, and she thinks it may be real. The quality of the video, the lighting, even the staging or lack thereof—all of it suggests that whoever filmed this wasn't worrying overmuch about presentation. It's more like he was intent on making a record of the act."

"Well, if it is real, and if this is our student..." Hannah trailed off, her gaze moving from the photograph to the two of them.

"Then we have a very real problem. And a ticking clock," Avery said.

"So what do we do now? Bring in the police?" Hannah asked.

"No. They have the same forty-eight-hour rule we do. And besides, Langley doesn't want to risk exposure by bringing in the locals. So for now we're on our own, which considering our resources isn't such a bad thing. And worst case, we'll call for help from the FBI."

"My old stomping grounds," Harrison said, his mind still on the missing girl.

"When's the last time anyone saw Sara?" Hannah asked with a frown.

"Last night. She was in the library studying and left sometime just after midnight. No one's seen her since."

"What about her roommate?" Harrison queried as he continued to type on his keyboard. "Wasn't she concerned?"

"Haven't been able to run her to ground either," Avery said. "Which made it seem as if they'd possibly gone off somewhere together. Although Tony swears they weren't really friends."

"Tony?" Hannah asked, her attention drawn back to the screen as Harrison switched back to the video, the grainy film work just as horrifying the second time.

"Marcuso," Avery said, his gaze also on the screen above them. "The boyfriend. Another junior. Econ major."

"Any reason to believe he might have something to do with the disappearance?" Harrison frowned as he magnified the picture on the monitor, the enlarged scene seeming even more ominous.

"Not so far. But we need to talk to him again. And the roommate, along with your TA, Hannah."

"Tina? She's definitely not a part of this, if that's what you're thinking. I saw her reaction to the video. She was as horrified as I was. There's no faking that kind of thing. Besides, if she were involved, she wouldn't have brought the video to me."

"She's not a suspect," Avery said. "Hell, we don't even know that we have a crime. But someone sent the video to her for a reason. And if we can figure that out, maybe it'll lead us to a source. Maybe there's a connection between Tina and Sara."

"Or the boyfriend," Hannah agreed. "I can talk to Tina."

"I was actually thinking you and Harrison could handle all the interviews since you're already running point on this. And to be honest, the two of you are more likely to get them to be honest with you. Being called before the dean of students tends to be off-putting."

"Especially when said dean is you." Harrison laughed, and then sobered as he adjusted the settings on his computer.

"I assume you're running some kind of diagnostics program," Avery said. "Any way to use it to ID the girl in the footage?"

"Not definitively, no." Harrison shook his head, entering something into the computer. "Basically the computer will use the algorithms in the program to try and fill in the details in the scene that are obliterated by the shadows, including the woman's face. It'll just be conjecture, of course, based on calculations the computer makes, but it might move us a step closer to figuring out if the woman in the video is in fact Sara Lauter. Sort of like an electronic sketch artist."

"So it's working now, right?" Hannah asked, pointing up at the screen.

"Yeah. It's filling in details. You can already see that the perimeter of the frame is coming into clearer focus."

"Over there in the corner, by the bed," Hannah said, squinting now as she studied the screen. "It looks like there's a chair. Can you freeze it and enlarge that area?"

"Sure," Harrison said, his gaze following hers as he moused over to the area in question, stopping the video as he enlarged the frame. "Holy shit," he whispered, as the object on the chair became clear.

The T-shirt was torn, almost shredded, but the insignia was still clear. The orange imprint bold against the black shirt. Harrison maneuvered the computer, pulling the image into sharper focus. The words printed on the shirt jumped off the screen—"Property of Sunderland College."

"Thanks for agreeing to see us," Hannah said, smiling as the young man took a seat across from Harrison in the Fischer Building's conference room. Tony Marcuso had the look of a typical college student—sweatshirt, jeans, overstuffed backpack. Although now that she thought about it, that pretty much described her most days as well.

She and Harrison had spent another hour or so going over the video, trying to find something in it that might lead to a location, or maybe an identification. Harrison's program had made the images clearer, but even though there were certain features that Sara and the woman in the video had in common, it was far from conclusive.

"Have you found Sara?" Tony asked, his face tightening with worry.

"I'm sorry," Harrison said, his voice kind. "We haven't. But we do have a few more questions for you. Nine times out of ten when someone goes missing like this, there's a reasonable explanation. Were you and Sara having any problems? An argument maybe?"

"No way," he shook his head. "I swear. Everything was great. We haven't really been dating that long, but our connection was pretty intense, if that makes sense. It's just kind of like I knew she was the one. And I think she feels the same way about me." Doubt chased across his face, competing with the worry, but Hannah had the feeling he meant everything he was saying.

"So you can't think of any reason why she might have run off?" Hannah probed. They'd already talked with Tina, trying to make some sense of her role in all of this. But nothing had come of that conversation either. Tina didn't even know Sara. So if there was a connection between the two women, it was clearly obscure.

"None at all," Tony said. "She was fine at the library. She only left because she had an early class and wanted to get some sleep. We agreed to meet for breakfast and that was the last . . . I saw of her." His voice cracked on the last few words, emotion clearly getting the best of him.

"What was her cellphone number?" Harrison asked, typing something into his computer. "We might be able to trace her through phone activity."

"It's 555-867-5209," he said, "but it won't do you any good. She lost it last week. She didn't want to tell her father. So she's been doing without. Oh, God, I need to call her parents."

"Why don't you let us handle that, Tony." Hannah reached across the table to cover the boy's hand with hers. "We need to be sure that we have all the facts before we contact them. There's no point in scaring them needlessly."

"But I'm telling you, Sara wouldn't just disappear like this. She's not like that."

"Well, until we have evidence to the contrary," she sucked in a breath, exchanging a glance with Harrison, "I have to assume otherwise. It's like we said, nine times out of ten—"

"I know. I heard you the first time. But there's no way she just ran off."

"What about her roommate? Maybe she went somewhere with her?"

"No way, she'd never go anywhere with Stephanie."

"Are you saying they didn't get along?" Harrison pushed back from his computer, eyeing the boy over the top of it.

"That'd be an understatement," he sighed, raking his fingers through his hair. "The two of them were a mismatch from the beginning. The only reason Sara was rooming with her was because she didn't want to pay for a single."

"I'm sorry, I'm not following," Hannah said, looking down at the papers she had in front of her. "According to my notes, Sara requested Stephanie."

"Yeah, but it was because Stephanie had been through a rough time. You remember the girl killed in the car wreck last year?"

"Donna something," Hannah frowned.

"Right. Donna Mayer. Well, Stephanie was her roommate. And it was really tough on her. So Sara moved in with her for the last couple of months. She was just being nice. And then when Stephanie asked her to room with her this year, Sara couldn't say no. But Stephanie's not the easiest person to be around." He shrugged, looking apologetic. "I'm not saying there's anything wrong with her. Just that she and Sara aren't a good fit. And they're certainly not friends."

"So there's no chance she'd have gone off with her on some kind of road trip," Harrison concluded.

"None at all."

"So is there any chance Stephanie could have done something to Sara?" Harrison asked. "Were their problems big enough to have caused that kind of over-reaction?"

"No," Tony shook his head. "Stephanie's a little weird,

but she's nothing like that. I mean, the worst thing she's ever done is unplug the clock so that the alarm doesn't go off. She's not a morning person, and Sara is." Despite the seriousness of the situation, he smiled. "Sara's one of those people who wakes up happy. Stephanie can't even function without a couple cups of coffee. So like I said, they just don't mesh. But Sara manages. Mainly by spending most of her time away from the room. With me. Or in the library. It's just easier that way."

"Okay, so how about we look at this from another angle," Hannah said. "Has Sara said or done anything to make you think she was unhappy? Or maybe had a problem with someone else. Someone you haven't mentioned."

He paused for a minute, clearly considering the question. Harrison was back to typing.

"I can't think of anyone. I wish I could. I just know something's really wrong, or I'd have heard from her. Phone or no phone. She's not thoughtless like that. That's why I love her." His eyes widened with the declaration. "Wow. I can't believe I said it out loud. But I do love her, you know? And I need for you to believe that she wouldn't just disappear like this. Something's really wrong. I know it."

Harrison paused for a moment, then clearly making a decision, turned his computer around. "Does anything about this place look familiar?" The still was from the video, but there was no sign of the girl on the bed or her tormentor.

Tony leaned forward, squinting as he studied the picture. "I don't think so. Should it be?"

"No." Harrison shook his head. "I was just hoping maybe it had some significance."

"You think Sara's there?" He nodded toward the screen. "Why would you think that?"

Harrison turned to Hannah, and she nodded. There was a risk in showing him, but everything in her gut told her that whatever the hell was going on, Tony wasn't involved in Sara's disappearance. Harrison hit a key and the picture dissolved into another. This time featuring the woman on the bed.

"Oh, my God," Tony gasped, pain lacing through his voice, "is that Sara?"

"You tell me," Harrison said.

Hannah reached out to squeeze the boy's shoulder, offering what comfort she could. "I know this is hard, but you know her better than anyone."

Tony studied the still for another minute or so and then shook his head. "I don't know. I can't tell. It's too grainy. The hair is right. And maybe the height. But I honestly can't say for sure." He clenched a fist, a muscle in his jaw twitching. "What the hell is this? Where did it come from?"

"It's a video that we found on the web," Harrison said, improvising a little bit. "We're not even sure it's depicting something real. But in light of Sara's disappearance, we have to consider the option that this could be her."

"Can you tell me what she was wearing the night she disappeared?" Hannah asked gently as Harrison turned the computer back around.

Tony was still staring at the back of the computer, the image clearly burned into his brain. For a moment, she thought he hadn't heard her, then he turned, his shoulders straightening as he pulled it together. "She was wearing jeans. The kind that come already torn. She thought they were really cool. And a jacket. You know, like photo-journalists wear."

"A flak jacket?" Hannah prompted.

"No, more like the kind with lots of pockets. Like in Africa."

"A safari jacket," Hannah nodded as Harrison typed. "What color?"

"Greenish. Um...khaki, I guess."

"And underneath the jacket?"

He shook his head, rubbing his forehead. "Gosh, I feel like such a jerk, but I can't remember. I should know what she was wearing."

"Just take a deep breath and think. You're dealing with a lot right now." Hannah shot a glance at Harrison, who was watching Tony, his eyes full of sympathy.

Tony nodded and closed his eyes, his forehead wrinkling as he concentrated. "No. I'm sorry. I just don't remember. Just the jacket." Tony's face turned ashen. "Oh, my God. The woman you showed me—was she wearing a jacket like Sara's?"

"No," Harrison said, trying to reassure the kid. There was no point in scaring him any more than necessary. At least not until they'd found something solid. "It'll just help us to find her if we know what she was wearing."

"So you believe what I'm telling you? That Sara wouldn't just leave without letting me know."

"We're treating this very seriously, Tony. And I promise you, if we find anything concrete, you'll be the first to know. But in the meantime, you need to keep quiet about this. If something has happened to Sara, the worst thing that can happen is for the news to get out before we understand what we're dealing with. Do you understand?"

He nodded, emotions playing across his face. "I just need you to find her. Before something awful happens." His eyes strayed to the computer again. "The woman in the pictures—she's in real trouble. And if there's any chance that could be Sara..."

"We're going to find her," Hannah said, even as Harrison signaled her to be quiet. She knew it wasn't professional. That it was an empty promise. But she couldn't help but respond to the pain in Tony's eyes. One thing was definitely clear—he loved Sara. And Hannah just wanted to give him something to hold on to.

CHAPTER 4

It seems like every time I move a step forward I wind up hitting a brick wall." Harrison pushed away from his computer with a sigh.

They'd adjourned to Hannah's house after their meetings with Tina and Tony, the goal to try to trace the video to its source and/or to figure out where the hell it had been shot. But so far, no luck; every lead had fizzled. Whoever was pulling the strings was good at hiding their tracks.

"Sounds to me like you're mixing your metaphors," Hannah said. "Besides, I've heard you say a thousand times that this kind of thing takes time."

"True enough," he agreed, looking at her over the top of his computer. It was amazing how easy it was to be with Hannah. He hadn't really had a friend like her since Madison.

Of course, he and Madison were still friends. Hell, he was probably officially still a member of Last Chance. But for now at least, it suited him better to stick with

A-Tac. Besides, Madison had Gabriel. And no matter how close they'd been, husband trumped best friend every time. Especially when said friend was a male.

He shook his head and glanced over at the clock on the mantel and wished he hadn't. It was almost midnight. "Problem is," he said, pulling his attention away from the past to the matter at hand, "we don't have time. Not if that girl is really in trouble. You know as well as I do that the first twenty-four hours are crucial."

"I do. And it makes me sick to think what might be happening to her. But we can't force the answers. So maybe what we need is a break." She pushed up from the chair at the table where she'd been working. "That way we'll be able to come back at it with fresh eyes. I could make us some coffee."

"Actually I could use a beer." Hannah had a weakness for English bitter and usually had a well-stocked refrigerator. "Any chance of a choice brew?"

"Absolutely. Owen just brought me some Samuel Smith," she said, already heading for the kitchen. Owen, an Englishman, was Tyler's husband. He was currently working with Homeland Security, but he still made the occasional trip back to the home country, and Harrison knew that Hannah had a standing order for beer.

Harrison followed, allowing his gaze to wander around the room. Like Hannah herself, the house was unique. Full of offbeat artwork and bright colors, it felt homey but still somehow empty. There were no photographs or personal memorabilia. Nothing that gave any hint of Hannah's life before A-Tac.

Although it wasn't unusual for people in their line of work to come from places they'd just as soon forget, he still found himself curious about Hannah's life. Crazy thought. Probably stemmed from their close call the other night. Almost dying had a way of bringing people together.

Or maybe it was the outfit. That skirt had been mouth-wateringly short and tight. And although he wasn't interested in relationships, he wasn't a eunuch either, and even in light of their dire circumstances—or maybe because of them—Hannah had looked pretty damn fine.

"You want it in a glass?" Hannah asked, rear end sticking out from behind the refrigerator door. "The only downside to having English beer delivered is that it has to come in a bottle." She straightened up, two bottles in hand, as he perched himself on a barstool at the breakfast counter. "So? Bottle or glass?"

"I know it's very pedestrian, but I grew up drinking Lone Star in a bottle."

"Bottle it is." She removed the top and handed it to him. "And just for the record, I like Texas beers. Particularly Shiner Bock."

"Ah, a girl with an open mind. I like that. So when were you in Texas?" The question was an honest one, but he found himself hoping for something to fill in the blanks of her past.

"We worked an operation with DEA a few years back. Trying to stop a Mexican drug cartel. We were based in Laredo." She hopped up onto the counter opposite him and took a long swig of beer.

"Not a hell of a lot else to do in Laredo except drink."

"Yeah, and I learned pretty fast that tequila wasn't the best choice. That stuff has a wicked kick."

"And usually about two beats after you've decided it won't affect you." He laughed, memories stirring.

"Sounds like you have personal experience with the stuff." Hannah tipped her head to the side, eyeing him through blue-rimmed glasses, the kitchen light playing on the magenta streaks in her hair.

"Not in a really long time. But when I was in college, I had a bad night. Some buddies and I decided to throw a party. And stupidly, I volunteered to play bartender. Rule was that every time someone had a shot, I had to have a shot, too. You can just imagine."

"Oh, God, makes me sick just thinking about it. I take it you took your duties seriously." She smiled, suppressing a laugh.

"Very seriously. And of course, as we just said, the most deadly thing about tequila is that it doesn't hit you right away. So when a bunch of us decided to go see a movie, I was more than game. *Apocalypse Now* was showing at the student union on campus. Part of some seventies film festival. So we went."

"Uh oh."

"Got it in one," he smiled, remembering. "We went into the theater, and I remember the opening. You know the fan blades going around above Martin Sheen's head, the sound swelling."

"Yeah." She nodded, sipping from her bottle. "It turns into the sound of a hovering helicopter, right?"

"Exactly. Anyway, the motion made me sort of sick so I made my way to the bathroom, and next thing I know, I'm waking up over the toilet bowl, and the credits of the movie are rolling."

"Oh, my God." She was laughing out loud now. "It's a three-hour movie."

"Suffice it to say, I haven't had tequila since. Just

thinking of it gives me the shudders. And Bree was really pissed because she had to leave her friends and take me home."

"Bree?" Hannah queried, her fingers picking at the label on the bottle.

"My sister," Harrison said, just the mention of her name sobering him. "She was at the movie, too. Saw me and my condition and swooped in to take me back to my dorm room. Probably a good thing in hindsight as I was still pretty drunk, even after crashing in the john. But I didn't think so at the time, which made it that much more difficult for her. Anyway, point is, I learned my lesson when it comes to tequila." He kept his voice light, praying that she wouldn't probe any further about his sister. It was just easier to keep the past separate from his life now.

"Well, my story isn't as spectacular," she said, her lips curling into a smile, "but it does begin with what I thought was a clear-headed game of pool. I leaned over the table to make a bank shot, and the next thing I remember, Jason and Nash were, literally, carrying me back to the hotel where we were staying. Needless to say, I still haven't lived it down. So I can truly sympathize."

Most women he knew wouldn't have been able to keep themselves from digging for more information. But not Hannah.

"I guess everyone has stories like ours."

"If they've ever drunk tequila." She leaned back, propping bare feet on the adjacent counter. "So after college you went to the FBI, right?"

He nodded, taking another sip from the bottle to order his thoughts. "I thought I could make a difference."

"And did you?"

"Not as much as I'd hoped," he shrugged. "Sometimes the bad guys win the day no matter what you do."

"Only you can't look at it that way," she said, "or it'll eat you alive. Jason always said it was about winning battles. And that the war might be never-ending, but that there were moments. The important thing is to celebrate the victories no matter how small rather than letting the losses weigh you down."

"It's good advice. And I suppose that's why I'm still here." He shrugged and hopped up. "Another round?" Hannah nodded, and he walked over to the refrigerator. "You and Jason were close. I could see that even in the short time I had with the two of you together. Was it ever something more?" He wasn't sure why he asked the question. There was no question that Jason had been in love with Lara. But still he couldn't help but wonder.

"Me and Jason?" she asked, clearly surprised as he handed her a beer. "No. Never. With him, it was always Lara."

"And with you?" Harrison asked, wondering if the beer was going to his head.

"I don't have time for relationships. At least not that kind. Jason was my friend. And I'll miss him until the day I die. But there was never anything more. On either side."

"I'm sorry," Harrison said, raising his hands in defense. "I shouldn't have asked. I'm just being nosy."

"It's a fair question." Hannah shrugged. "I know I talk about him all the time. I still wake up in the middle of the night wanting to call him about something, and it takes a moment to realize that he's not there. And even more strange, I thought it would be easier with Lara gone. But it's not. It's only made it harder somehow. As if in seeing her and talking to her, I was still somehow in touch with Jason. Stupid, right?"

"Not at all," he assured her. "When we care about someone—no matter the context—and then we lose that person, I think it's sort of like a part of us dies, too. And we want it back. That's perfectly normal." He paused, realizing the danger of the ground they were treading. "Or at least that's what they kept telling us at Quantico."

"That's right. I forgot," she said, fortunately following his conversational lead. "You worked with the serial killer unit, didn't you? That must have been horrific."

"More than you can possibly know."

"And now all of this with Sara. It must be bringing up all kinds of memories." She sounded so caring he almost told her the truth.

Almost.

"You have no idea."

She studied him for a moment and then nodded. "I can't imagine dealing with that kind of thing day in and day out. I guess it's not surprising you moved on. And now thanks to A-Tac, you're potentially right back in the middle of it."

"Well, we don't know that for sure. There's still the possibility that Sara's disappearance and the video are unrelated."

"But you don't believe that, do you?" she asked, shoving her glasses farther up onto her nose as she opened the beer he'd handed her.

"No," he shook his head, wishing it weren't the truth. "I don't."

"Which means that you think Sara's already dead,"

Hannah said, putting voice to the words he couldn't bring himself to say.

"We don't know that either. And for now at least, we've got to keep operating as if we can still help her. And the best thing we can do now is get back to work." He pushed off the stool as Hannah's cellphone started to ring.

Pulling it from her pocket, she answered, nodded as she listened to the conversation on the other side, and then flipped the phone shut again.

"What?" Harrison asked, his mind running through the possibilities.

"That was Avery," she said. "They've found Sara's roommate, Stephanie."

Regan Hall was the newest women's dorm on campus. Which meant the 1940s. So not exactly "new." But still it boasted larger rooms and better bathroom facilities. And though there was fierce loyalty to all the dorms, Regan was the most popular by far.

Stephanie Blackwell sat at the table in the Regan dining room, her hands clasped tightly together as she watched Harrison and Hannah. "I swear to you I had nothing to do with Sara's disappearance. I'm sure Tony told you, we barely talk."

"So where have you been?" Harrison asked. He was standing by the window, hand braced on the frame.

"I went home," Stephanie said, her voice trembling. "My mother's been sick, and they put her in the hospital. I wanted to be there. You can call my dad or the hospital."

"It's okay," Hannah said, careful to keep her voice reassuring. "We're not the police. We're just trying to find Sara."

"Well, I don't know where she is. I haven't seen her since yesterday morning just before I left."

"And was there anything wrong? Had she been acting strangely? Like something was bothering her maybe?"

"No," Stephanie shook her head. "It was the opposite actually. She was really happy. It was Tony."

"I thought you didn't talk," Hannah queried, more to keep the conversation going than because she thought Stephanie had anything to do with Sara's disappearance.

"I said we weren't close, but we do still live together. And I have eyes. Obviously I saw Tony coming and going. And she spent a lot of nights in his dorm room. I had to cover if her parents called."

Hannah listened for any sign of jealousy. But except for a trace of resignation there seemed to be no malice. "So as far as you know, there was no reason for her to run off."

"Even if there were, she wouldn't do it. She's the overly responsible type, you know? She'd never just disappear. She'd tell somebody. Just not me."

"So who were her friends? Besides Tony, I mean. Who would she have confided in?"

"I don't know," Stephanie shook her head. "I truly don't. She's friends with pretty much everyone in the dorm."

"Has anything unusual happened?" Harrison asked. "Something out of place. Mail, email. Or maybe someone nosing around?"

"No," Stephanie shook her head. "I don't think so." She paused, a little frown marking her concentration. "Wait. There was something. An email, I think. Or maybe a podcast or an online post of some kind. Whatever it was, she found it on her computer."

Harrison and Hannah exchanged a glance, the hair on Hannah's arms rising. "So it could have been an mpeg?"

"I don't know what that is."

"It's a computer suffix denoting a video."

"Yeah, maybe...I don't really know for sure. She didn't want to talk about it. I just remember that she thought it was really weird. She said she was going to take it to Tony."

"When was this?" Harrison probed.

"I don't know, a day ago, maybe two."

"Can you walk us through it? You'd be surprised at what you might remember." Harrison moved over to the table, perching on the edge, his proximity meant to reassure her. "And anything you can tell us will be helpful."

"I can try," Stephanie said with a faint smile, her eyes locked on his. "Sara was sitting at her desk, and the computer beeped. She opened whatever it was and then frowned, clearly confused. I asked what was going on, and she said it was nothing and that she was going to talk to Tony. Then she left. I figured it was just something on Facebook."

"So the last time you saw her was yesterday morning?" Harrison asked.

"Yes. Right before I left for home. She was on her way out the door—heading for class."

"And there's nothing in the room to indicate she got home. No books or anything that would indicate she made it back to the room from the library?"

"Nothing." Stephanie shook her head, and this time she sounded positive. "She always carried everything in this big messenger bag. You know, the canvas kind you carry over your shoulder. And it's definitely not in the room."

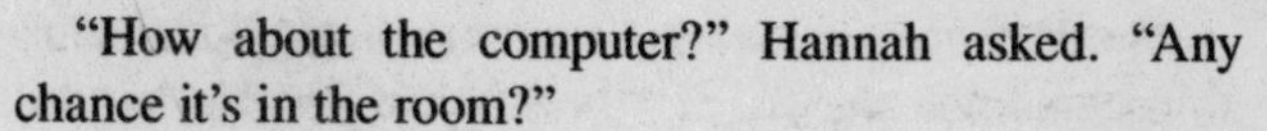

"How about the computer?" Hannah asked. "Any chance it's in the room?"

"No. And I actually checked. She's got one of those notebooks, and she carries it with her everywhere—in the bag. She never goes anywhere without it."

"Makes sense," Harrison said. "But it was worth asking." He smiled at her, and for the first time since they'd walked into the room, she relaxed, giving him a timid smile, a dimple playing at the corner of her mouth.

"You've really been a lot of help, Stephanie," he continued. "And we just have one more thing we need to run by you. That okay?"

Despite the gravity of the situation, Hannah swallowed her own smile. Obviously Harrison had chosen to play the good cop.

Stephanie nodded. "I want to help. Really, I do."

"Okay, then I need for you to look at this photograph and see if you recognize anything about it." Harrison handed her his cell, the still of the bedroom from the video on the screen minus the man and woman.

Stephanie studied it and then shook her head. "I've never seen this place. Is it important?"

"We don't know," Harrison said. "We're not even sure there's a connection. We're just trying to follow all possible leads. So nothing rings a bell?"

She moved the phone so that it was in direct light, her eyes on the screen. "No. I'm sorry." She looked up at him, frowning, her eyes full of apology.

"No worries." Harrison blew out a breath and reached for the phone. "It was a long shot, anyway."

"Wait a minute," Stephanie held out her hand, reaching for the phone. "Is there any way to enlarge the picture?"

"Sure," Harrison said, his gaze locking with Hannah's as he enlarged the frame. "Is this better?" He handed Stephanie the phone again.

"Yeah." She nodded, as she squinted at the screen. "I don't know if it helps, but isn't that Sapphire Lake just outside the window?" The lake was about five miles from Sunderland and a popular student hangout.

"I'll admit it looks like water," Harrison said, shifting so that he could see better. "But there's no reason to believe that it's our lake."

Hannah and Stephanie shook their heads in unison.

"You haven't been here long enough," Hannah said. "Sapphire Lake got its name for a reason. The water is saturated with a unique blend of minerals. They turn it a really deep blue. There's nothing quite like it."

"So have either of you seen a building that could house this room?" Harrison asked, still looking at the photo. "A farmhouse, an old warehouse? Something?"

"No." Stephanie shook her head. "It's in a state forest. There aren't many buildings."

Hannah nodded to concur.

"Okay, so what about this—I know it's hard to see, but is there anything about the area outside the window that gives a clue as to where on the lake it might be?"

"I don't see anything that looks familiar," Stephanie said. "I mean you can only see a tiny snippet of the water, and it's a really big lake."

"I'd say at least five or six miles from end to end," Hannah agreed. "But at least it's something."

"And you think it might help you find Sara?" Stephanie asked, worry making her sound much younger.

"It's definitely a start," Harrison said, smiling across

at her. "We're really grateful for your help." He reached out to shake her hand, and she looked up at him with the blind adoration only the young can achieve.

"And I promise to get back to you as soon as we know anything," Hannah added.

She nodded, looked quickly at Hannah and then back to Harrison, and then turned to go.

"Hang on," Harrison said, as Stephanie turned back to him. "One more question. Do you remember what Sara was wearing the morning she left?"

Stephanie frowned, then smiled. "Yeah. This I do know. She was wearing jeans and a shirt. Mine, actually. She hadn't done laundry. It was a Sunderland T-shirt. Black with orange writing that said 'Property of Sunderland.'"

CHAPTER 5

The scene was overly bright, despite the fact that it was nearly three in the morning. Local police cars were lined up in the rutted lane that fronted the old building, lights flashing a garish red. Harrison killed the engine and was out of the car almost before it stopped, heart pounding as he made his way past the requisite crime scene tape, a halfhearted effort to contain access to the site. In truth, there was nothing to contain, the out-of-the way house surrounded by the twisted cedars and rocky inclines that marked the Texas Hill country.

He flashed his FBI credentials at a policeman standing guard on the front walk and then stopped on the weather-beaten porch as his partner Madison emerged from inside. With an unbidden intake of breath, he waited.

"It's her," Madison said, her eyes dark with emotion.

"Is she…"

"Yeah. ME says maybe as long as twelve hours. They'll know more when they get the body back to the lab."

His stomach threatened revolt, but he started forward anyway, determined to get to her even though it made no sense. He'd arrived too late to be of any help. Hell, even with all his training, all his connections, he hadn't been able to make the difference. He hadn't been able to find her in time. But he still needed to see her, if for no other reason than to prove that this was real.

Brianna was dead.

"No," Madison whispered, her hand on his arm preventing forward motion. "You don't want to go in there. You don't want your last memory to be..." She swallowed, a shudder rippling across her frame.

"She's my sister, Madison. I don't have a choice." He shook off her hand and stepped inside the little house. The living room looked almost quaint, but he ignored the homespun comfort and headed down the hall to the room in the back where the forensic techs were hard at work, their bright lights cutting across the shadowed hallway with a garish glow.

The harsh metallic smell of blood filled the room. And even though the odor wasn't something new, it still made his skin crawl and his gut clench. There were bloodstains on the bed, the spatter on the wall behind the headboard looking like some kind of macabre painting. A piece of rope had fallen to the floor, the hemp also stained with blood. But despite the signs of violence, there was no body.

"Where is she?" Harrison asked, his voice sounding overly loud against the forced hush within the room.

Tracy Braxton, the ME, blinked once, her chocolate eyes taking a moment to focus as she pulled herself from her train of thought. "She's downstairs. In the basement. But you don't want to go down there, Harrison." Like Madison, she was trying to protect him. He knew that. Knew also that she was probably right. But he didn't have a choice. Bree was a part of him.

Exactly two minutes older, he'd always been quick to remind people that he was the eldest sibling. But in truth, Bree had been the wise one, the calming influence that tamed his wilder instincts. He'd been the one who'd walked the razor's edge. And she'd always been there, waiting until he'd needed her to rescue him—mostly from himself.

And now, the one time she'd truly needed him…

With an apologetic shrug to Tracy, he turned and made his way back down the hallway to the cellar door. In his haste, he'd missed it the first time, the faint light from below barely visible at the top of the stairs.

As in the bedroom, the first thing that hit him was the smell. And he stopped for a moment, reaching inside for strength. Then with a slow exhalation, he made his way to the bottom of the stairs, nodding at a uniform and again flashing his credentials, before making his way to the back of the brick-lined room.

It was cold. Colder than he'd have thought considering it was spring. Like a grave. He pushed aside the thought and turned the corner, walking into the little alcove that marked the center of activity, his mind revolting at the sight before him. She was naked, strung up by the arms, her position reminiscent of ancient crucifixion. The disrespect was evident not just in the horrific way she'd been left to die, but in the carvings on her skin. Each cut, surgically precise, was accentuated with a trail of dried blood, the garish result making her look more like a battered doll than a human being.

His sister. Bree.

White-hot rage ripped through him, the pain doubled by the feeling of impotence. Nothing he'd done had mattered. He hadn't been fast enough. And now the bastard behind this…this carnage was out there somewhere, waiting to do it all over again.

He reached up to touch her face, ignoring the tech trying to shoo him away, praying that somehow he'd wake up and find it all a dream. His fingers touched the cold flesh of her cheek, and her eyes fluttered open, the condemnation there shattering his heart.

"Why didn't you come?" she asked, her brownish-green eyes the exact mirror of his, the anguish reflected there sucking the breath from his body.

He opened his mouth, but there were no words, and still she held his gaze, imploring him, condemning him. "I believed in you," she whispered, and then slowly the life began to fade. He screamed her name, trying to pull her back to him. To will her to life.

"Harrison."

The voice pulled him from sleep, relief making him giddy.

"Bree." He reached out and grabbed her, his fingers digging into her arms. "You're all right. You're really okay."

"Harrison. Wake up."

And then it hit him. As it had a thousand times before. Bree was dead and gone. He hadn't saved her then, and he couldn't save her now. Disoriented, he fought against the last remnants of the dream—the sensory memory as strong now as it had been all those years ago in Texas.

"Harrison," the voice called again, and this time reality surfaced. It was Hannah. His eyes flickered open, and her face swam into view. "It's okay," she whispered. "It was just a dream." She was leaning over him, concern stretched tight across her face.

The room came into focus. He was in Hannah's house on the sofa. They'd been working late, trying to find the place at the lake. He must have fallen asleep. The events of the day had clearly brought on the nightmare, and he was gripping her arms as if there were no tomorrow.

"Oh, my God," he said, releasing her. "I'm so sorry. Did I hurt you?"

"No," she said, as she rubbed her arm, the action negating the words. "I'm fine. It's you I'm worried about." She sat down next to him. "You were calling for someone. Your sister, I think."

He blew out a breath, still trying to assimilate his thoughts. "I'm sorry. I didn't mean to scare you." He'd never had the dream when someone else was present. And now, he wasn't sure how much to share. He trusted Hannah, but he liked the idea of his past staying just that.

Except that with Sara's disappearance, past and present seemed to be set on a collision course, every nerve in his body screaming that history was repeating itself.

"You didn't scare me," Hannah said, reaching over to

brush the hair out of his face, the gesture soothing in its simplicity. "I was just worried." She searched his face. "Do you want to tell me about it?"

He didn't. And yet, he couldn't seem to stop the words. "You were right. The dream was about my sister. Bree was murdered."

"Oh, God, Harrison, I..." Hannah trailed off, her eyes filling with tears. "I can't imagine."

"It was a long time ago."

"Yes, but that kind of thing never goes away. And all this stuff with Sara Lauter, it's bringing it all back."

He nodded. "After it first happened, I had the dream almost every night."

"Sometimes the mind just needs an outlet." She talked as if she really understood. "A way to cope."

"Yeah, I guess. But I can think of more productive ways to deal."

"I don't know." She shook her head. "Sometimes it's just easier to put it in abstract."

"Believe me, this dream is anything but abstract. It's like I'm there, experiencing it all over again." He tried, but couldn't contain a shudder, his body still drenched with sweat.

Hannah waited, and he realized she wasn't going to press. This was his chance to pull away. To keep his secrets. But suddenly, sitting here with her, he realized he didn't want to deal with it all alone. He wanted to talk about it. Because it was Hannah.

"Brianna was my ground wire. She was the one who always cleaned up my messes when we were young."

"Was she older than you?"

"No. That honor goes to me. By two minutes," he

paused, looking down at her hands. "We were twins. She was my best friend."

"So what happened?" Hannah asked, her voice gentle.

"It was a serial killer. The press dubbed him the cyber killer because he always sent his victims an email. The first one was simply a warning. The rest mentioned the names of the previous victims..." he trailed off, images of Bree filling his head.

Hannah reached for his hand, her fingers giving him strength. "So this happened while you were at the FBI?"

"Yeah. I was two years in. But I wasn't on the case. It had been assigned to someone else. Hell, I didn't even know the bastard existed until he took my sister. He was a real piece of work. A sadistic son of a bitch that tortured his victims before killing them. I can't even imagine what it must have been like."

"And you shouldn't have to. If nothing else, Bree wouldn't want that."

"Yes, but if I'd been better at my job, if I'd done something differently, maybe I could have gotten to her in time."

"You know as well as I do that once someone's been abducted the odds are against finding them alive. No matter who is working the case. Besides, I know you, Harrison. And I'm certain that you did everything humanly possible to help your sister. But that's the hard part. Sometimes no matter how much we try, it still isn't enough."

"I know you're right, but it's a little more difficult to accept. Bree was always there for me. And yet when she needed me most, I let her down. And because of that she died."

"She died because some sick son of a bitch took her. He's responsible, Harrison, not you." She squeezed her hand, her gaze holding his. "You can't blame yourself for your sister's death."

"I wish it was that easy." He tried for a smile but missed by a mile. "Anyway, it was a long time ago. And I've moved on. It's just this thing with Sara and the video. It's bringing it back."

"So did you ever catch the guy?"

"No." He shook his head. "And not for lack of trying. We really got close a couple of times. But never enough to figure out for certain who he was."

"So how many victims were there?" Hannah asked.

"There were five altogether. Bree was the third. They were spread in and around Austin, Texas. The killing ritual was the same, and the victims were all twenty-something, brunette, and single. We never found anything else to tie them together. Except for the emails, and we discovered that pretty late in the game."

"So were the emails sent beforehand?"

"Actually almost simultaneously. That's why we missed them at first. The women were taken about the same time that the emails arrived. Sort of a cyber-version of 'gotcha.' Almost as if he were gloating."

"You said there were five. I'm no expert on serial killings, but unless they're stopped, don't people like that typically keep going?" She was still holding his hand, and although the horror of the dream had faded, he found he had no desire to break the contact.

"It varies. There are a lot of things that play into

something like that. Sometimes killers fulfill the fantasy and let it go. Sometimes external forces keep them from continuing. And sometimes they change their MO, and so we think they've stopped, but in fact they haven't. Anyway, this guy just dropped off the map after victim number five. And despite our efforts, the trail went cold."

"And so you left the FBI."

He was surprised that she'd put it together, but then he should have expected it, he supposed. Hannah was nothing if not astute.

"I'm just following the time line," she said, by way of explanation, pulling her hand free to hold it up in apology. "And I know you worked for Phoenix, right? John Brighton's company."

"Yes. They were doing cutting-edge stuff with computers. Developing tools and databases for law enforcement agencies at all levels. There was a new program, correlating data on serial killers."

"And you thought maybe you'd be able to use it to help identify Brianna's killer."

"That was the plan. But even with that kind of sophisticated analysis, the guy was still a ghost. And then Madison, my old partner at the FBI, called me in to work on the task force."

"And you figured there was nothing more you could do at Phoenix so you left. It must have been hard to let go."

"Oh, I haven't let it go. It's always there with me. Waiting. Look, I'm sorry you had to listen to all of this." He pulled free and pushed to his feet. "I didn't mean to dump all my crap on you."

"Hey," she said, coming to stand beside him, "that's what friends are for."

She was inches away from him. So close he could feel the rise and fall of her breasts as she breathed. He reached out a hand to cup her face, his gaze moving across the curve of her cheek and the ripe swelling of her lips.

She really was a beautiful woman. And the amazing thing about her was that she had absolutely no idea. Always hiding behind a pair of glasses and the wild streak of colors in her hair. A mixture of fearless and guarded, she'd intrigued him from the beginning, but it wasn't until just now that he'd realized how very much he'd come to depend on her.

She swallowed nervously, the skin on her throat rippling with the action. He wanted to kiss it. To follow the smooth skin to the valley between her breasts. To taste her nipples and feel them bud beneath his tongue. Just the thought made his body grow hard. Desire rose, hot and insistent, as he closed the distance between them, wanting nothing more than to feel her moving beneath him.

Hannah tilted her head back, her eyes closing as he slanted his mouth over hers, his lips taking possession. His mind emptied, everything that had been bothering him gone in the wake of the heat of her tongue moving against his. All he wanted now was to bury himself inside her and forget—at least for a little while.

He slid his hands to her hips, pulling her closer and then closer still. She moaned as his fingers began to explore, sliding under her shirt to caress her skin, moving in slow circles as he deepened the kiss, his tongue thrusting, each stroke mirroring his rising need.

Then a harsh insistent buzzing cut through the

pheromone-induced haze, breaking the spell, and they sprang apart. Hannah's gasp for breath a reflection of his own disarray.

"It's my computer," he said, his body still reacting to her nearness. "I was running a program analyzing light patterns and details from the tiny bit of the lake we can see in the video. Comparing it to the topography in the area in the hopes that we might narrow down the search."

She nodded, pushing her shirt back into place, color staining her cheeks.

"Hannah, I—" he started, but she cut him off with a wave of her hand.

"It's okay. It was nothing. We just got lost in the moment. That's all." She turned away from him, walking over to the computer. "What we need to do now is concentrate on finding Sara."

He opened his mouth to argue, to tell her that kissing her had been about a lot more than nothing, but the truth was that he wasn't sure what the hell it had meant. Maybe she was right and it was just a reaction.

"So did the computer find something?" she asked, her attention planted firmly on the screen, but her breathing still reflected the fallout from their passion.

"Looks like it," he said, reaching over to hit a key, pulling his mind away from Hannah and the heat of their kiss.

There'd be time to deal with the implications later. Right now, Hannah was right, he needed to concentrate on the matter at hand. The computer whirred to life, and a new screen opened displaying the search results.

"According to this, we've got a probable match. An old farmhouse on the northwest edge of the lake."

"You said 'probable.'" Hannah lifted her gaze to his. "What does that mean?"

"It means that right now, it's the only lead we've got. And if we're right about the connection between the disappearance and the video, then it's also our best shot at finding Sara."

CHAPTER 6

All right, everyone in place?" Avery asked, the comlink in Hannah's ear bursting to life. They'd surrounded the farmhouse set deep in the woods on the northwest shore of Sapphire Lake. It was hard to tell from the outside, but the view was right, and the weathered exterior mirrored the wood planked walls in the video.

Avery, Harrison, and Hannah were coming in from the front, with Drake and Simon taking the back. They'd done this sort of thing a thousand times, and yet somehow, today it felt different. Hannah wasn't sure why. Maybe it was Harrison's talk of a serial killer. Or maybe it was just the idea that it was a Sunderland student. Or maybe it was because she was remembering her own past.

There were certainly parallels.

"We're all set," Simon said, his voice breaking up slightly at the end. "And I'm not seeing any sign of movement from back here."

Hannah swallowed, automatically looking over at

Harrison. If they were in the right place, no movement could be construed as a bad thing.

"It only means there's no one coming, and no obvious threat from inside," Harrison said, his voice reassuring, but his face reflected her concern.

Hannah nodded and pulled her gun from beneath her Kevlar vest. If it weren't for the seriousness of the situation, the moment would be almost comical. Just a couple of hours ago she'd been kissing Harrison in her kitchen. If his computer hadn't intervened, she'd probably have given in to the pleasure. And that would have changed everything. And not in a good way.

"All right, people," Avery said, and Hannah felt her face go hot as she pulled her attention back to the situation at hand. "We're silent from here on out. We have no idea what we're going to find in there so move quickly and stay alert."

Harrison nodded. And Hannah tightened her hold on her gun, moving into place as they started toward the house, using the trees for cover. She could just see the lake in the distance, the angle eerily like the photograph Harrison had pulled from the video. Heart pounding, she inched forward, leading with her gun, Harrison flanking her, Avery on point.

The house was dilapidated, with peeling paint and broken window glass. It was hard to believe anyone could be inside, and Hannah felt hope slipping away. They moved quietly to the edge of the porch. The forest had already reclaimed parts of it, a sapling actually springing up through broken boards.

Avery motioned Hannah to one side and Harrison to the other as they climbed the steps, guns drawn. Backs to the wall, Avery reached out to try the doorknob. Surprisingly, it swung inward. He motioned them forward again, and they stepped into the living room. Harrison went first, turning in a slow circle, pointing his weapon.

"It's clear," he said, motioning them forward. Avery took the hallway leading off to the right, while Hannah moved into the one on the left, Harrison staying behind them to watch their backs.

Leading with her gun, Hannah moved slowly. The hallway was dark, the walls rough and bare. The rug beneath her feet was stained and torn, and in places missing completely, exposing a subflooring composed of the same wooden panels as the walls. There were three doors leading off of the hall. One to the right, another to the left, and at the end, swathed in shadows, the final opening.

Heart pounding, she opened the first door—an empty bathroom. From the looks of the place, it hadn't been used any time recently. She edged back into the hallway, heading for the second door, this one open. From somewhere behind and to the right, she heard Avery call "clear" as she swung into the doorway, holding her position as her gaze traveled across the room.

It was empty except for a table and a couple of chairs. The window was broken, and the wind whistled through it. The breeze had deposited a fine layer of dust on everything—including the floor. Which meant that no one had been inside the room in a very long time. She could hear Simon now, as he, too, called "clear." And then more voices as the men moved into the living room.

On an exhalation of breath, she moved back into the hallway and headed for the doorway at the end. Last stop. She hit the switch on her handgun's tac-light, aiming the resulting beam toward the door. It was closed, and the first thing she noticed was that, unlike the rest of the house, the door was new.

She heard movement behind her and signaled the team quiet with her hand. She pressed flat against the wall, straining for any sound. But there was only a soft rustling as Harrison came up behind her, moving to the opposite wall.

She pointed toward the doorknob, and he nodded—lifting his gun, ready to intercept whatever the hell they might find inside.

On a silent count of three, she reached for the knob. Turning it slowly, she pushed the door open, and Harrison rushed into the room, gun leveled as she followed, her weapon ready as well. But there was no need. Whoever had been here was gone.

Leaving behind the scene of the crime.

It looked exactly as it had in the video, right down to the view from the window. It was all there. The bed. The torn T-shirt. There was rope still tied to the headboard, and the wall behind it was stained a muddy brown.

Blood.

There were stains, too, on the mattress, a deeper brown than the spatter on the wall. Hannah reached out to touch one with a fingertip.

"It's still wet," she whispered, as her mind tried to process the scene. Beyond the ropes and the blood, there was no other sign of violence. No overturned furniture or broken glass. The windows in the room were intact. And the headboard and mattress, though damaged now, appeared to be new.

"Son of a bitch." Simon stopped just inside the doorway, his eyes on the bed. "I don't think this is going to have a happy ending."

Avery moved past Simon into the room, his gaze taking in the scene. "Everything's new," he said. "Someone definitely planned this."

"So where the hell are they now?" Hannah asked, wiping the blood off her finger. "You think the killer knew we were coming?"

"I don't see how." Avery frowned. "We took every precaution."

"Could be he just wanted to move to a new location," Drake offered, as he joined Simon at the doorway. "These guys get off on playing out a fantasy. Maybe his included alternate locations."

"Look for a cellar," Harrison said, speaking for the first time, a tiny muscle in his jaw ticking.

"There isn't one." Simon shook his head. "We checked the whole back of the house."

"How about outside?" Harrison walked over to the window, peering out the grimy glass. "Anyone check there?"

"On the way in," Drake said with a frown as Harrison turned back toward the door, clearly agitated. "There was nothing. I swear."

"Well, maybe a trap door in the floor. Or something hidden behind furniture. I don't know. But I'm telling you it's here somewhere." Harrison dropped down to look under the bed. Then pushed back to his feet to move a chair and then the bedside table.

"Harrison—" Avery started only to be cut off as Harrison waved him off.

"Trust me. If it's not in this room, then it's got to be

out there somewhere." He gestured toward the hallway, his tone brooking no argument.

"Drake," Avery said, "you and Simon take the back of the house. Check again, this time concentrating on looking for egress either through the floor or through the walls. Hannah, you take the two front rooms, and I'll help Harrison here."

Hannah nodded, fighting the urge to reach out for Harrison. She could almost see the tension radiating from him, the situation hitting too close to home. But there was nothing she could say to make it better. And besides, it wasn't really her place.

With a last look, she headed back down the hall and into the living room. It was small, and sparsely furnished. She checked beneath the old sofa. And then behind a dilapidated bookshelf, carefully tapping the wall, listening for anything that might indicate a hollow space hidden behind the boards. But there was nothing.

She continued to search, until she was certain she'd exhausted all possibility, and then moved into the small adjoining room. It wasn't more than about twelve feet square and except for a three-legged table propped beneath a window, there was no furniture. Just a rotting quilt in a corner across the room. At some point it had probably covered the wall, but gravity, with the help of the wind, had managed to relocate it.

As if echoing the thought, the far edge of the quilt moved in the breeze from the window, and just for a moment, Hannah thought she saw the glint of metal beneath. Adrenaline surging, she drew her gun and moved toward the swaying cloth. Then, holding her breath, she yanked back the quilt to expose a door.

Heart pounding now, she reached out to pull it open, half expecting it to be locked, but the door obediently swung inward and again Hannah turned on the light attached to her gun. The beam cut into the dark, abolishing the shadows, and Hannah's spirits sank. It was only a closet.

She moved the beam of light across the space, but except for a cardboard box in the corner the closet was empty. She blew out a breath and turned to go, but just as she started to step back into the room her mind presented an image of the box.

Something about it didn't quite fit.

She turned back, shining the light on the cardboard container, the incongruity immediately clear. The box, like the bedroom door, was new. Frowning, she knelt beside it, and pulled it open. There was a coil of rope inside. The same kind that had been fastened to the headboard. And a roll of duct tape, the beam of her tac-light catching the silver of the tape.

Although the find was insignificant in light of the missing girl, it was still possible that there might be prints on the contents. She pushed back to her feet, intent on telling the team what she'd found, but as she started to move, she tripped on the corner of the box and went flying, arms pinwheeling as she fell, her gun spinning across the floor.

For a moment the world swam crazily, and then her head cleared. Chagrined, she sat up, rubbing one knee, grateful that no one had been there to see her make a fool of herself. The box had slid across the floor, and her gun, its light still shining, was resting a foot or so away. With a resigned sigh, she reached for it, but froze as her gaze landed on the illuminated spot where the box had been.

The flooring here was different from the rest, the planks cut perpendicularly by what looked to be a frame. Or an edge—marking a trap door.

Although it was tempting to go in herself, Hannah resisted the urge. She knew from experience that grandstanding usually ended badly. Besides, if someone was down there, he'd have heard her fall, and if said person was a hostile, then he'd be ready.

Better to get help.

She rose to her feet and reached to push aside the quilt, but before she could step free, she heard something moving and froze, her fingers tightening on her gun.

"Hannah, are you okay?" Harrison's voice filtered through the rotting cotton, and she almost dropped the gun in her relief.

"I'm here," she said, pushing past the quilt. "In the closet."

"Well, there's an opening if ever I heard one," he said, relief playing across his face.

"Except that you know better," she shot back without thinking, the words immediately sending blood coursing to her cheeks. "I'm sorry that didn't come out right."

"Seemed pretty on point to me." He smiled, but then sobered as he studied the opening behind her. "You found something."

"Yes," she nodded, grateful to be back on safer ground. "I think there's a trap door. But I didn't want to go in by myself."

"Smart girl," he said, pulling his gun as he moved past her into the closet. "Where is it?"

"In the corner," she aimed her gun so that the light shone on the area of floor where the trap door was. "It was under a box. I saw it after I fell."

Harrison shot her a concerned look.

"It was nothing. I'm fine," she said, resisting the urge to rub her throbbing knee.

He nodded, his attention already back on the trap door, as he traced the edges to try to find a handle or latch or something. "You need to get Avery."

"You can't go down there by yourself," she protested. "I'll just radio him. Not much point in going dark. After my fall, if anyone's down there, they'd have to be deaf not to have heard me."

"Or dead," Harrison mumbled under his breath, and Hannah shivered.

Pushing aside all thoughts of Sara, she adjusted her comlink. "Avery, are you there?"

"Yeah," came the crackling reply. "You guys in trouble?"

"Negative," she said. "But I've found a trap door. It's in a closet in the room next to the living area. Harrison's here and we're going to try to open it."

"Copy that," Avery answered. "We're on our way. Be careful."

Silence loomed for a moment, and then with a sharp intake of breath, Harrison pulled upward, the trap door opening with a mechanical groan.

They shined their lights on the opening, a series of steep steps leading downward. They held position for a moment, listening, but nothing moved. There was no sound at all except the slow dripping of water somewhere.

"You ready?" Harrison whispered.

Hannah nodded, not completely sure she meant it. If there was something down there, she had the feeling it wasn't going to be anything good.

Harrison moved first, shining the tac-light attached to his gun ahead of them. Moisture filled the air, the dampness cold and cloying. Shadows stretched across the floor, moving like living things in the flickering beams of their lights.

They reached the bottom, and Harrison swept his light across the room. Dust-coated boxes were stacked in a corner, and an empty shelving unit stood against the far wall. Like the boxes, it was coated in grime, the filth making it clear that no one had touched it in decades.

"There's nothing here," Hannah said, turning in a slow circle moving the beam from her tac-light across the walls and floors. "It doesn't look like anyone's been down here in years."

"Yeah, but look," Harrison pointed down at the floor just by the stairs, "there's no dust here. It's been swept clean."

Hannah shifted, lowering her light so that she could see. "So what are we missing?"

"I don't know." Harrison shook his head. "But if I had to call it, I'd say it's under the stairs."

He pushed aside a stack of boxes and ducked into the space beneath the steps. "See anything?" she asked, his back blocking her view.

"There's a door in the back wall," he said. "A new one. Looks the same as the one upstairs."

Above them they could hear footsteps on the stairs. "Avery?" Hannah whispered, clutching her gun. "That you?"

"Roger that," he replied. "What have you got?"

"Harrison's found another door."

"All right," Avery said. "Hold position until we get there."

Harrison nodded, indicating that he'd heard Avery's order.

"Is it locked?" Hannah asked.

"I don't think so," he said, training his light just above the knob as he moved to the side so that she could see. "There's a deadbolt on the outside. Whatever this was used for, it was for keeping people in, not out."

Again Hannah shivered. Avery, Drake, and Simon hit the bottom of the stairs, the big men filling the small cellar.

"Am I clear to go?" Harrison asked, his expression grim.

"Yes," Avery acknowledged. "Just be careful."

Harrison nodded and then reached for the knob. Hannah held her breath as the door squeaked open, the smell emanating from the opening drawing bile into her throat.

"Oh, my God," she whispered, fighting her rising nausea. "Is that..." she trailed off, not able to form the words.

Harrison nodded, his mouth drawn into a thin, tight line as he stepped through the doorway into the room. Sucking in a breath, Hannah followed, mentally steeling herself for what she already knew they'd find.

Sara was strung by her arms from the wall. Naked. Blood pooling at her feet. Precision cuts and slashes snaked across her body like some kind of macabre tattoo.

Hannah fought against another wave of nausea. "Is she—"

"Dead?" Harrison finished for her, as the rest of the team made their way into the room. "Yes. From the looks of the blood on the floor, I'd say she's been that way for quite a while."

"So we couldn't have—" Again Hannah had trouble finding the words, tears filling her eyes as the horror enveloped her.

"Saved her?" Drake finished, his voice echoing in the eerily lit room. "No way. We never had a chance."

"Neither did she," Harrison said, his voice hushed, his face tight with emotion.

"How did you know?" Hannah asked, the words coming of their own volition. "To look for a cellar, I mean?" She lifted her gaze to his, and the pain she saw reflected there almost took her breath away.

He shook his head, his eyes moving back to Sara, hanging on the wall. "Because that's where they found my sister."

CHAPTER 7

Harrison sat on the front porch steps of the house by the lake, his thoughts rioting. Despite the fact that nine years had passed since his sister's death, it might as well have been yesterday. Especially in light of the body they'd found inside. The forensics people were at work in the basement and bedroom. And the rest of the team was either inside helping or back at Sunderland trying to run interference.

There was no avoiding publicity now. And that meant that Avery would have his hands full dealing with the fallout. Parents, students, even professors—all with legitimate concerns—who'd be bombarding the college with questions and fears. Harrison was glad he wasn't the one who had to cope.

"You okay?" Hannah asked, sitting down beside him on the steps, her voice laced with concern.

"Hey, this isn't about me," he said, lifting his hands. "Sara's family members are the ones who are going to have to deal with all of this."

"I know that. But you were already thinking about your sister, and now this. It can't be easy."

"It is what it is, Hannah. And talking about it isn't going to help."

"Okay," she said, her face shuttering. "I guess I just thought that..." She trailed off, staring down at her hands, and he hated himself for being so short with her, but right now, more than anything, he needed to maintain control.

"I know you mean well," he said, "but we need to focus on Sara's murder, not my sister's."

She nodded and stood up, but not before he saw a flicker of hurt in her eyes.

This was why he didn't do relationships. But with Hannah somehow it was different. He just couldn't stand the idea that he'd caused her pain.

"I'm sorry. I'm not exactly at my best." He stood up, reaching out to take her hand, the action surprising him almost as much as it surprised her. "But I didn't mean to snap at you."

"I understand. But you need to know that I... that we all care about you. And whatever you need—even if it's just space—we're here to give it to you."

"That means a lot to me."

He was standing on the bottom step and Hannah was on the top, so for once they were almost eye level. "I value our friendship, Hannah." More than he was ready to tell her actually. Hell, more than he wanted to admit. "But right now, the best thing we can do for my sister is figure out who did this to Sara and stop him before he strikes again."

"So you do think we've got a serial killer?" Avery

asked, striding out onto the porch, snapping his phone shut. Drake and Simon right behind him.

"I think it's a definite possibility," Harrison said as Hannah pulled her hand free, the color rising in her cheeks. Hannah always had trouble concealing her emotions. It was one of the things he liked best about her. She was always honest.

"That's what the ME thinks, too." Avery nodded. "But he doesn't have the same degree of experience with serial killers that you do."

"Hey, it's been a long time since I worked for the FBI," Harrison said. "I'm hardly an expert anymore."

"Well, you're the closest thing we've got right now. And I value your opinion."

"So what does the brass say?" Hannah asked.

Avery had been talking to Langley trying to figure out who was going to take the lead in the investigation. Normally it would fall to the FBI, but with A-Tac undercover at Sunderland there were extenuating circumstances.

"They're deferring to us—for now," Avery responded, perching on the windowsill. Drake settled in next to Simon on the porch railing, Hannah dropping down onto a weathered bench next to the door. Harrison sighed and leaned back against a support column, itching for his computer.

"Meaning what?" Drake asked.

"Well, we're clearly not set up for this kind of thing, but under the circumstances Langley feels like it needs to stay in-house. So we're taking lead on the investigation. But there's no way we'll be able to keep this out of the press, so we've got to at least make it look like we're routing things through proper channels. As far as the world is concerned, we're just a bunch of professors. And the brass wants to be sure it stays that way."

"So how do we do that?" Drake frowned.

"Langley's sending some operatives. They'll pose as FBI agents. As far as the public is concerned everything will be coming from Quantico. But in reality we'll be running the show."

"There's no way we're going to contain this," Simon said. "A serial killer is big news. The public is going to want to know what's happening."

"And they will. Everything except the fact that the professors of the college are actually CIA agents working the case. Look, it's a difficult situation. But we're still in the game, and that's what matters."

"Except that you were right the first time," Hannah said, leaning forward, pushing her glasses up on her nose, the light catching the blue streaks in her hair. "We're not fully equipped to handle this. I mean, Harrison has experience. But we need more than that." She shot him an apologetic look and then continued. "We need a profiler."

"Already ahead of you on that," Harrison said. "If you think we can get it approved, I've got a couple of friends that can fill those roles. People I worked with when I was with the Bureau and Last Chance. Madison Roarke is a profiler. One of the best in the country. And Tracy Braxton runs Braxton Labs."

Drake whistled. "You run in some pretty elite circles. I've worked with Braxton Labs before. On an archeological find. The outfit is tops when it comes to forensic pathology."

"Can we trust them with our unusual situation?" Avery asked.

"Absolutely. They're good people, both of them. Madison and I started at the FBI together. We were partners." And friends. She'd been the one who'd forced him back to life after his sister's death. Brought him back into the fold, so to speak.

"All right then, you contact them, and I'll clear it through Langley."

"What about Sara's parents?" Hannah asked, leaning forward and propping her chin in her hands. "Who's going to tell them?"

"I will. It's my job as dean," Avery replied. "And until we have a better handle on what's happening, I'll feel better if we keep our personnel limited to just the five of us. We're going to have enough to deal with when you factor in the people Langley's sending, and if approved, Harrison's friends."

"So besides calling in reinforcements," Simon said, "what's our next move?"

"I'm going to close the campus. No one in or out without clearance. For obvious reasons, we're overly cautious about who we hire, so I'm thinking our man isn't on staff at Sunderland. I'm also canceling classes for the rest of the week. Again it's not a failsafe, but it gives students the option of going home without missing anything."

"What about the ones who stay?" Hannah asked.

"I've issued an alert advising that everyone stay inside after dark, and if they can't do that, then they're to travel in groups. We know that there's safety in numbers. These guys don't like crowds."

"Actually, some of them get off on that," Harrison said. "But I'm not seeing anything here to make me think the unsub is playing that kind of game."

"Unsub?" Simon frowned.

"Sorry." Harrison shrugged. "Old habits. In the FBI we called the object of our investigations unknown subjects."

"Unsubs," Hannah repeated. "Has a certain ring to it. Although I like perp better."

"You always did have a slant toward law enforcement." Harrison grinned at her, feeling relieved that they were back to their usual banter.

"Well, whatever we call the bastard, we need to take him very seriously," Avery said. "He's already murdered a student, and it's our job to make sure he doesn't get the chance to kill another."

"How do we know he's only after students?"

"We don't." Harrison shook his head. "But for now, it's the obvious assumption. And in the meantime, we need to start digging into Sara's background. Try to find out if there's anything there that might point us toward some other connection to the killer."

"But you just said he was an unsub," Simon said, "so how do we know what might connect Sara to him?"

"There are obvious links. If, say, Sara had been working at a club for extra money. Or if she'd been volunteering with prisoners or the homeless. Any little detail might help us as we try to see a pattern. In addition to that, we need to find out if there have been any other similar murders in, say, the last three months. That's another way to establish a connection."

"Sounds like something I can do," Hannah said, flexing her fingers, clearly wishing for a laptop as much as Harrison was.

"Good," Avery said. "And while you're at it, look for a connection between Sara and Tina."

"But we already talked to her," Hannah protested. "And there isn't one."

"Well, maybe it's something she's not aware of. Just do a little digging and see what pops up. See what parallels she might have with Sara. Something that puts them in the same victim pool. Start with the basics, physical characteristics, common interests, background information. Anything you can think of that might prove to be a parallel between the two women. I don't believe for a moment that Tina was chosen randomly."

Hannah nodded, hating the idea of digging into Tina's life without her knowing, but accepting that, for now at least, it was the best course of action.

"Drake," Avery was saying, "I want you to interview Sara's parents and friends. It won't hurt to talk to the boyfriend again either."

"Roger that," Drake agreed.

"And in the meantime," Avery said, "I'll coordinate with Langley and the locals while Harrison contacts his friends. And, Simon, you'll stay here and oversee the crime scene until reinforcements arrive. The important thing right now is to amass as much information as possible. That'll make it that much easier for Harrison's people to hit the ground running."

"So we're going to just let them take over when they get here?" Drake asked, his face reflecting his disapproval.

"No. We're going to make them a part of the team. And together, we're going to do whatever it takes to find this guy and bring him down before he has the chance to kill someone else."

Avery stepped off the porch, pulling his phone from his pocket, the action signaling an end to the conversation.

Simon and Drake headed back into the house, leaving Harrison alone with Hannah.

"So I guess I'm heading back to Sunderland," Hannah said, pushing to her feet to stand beside him. "I figure I'll work faster if I have my computer. You coming?"

"In a little while." Harrison turned to look at the house, the smell of blood sharp as it assaulted his nostrils. He closed his eyes, Bree's smile filling his mind. "I want to stay here until they bring her out."

Hannah reached out to touch his arm, her fingers gentle. "Harrison, it's not Bree in there. You know that, right?"

Her words pulled him sharply back into the present, the image of his sister vanishing, the feel of Hannah's hand warm against his skin. And for a moment, all he wanted was to hold her. To anchor himself in the here and now. But then the door swung open and a couple of techs walked out holding a bag with bloody evidence, and once again his mind was filled with images of his sister, his gut tightening with frustration and rage.

"I won't let it happen again," he whispered, fists clenching. "No matter what it takes. I owe it to Bree. Hell, I owe it to Sara."

"Well, for what it's worth," Hannah said, her gaze locking with his, "we're in this together. And I promise I'll be with you—every step of the way."

CHAPTER 8

Gin," Tina said as Hannah walked into the rooms where her TA had been sequestered. It was a small apartment on the top floor of the administration building, primarily used for visiting board members and dignitaries.

"I can't catch a break with you," Jasmine Washington grumbled, throwing her cards on the table. "She's beaten me five times in a row. I hope you don't mind that I'm here?" She looked up at Hannah, her dark eyes sparking with mischief. "I told the guy outside I was dropping off coffee. She waved at the Java Joe cups on the table. "But I just stayed."

"I begged her to," Tina added. "And the FBI dude hasn't said anything about it. So it's okay, right?"

The "dude" outside was actually CIA out of the New York office. But with his suit and tie, Reid Kotchner certainly looked the part of a G-man. There were also men situated at the entrance to the building. Avery had decided that, until they better understood Tina's role in all that was happening, it was best to keep an eye on her. And the suite had the added benefit of on-campus security.

"Yeah, it's fine," Hannah said. "I just came to check on you. I wanted to be sure you were okay with all of this."

Tina grimaced. "I don't know that I have much of a choice. But under the circumstances, I do feel safer here than I would at my place." Tina lived by herself in a rental house off-campus. Yet another reason why it had seemed safer to put her here, rather than send Reid and company out there.

"Well, I'm sorry you have to go through any of this. But until we figure out your connection with the killer, it's just better if someone keeps watch. And it's easier to do it here."

Jasmine leaned back in her chair, frowning. Tall and lanky, she had the natural grace of an athlete. "I still can't believe any of this is happening. I mean the idea that some crazy asshole is out there stalking students just feels so surreal."

"I know it's scary. But the truth is that we don't know for sure that he's stalking anyone. It's possible that this thing with Sara was a one-off."

"But you don't think that's true." Jasmine's eyes narrowed as she studied Hannah's face.

"No," Hannah shook her head, figuring that under the circumstances at least that much honesty was warranted. "But it is possible that now that the murder's gone public, he'll avoid the campus. I mean, he's bound to know there will be heightened security."

"Great, so now he'll turn to the women in town." Jasmine shuddered at the thought.

"I'm sure the police department is working closely with the FBI on this one," Hannah assured her. The police had actually been brought up to speed by one of the men from Langley, but it was only semantics.

"So why didn't they just send me home?" Tina asked. "I mean that's what everyone else is doing."

"Not everyone," Hannah said with a sigh. "You wouldn't believe how many students are staying put." In point of fact, it seemed that most everyone was staying, which only meant a bigger headache for A-Tac as the team tried to maintain security on campus.

"I guess they're just trying not to give in to their fears," Tina said, reaching out to gather the cards. "I mean, we can't let this guy run our lives, right?"

"Yes, but we do need to exercise caution," Hannah warned. "Which is why you're here. Until this is over, you need protection."

"Well, I've certainly got that," Tina said with a sigh. "I mean, the guy outside has a gun. And he doesn't look like he'd hesitate to use it. Which probably makes me the safest person in town."

"As long as you stay put."

"Hey, I'm not going anywhere. At least until next Friday."

"What happens next Friday?" Hannah asked.

"Matchbox Twenty is playing at the Garden. Roger scored tickets—on the floor." Roger Jameson was Tina's boyfriend, a recent Sunderland alum who worked in Manhattan. "It's going to be awesome. I can't wait." Her fear forgotten for the moment, Tina jumped to her feet, excitement bringing color to her cheeks.

"I'd kill to see them in concert," Jasmine said, her enthusiasm matching Tina's. "I've got like fifteen of their songs on my iPhone."

"I will be able to go, right?" Tina turned to Hannah, her eyes pleading.

"I can't promise anything," Hannah said. "It's up to the FBI. But if it looks like it's going to be a problem, maybe I can talk to them."

"That'd be great. It's super important that I go. We've been planning it forever. Which reminds me. I need to call and let him know that I'm all right. I'm sure he's been worried sick. Only you've still got my phone."

"I know." Hannah nodded. "That's actually one of the reasons I came over here. I wanted to return it. But you need to limit usage."

Tina folded her arms, her eyes turning mutinous, but before she could speak, Hannah cut her off.

"I'm not saying you can't use it at all," she said, reaching into her pocket to produce the phone. "You just need to be cautious. No Internet browsing and no email to anyone you don't know."

"What about social networks?"

"Better to stay off of them. Look, we don't know how this guy found you. And until we figure that out, you need to limit your exposure."

"But I can call people?"

"Yes, but even with that, you need to be careful. If you want pizza delivered or something, Reid can do it for you."

"This is all just a little too much," Tina said. "I mean this morning the only real concern I had was whether I'd have enough time to finish grading papers. And now I'm here in the middle of what's starting to feel like my own personal episode of *Criminal Minds*."

"Now if only the guy outside will morph into Morgan," Jasmine said, her gaze shooting to the door.

"Who?" Hannah asked, shaking her head. Truth was, she never had time to watch TV.

"You know, the hot guy," Jasmine and Tina said, almost in unison, and Hannah smiled, happy that they'd found something to lighten the mood.

"Well, on that note, I think maybe I'll leave you to your fantasies." Hannah reached out to give Tina a hug. "Call me if you need me. I'll just be a phone call away."

Tina nodded. "Thanks. It's nice to know you're in my corner."

"Yeah, well, I'm thinking even better to have him on your side." Hannah tipped her head toward the door and the man outside. "Stay safe. Jasmine, are you staying?"

"For a little while longer." Jasmine lifted the deck of cards. "I've still got to prove that I can win a game."

"All right, but be sure to ask Reid for a security escort when you leave." The cell in her pocket began to ring, but she waited for Jasmine to nod her agreement before answering. "Hello?"

"Hannah. Good, I'm glad I caught you." Harrison's voice filled her ear. Speaking of hot guys and fantasies. "I need you to get over here as quickly as you can." All levity vanished at the tone in his voice.

"What's up?"

"We found Sara's book bag," Harrison said, "and her computer."

"So where did you find it?" Hannah asked as she walked into the A-Tac computer room.

"It was in the bushes between the Union and Varsley Hall," Harrison said, looking up from the laptop.

Hannah as always looked somewhere between hip

and disheveled, her hair going in crazy directions, the word bedhead taking on a whole new meaning. His eyes drifted downward to the soft curves of her body and he wondered when he'd moved from thinking of Hannah as a friend to thinking of her as someone he wanted to get between the sheets. Maybe it was the night on the roof with her skirt slit to her ass and her eyes flashing fire as she crossed the ladder to escape the Consortium shooters.

All he knew was that he wanted her in the worst way and that his timing sucked.

Drake, who was reading through the preliminary coroner's report, glanced up at the two of them. Harrison mumbled a curse and forced his attention back to the computer.

"So have you found anything?" Hannah asked, dropping into the chair next to his. Hell, he could feel the heat of her body, smell the scent of her shampoo. It took every ounce of determination he could muster to keep from reaching out to touch her.

Son of a bitch.

"Nothing yet," he said, shaking his head to clear his mind. "I've been through her emails, and there wasn't anything to indicate she'd had any contact with the killer. And nothing to point us toward someone she knew. I'm going through her files now."

"So what have you got?" Hannah asked Drake, fortunately oblivious to the turn of Harrison's thoughts.

"ME's report," Drake said. "So far no surprises. The blood they found in the house was Sara's. Which we already knew. There's evidence of sexual assault, but no semen."

"So this was an act of rage," Hannah said.

"Or he used a condom." Drake shrugged.

"Did they establish time of death?" she asked.

"Yeah." He looked at her over the top of the file, his expression grim. "About six hours before we got there. She was probably already dead when your TA got the video."

"So we were right, she never had a chance," Hannah said.

"Doesn't look like it, no."

"This is all just so unbelievable." Hannah ran a hand through her hair. "I mean, we deal with some pretty awful people on a rather regular basis. But nothing like this. Nothing so pointed. A terrorist wants maximum damage. Biggest bang for the buck. And the loss of life is awful. But this is more than that. This is someone who thrives on death and fear. I can't even imagine what the last hours of Sara's life must have been like."

"You can't let yourself go there," Harrison said. "It's too easy to get sucked into the horror. You have to divorce yourself from the reality of the acts. Keep your mind separated from your emotions."

"Good luck with that," Drake said. "I've been looking at these pictures for over an hour now, and my stomach is still churning. And I've seen a hell of a lot in my time with A-Tac. But Hannah's right—nothing like this. I don't see how you did it, bro."

"I didn't do it for that long. And most of the time I spent in the unit was on the computer, not in the field."

"So I'm guessing there was nothing at the scene to give us a lead on identifying the killer?"

"Nothing concrete," Drake said. "No prints. No DNA. Nothing to tie the scene to anyone but Sara. Most of the action seems to have taken place in the upstairs bedroom."

"So why the change in location?" Hannah asked, chewing the side of her lip as she considered the question. "I mean, the place was deserted. So what reason is there to move her?"

"I'm betting that it's got to do with the ritual," Harrison said.

"I'm not following." Hannah shook her head with a frown.

"Every serial killer develops a ritual. A set plan of action guaranteed to get his rocks off. In this case, it appears that the first act of his fantasy plays out in the bedroom, with the finale in the cellar."

"That fits the facts," Drake said. "The sexual acts and the killing appeared to have occurred in the bedroom. So she was already dead or dying when she was taken downstairs where he finished her off."

"And you've got nothing there to give us a clue as to who it might have been?" Hannah asked, turning back to Harrison.

"Not so far. I've authenticated all the files. There's nothing here that jumps off the page or seems out of place. Just the kinds of files you'd expect to find on a college kid's computer."

"What about Facebook or other social networking sites?" Hannah suggested. "Didn't Tony give us the info we need to get into her accounts?"

"He did, and I've already searched there. Even before we found the computer. And again, there was nothing out of the ordinary. She had a Twitter account, but didn't really use it. And her Facebook page was limited to friends, which seems to have included pretty much everyone on campus. But as Facebook pages go, this one is pretty tame. There's nothing that would seem to have been a hook for a killer."

"Hell, for all we know, this was just random," Drake said. "Right place, wrong time."

"It's possible. But this guy is already pretty far into building the fantasy," Harrison said. "Which means this most likely isn't his first time at the party. And we can't ignore the parallel to the cyber killer. I'm hoping that when Madison and Tracy arrive they'll have some insight."

"So when are they getting here?" Drake asked.

Drake didn't mention his sister, and Harrison was grateful for the reprieve. He'd told Avery everything. And Avery in turn had told the team.

"They'll be here in the morning. Tracy's flying in from Texas, and Madison's coming in from D.C. She's actually working another case right now, so she won't have a lot of time, but I faxed her everything we've got so she'll already be up to speed when she gets here. She's a hell of a profiler. And when you combine that with Tracy's forensic expertise, hopefully, we'll know a lot more by tomorrow night."

"And in the meantime, we've just got to hold the fort," Drake said.

"And pray that he doesn't take someone else," Hannah added, her attention on the computer screen. "What about erased emails? Is there any way to retrieve them? Maybe there's a clue in something she got rid of."

"Already ahead of you," Harrison nodded. "I contacted her Internet provider and they downloaded everything they had on their server. They refresh fairly frequently, so there's not too much. And what was there was innocuous."

"What about IMing?" she asked, leaning closer as she studied the screen. "I see a link to AIM on her desktop."

"There's nothing there either. Apparently she didn't use it all that much. Same goes for her Skype account. And when I searched her Internet history, I didn't see anything to indicate she'd been involved in online chats or stumbled onto a website she should have avoided. Basically, there's no record of her doing anything online that might set her up to attract the wrong kind of attention."

"So we're back to random," Drake said.

"Or maybe he's been watching her. Physical stalking rather than cyber. Although I'd have thought that considering his use of the Internet to send out a record of his act, he'd have been more inclined to use cyberspace to find his prey."

"Yeah, but if he's as good as we think he is," Harrison said, "he wouldn't do anything that might leave a trail. It's pretty easy to hack into Facebook or other social media accounts. One thing she did do was post a lot of pictures. So maybe our guy just liked the way she looked. There's usually something specific that draws these guys to their prey."

"What about her trash can?" Hannah asked.

"In her dorm room?" Drake laid down the report with a frown.

"No." Hannah shook her head. "On her computer. I never remember to empty mine. It's usually crammed full of stuff. Most of which I've completely forgotten about. If Sara's like me, maybe she deleted something important."

"It's worth taking a look," Harrison said, moving to

the desktop and clicking on the trash can icon. The list of deleted files was indeed long. Some of them dating back more than a year.

"We'd be looking for something recent, I'd think," Hannah said, leaning over his shoulder now.

"Makes sense." He typed in a command and the images were reorganized by date. The documents were ones he recognized from other, newer versions in her actual files. But there were also a bunch of photographs. Mostly loaded from her phone, but also a few taken from the Net.

"I'm not seeing anything suspicious." Hannah frowned, staring down at the screen.

"Yeah, but they're all too little to really be able to tell for certain," Drake said, coming to stand beside them. "Any way you can make the pictures bigger? I don't know, like a slide show or something?"

"No problem," Harrison said, highlighting a large group of photos and then opening them with Sara's photo gallery software. The pictures started to flash by. Mostly out-of-focus pictures taken around campus. The viewer stopped on a picture of Sara and Tony, cups of beer in hand, a keg clearly visible in the background.

"Well, that explains why the pictures are out of focus." Hannah sighed. "But it doesn't help us find the killer." She tilted her head back, rubbing her neck. "I guess this was a bad idea."

"No, wait," Drake said, still studying the screen. Upcoming pictures displayed on an icon bar below the keg party picture. "What about that one? I can't make out the subject, but it's in black and white. And the rest of these are in color."

Harrison opened the shot. It was grainy and full of shadows, making it hard to decipher content, but something about it seemed familiar. "Hang on, I'm going to try to enlarge it." He hit a button, and then another, and the shot came into better focus. "What the hell?" he whispered as he stared at the photograph.

"What is it?" Hannah asked, tilting her head as she studied the shot. "It's just an old house."

"It's more than that," Harrison said, his mind spinning, as he tried to order his thoughts. "It's a crime scene. From nine years ago. I recognize it, because I was there. This is where we found the cyber killer's last victim."

"And you're sure it's the same place."

"More than sure," Harrison said. "Look there on the porch." He pointed to the upper half of the picture. "You can see the crime tape."

"So was this picture out there on the web somehow? I mean, maybe Sara was researching the case for some reason. Is there any way to tell where the file came from?"

"No. But according to the properties, it was created a few days before Sara died. And then deleted a couple of hours later." Harrison hit another key. "What that tells me is that she opened the file, and either it was automatically saved or she saved it—and then down the road at some point decided to delete it."

"So the picture could have been what Stephanie was referring to when she mentioned Sara opening a file that seemed to upset her," Hannah said.

"It's possible," Harrison agreed. "It would fit the time line."

"Is there a file name?" Drake asked.

"Just a number. Which could mean anything. And

probably isn't relevant. The real question here is what the hell this picture is doing on Sara Lauter's computer." He turned, his gaze meeting Hannah's.

"Yeah." She sighed. "Except that I'm not sure we want to hear the answer."

CHAPTER 9

Hannah sat in the rocker on her front porch, trying not to stare over at Harrison's house. There was a light on so she knew he was home, and if she were perfectly honest with herself, all she could think about was going over there.

The night was crisp, the chill in the air penetrating, and she pulled her sweater tighter, snuggling into its warmth. Professor's Cove was quiet. The cul-de-sac housed all of the A-Tac members. With Drake and Madeline's house undergoing renovations, it was dark, along with Annie and Nash's next door. And Tyler and Owen's next to them, although Simon was currently staying in the guest house out back so she could see faint light reflecting off the trees.

Avery's house was at the end of the cul-de-sac, and from her porch, she could see the blue flicker of his television screen. Avery and Drake no doubt were watching the baseball game. Lara's house, next to Hannah's on the right, was also dark. She'd left A-Tac shortly after Jason's death. Not that Hannah blamed her. It would have been hard to stay. To be reminded daily of everything that had gone down. But at least she was getting a second chance—building a new life with Rafe Winter.

Some people were just lucky like that. Two great loves in one lifetime.

The minute she had the thought she regretted it. Lara had suffered so much, losing Jason. And then she'd almost died in Africa. Luck was the last word she'd associate with her friend. But the point remained that Lara seemed to have gotten her happy ending. And Hannah was happy for her.

And maybe a little jealous.

She smiled at her own foolishness, her eyes drawn again by the light coming from Harrison's house between hers and Avery's. It had belonged to Emmett originally. But Avery had ordered it remodeled, wiping out the past and opening it up to the future. Emmett's traitorous actions had changed A-Tac forever. But they'd all survived. And remained strong.

And now, in the wake of their latest brush with the Consortium, they were being challenged by a new threat. A woman was dead. Raped and tortured by a sadistic bastard intent on playing a game of cat and mouse. Hannah blew out a breath. It was all hitting too close to home. Memories she'd buried long ago, threatening to surface.

She closed her eyes, pushing the thoughts away, concentrating instead on remembering the feel of Harrison's lips when he'd kissed her, the heat from the palms of his hands against her skin. Her body tightened with need. And she swallowed a sigh.

It hadn't meant anything, that kiss. It was a moment out of time. Her reaction to his saving her life. And his need to forget the horror of his sister's death. They were friends. Nothing more. And yet she ached for his touch. Wanted him so badly she was willing to go over there and throw herself at him.

But she was also smart enough to know that once they crossed that line, they could never go back. *Too late*, the little voice in her head whispered. *Way, way too late.* Maybe it had started when he'd saved her life. Or maybe when he'd bared his soul about his sister. Or maybe it was the first time she'd seen him, looking up from his computer with his crooked grin and tousled hair.

Hannah pushed to her feet, took a step forward, and then sat back down again. She was a fool. And she had more important things to deal with than her surging hormones. She was overwrought and alone. Never a good state. Still, they'd kissed. That much at least was real. And who could blame her for wanting more?

Harrison Blake was hot. There was no denying that fact.

But he was also her friend. And in the end, she knew that was most important. Neither of them wanted a relationship. And having sex was a game-changer. There was no such thing as friends with benefits.

She pushed back her hair with a deep sigh. She needed to focus. Quit thinking about Harrison and concentrate on figuring out how to find Sara's killer before he could strike again.

She'd been trying to find something to connect Sara and Tina but so far there was nothing except that they were both attending Sunderland. And even that analogy wasn't perfect since Sara was a junior and Tina was a graduate student. Despite the fact that the campus was small, their paths rarely intersected. They had different friends, different interests, and physically very little in common.

Frustrated, Hannah had started researching the cyber killer. Looking to see if maybe the photograph they'd found was out there somewhere on the Internet. But the deeper she'd dug, the more her thoughts had centered on Harrison—and the kiss. So she'd come out here to clear her head, and instead, she was staring at his house like a lovesick teenager. Wishing for a sign.

"Hannah?" His voice was so low that at first she thought she'd imagined it. But then he was standing there, on her porch. "I couldn't sleep."

"Me either." She shook her head, rising to her feet, tipping her head back so that she could see his eyes. "I'm sorry about earlier. At the house, when I pushed. I was just trying..."

He shook his head, covering her lips with his finger. "No more talk." Then he bent his head, replacing the finger with his mouth, his lips hard against hers, taking possession. Hannah's stomach lurched as he threaded his fingers through hers, her desire rising as their kiss intensified. She arched against him, wanting more, the thrust of his tongue against hers a promise of things to come.

He lifted his hands, carrying hers with them until her arms were over her head, his body pressing against hers, the bricks from her house cold against her back. His mouth moved, his tongue finding the soft whorl of her ear, and she shivered in response, tipping her head back as he trailed kisses down her neck to the hollow at the base of her throat.

She knew she should stop him, but she didn't want to pull away. The events of the past few days had taken more of a toll than she'd realized. Truth was, she just wanted to forget, to escape into the silent seduction of his kiss.

The leaves rustled in the wind, and she shivered, the vibration running through them like an electric current. She pressed closer, feeling his arousal hard against her thigh. There was power in knowing that the seduction was mutual, her strength matching his.

The thought both elated her and frightened her.

As if sensing her dilemma, he pulled back, his multi-colored eyes dark with both passion and concern.

"What are we doing?" Hannah whispered, her voice raspy from emotion.

"Forgetting," he answered, releasing her hands to push the hair back from her face. "I thought you wanted this, too." He frowned, his eyes searching hers. "But if I was wrong..."

"You weren't," she said, reaching up to stroke the side of his face, desire mixing with something stronger, something she wasn't even certain she recognized. "I do want you, Harrison. The truth is, I was sitting here on the porch fantasizing about it. But if we do this..." It was her turn to trail off.

"We'll be crossing a line," he finished for her, his hands framing her face as his gaze collided with hers.

She nodded, her need so strong now it almost seemed to have a life of its own. She whimpered softly, and with a groan, he pulled her to him again, his mouth crushing down on hers.

The feel of his skin moving against hers was exquisite—sensual beyond belief. For the moment, there was nothing but him. His lips, his hands, the hard masculinity of his body. She needed him like she needed air or water.

She reached behind her to open the door, and without breaking their kiss, he swung her up into his arms and carried her into the foyer, away from prying eyes, closing the door behind him. He released her, and she pressed herself closer, letting the smell of him surround her. Almost a tangible thing, it caressed her senses, leaving her reeling.

His hand found her breast through the soft cotton of her sweater, the movement of his fingers leaving her quivering for more. It was almost as if she'd been waiting for him. Holding some part of herself in reserve. His tongue dove deep into her mouth, and she opened for him, giving as good as she got.

Then he stepped back, his eyes devouring her as he pulled off her shirt and sweater, tossing them across the foyer into the living room. Cool air rippled across her skin, and then he was kissing her again, her back to the wall as his hands slid down to settle against her hips.

She fumbled with the buttons on his shirt, fingers shaking as she finally pushed it off, reveling in the feel of his skin next to hers. His mouth moved hungrily, his need laid bare with his kiss. Passion rose inside her, and she gave it to him freely, wanting him as much as he wanted her.

He cupped one of her breasts in his hand, kneading it slowly, his thumb rasping across her nipple. The sensation ignited pools of liquid heat between her thighs, and she arched back, offering herself to him. He trailed hot kisses along the line of her neck and down the slope of her breast, the soft silk of his hair adding torment to the already unbearable heat.

When his lips closed around her areola, tugging gently, she fought to contain a moan, the sound coming out a muted gasp. His tongue circled, drawing her nipple farther into his mouth. Still braced against the wall, her body responded with a fervor she hadn't known she possessed.

Then he shifted, his mouth slanting over hers, his hands cupping her bottom, his erection pressing against her. His kiss was possessive now. A take-no-prisoners approach that demanded everything. And suddenly she was afraid. She jerked free, covering her breasts, her breath coming in gasps. But he reached for her hands, his eyes dark with passion, a crooked smile twisting his lips.

This was Harrison. Her friend. Her soon-to-be lover.

And with a sigh, she let go of any doubt, intent upon riding the wave. Life was too damn short to overthink everything. There'd be time for regret tomorrow.

What she wanted, what she craved, was to feel him moving inside her. It wasn't wise, it probably wasn't even rational, but at the moment, she didn't care. With a groan, he swung her into his arms and carried her up the stairs to her bedroom, laying her against the cool cotton sheets. After making quick work of the rest of their clothing, he knelt beside her, his mouth on her breasts again. Sucking, licking.

And then he let his mouth trail lower, his fingers massaging the soft flesh of her inner thighs, his tongue finding the soft indentation of her navel, driving in, pressing skin against skin in a way that made her writhe against him, wanting more. Needing more.

She arched upward, and he slid his fingers inside her, his tongue still twisting into her belly button. She swallowed, the delicious tension inside her reaching a level beyond anything she'd ever experienced.

His thumb flicked against her, and she threw back her head and moaned, the sound guttural, coming from deep inside her. His mouth found her center then, tongue replacing thumb with moist heat that made her buck against him, then struggle to escape the finely drawn pain he was instigating.

But his hands found her hips, cupping her bottom and holding her in place, his tongue moving faster and faster, lightning streaking through her with each and every touch. She wanted more, and yet she wasn't certain she could survive the passion he was unleashing inside her.

He sucked then, the pull deep and strong, and she climaxed, white-hot sensation breaking in icy shards around her, sending her beyond all reason. The internal contractions were so powerful that she knew with clarity why it was called a little death. She fought for breath, her mind swirling, and then cried out as the heat enshrouded her and there was nothing but sensation and the feel of his mouth upon her.

Then just as suddenly he was gone. She opened her eyes, startled, but then he was with her again, his hard body sliding along hers, until they lay pressed together, fitting like two pieces of a puzzle. She reached for him and pulled his lips to hers, the kiss slower than before, but no less wanting. This time she explored the hot crevices of his mouth, the smooth surface of his teeth, feeling the heat rising in her again.

With a groan, his kiss turned demanding, absorbing her with each taste, each touch. She felt him shiver as her fingers caressed the hard planes of his chest to land firmly against his abdomen, her palm tracing circles on his skin.

There was power in touching him. And she delighted in the feel and smell of him. Velvet and steel. She kissed the scar that ran along his collar bone, then slid down farther to take his nipple into her mouth. Sucking and nipping, she savored him, reveling in his strength—and hers. His penis tightened, throbbing against her thigh, and with a smile, she closed her hand around him.

"Oh, God," he groaned, his eyes closed now. "I need you, Hannah. I need you now." The words were rough, almost garbled. As if they'd cost him everything. And Hannah took the gift, her heart swelling in response. She needed him, too. As if some part of her were missing. As if joining with him was the only way to feel whole again.

She smiled up at him and slid farther down, taking him into her mouth, circling him with her tongue. She moved her hand as well, the rhythms combining in an effort to bring him the same pleasure he'd brought her. Up and down, squeezing, stroking. He writhed on the bed, then with one swift move, he flipped them over, gaining control.

"I want to be inside you." His voice was still hoarse, his need showing raw across his face. "Now."

She nodded, spreading her legs, offering herself.

Bracing himself on his elbows, he looked down at her, eyes glazed with passion as he thrust home, the power of his heat stealing her breath away. They stayed still for a moment, eye to eye, their breathing in sync, linked together as man and woman.

The pleasure was exquisite, and she pushed against him, taking him even deeper.

There was passion reflected in the depths of his eyes and something else—something so tender it almost took her breath away. She lost herself then in the brown and green of his eyes.

Together they began to move, rocking slowly at first, savoring the moment—the connection—then gradually they began to move faster, each stroke bringing them tantalizingly close to the edge of the precipice.

Tension built between them like a delicately strung wire, pulling tighter and tighter, pleasure and pain mixing as one, need driving every move. She reached up to grab the railing of the headboard, arching her back, pulling him deeper. And balanced on his elbows, he yielded to her demand, the pounding of her heart echoing the motion.

Amazingly the tension inside her was building again, stronger than before, demanding release, promising pleasure beyond imagination, the only reality the sensation between her thighs.

His hands circled her hips, and he began to move with her. Up, down, in, out. Over and over again, deeper and deeper, their eyes locked together, a connection beyond the physical.

The heat between them built, flames of passion licking at them both, winding them tighter and tighter, pulling the thread taut, and then with a moan, she slammed upward, driving him deeper, and the fury erupted, the storm reaching crescendo.

Calling his name, Hannah wound her fingers in the soft swirl of his hair and surrendered herself to the fire, feeling his spasms as he, too, climaxed. She tightened her legs around him as if trying to bind them together. To hold on to this moment.

She wasn't naïve. And this certainly wasn't her first time. But somehow, she knew that with Harrison it was different—special. Of course she also knew that soon the feelings would fade, rational thought taking precedence over emotion.

Harrison rolled to his side, pulling her with him, staying connected, as if he, too, wasn't quite ready to let go. She reached out to smooth back the hair from his face, the gesture somehow more intimate than the acts preceding it.

Tomorrow she'd have to face reality. But for now, she was content just to lie there listening to the cadence of his heartbeat. If there was no such thing as happily ever after, then that was all the more reason to savor the moment.

CHAPTER 10

Jasmine stopped at the front door of Tina's house, holding a small duffle. Tina had been totally freaked about her cat. The FBI agents hadn't been able to find him, and she was worried something had happened. So Jasmine had agreed to check on Asha and gather some things the FBI agents hadn't thought to get for her. She figured she'd deal with the cat now, and deliver Tina's things this afternoon. She glanced at her watch, satisfied that she had plenty of time before she was due to open the coffee shop.

The sun was just visible above the horizon, pink lines spreading upward into the still blue-black sky. If she hadn't been in such a hurry, it would have been a moment to savor. But in all honesty, Jasmine couldn't remember the last time she'd had a minute to enjoy anything. Which was totally her own fault. Had she known how difficult it would be to create a successful coffee house in the era of Starbucks, she might have had second thoughts.

But Jasmine wasn't given to introspection. She'd always just jumped feet first, no time for considering things. She'd set her goal and stuck to it. So when an old house on the edge of campus had gone up for sale, she'd bought it. And six months and a hell of a lot of red tape later, she'd opened Java Joe. And the rest, as they said, was history.

She reached into the geranium pot for Tina's spare key, and then slid it into the lock and opened the door. The house was small, but charming, decorated with a touch of whimsy. Jasmine's eyes fell to a wall sculpture of three dancing women—their arms and legs spread in abandon. Cut from an old oil drum, the metallic art piece was the work of a former student. A boy Tina had once dated.

Jasmine struggled to remember his name, but came up empty as she took the stairs two at a time, heading for Tina's bedroom. Asha's favorite hiding place. The room looked as if Tina had just left it. The bed unmade, stuff scattered everywhere. They'd roomed together when Jasmine was a sophomore and Tina a freshman. And there hadn't been any space left uncovered by something of Tina's.

Nothing had changed.

"Asha?" she called, checking the closet carefully for signs of the cat. But he was evidently hiding elsewhere.

She checked under the bed, and then stopped at the bureau to grab the underthings Tina had requested. She hadn't allowed herself to dwell on the reason she was here in the first place. It was just too awful. And inconceivable. Sunderland had always been a safe haven. And the idea that some crazy dude was out there hurting women... well, it was just too much to consider.

She opened another drawer and added Tina's favorite T-shirt to the duffle and then turned to face the room, the lingering shadows making it seem suddenly less than inviting. Sucking in a breath, she searched quickly for the boots, finally finding them under the bedside table.

All that was left was to gather some toiletries, then she'd be on her way. Screw the damn cat. Glancing at her watch, Jasmine quickened her pace as she walked back into the hall, heading to the bathroom.

The house was quiet except for the wind whistling through the trees outside. She could see the clouds gathering in the distance, the pink-tinted sky turning to a steely gray. It looked like it was going to be a blustery day. Jasmine shivered, pulling her sweater closer, quickening her pace. At least that meant folks would be wanting coffee.

She stopped in the hallway just outside the bathroom, frowning, something somewhere setting off alarm bells. Standing perfectly still, she waited, heart pounding, but the house remained quiet. Blowing out a breath, she started into the bathroom, but swung around again as the sound of something rustling emanated from the spare room across from her.

Asha.

Shaking her head, she started for the spare room, but froze when she heard a crash followed by a thump as something heavy hit the floor. Adrenaline pumping, she sprinted for the stairway, figuring retreat was her best option. But she hadn't made it very far when something dashed past her, a long silky tail brushing against her leg.

"Damn it, Asha," she yelled at the retreating cat. "You scared the life out of me." Said feline stopped a few feet away, inspecting a paw, feigning indifference, and Jasmine bent to rub between the cat's ears, heart still pounding.

"What has you all in a tizzy?" she asked, forcing herself to retrace her steps and check the spare room. A storage box lay on the floor, the contents scattered. And next to it, a broken vase and some silk roses. With a sigh, she bent to straighten Asha's mess. The cat was a certified kamikaze. Always trying to climb to the top of everything. And more often than not, missing by a mile.

She tucked the box back on top of the bookshelf and threw out the shards of glass, then grabbed the duffle again and went back to the bathroom. Picking out the moisturizer and face cream Tina had requested, she shoved them into the bag and headed for the staircase. Asha had disappeared, but Jasmine didn't have time to look for him.

"It'd serve you right if I left without feeding you," she called as she headed down the stairs, duffle in hand. She stopped in the kitchen and opened the pantry to grab the bag of cat food. After opening it, she turned to the bowls by the back door, surprised to find that they'd been turned over—water pooling beside them on the floor.

More of Asha's antics.

She cleaned up the floor and then filled both bowls, returning them to their proper places. "Tina, you're going to owe me big time." She laughed to herself and then headed for the front door, remembering at the last minute that she'd forgotten the duffle. Turning back, she walked into the kitchen and reached for the duffle on the counter where she'd left it.

But just as her hand closed around the strap, someone grabbed her from behind, a hard calloused palm pressing against her mouth. She slammed an elbow backward, satisfied to hear a grunt of pain, and jerked free for a moment. But her attacker was bigger and faster.

His arm circled her waist, pulling her backward, but she kicked out, fighting against him, the momentum sending them both crashing into the counter. Scrambling, she pulled an arm free and made a grab for the knife block. But before she could reach it, his fist closed around her braids, and he yanked her back, the pain making her dizzy.

Above her she saw Asha, on the top of the cabinets, back arched, spitting with fury. With a scream worthy of a Scottish banshee, the cat launched himself at the man, hitting him square on the shoulders. With a muffled curse, he swung at the cat, knocking the animal aside. But it was the opportunity Jasmine needed. Breaking free, she ran full-out for the front door, yanking at it only to remember that it was locked.

She struggled with the deadbolt, trying to turn the latch with shaking fingers. Finally, it turned, but she was too late. The man grabbed her from behind, pulling her away from the door and freedom. This time it was a handkerchief that covered her mouth and nose, the sickly sweet smell making her woozy. She tried to fight him, but her limbs had gone rubbery, her mind filling with cotton.

It was like trying to swim through a fierce current. The harder she tried, the deeper she was dragged, until there was no more air to breathe. With a sigh, she let go, realizing that Professor Marshall had been right—the man who'd killed Sara Lauter was going to kill again.

Hannah stood in the doorway of the war room, trying to calm her nerves. Inside, huddled together over the computer, stood Harrison with two beautiful women. One the blonde all-American type and the other a statuesque black woman with full lips and perfectly carved cheekbones.

The kind of women men went wild over.

She shook her head, embarrassed by her jealousy. She and Harrison had slept together. A one-night stand to relieve pressure. They'd both entered into the liaison willingly, and neither of them had made promises they couldn't keep. It was just the way she liked things.

Except that this morning, when she'd awoken to an empty bed, she'd felt a profound sense of loss. A gut-level ache that she wasn't willing to examine too closely. And now, standing here watching him flirt with the two women, the pain was even more acute.

Damn it all to hell—she hadn't fallen for the man. She couldn't. She wouldn't.

Squaring her shoulders, Hannah walked into the room. Avery was standing in the corner, on his cellphone, and Simon and Drake were huddled over the same files Drake had been culling last night. Upon seeing Hannah, Avery snapped the phone shut and, with a quick nod, headed for the front of the room.

"Now that everyone's here," he said, "we'll get started."

The blonde looked up from the computer, her face classically lovely. But there was a spark of something else there. A strength that Hannah couldn't help but admire. This woman was more than the skin she wore.

With a warm smile for Harrison, she moved from behind the computer desk, her stomach preceding her. Madison Roarke was at least five months pregnant. Hannah hated the fact that she felt an acute sense of relief.

Where the hell was her pride? She'd slept with the guy, not married him.

"So before we begin, let me officially introduce our guests," Avery said, as everyone gathered around the table.

Harrison was sitting between the two women, his attention, as usual, on his computer. He had yet to make eye contact. And real or imagined, Hannah could feel the tension radiating between them. This was why it was a stupid idea to sleep with a colleague.

"Special Agent Madison Roarke." Avery gestured toward the blonde. "And forensic pathologist Tracy Braxton. We really appreciate your coming on such short notice."

"Anything for Harrison," Madison said, with another fond smile. "And besides, this is what we do. Although usually with a full team." Madison worked with the Behavioral Analysis Unit, a group within the FBI dedicated to profiling and tracking serial killers.

"Hey, you've got Harrison and me. What more do you need?" Tracy's eyes danced with amusement. "It's like old home week. Not sure it gets any better than that."

Again, Hannah felt the surge of jealousy. She'd known, of course, that Harrison had had a life before A-Tac, but somehow it hadn't seemed to matter. But now, faced with the reality of these two women, both of them clearly close to Harrison, she wasn't at all comfortable with the idea. Harrison belonged with A-Tac. They were family.

Not to mention the intimacy of the night before.

As if reading her mind, Harrison looked up, his expression unreadable, but the small smile at the corner of his lips twisted her stomach, her pheromones not the least bit interested in the logic that she shouldn't let herself get any more involved.

Love caused pain. Period. It had destroyed her when she was young, and then she'd faced a different sort of loss with Jason's death. She wasn't willing to go there again. Which meant that Harrison's defection this morning should have pleased her. It just made it easier to pretend that nothing had happened, but somehow her heart hadn't gotten the memo.

"Actually, it can be better," Harrison was saying. "You've also got A-Tac on your side. And trust me when I say, it doesn't get any better than these guys." He smiled at her then, the warmth in his eyes almost her undoing. At least they were still friends.

"As much as I appreciate the accolades," Avery said, "we've got a killer out there. And if I understand correctly, Madison can't afford more than a couple of days with us. So we need to hit the ground running."

"So what have you got?" Drake asked, pushing back in his chair so that it was propped on two legs as he leaned back against the wall. He and Simon were watching the two newcomers warily. And Hannah suppressed a smile. Some things at least hadn't changed, the alpha males clearly marking their territory.

"Not as much as I'd like," Madison said. "Right now, you've got what appears to be an isolated incident. Which makes it harder to profile. But there are certain tells that would seem to point to the fact that this isn't the killer's first time around the block."

"Meaning you think he's killed before?" Simon asked, his gaze speculative.

"Yes. I do." Madison nodded, standing up to move

to the front of the room, her hand resting protectively against her swollen belly. "People don't just jump into this kind of organized sadistic torture. They work their way up to it."

"So have you found anything that looks like this guy's warm-up act?" Simon asked, his gaze moving to Harrison.

"No. Nothing in the area," Harrison replied. "Which makes the whole thing a little bit weirder. These guys usually don't stray very far from their comfort zone. So you'd expect to find something local with a similar MO. Or at least some sign of a killer building his fantasy. But so far, we haven't found anything."

"What about widening the search radius?" Avery asked. "I know these guys like to keep to their own backyards, but in our business, sometimes it's all about the exception."

"Well, profiling works off of predicting behavior. But I agree there are always people who fall outside the parameters," Madison agreed.

"Unfortunately, the only parallel we found when we widened the search was the cyber killer," Tracy said, her voice low and husky. Sexy. Hannah shook her head—angry at the train of her thoughts. She wasn't in the running for Harrison. And even if she was, every other woman wouldn't automatically be competition.

"The guy that killed Harrison's sister?" Simon asked, eyebrows raising. "But wasn't that like nine years ago? I mean, isn't it weird for someone like that to suddenly resurface after all this time?"

"It's rare, but not unheard of," Madison said. "Sometimes there are extenuating circumstances. An unsub winds up in prison. Or some change in his life prevents his continuing to kill. Or maybe something happens to relieve the stressor. Most of these guys are reacting to something negative that happened in their lives. Sometimes real, sometimes imagined. Then when something happens to change any of those circumstances—"

"Like being released from jail," Drake prompted.

"Exactly." Madison nodded. "In that case, they're free to resume."

"So if this guy found something to tame the beast, so to speak," Hannah said, "and then for some reason that situation changed, he could be right back where he started."

"Sometimes it's even worse," Madison added. "But we don't think this is the work of the cyber killer."

"What about the photograph on Sara's computer?" Hannah asked. "Surely that would indicate a connection to the cyber killer."

"A connection, yes, but nothing that links concretely to the actual killer," Madison said, as Harrison brought the photograph up on the overhead screen. "Anyone could have taken this. At any time."

"But the black and white and the crime scene tape—" Hannah began, but Harrison interrupted.

"I analyzed the digital image early this morning and couldn't find anything that proves it's an old shot. But I also couldn't find any evidence of tampering either. Which indicates it wasn't photoshopped. So it could be the real deal. Or someone could have physically staged the shot. There's just no way to verify for certain."

"Do we know if the house still exists?" Simon asked.

"It does," Tracy nodded. "And the appearance, especially at night, is still pretty much the same."

Harrison hit a key on the computer, and a second photo came up next to the first. "As you can see, when I adjust for darkness and switch to black and white, it could easily pass for nine years ago. Even the tree is similar enough to provide doubt."

"And besides," Madison said, "even nine years ago, anyone could have taken a photo at the scene. It was a busy block in Marble Falls, Texas. And although the actual scene was closed off, the street wasn't."

"So if our killer took the shot, he could have taken it any time after the murder," Drake said. "And it would still look as if he'd been there in the moment."

"Or it's possible someone else took it, and somehow our killer got his hands on it," Madison offered. "Finding something like that can often act as a trigger."

"Then we're saying it's a copycat." Avery's words were a statement, not a question.

"I think it's possible." Madison absently rubbed the top of her belly, clearly ordering her thoughts. "There are definite similarities between this murder and the ones committed by the cyber killer. Particularly the ritual, which for both apparently involves two stages. The bedroom where the victim was sexually assaulted and killed. And a second scene in the cellar where the victim was strung up crucifixion-style. But there are also definite differences."

"Like?" Simon asked, leaning forward, palms on the table. An ex-SEAL, Simon was a cut-to-the-chase kind of guy.

"Well, for starters," Tracy said, "the knife wounds from your vic were administered postmortem. The cyber killer used his scalpel to inflict torture. Every slice was designed to produce maximum pain without threatening death."

"Sadistic bastard," Drake mumbled under his breath.

"And then some," Madison agreed. "But Tracy's right. That kind of act, that kind of anger, isn't something that goes away. If he were back, I'd expect the anger to have escalated, not diminished. And certainly not to have disappeared altogether. There's pleasure derived from postmortem disfigurement, but it's not the same as the kind elicited from torturing someone."

"And in addition to that," Tracy said, "this unsub slit his victim's throat in a way that guaranteed instant death. Sara died within seconds. The cyber killer, on the other hand, had refined his cutting so that the victim bled out slowly in an effort to continue the torture. There were also two other deviations physically."

"The original killer gained access to the women's homes without any sign of forced entry," Harrison said.

"Which means he had social skills our new unsub is lacking," Tracy added. "According to my preliminary examination, I'd say that Sara Lauter was drugged. I've ordered a tox screen to confirm, but the signs are pretty clear."

"So the only way he could subdue her was to drug her."

"It seems likely." Tracy nodded. "And there's one more big difference. The original killer raped his victims. It was a power play. A way to show his dominance. But this guy isn't into that."

"But Sara was sexually assaulted," Hannah said. "I saw it in the report."

"Yes, she was." Tracy nodded. "But not in the usual way you think of rape. The vaginal tearing and bruising of the labia indicate that Sara was assaulted with an inanimate object. Something fairly large with a sharp end."

Hannah swallowed rising bile, her mind conjuring the image of the bright young woman she'd had in class.

"I've got people at the scene now, checking to see if maybe we missed something. But my guess is that the unsub took whatever it was with him. This guy was nothing if not careful."

"Jesus, I can't believe we're sitting around talking about this stuff." Simon blew out a breath and pushed back from the table, arms crossed as he studied Tracy and Madison. "How the hell do you guys deal with this kind of thing day in and day out?"

"Same way you deal with the fallout from terrorism, drug cartels, nuclear bombs—all the things you're called upon to handle." Madison shrugged.

"Point taken." He nodded, a rueful smile playing at the corners of his lips.

"Okay, so we've got the differences in the way the abduction, torture, and killing were handled. What else?" Avery prompted.

"The original killer was organized," Madison said. "He planned his attacks with meticulous care. Researching the right victims and the perfect surroundings."

"Meaning what?" Drake asked.

"Each of the women was taken to a house with a cellar. We believe this was a crucial part of his ritual. Part of his fantasy, if you will. Something happened to him involving a cellar and each time he killed, he was replaying or rewriting that incident. It took planning to find women who fit the victimology and then to find the right houses with cellars."

"Victimology? Are you talking about the type of women he chose?" Simon asked.

"Yes," Tracy said. "It's almost as important to understand the victims as it is to understand the unsub. Maybe more so when you consider that the commonalities between victims can tell you a hell of a lot about the killer."

"And the cyber killer picked young women. Midtwenties. Brunettes. Right?" Drake asked.

"Someone's been doing their homework," Harrison noted. "And yes. That's the basic profile. In addition, they were also all successful. They came from an upper-middle-class background. They all lived alone and within roughly a fifty-mile radius just slightly north of Austin."

"His comfort zone," Hannah said.

Harrison nodded. "Which is another major difference. If it were the same guy, he'd be a hell of a long way from home."

"Which isn't unprecedented but certainly isn't the norm," Madison added. "Anyway, my original point was that while the cyber killer was highly organized, this guy is presenting mixed signals. On the one hand, he's shown evidence of planning, and he's meticulous about removing trace evidence that could tie him to the scene. But there are also some signs of spontaneity. Maybe even in choosing the victim. And if it is a copycat, it could be that the planning isn't really his own."

"You mean that he's just following a template and improvising along the way."

"It seems possible," Madison agreed.

"And if you consider the differences in their victimology," Tracy said, "it only makes it seem more certain that we're talking about someone other than the original killer. Sara Lauter was a good five years younger than the original victims. She's a college student. She lived in a dorm. She had a serious boyfriend. She basically isn't his type."

"And then there's the video footage," Harrison said. "That's totally new. And clearly aimed at garnering attention—preferably from the authorities. The cyber killer wasn't interested in attention like that."

"But he sent emails, right?" Simon asked.

"Yes. But just emails. No visual. And in all five instances, we didn't even find the emails until after the fact. In this case, it's pretty clear the killer wanted the video to be found and broadcast."

"So why not send it to the paper or the police? Why send it to Tina?" Hannah asked.

"There's probably an element of fear involved. But something as graphic as what he sent was bound to be brought to the attention of someone in authority. In this case, Hannah." Madison smiled at her, the gesture making her feel guilty for her earlier thoughts. "The killer's flaunting his power. He's giving us enough to solve the mystery but not enough to save Sara. And of course, if he really is basing his killing on the cyber killer's work, then we can't ignore the possibility that Tina is the next target."

"Except that we've made it next to impossible for him to get to her," Simon said.

"True," Madison nodded. "But that may only serve to increase his determination. Men like him live to outmaneuver and outplay."

"Should have been on *Survivor*," Harrison quipped, in

an effort to lighten the mood. Hannah smiled, meeting his gaze, relieved when he grinned in return.

"You'd be surprised, actually, how many of the people portrayed in the show actually do exhibit signs of personality disorders." Madison shrugged. "Although so far, no serial killers."

"That'd certainly up the ratings," Drake suggested with a wicked smile. "So what else do we know about our guy? Besides the correlations or lack thereof to the cyber killer."

"We know that he's operating alone," Harrison said. "The film angles indicate a tripod, which means he didn't need anyone to run the camera."

"He's white," Madison continued. "Moderately educated. Probably a loner. He's had some knowledge of anatomy and medical procedure but he isn't a doctor. And he most likely has experience with computers and video equipment."

"The forged email and the streaming video." Drake nodded, as Avery rose to answer his phone.

"It's also possible he was in the military or has a background in hunting," Tracy continued. "That would explain his expertise in cutting a throat. And he's going to be big. Strong. Sara wasn't a large woman, but getting her subdued and transported, even drugged, would have taken muscle. Not to mention stringing up her body the way he did."

"As we said before, he's an organized killer, but with a modicum of spontaneity. Probably proving that he's still fairly new to the game, although he'll have had at least some experience," Madison said. "Finding the house where he kept Sara implies an extensive knowledge of the area around Sunderland."

"And he's most likely got some connection to Texas and through that, the cyber killer," Harrison said, trailing off, pain radiating across his face, the conversation obviously hitting too close to home.

"Right," Madison continued, clearly recognizing Harrison's discomfort and coming to the rescue in a way Hannah could not. "Either directly or possibly through secondary sources. Like newspaper accounts or police files or both. The bottom line, here, is that in all probability, we have a serial killer on our hands. One who is most likely copying the cyber killer. Maybe even believing that he's continuing his work. And bottom line, he's going to strike again."

"Sooner rather than later," Avery said, snapping his phone closed, his expression grim. "That was Reid. The killer's sent Tina another video."

CHAPTER 11

I really shouldn't have opened the damn thing," Tina said, chewing the inside of her lip. "But this time it wasn't from Princeton. It was from you." The girl looked apologetically over at Hannah. "I thought maybe you'd found something new, so I just opened it without thinking."

"I didn't send anything." Hannah shook her head, her gaze moving from Tina to Harrison.

"I'm checking," Harrison said, looking up from his computer. They were back in the Fischer Hall conference room, Reid situated near the door to keep watch. Madison and Hannah were sitting with Tina, who was looking incredibly shell-shocked. Not that he blamed her. "I've got the phone connected to my computer, and I'm in the process of copying the mpeg. I'm also trying to trace the source of the original email, but this guy's using proxy servers to disguise the search."

"But it didn't come from me?" Hannah asked.

"Not literally, no," Harrison shook his head, his eyes on the map displaying his search as he pinged off various servers. "Jesus, he's utilizing one in Belarus and another in Western Australia. This dude's good." He frowned at the screen, hitting a key to stop the action.

"What is it?" Hannah asked as she rose to stand behind him. He could feel her breath on his neck, making it more difficult to concentrate than he cared to admit. Which was frustrating on too many levels to count.

"The message does appear to originate from your account," he said. "The IP through Sunderland.edu."

"Shit. So he hacked me?"

"Maybe. But more likely he just mirrored the IP. Sort of the same as using proxy servers."

"But why me?" Hannah asked, confusion playing across her face.

"No way to know for sure," Madison said. "Unless we can catch the bastard and get him to tell us. Most likely it was someone he knew Tina would trust."

"So he's watching me?" Tina asked, her voice coming out on a squeak.

"Not necessarily," Madison assured her. "It's far more likely that he just hacked into your email account. Both Professor Marshall and your contact from Princeton would have been listed there. And if he got into your emails, it'd be fairly simple to figure out your relationships with both of them."

Tina nodded, clearly not convinced.

"Look, these men like to play off your fears. But to do that, they have to reach you first. And in this guy's case, he's trying to do it through these videos. And for them to work, you've got to open them, so he needs to be sure that they appear to be from trusted sources. People you'd have faith in."

"In my case, that'd be my professors," Tina said.

"Exactly," Madison nodded. "And after he hooks you into opening the thing, he clearly expects you to share what you find. That's probably the whole point of sending them in the first place. He needs validation."

"So I'm just a means to an end?"

"It seems that way," Madison agreed. "But we really don't have enough information yet to know for sure. Maybe we'll find something here. Did you watch the whole thing?"

"No." She shook her head. "I couldn't. I just closed it as fast as I could and called Professor Marshall."

"I think considering the circumstances, it'll be all right if you call me Hannah." She smiled, reaching out to touch Tina's shoulder.

"Wow." Tina laughed, the sound strangled. "I've always wanted to be on a first-name basis with my professors, but this wasn't exactly the way I'd envisioned it."

"I know. And you're being really brave about all of this," Hannah said.

"Well, I'd just as soon opt out of the whole thing, if you don't mind. I didn't look at the video because I didn't want to see it. I'm still having nightmares about that man and...and Sara." She stared down at her hands.

"Look, sweetie," Hannah said, dropping down in the chair next to Tina, swiveling it so that she was facing her. "I know this is really scary. Hell, it scares me, too. But Madison here is really good at what she does. And the best way we can help her is to provide any information we can." She took Tina's hands and waited until the girl raised her eyes. "And since this man, whoever he is, seems to have targeted you in some way, it follows that you may be in a unique position to help."

"But I don't know him. I don't. No one I know could have murdered Sara." Her voice broke on the name.

"If he does know you, Tina," Madison said, coming to sit on the other side of her, "it doesn't mean that you know him. These kinds of predators don't make friends easily. It could just be someone you came in contact with in a casual way. But for whatever reason, he wants you to know what he's doing. And if you let him get to you, then he wins."

Hannah nodded. "She's right, Tina. This is all about power. And as long as you don't give in, he's not going to get it."

"Well, I sure as hell don't want that son of a bitch taking anything from me. So if it helps, I'll stay. And I'll watch the video." She nodded, sucking in a big breath. "But, Dr. Marshall . . . *Hannah* . . . you're going to be here the whole time," she said. "Right?"

"Absolutely, I'm right here. And so are Madison and Harrison."

"Okay, then, you think you're ready?" Madison asked gently, pushing to her feet.

"Yes." Tina squared her shoulders clearly trying to rein in her fear.

"I'm assuming, now that it's downloaded onto your computer, you'll be able to project it up there?" Madison tipped her head toward the large monitor on the back wall of the conference room.

"Not a problem," Harrison said, hitting a key to open the mpeg in a program that would project it onto the screen above them.

It was grainy. Like the other video, the shadows masked most of the scene. This time, however, unlike before, the camera wasn't stationary. It was moving. Almost point of view. A piece of wooden flooring. Maybe a porch. And then a painted wall. Everything was shot in black and white, which made it even harder to make out details. And this time, there was sound. Slow, rhythmic breathing, accentuated by the occasional creak of the floor.

"He's moved inside somewhere," Hannah said, narrowing her eyes as she studied the video.

"A hallway from the looks of it," Madison nodded. "But he's being careful not to give anything away. He's playing with us, I think."

"At least he doesn't seem to have a victim," Harrison noted, as he multitasked, watching the video and still trying to trace the source of the email.

"Yet," Madison said, then frowned, clearly regretting her choice of words as Tina cringed.

"I think it's a kitchen," Tina said, frowning at the grainy image of tile and the edge of something wooden. "But it's—" Her voice was cut off by the sound of a scream, as a hand filled the screen, and then an elbow, followed by what looked like a dark woven material of some kind. The scream stopped abruptly, followed by a grunt of pain and what looked to be a struggle.

Hannah winced, and Tina had hidden her eyes.

"What's that?" Madison asked as she studied the screen above them. "Right there, and then again there."

"It looks like hair," Harrison said, freezing the screen and enlarging the frame.

"Human hair," Hannah added, her voice barely audible. "I think it's braided."

Harrison hit a key and the video resumed as something flashed across the screen and another scream erupted—this one clearly feline.

The camera, or the person holding it, shifted, a white cat coming front and center—pupils dilated as it leaped forward, hissing, claws bared.

"Oh, my God," Tina whispered, her eyes almost as wide as the cat's. "That's Asha, my cat. And the hair—I think it's Jasmine's."

Drake and Harrison flanked either side of the door to Tina's house, Simon and Avery moving toward the back. Hannah held her breath as she drew her gun and waited for Drake's signal.

Because of the baby, Madison had stayed behind with Tina. Hannah almost wished she'd volunteered to stay behind as well, but she felt like she owed it to Tina to be here when they found—whatever the hell it was they found.

Apparently Jasmine had volunteered to stop by Tina's house to check on her cat. And a quick check at the coffee house had proved damning. Jasmine had been supposed to open up, but she'd never showed. Hannah's heart pounded as Avery radioed that he and Simon were in place.

Using his fingers, Drake counted down to one, and Harrison reached out for the doorknob. It turned easily, and the door swung open, Drake moving into the entry hall, leading with his gun, she and Harrison following close behind.

Harrison edged toward the staircase as Drake moved into the living room and she stepped cautiously into the dining room. She turned slowly, gun at the ready, then called, “clear,” as soon as she was certain the room was empty.

Behind her, she heard Drake call out the same, and the squeak of Harrison’s shoe on the staircase. Stepping back into the foyer, Drake motioned her upward—following Harrison, and with a quick nod, she started up the stairs behind him.

Below, she could hear Avery and Simon in the kitchen, and she flashed to memories of the house in the woods and Sara’s body. She shook her head, pushing aside the image. Best to concentrate on the here and now. And, she hoped, the living.

Harrison was already at the door to the bathroom when she hit the landing. And with a nod in her direction, he swung inside, then reappeared with a shake of his head. She moved forward, stopping in the door of the extra room, waiting until he had her back. Then with a quick intake of breath, she stepped into the room, leveling her gun.

It was empty. Like the dining room, perfectly in order.

She walked back into the hallway and followed Harrison to the bedroom. He swung into the doorway, then shook his head.

“All clear here, too. Although it looks like someone has been here. The place is a mess.”

Hannah laughed, relief making her giddy. “It’s just Tina. She’s a slob. Anywhere she goes, it’s like liquid—she fills every single inch of space.”

Harrison pressed the button on his comlink. “Avery, we’re clear up here.”

“Wish I could say the same,” Avery replied. “We’ve got signs of a struggle in the kitchen.”

Hannah suppressed a shiver, her mind going back to the scene of Sara's murder. Jasmine was a friend.

"You okay?" Harrison asked, his brown and green eyes filled with concern as they headed back to the staircase.

"Yeah," she shook her head, realizing that the gesture negated her words. "It's just that I can't seem to keep the image of Sara strung up at that house out of my mind. And now it could be Jasmine..." She trailed off, angry that she'd let her emotions get the best of her.

"It's okay to care, Hannah," he said, his fingers warm against her arm as they started down the stairs. "It's what lets us know we're still human. The day you stop, that's when you need to worry."

She knew he was right. But it didn't make it any easier.

They walked into the kitchen to find Avery and Drake already there. Avery on the phone, presumably to call in the forensics people. There was no sign of Simon. The sunny kitchen had always seemed so cheerful to Hannah, but now the floor was littered with cat food and broken dishes, the signs of the struggle they'd witnessed on the video almost seeming more ominous after the fact.

"So what have we got?" Harrison asked, as he knelt to touch his fingertip to a small pool of drying blood.

"Not enough to have been a kill," Drake said. "But it's pretty clear that someone was on the losing end of this fight."

"Or some*thing*," Hannah amended, searching the kitchen for signs of Asha. "Any sign of the cat?"

"Not so far," Avery said, flipping his phone closed. "But I suspect he headed for the hills when he heard all the noise. This didn't happen in a vacuum." He waved a hand at the paraphernalia littering the floor and countertops. "Anyway, whoever was here, we can be pretty sure it was our killer. The scene seems to match up with the video."

"Forensics on the way?" Harrison asked, straightening up again, his gaze moving across the kitchen.

"Yeah. That was Tracy. She's coming with the locals. She'll make sure nothing's missed."

"Speaking of missing—looks like we're down a knife." Drake frowned, nodding toward a large knife block. "It might be nothing but it's worth checking with Tina."

"And when we do, we can give her a little good news," Simon said, walking into the kitchen holding a still agitated Asha. "Found him in the linen closet." He set the cat down in front of his food bowl, and after a lap at the water, he leaped up into a kitchen chair, watching them through emerald eyes.

"He seems to be no worse for wear," Avery observed. "Which I guess rules him out as the source of the bloodstain. What made you look in the linen closet?"

"I had cats when I was a kid. And when they're scared, they like small, dark places," he said. "Plus I was looking for a cellar."

"For the body," Hannah said, the words coming of their own volition.

"Yeah. But there isn't one—a cellar, I mean. Hell, best I can tell, there isn't a body either."

"But judging from this duffle," Harrison said, lifting a navy bag that had been thrown into the corner, "I'm guessing that Jasmine was here. It's full of clothes and toiletries. I'm guessing stuff she was bringing to Tina."

"Which means what?" Hannah asked. "The killer subdued her here and then took her somewhere else?"

"That's what happened with Sara Lauter," Simon said.

"But Jasmine and Sara have nothing in common," Hannah said. "What was it Madison said about victimology? Killers usually stick to a type? Jasmine is older than Sara, she's successful, she's not a student, and she's black. Seems like sort of a stretch to put the two women in the same category."

"Unless there's a common thread we're missing," Drake replied.

"Or Jasmine wasn't the real target." Avery was staring at the bag, eyes narrowed. "What if the killer didn't know that Jasmine was coming. What if he was waiting for Tina?"

"You think that because she got the video, she was targeted next?" Simon frowned, considering the idea.

"That's pretty much what the cyber killer did." Harrison shrugged. "But we already established that he'd know that we'd sequester Tina as soon as we found out she'd gotten the mpeg."

"Maybe he thought we'd do it at her house. So he was waiting."

"Yeah, but if he wanted Tina, why not just walk away when he realized it wasn't her?" Hannah asked. "I'm no expert, but if this guy had a plan, then wouldn't he have just waited?"

"Maybe she surprised him," Simon suggested, reaching down to pet Asha, who was purring contentedly now. Whatever had happened here, the cat had already put it behind him.

"Okay, but then why move the body? If she didn't have the profile to get his rocks off—why take her?"

"To hide the body?" Hannah knew even as she said it that it didn't make sense.

"If that were the case," Simon said, reading her mind, "he would have cleaned up as well. Although I'm willing to bet that the blood is Jasmine's and that there's nothing else here to incriminate him. He was too careful before to make that kind of mistake now."

"Could be he's rattled," Drake suggested.

"I don't think so." Harrison shook his head. "You're forgetting that the bastard had the presence of mind not only to videotape the attack but to send it to Tina—and through her, to us. There's a message here somewhere, I just don't know what the hell it is."

"Well, if there's a trace, we'll find out soon enough," Avery said, his words reflected in the sound of approaching sirens. Behind them, from somewhere in the living room, a snippet of music filled the air.

"What the hell was that?" Drake asked.

"Unless I'm off my game," Harrison said, already striding toward the door, "that was the sound of a computer booting. There's no mistaking the Windows theme."

Hannah and the others followed him into the room. He was standing in front of a small laptop set on the corner of the coffee table, situated so that it was facing the kitchen. The screen was up.

"Was it like this when you first came in here?" Harrison asked, his hand on his holstered gun.

"Yeah." Drake nodded. "We didn't touch anything."

"It's Tina's," Hannah said, "I've seen her with it on campus. So why did it boot up?"

"Because it's streaming another video." Harrison stepped back so that everyone could see.

The room was different, but the scene was the same as the first one. A woman, naked and tied to a bed. The shadowy shape of a man with a knife. Hannah's stomach tightened.

"Son of a bitch must be operating the computer remotely," Harrison said. "I won't be able to tell for sure until I get it back to Sunderland."

"But that means he knows we're here..." Hannah trailed off as the scene on the computer changed, the camera zooming in.

The woman's face was illuminated in the light, her eyes wide with fear. This time there was no question as to identity. It was Jasmine. And if things continued to play out like before—she was about to die.

CHAPTER 12

I've been over this thing like ten times now, and I'm not finding anything that's going to get us any closer to finding out where he's taken Jasmine." Harrison ran a hand through his hair and sat back, staring at his computer screen.

He and Madison were in A-Tac's computer room trying to make sense of the video. Unlike the emails, this one had been broadcast via a program installed on Tina's computer. It was a remote feed, using the Internet, but so far, Harrison hadn't been able to trace it back to the source. Hannah was with Tina. And the rest of the team was on site with Tracy and the forensic techs.

"So he's covered his tracks," Madison said, her eyes narrowed in thought.

"And then some. I tracked him through at least eight proxy servers, and now I'm linked into Tina's IP address. He's just made an endless loop with absolutely no way to isolate the real source. Whoever he is, he definitely knows his way around the Internet."

"Which is part of what bothers me," Madison said. "This guy's skill set doesn't seem to mesh. On the one hand, he presents as a techy. Organized and definitely operating with a plan. But on the other side, when you look at his victims, it seems more like a crime of opportunity."

"Except when you factor in the photo he sent Sara."

"But he didn't send anything to Jasmine," Harrison reminded her.

"That we know of." Madison shook her head. "Without a second body, the truth is that we don't have all that much to go on in the first place. But even so, this all feels contrived somehow."

"So maybe, like we said, he's following a template. Which would mean the murders themselves are based on the cyber killer, but the technical touches are his own."

"And yet, he's really good at killing, but we don't have any record of a local with an MO anywhere close to this guy."

"So maybe he learned the skills somewhere else?" Harrison suggested. "I mean, you said he might have military training. That could potentially have him moving around all over the place."

"It's definitely a possibility. As are a dozen other scenarios. The truth is we need more to go on. And to get that..." She trailed off.

"We need someone else to die." Harrison looked up to meet her gaze. "I know. It's awful. But I suspect it's already out of our hands. This guy wants us to know what he's doing, but he sure as hell doesn't want us to figure it out until it's too late. So if he's following the pattern, the fact that we have the mpeg means that Jasmine Washington is already dead."

"But why?" Madison asked, frowning as she rubbed her swollen stomach. "I mean sure he's showing his power over us. And that's certainly a profile we see a lot with these guys. But I feel like there's something more to it. Something we're missing."

"Like the fact that this asshole just happens to choose the community where I live to resurrect the work of the cyber killer?"

"The thought had occurred to me," Madison said on a sigh. "But it doesn't really make any sense. I mean why now?"

"Because maybe I'm finally starting to put it behind me?"

"Yes, but that would mean that the killer is fixated on you. And if that were the case, why hit women you don't know? Seems like the emotional impact would be a lot stronger if he attacked someone like Hannah."

"Well, he'd have his work cut out for him if he tried something like that. Hannah isn't exactly an easy mark." The words were meant to deflect the real meaning of Madison's words.

"No, she isn't. But I stand by what I said. If the guy were out to get you, she's a much more likely target."

Harrison clenched a fist, the idea of anyone hurting Hannah making him want to hit something—or someone.

"You really do care about her, don't you?" Madison observed, her voice soft.

"Of course. She's a friend. I wouldn't want anything to happen to her, or to any of them."

"Right." Madison nodded in that superior I-know-what-you're-really-thinking kind of way.

"Look, you're wrong if you believe it's anything more than that. I don't do relationships, remember?"

"Sometimes we don't have a choice," she said. "The heart wants what it wants. Even when we're determined to ignore the fact. And a person would have to be blind not to see that there's something going on with the two of you."

"We slept together. All right?" He held up a hand in surrender. "But that doesn't mean we made a commitment. In fact, it probably shouldn't have happened at all. But we've both been through a lot lately. And one thing just led to another." Sort of.

The truth was, he hadn't been able to quit thinking about her. So he'd taken action, assuming that having sex with her would solve the problem. But it hadn't. And in spite of everything that was happening—or maybe because of it—the truth was that he wanted her now more than ever.

"It's not wrong for you to be happy, you know. Bree wouldn't have wanted you to stop living."

"I am living," he protested, albeit a bit too loudly. "But that doesn't mean I want a relationship with anyone. Hannah included."

"Who are you telling that to? Me or yourself?" she asked, her smile gentle.

"You," he snapped. "Or me... Hell, I don't know. And it doesn't matter, because even if I did want to move forward—she most certainly does not."

"I wouldn't be too sure of that. I've seen her looking at you."

"I told you she's just a friend."

"Well, then you and I have a completely different idea of friendship." Madison grinned.

"I'll admit Hannah and I are connected. But not in the

way you're implying. Besides, Hannah made it more than clear that she's not interested in a relationship."

"She's closed off. I'll give you that." Madison shrugged. "The hair and the glasses are a giveaway. I'm guessing that somewhere along the way she got hurt pretty badly. And she learned to hide behind her intellect and keep her feelings locked away. But that doesn't mean she's incapable of having a relationship. It just means it'll take the right guy."

"Well, then I'm even more sure that it's not me. I'm not ready to take on someone else's problems, Madison. Hell, I have enough trouble living with my own."

"Sometimes it takes someone who can understand."

He thought about last night and sharing his sister's story with Hannah. It wasn't something he usually did. He'd put it down to the heat of the moment, but maybe Madison was right, maybe it was something more. The minute he had the thought, he shook it away. "You're making too much out of it. Trying to read something into nothing. It was a one-off."

"Maybe you're right. Maybe she's too damaged," Madison said, turning her attention back to the computer.

"She sure as hell is not. She's amazing," Harrison said, anger rising. "You saw her with Tina. She genuinely cared about the woman. And she's like that with everyone. Hannah may have secrets in her past. We all do. But believe me, she's not damaged."

"And you care. A lot." Madison's smile held a hint of triumph.

"Never try and argue with a profiler," he grumbled. "But I still stick to my original point. Hannah doesn't want anything more from me than what we already have. And neither do I. So just let it go."

"Okay," Madison said, holding up her hands in surrender. "I will. But this isn't about me. And if I'm right, the very fact that Hannah let down her guard to sleep with you means that she cares as much as you do. And that is a very rare thing, indeed."

"And you, my friend, have turned into a romantic," Harrison said. "Baby number two is addling your brain."

"Gabriel actually says the same. But the truth is that I'm deliriously happy. And there's nothing at all wrong with wishing the same for a friend."

"Well, I appreciate the thought. But I'm fine with things just the way they are."

Famous last words.

"So far we've got nothing to give us a bead on the killer," Tracy Braxton said, her brow furrowed as she considered the evidence before her. The techs had almost finished their work, yellow tape and plastic evidence markers somehow only making the scene in Tina's kitchen seem more macabre. "The blood on the floor is definitely Jasmine Washington's."

"I didn't think you could process DNA evidence that quickly," Hannah said, looking up from the table where she'd been studying a copy of the video of the attack. Something about it kept niggling at her brain, but so far she hadn't been able to figure out what it was.

"We can't. But Jasmine was an autologous blood donor. So we compared our sample to the one at the hospital, and there was enough similarity for me to identify it as Jasmine's. We'll follow up with the DNA panel to verify for certain."

"And there weren't any fingerprints?" Hannah asked.

She'd only just arrived, having spent the last hour or so with Tina, who, understandably, was completely freaked.

"Lots," Drake responded from a corner where he was examining blood spatter. "It'll take days to go through them all. But there's not much chance any of them belong to the killer. If you'll notice in the video, he's wearing gloves."

Hannah turned back to the phone she was using as a monitor, rewinding and then hitting play. Without the volume, the video seemed more surreal, less frightening. But the sight of the struggle still set her stomach on edge. Then, just before the cat launched himself at the camera, Hannah could clearly see a gloved hand as the unsub attacked Jasmine.

"So we've got nothing?" she asked.

"I've got a list of names from the local police," Tracy said. "Men who have a history of sexual violence. But there are only ten, and eight of those are in prison or have moved out of the area."

"What about the other two?"

"Avery and Simon are checking them out now," Drake said. "But neither of them really fits the profile. The first one leans toward older victims. And the other one is old. Seventy-eight, to be exact."

"What about the second video? The one we found here. Has Harrison managed to isolate anything to give us a location?"

"Not yet," Drake shook his head regretfully. "How's Tina doing?"

"As well as can be expected, I guess," Hannah said, blowing out a long breath. "Considering what happened to Jasmine..." She trailed off, shaking her head.

"I think it's almost harder not knowing," Tracy agreed. "I wish there was more we could do for her. But this guy isn't cooperating. So far he's given us nothing."

"This place is a mess." Drake frowned. "I mean there's been no effort to clean it up at all. Surely there's something here."

"You'd think." Tracy shook her head. "But the things he's left—broken dishes, the bloodstain—none of them have any trace that could link back to him. He was careful where it mattered."

"And the rest?" Hannah asked, pretty certain she already knew the answer.

"The rest he wanted us to find," Tracy said. "This guy is all about sharing. He's almost going out of his way to make sure we have a front-row seat to the murders."

"It's like he's getting off on jerking us around." Drake frowned as his gaze swept across the scene.

"He is. After a fashion," Tracy agreed. "It's a show of power. A way for him to prove that he's better than we are. Always one step ahead of the game. He probably likes the danger, too. Although most likely he doesn't really believe we'll be able to catch him. And he's escalating."

"How do you know?" Hannah laid down the phone, twisting in her chair so that she could better see Tracy.

"Two things. First off, it's been less than twenty-four hours since we found the first body. And he's already striking again. The cyber killer, if that's who he's emulating, was much less rushed. Five murders over a two-year period."

"So either this guy is much more driven to find release, or he's following his own damn drummer," Drake said, dropping down in the chair next to Hannah at the table.

"Could be either one. But it means that he's moving quickly, and that gives us less time to try to find him."

"You said there were two things," Hannah prompted.

"Yes. The video of his attack. He didn't wear a camera when he took Sara Lauter. Or if he did, he didn't have success sending it. But I'm guessing it was the former. Somehow filming the murder isn't enough. He needs more."

"Which is why you say he's escalating. Whatever his fantasy, it most definitely involves a need to get one over on authority figures. He wants validation."

"And we're fulfilling that need."

"Exactly. Although in point of fact, it's the FBI he's making grandstands for. You guys are just professors as far as he's concerned."

"Well, that's par for the course for us," Hannah said. "The whole idea is that no one knows who we really are."

"Except the Consortium," Drake sighed.

Tracy looked askance, and Hannah shrugged. "They're a lot like the killer. Always one step ahead. Taunting us with their ability to stay under the radar. So far we've been able to avert the worst of their activities, but we're not even close to shutting them down. It's like fighting a terminator. They just keep coming back."

"Well, everyone makes mistakes sooner or later," Tracy said. "Even the most talented unsubs. And if I had to put money on it, I'd pick you guys against any organization, no matter how good they are at covering their tracks. Anyway, bottom line here," her gaze moved to the scene, "whatever the stressor that started all of this, broadcasting the kill isn't enough anymore. He needs to feel like he's manipulating everything. That he's calling all the shots."

"I thought Madison was the profiler," Drake said with a crooked smile.

Tracy laughed, the levity at odds with the situation. But sometimes it was the only way to stay sane. "I'm a fast learner. And you can't hang around with people like Madison and Harrison and not pick up a thing or two."

"So you were working with them when his sister died?" Hannah asked, curiosity getting the better of her.

"Yeah," Tracy said, sobering. "I was a consultant for the FBI at the time. Still am, actually. So I work a lot of their cases. I was there when they found Bree."

"I can't even imagine what that must have been like." Hannah sat back, watching the other woman. "Losing a sibling. A twin to boot."

"He told you about it?" Her dark eyes widened in surprise.

"He sort of had to," Drake said. "With everything that's been happening, it was crucial to bring us up to speed. And since this guy seems to be doing a pretty good imitation of the cyber killer, that meant telling us about Brianna. He'd never mentioned any of it before, though."

Tracy shrugged. "For such a genial guy, Harrison's not big on sharing."

That was something Hannah could understand. "Sometimes the past is just better off staying buried." She hadn't meant to say the words out loud, but then they thought she was still talking about Harrison.

"Until it comes back to bite you in the butt," Drake said. "Anyway, I'm sorry he's having to relive all of this. And when we get our hands on this bastard..." he trailed off with a shrug.

"I'm just glad that Harrison landed in a good place. He's been through a lot. And I don't think he's ever really found somewhere where he felt like he really belonged."

"But I thought he and Madison..." Hannah broke off, embarrassed to have asked the question.

"They were close. Really close," Tracy said. "I'm not sure he could have gotten through it all without her help. But they were never more than friends, if that's what you're implying. To be honest, after what happened to Bree, I don't think Harrison is capable of having that kind of relationship. He's just lost too much to ever be able to give like that again."

It wasn't anything Hannah didn't already know, and yet, she was surprised at how much the thought hurt. Maybe it was hearing it from someone else. Or maybe she'd been holding out some small hope that...She shook her head, angry at herself for even considering the idea. Harrison was her friend. And she was lucky to have that. People like her were too dysfunctional for anything more. Isn't that what the social worker had drilled into her head all those years ago?

"Well, I'm living proof it's possible," Drake was saying, the words pulling her from her thoughts. "If you'd have told me a couple of years ago that I'd wind up with an amazing wife and a baby on the way, I'd have told you to go screw yourself. If I can find that kind of happiness—believe me, anyone can."

Hannah stared down at her hands, trying not to let Drake's words turn personal. She was letting the emotions of the past few days get to her. They needed to find this guy and stop him, then everything would go back to normal.

"I see Drake is emoting about the glories of married life again," Simon said, as he and Avery walked into the room.

"Hey," Drake said, his smile widening, "don't knock it until you've tried it."

"No, thank you." Simon shook his head, while Tracy laughed. "I'm just fine with love 'em and leave 'em, believe me. As far as I'm concerned, permanence is highly overrated."

"You and me both," Hannah said, forcing a laugh. "So how did it go with the suspects?"

"It was a wash," Avery said, his frustration evident in his expression. "The first guy had an airtight alibi. And the second is so old he can barely breathe. So we've still got nothing."

"Madison and Harrison are batting zero, too," Drake said, pushing away from the table. "So far there's nothing on the latest video to help us ID where he's keeping the girl."

"And every minute that goes by it's less likely that we'll find Jasmine alive." Avery frowned, his gaze moving to Tracy. "You almost done here?"

"Yeah. Just a little while longer," Tracy said as the two of them walked into the next room, Drake trailing behind them.

"So what are you doing?" Simon asked, dropping down into the chair Drake had vacated.

"I don't know for sure," Hannah said. "I've been going over the footage the killer sent to Tina. Something about it bugs me. But I can't figure out what it is exactly."

"Want me watch it with you? Maybe I'll see something you missed."

"That'd be great," she said, queueing it up. "It's toward the end that I start feeling like there's more." They sat back, watching as the camera caught the edge of a cutting board against the tiled countertop and then swung forward as the killer grabbed Jasmine, the sounds of their struggle still nauseating even after multiple viewings.

"Okay, now," Hannah said, nodding at the screen. "Something here." The sound of Jasmine's scream was replaced by the yowl of the cat as the camera swung around to face Asha. The animal crouched and then sprang at the camera.

"Wait," Simon said. "What's that sound?"

Hannah rewound slightly and then started it again, straining to listen. "A curse, maybe? From the killer?"

"Makes sense." Simon nodded, still staring at the screen. "Cat gets freaked, takes a flying leap at the unsub, and the guy gets pissed and mouths off."

"But it's really hard to understand." Hannah shook her head, the niggling feeling still there.

"So maybe Harrison can work his magic on it. I know there are programs that can pull out the interference of background noise. All we need is to enhance it. Cut out the cat's scream and bring up the level of the voice. Seems simple enough. We just need the right equipment."

Hannah nodded, still considering Simon's words. The cat had attacked the killer. It was right there on the screen. Suddenly the niggle blossomed.

"Does Asha still have his claws?"

Simon frowned, trying to follow her train of thought. "Definitely, I felt them when I pulled him out of the laundry basket. But I don't see why..."

"Hang on a minute." Hannah ran the footage back

again to right before the cat entered the scene. "Tracy said the killer was wearing the camera, right? Giving us his point of view."

"Yeah." Simon nodded, his eyes on the screen now, too.

"So when the cat jumps," Hannah froze the video just as the cat yowled, crouching to pounce, "he's aiming for something in front of him. Something that's pissing him off. And if the camera is on the killer then—"

"Then it has to be the killer he's attacking," Simon said, comprehension dawning. "And when a cat attacks, it uses its claws."

"And if Asha drew blood, then we just might have a shot at the killer's DNA."

CHAPTER 13

We need to talk," Harrison said, walking into the war room where Hannah was reading a report. He wasn't really sure what he wanted to say, but he could feel the tension between them growing and he hated the idea of anything—even their own stupidity—coming between them. "I know now isn't the right time, but with everything happening, I'm not sure there is such a thing. And I really regret what happened last night."

She sighed, putting the report on the table as she lifted her gaze to his. "I'm not exactly sure 'regret' is the word a woman wants to hear from a man she just spent the night with."

"You know I didn't mean it like that," Harrison protested, wishing he hadn't opened his mouth at all. "I suck when it comes to words. I just don't want what happened to come between us. I value your friendship."

"And that's all you want?"

He sucked in a breath, suddenly certain that whatever

he said it was going to be the wrong thing. "Yes. No. Hell, I don't know. I just know that you're important to me. Too important to let casual sex fuck it all up." Fuck being the operative word.

Friends with benefits.

He'd always thought the phrase sounded crass. And now here he was trying to compartmentalize last night's foray in exactly that way.

"Look, Harrison," Hannah said with a soft smile. "I don't regret last night. But that doesn't mean it's a 'big deal' either. So if you're worried that I'm reading more into it than I should—I'm not. It was a great night. We both needed to let off steam, and I'd say we accomplished that in spades. But now it's over. And so everything can go back to normal."

He searched her face, trying to read between the lines, but she looked just as she always did. Slightly disheveled and wonderfully sexy all at the same time. And despite the fact that they were, for all practical purposes, saying that last night had meant nothing, he felt his body stirring, desire rising. The woman had a way of affecting him like that.

"We're good?" he asked, tamping down his libido.

"Absolutely." She nodded, her expression resolute.

"And things can go back to the way they were?" The question came of its own accord, and just for a moment, he thought he saw a shadow cross her face.

"Stop worrying, Harrison. Nothing's changed," she said, reaching out to touch his hand, their gazes locking, the pheromones surging between them negating their attempts at denial.

"Hannah, I..."

"You were right," Drake said, bursting into the room completely oblivious of the rising tension. "There was blood and skin residue on the cat's front claws. Good catch, Hannah."

"Thanks," she said, pulling her hand free and turning to Drake, the moment between them evaporating as quickly as it had come. "So did it tell us anything?"

"Nothing yet." Drake shook his head. "Tracy's working to extract the DNA. And then we'll have to run it against existing databases to see if we get a hit. But right now it's our best shot."

"Yes, but we're not going to get the information soon enough to help Jasmine Washington. No matter how you look at it, her time's running out." Simon walked into the war room, radiating frustration. Avery followed on his heels, talking with Tracy.

"Or it already has," Drake said, his tone matter-of-fact, but his face reflecting the harsh reality of the situation.

"All the more reason to nail this bastard," Avery said as the team found seats around the table.

"Where's Madison?" Simon asked, his gaze encompassing the group.

"She got called back to Quantico," Avery responded. "Her team's working on a case in Portland. And they need her there. But she promised to stay connected via cellphone and email. And we've still got Tracy." He shot a smile in her direction. "So we're in good hands."

"Well, I don't know that I'm on the same level as Madison when it comes to predicting behavior, but I've got my talents. I managed to extract the DNA from the blood sample you gave me. And it definitely isn't a match to Jasmine Washington. Which means it's most likely from the unsub. I'm running it against the FBI databases now."

"If you'll send me the details, I can run it against CIA records as well," Hannah said, pushing her glasses up on the bridge of her nose. "And I can also cross-check it against Homeland Security's databases. I realize it's not as likely that we'll get a hit, but you never know."

"The more places we search, the better," Avery agreed. "I'll also forward the info to the local police. It's important that we keep them in the loop. And you never know, maybe they've got a local we missed when we did our search. There are definitely aspects of Sara's murder that don't fit the profile of a sexual predator."

"I'm not following." Simon frowned, shaking his head.

"Just that there's a detachment about the way she was killed. Even the rape. It's almost as if the killer is just going through the motions," Tracy said.

"Yeah, well the end result is the same. Sara's dead. And Jasmine Washington is next on the list." Drake leaned forward, anger coloring his words.

"I'm just trying to point out that our unsub may not be a sexual offender. And least not in the usual sense."

"Well, maybe we'll get something from the public," Avery said. "Madison did a press conference before she left, releasing selected parts of the profile and warning everyone in the area that we've got a dangerous man on the loose. Who knows, maybe the information she shared will trigger a memory with someone and they'll call it in. How's Tina holding up?"

Hannah shook her head, her face lined with worry. "Not good. Not that it's surprising. She and Jasmine were really close. But she's hanging in there. And she's got guards 24/7 so at least she's safe. Oh, and she confirmed that the knife set in her kitchen was complete. Which means Simon's right, and there's a knife missing."

"Maybe he used it to get Jasmine to cooperate," Harrison suggested. "Nothing like a knife to the neck to get someone moving."

"Yes, but again it doesn't fit with our initial profile. And certainly not with the original cyber killer. Taking a knife from the scene is sloppy." Tracy frowned, jotting something down on a legal pad. "This guy is just full of contradictions. Maybe it's just because we have so little to go on. But it's really making me uneasy."

"Like there's something else going on, and we're missing it," Avery agreed. "Harrison, have you and Simon been able to isolate the voice from the video at Tina's house?"

"We did." Harrison nodded, exchanging a glance with Simon. "And Madison ran it against the FBI's database using voice recognition software. But there weren't any hits."

"Maybe we should broaden the search," Drake suggested. "The CIA has voice databases, too, right?"

"They do," Hannah confirmed. "And if you'll send me the file, Harrison, I'll get it to Langley." She didn't actually look at him, and he worried that somehow his attempt to discuss things had only made it worse between them. Understanding women was just too damn difficult.

"All right then, between the DNA and the voiceprint, we've got a good shot at identifying this guy, but in the meantime we need to concentrate on finding Jasmine. Where are we with the mpeg?" Avery asked.

"Madison and I have been over it numerous times,"

Harrison said, running a hand through his hair. "And I've still got nothing. Last time, he left us a clearly visible clue with the view of the lake. But there's nothing identifiable here. I even had Drake look at it. He's lived here longer. I thought maybe he'd see something I didn't. But there's nothing."

"Which doesn't make sense," Tracy said. "This guy wants us to find him. It's probably the most important part of his fantasy. I know we've said it before, but he needs the validation."

"So why the hell is he making this so difficult?" Harrison asked, the question for no one in particular. They all knew it was probably too late, but that didn't change the feeling of urgency.

"Maybe we're coming at this the wrong way," Hannah said, pushing a strand of purple-streaked hair out of her face. "What if this isn't about what we can see?"

"Come again?" Drake asked, leaning forward, brow furrowed.

"Well, the first video was all about what we could see, right? And the second one was shot from the killer's point of view to a degree that meant it was impossible to get a big picture of what was happening. In fact, it might not have been comprehensible at all, except that there was a difference."

"Sound," Harrison said, already pulling the video back up onto the computer. "The second video had sound."

"And so did the third," Avery concluded. "So maybe the clue is in the audio."

"It's certainly worth a try." Harrison hit play and sat back as the video was projected onto the screen above the war room conference table.

The feed was still horrifying. The screaming seemed to drown out almost everything else, and as much as Harrison wanted to adjust the sound to screen it out, his hand refused to move, his mind instead superimposing the images of Jasmine with his sister, the memories threatening to overwhelm him.

"It's all right," Hannah said, materializing beside him, her breath warm against his neck as she reached across to freeze the video. "I can handle this. You don't have to do it."

He closed his eyes for a second, summoning all of his strength. "I'm fine. I don't need your help." He hadn't meant to sound so harsh, but it was all he could do to squeeze out the words.

"Harrison," Avery began, his deep voice laced with concern.

"I said I'm fine." He pulled free of Hannah, concentrating on the program's controls. "I need to do this myself." With a sharp exhalation, he adjusted the feed so that the scream was replaced by the ambient background noises.

Simon leaned forward, listening. Drake was still watching Harrison, his eyes concerned. But at Harrison's nod, he dropped his gaze, instead joining the others as they listened for something—anything—that might give a hint to the location.

At first there was nothing but the creak of floorboards and the soft intake of the killer's breathing. Then, from farther away, another noise filtered through the scene.

"Wait—" Hannah said, pushing her glasses up as she stared up at the screen. She was sitting beside him now, her fingers splayed on the table as she strained to hear. "There. What's that? It's metallic, right?"

"A clanging," Tracy agreed.

The noise swelled, then faded, the sickening "thwick" of the killer's knife taking precedence.

"Can you play it again?" Avery asked, his gaze moving to Harrison, assessing him as much as the video.

"Yes." Harrison rewound and adjusted the sound levels again, trying to bring the noise they'd heard to the forefront. The result was a bit stronger, although still muffled, the other more horrifying sounds now reduced to the background.

"It's rhythmic," Simon said, lines forming on his forehead as he concentrated. "A bell maybe."

"Or a clanger," Hannah said, pushing to her feet. "Like a railroad crossing signal."

"That's it," Drake echoed. "They must be near the railroad tracks." The tracks bisected the far west side of the town.

"But that's got to be at least five miles," Simon said. "And there are houses all along the line."

"Yes, but in order to be able to hear the signal, you've got to be at or near a corner. That should narrow it down some," Avery observed.

Hannah was typing on her computer console. "According to web, there are five corners with audible signals."

"And we can be fairly certain that he's chosen the most remote of the five. Fewest houses. Any way to narrow the search down to include that?"

"Doing it now," Hannah acknowledged, and Harrison marveled at her ability to concentrate and sort through the chaff so quickly.

"All right," Avery said, pushing out of his chair. "I want everyone else to mobilize. As soon as Hannah's got something, we need to be ready. Hannah, you have an address for us yet?"

"I've got four possibilities—I'm cross-checking them now against rental properties and empty houses." She typed something else into the computer, her eyes glued to the screen. "Okay, that narrowed it down to two."

"Do either of them have a cellar?" Simon asked. "We know that's part of the fantasy."

"Checking now. But that's going to be a little harder. There should be a blueprint through the county planner's office. But it's all secured."

"Move over." Harrison slid his chair up next to hers so that he could access her keyboard. "Shouldn't be that hard to get in." He opened a utility panel and searched the scrolling list of programming, looking for a back door. "There," he said in triumph. "I'm in."

Hannah grabbed the keyboard back, typing in the first of the addresses, shaking her head when the computer verified that there was no cellar.

"Try the other one," Harrison said, eyes on the screen as she typed.

It remained frustratingly blank for a moment and then filled with data. Hannah hit another key, and a blueprint appeared, the line drawing showing both the proximity of the railroad crossing and, even more damning, the presence of a cellar.

CHAPTER 14

The white clapboard house showed no sign of habitation. Set back from the street on a corner, it was surrounded by overgrown shrubbery, the tall tangle of bushes isolating it from its only neighbor. To the left and just behind the house, a pair of red lights and the requisite black and white X marked the railroad crossing. The windows were covered with plywood, the porch overgrown with weeds rising up through the floorboards.

Daylight was fading, the cold October wind biting. Red and yellow leaves whirled in unseen eddies, empty tree limbs reaching up toward the sky as the shadows of evening deepened. They approached the house, this time with backup from the local police.

Hannah was filled with a sense of dread as they broke through the front door and made their way through sheet-shrouded rooms until they reached a bedroom in the back. As with the scene before, there was blood everywhere. The bed and the wall behind it were covered with spatter, a deep stain spreading across the sheets, the remnants of restraints still tied to the bedposts.

"Goddamn it," Harrison said, turning heel, already heading to the cellar.

Hannah started after him, and then stopped, looking to Avery, who motioned her to go. Sprinting, she followed behind as he took the cellar steps two at a time. There was only one room, and like Sara Lauter, Jasmine Washington was strung up from the rafters crucifixion style, legs and arms splayed, hair matted, her body spattered with blood.

Harrison searched for a pulse as Avery and the rest of the team arrived. "She's dead. But she's still warm. It can't have been that long."

The words made Hannah's gut churn. They'd been so close.

"He wanted us to find her," Harrison said to no one in particular as Tracy moved forward to examine the body. "He needed to prove that he's still one step ahead of us. That he's still capable of jerking us around."

"This isn't personal," Avery said.

"The hell it's not." Harrison bit out the words, his jaw tight with anger. "This bastard has done his homework. Remember? He sent Sara the picture. He knows about the cyber killer. And if he knows that, then he probably knows about my sister. And me. It wouldn't be that hard to put the pieces together."

"Yes, but if he were after you specifically, wouldn't he have selected more personal targets?" Simon asked.

"That's what Madison said. But maybe having me involved just feeds the fantasy that he's recreating the work of the cyber killer."

"Actually there's some logic to that," Tracy said,

looking up from where she was examining Jasmine's body. "I mean, your being involved pulled Madison and me in as well. And the three of us were part of the team that took over the investigation after Bree's death."

"So you're thinking that the change of locale might have been because Harrison was working at Sunderland." Drake frowned as he considered the idea.

"It makes sense." Tracy shrugged, inserting a probe in the body to obtain a liver temperature. "You guys keep a lid on the CIA side of Sunderland, but your professorial roles are public knowledge. And it was a coup for Sunderland to get someone with Harrison's background. Not only for IT but for your criminology courses. So I'm guessing it made the news. At least among academic circles."

"And here in New York," Avery agreed. "We should have seen it before."

"We haven't had the time to put it together. Everything has been happening so quickly," Hannah said. "And even if we had, I don't think it would have helped us find Jasmine any faster." The last was meant for Harrison, whose hands were clenched as he fought against his demons.

"Hannah's right. According to temp and lividity, I'd say Jasmine's been dead about eight hours." Tracy pushed to her feet, signaling the hovering forensic tech that it was okay to take photographs.

"But when I touched her, she was warm," Harrison protested.

"The body loses about one-point-five degrees an hour depending on the surrounding environment," Tracy said. "It's cold in here. So even at eighty-six degrees, she's going to feel a little warm."

"If she's been dead eight hours—" Avery began.

"That's approximate, of course," Tracy interrupted. "I can be a little more exact after I get her back to the lab for an autopsy. But for all practical purposes, the killer is the only one who can give us an exact time of death."

"Okay, but the point is, if she's been dead that long, then he didn't spend much time with her."

"You're right." Hannah nodded, her mind running over the facts. "Tina said that Jasmine was going to check on Asha this morning. And we know she never opened her shop. So that means it was sometime before seven."

"And assuming she stuck to the plan and went to the house on her way to work," Simon said, "I'm guessing that'd mean sometime between six and six-thirty. It's only a few minutes' drive from Tina's house to Java Joe."

"And this is important because...?" Drake asked.

"Because the cyber killer's ritual was all about torture." Harrison ran a hand through his hair, his breathing calmer, but the muscle in his jaw still ticking. "He wanted them to suffer and then die slowly. They estimated he tortured his victims at least twenty-four hours before he killed them."

"So this is another break with the original," Avery said. "If he's a copycat he's gone way off script."

"Maybe he let it build into his own fantasy," Tracy said. "There's some similarity to the first kill. He raped her. Same MO. A blunt object. But there's no sign of torture here at all."

"What about the knife wounds?" Hannah asked, forcing herself to depersonalize the body. "There have to be at least fifteen."

"They're all really shallow," Tracy replied with a shake of her head. "And most of them are postmortem."

"Meaning that Jasmine was dead when he inflicted the bulk of them?" Simon asked.

"Exactly. Last time, with Sara," Tracy said, "there were postmortem wounds too, but there were also five or six deeper lacerations inflicted before she died." She sighed, her eyes moving to the tech who was now carefully photographing Jasmine's body. "You'll remember that I told you that the cut to the throat was designed for instant death."

"Unlike the cyber killer, who wanted to inflict maximum pain," Harrison added.

"Yes," Avery said. "And you're telling us that he's done that again."

"Absolutely. Jasmine was dead before she ever left the bedroom. But last time, lividity showed that there was pooling of the blood in Sara's buttocks and back."

"Which would mean she was left lying prone for a least a little while after she was dead before being moved downstairs." Hannah winced as the body moved slightly as a tech slipped by.

"Right." Tracy nodded. "But this time, all the blood is in the ankles and feet. Which means he didn't wait. He moved her almost immediately. And she wasn't as artfully arranged as Sara was. It's almost like he's giving us the signature we're looking for."

"Except that we're finding the differences almost immediately," Drake said, his frustration mirroring everyone else's in the room. "Or more accurately, *you're* finding them."

"Only because I'm trained to." Tracy shrugged.

"So what are we missing?" Hannah asked, her mind running in circles now.

"The big picture," Simon agreed. "But how the hell are we supposed to put it together?"

"Well, we've got the DNA sample," Avery reminded them. "Maybe we'll get a hit off the databases. If we know who we're up against, it'll be a lot easier to figure out why he's here. And where he might strike next."

"Or if we're lucky," Drake added, his gaze dropping to Jasmine's mutilated body, "we'll be able to stop him before this happens again."

"Any progress?" Avery asked as he walked into the A-Tac computer room where Harrison was working. Hannah had been designated to be the one to break the news to Tina again, and Drake and Simon were still at the scene helping Tracy and her team.

"No. It's like this guy just came out of nowhere. I've been running cross-checks against cases I worked back in the day. But most of the people we convicted are still in prison. Three are dead. And the ones that don't fit any of those categories are still accounted for. And none of them are anywhere near Sunderland."

"So maybe it's someone who was peripherally connected to the cyber killer case," Avery suggested.

"I thought of that," Harrison acknowledged. "So I checked all the interview notes and made a list of all the people we talked to. Then I checked them for proximity to Sunderland or local criminal activity, and nothing popped. I've got a field agent from the Austin FBI office verifying that everyone's where they're supposed to be. But I'm not expecting him to find any aberrations."

"So maybe the connection isn't from your FBI days," Avery said, perching on the arm of a chair. "Maybe it's something from after that. Someone you investigated when you were a part of Last Chance. Or someone you came across through your work with Phoenix."

"It's worth considering. And I've run cursory checks. But the truth is, the cases we pursued at the task force didn't involve the kinds of people who'd revert to serial killings. There's got to be a basic psychology there. And even allowing for variations in profile, the people we dealt with just aren't the type. And at Phoenix, it was just program development."

"Any problems with any of the employees?"

"None that I can remember. And believe me, I've been over it. I even gave John Brighton a call. It's his company. He's got his people looking, too. But I don't think they'll find anything. If this guy is connected to me in some way, it's nothing that obvious."

"Well, keep digging." Avery said. "And concentrate on your time at the FBI. Maybe narrow the focus to cases that you and Madison and Tracy worked. It could be that she was right, and whoever is behind this wanted the three of you back together for some reason."

The door behind them opened, and Hannah walked in, her expression so grim that Harrison was instantly on alert. "Has something happened?"

"No, thank God." She shook her head, dropping down into the chair beside Avery. "But I just came from Tina's, and she's a wreck. And even though there's no way this is her fault, I think she's blaming herself for what happened. If she hadn't sent Jasmine to her house..."

"He'd probably have found her somewhere else," Avery said. "Remember, these guys pick their victims."

"Yes, but we've already established that our killer is

coloring outside the lines when it comes to behavior. He's not following a script. He's organized and disorganized. And he seems to have been targeting Tina, at least to some extent. I mean, he sent her two videos." Hannah ran a hand through her hair, the spikey ends sticking up every which way. "I just wish there was something I could say that would make it better."

"Well, at least she's safe," Harrison said. "The CIA guys are still there, right?"

"Yes. Reid is still stationed outside the apartment, and there are two more men situated outside the building. Not to mention Sunderland security's eyes and ears all over the campus."

"Good. If she is a target, I just want to be sure she's protected."

"Actually, we were just discussing the fact that it's looking more and more likely that Tina was only a conduit—possibly to get to Harrison."

"Then why not use Harrison's TA?" she asked, her face scrunching up as she considered the idea.

"Mainly because I don't have one," Harrison said. "I haven't been able to find anyone I want to work with on that regular a basis. Yet." He added the last for Avery, who'd been on him for a while now to find a suitable candidate. They were gone so often it was important to have someone who could maintain continuity in class. "I'm working on it, I promise. And in the meantime, other members of the department have been picking up the slack. It helps when you're the chair."

"Okay, so that still doesn't explain why the killer would have picked my TA. She's not even remotely connected to the IT department."

Avery sat back, eyeing them both, his message crystal clear.

"Oh, please," Harrison said, before he had the chance to think about his words. "Not you, too. Why is everyone so damned determined to link Hannah and me together?" Hannah shot him an indecipherable look, but he was pretty sure it wasn't anything good. "I'm sorry that came out wrong. I seem to be doing a lot of that lately. What I meant was that there seems to be a consensus that there's something going on between the two of us. And there isn't." God, he was rambling like a schoolboy.

Avery was looking amused, and Hannah—well, she was staring at her hands, her expression clearly now one of complete horror.

"I'm just saying that maybe the killer connected the two of you somehow. *As friends.*" Avery's emphasis on the last did little to cover Harrison's gaffe, but hopefully he'd be able to heal the rift he'd caused with Hannah later. He'd tell her the truth. That he was a total ass.

"Well, I suppose it's possible," Hannah said, lifting her head with a nod, clearly delighted to be on safer ground. "We do work together a lot. And Harrison does teach the advanced criminology classes in my department. So I guess there's a connection to Tina indirectly that way. But wouldn't it have just been easier to go after Harrison directly?"

"Maybe the guy wants him to work for it," Avery suggested. "I don't know. Hell, this whole thing is just conjecture. But I don't think we can afford to ignore the possibility that there's some kind of connection between Harrison and the killer."

"So does that mean he's not a serial killer?" Hannah

asked. "And that Sara and Jasmine got caught in the cross fire?"

"Jesus," Harrison said, past and the present colliding, the pain over his sister's death augmenting the rage he felt now. "How the hell am I supposed to deal with that?"

"The same way you did nine years ago," Tracy said, walking into the room, Simon and Drake behind her. "Look, this unsub is definitely playing some kind of mind game with all of us. But that doesn't make him any less a serial killer. His goal is to fulfill his fantasy. And unfortunately that includes manipulating authority figures to make himself feel powerful."

"And by authority figures—you mean me." Harrison dropped down into his chair again.

"I mean all of us," Tracy said. "I do believe there's some kind of connection to Harrison. But it isn't as cut and dried as his just having been involved with the cyber killer. It's more complex than that. This guy has his own motivation. And if I had to call it, I'd say he's starting to break down. One minute these guys are changing—growing, if you will, and then something happens and they're losing control."

"And becoming more dangerous," Simon said.

"Exactly. As it becomes harder and harder to fulfill the fantasy, he takes bigger and bigger risks." Tracy crossed her arms, her eyes narrowed in thought.

"You're talking about his taking Jasmine even though she most likely wasn't the intended target," Hannah said.

"That and the speed of the attack and subsequent killing," Tracy allowed. "The ritual is devolving."

"Or maybe we were wrong, and the connection to the cyber killer was spurious," Harrison said, pushing aside his personal problems. There were more important things at stake.

"I'm not sure that it matters anymore," Avery said. "In fact, I'm not sure there's any reason to continue comparing the unsub with the cyber killer. He's gone so far off book now, there's no real value."

"He's right." Tracy nodded. "The unsub may have used the case as a starting point. But he's definitely playing his own deadly game now."

"Yeah," Drake said. "The key word being deadly."

CHAPTER 15

We could have just worked at your house," Hannah said, as Harrison attached cable to the computer he'd set up on her dining room table. The room, formal and mostly unused, was now covered with equipment.

"I know that," his disembodied voice came from underneath the table. "But you have food and beer here." He pushed back into view, his smile apologetic. "I tend to run to half-empty bottles of scotch and a stack of take-out menus."

"Well, you've certainly managed to make yourself at home," she said, her gaze encompassing the growing array of computers and monitors.

"Sorry—comes with the job. I guess I'm never really happy unless I'm wired for sound, so to speak."

"Beer's in the fridge," she said with a smile.

She had to admit, she was happy to have him here. It's just that between their earlier conversation and his reaction to Avery's insinuation, she was pretty sure there wasn't much chance of anything more developing between them. She should have been relieved, but she wasn't. Instead, she was standing here wondering what it would be like to have something more.

"You okay?" he asked, coming back into the room, holding out a beer. Behind him lightning flashed in the kitchen window. It was late, and with the approaching storm, the night seemed even darker than usual.

"I'm fine. Just kind of overwhelmed with everything that's happening," she said, taking the cold bottle. "I know it's our job to deal with this kind of thing, but Sara and Jasmine—they didn't sign on for any of this." She waved at the computer array.

"We're going to stop this guy," Harrison said. "I promise."

"You can't guarantee that." Hannah shook her head, taking a seat on one of the dining room chairs. "And even if we do catch him, those girls are still dead."

"And you think that's my fault?"

The question came out of left field, and Hannah shook her head. "Of course not. Why would you say that?"

"Because this guy seems to have come here because of me."

"We don't know that for certain. And even if this guy is connected to you—he's not killing for you or because of you—he's just trying to get your attention. You're as much a victim as Sara or Jasmine."

"Except that I'm not dead."

"Well, sometimes that's the hardest part."

"How do you figure?" he asked, looking up from the monitor he was connecting to a computer.

"For them it's over. Either they've moved on to a better

place—or they've just ceased to be. Bottom line. They don't have to live with the pain anymore."

"Do you believe in heaven?" he asked, sitting across from her, sipping his beer.

"Loaded question." She smiled, knowing it didn't quite reach her eyes. "I suppose I want to believe. But with the things I've been through, the things I've survived—I don't know. Since I've been with A-Tac, I've seen a lot of bad things happen to good people. Which makes believing in a higher power really difficult. And either way, it's the living who are left to deal with the fallout. Sorry—didn't mean to go all cynical on you."

"I'm not sure my thinking is all that different," Harrison said, his thoughts clearly turning inward. "When Bree died, I really lost faith. Not so much in God, but in man. And the ability of the good guys to play the winning hand. I guess, the truth is, I lost faith in myself."

"But you found it again. I mean, look at all you've accomplished."

"Maybe. I don't know." He shook his head. "I couldn't save my sister. Hell, I couldn't even find her killer."

"Well, you're right about one thing. Sometimes good people do lose. But like I said before, there'll be other battles."

"Like the one we're fighting now."

They sipped their beers in silence, the only sound the wind in the trees outside. It should have been comfortable, but there were shadows between them. Mostly of their own making.

"So what's with the anonymity around here?" Harrison asked, his eyes moving slowly around the room.

"There aren't any mementos, no pictures. Nothing to indicate you have a past at all."

"I just don't like clutter." She shrugged, trying to keep her tone even. She wasn't going to go there. Not even with Harrison.

"No. I don't buy that." He leaned forward, his gaze assessing. "There's got to be more to it. A minute ago, when you talked about bad things happening to other people, you limited it to your time with A-Tac." He frowned, clearly ordering his thoughts. "But when you said you'd been through some awful things in your life, you said that first and without the qualification. So what is it? What happened to you?"

"None of your damn business," Hannah said, pushing out of her seat and walking over to the window. "I'm not a suspect. I don't need to be profiled."

"I'm not trying to profile you. I was just trying to learn more about you. The truth is, you never talk about anything that happened to you before A-Tac."

"And now suddenly you're curious? Why, because you slept with me?" she snapped, her fingers locking around the windowsill as she fought against confusion and anger. She knew she should shut up, but she couldn't help herself. He'd hit a nerve. "You've made it more than clear that it was a mistake and that you're not interested in a relationship. So why the need to dig into my past?"

"I asked because I care about you. You're my friend."

"If I hear that word one more time today..." Her jaw tightened, fingers still clutching the windowsill.

"Look, Hannah, I'm sorry. I know I fucked up earlier. I said all the wrong things. But it isn't because I don't care. It's because I don't know how to handle what I'm feeling. All right?" He took her shoulders, forcing her to face him. "And now I've obviously made things a hell of a lot worse. And I swear that wasn't my intention. But you need to know that you can trust me. That I'll always have your back."

"I don't know what to think except that I'm starting to feel more for you than just friendship. And I don't like how vulnerable that makes me feel. And then when you say things like you did earlier about regret and friendship, it hurts. A lot. And that scares me, too. I don't want to care about you, Harrison. But I do."

Tears pounded at the back of her eyes, but she fought them off, ashamed of her own weakness. He'd flat out told her there was no chance of anything beyond friendship, and here she was practically declaring herself to the man.

"Hannah, I don't want to hurt you," he said, his brown and green eyes full of concern. "Hell, I don't want to let you out of my sight. And not just because I'm worried about the madman out there, but because I want you close by. You give me strength. I don't think I could have faced all of this again if you hadn't been there. I need you, and that scares *me*."

"So what do we do about it?" she asked, her words coming on a strangled whisper.

"I'm not sure...but I know that walking away isn't an option. At least not for me." Their gazes met and held, her heart constricting at the raw emotion reflected in his eyes.

One minute they were standing there staring at each other, and the next he was crushing his mouth to hers, his lips and tongue taking possession. The wind increased its fury, wailing down the chimney in the fireplace behind them. And Hannah felt the house shudder as lightning split the sky, and thunder crashed through the silence of the night.

Rain lashed against the window, and she tilted her head back, offering herself to him. He kissed her nose, her eyes, his tongue tracing the shell of her ear. Heat rose inside her, echoing the power of the rising storm. And then he was kissing her again, and she opened her mouth, welcoming him inside. A prelude.

He lifted her up onto the windowsill, and she wrapped her legs around him, feeling his arousal against her thighs. God, she wanted him. It was like an obsession. She wanted him inside her. It was a driving hunger like nothing she'd ever felt before. As if somehow in joining they were better—stronger.

He pushed the sweater off her shoulders and licked the soft curve of her neck. She shivered in anticipation as his hands cupped her breasts, his fingers moving in slow circles, his heat penetrating the thin cotton of her camisole. She felt her nipples bud hard against his calloused touch, and she pressed closer—needing more.

As if he'd read her mind, he pushed a strap down, his palm covering one breast, his touch sending spirals of desire coursing through her. Then he began to roll her nipple between his fingers, slowly at first, then harder, squeezing, the pressure making her cry out, even as she squirmed closer, her tongue tracing the line of his lips—tasting, nipping, teasing—wanting to give him the same pleasure he was giving her.

With a groan, he bent his head and took her breast into

his mouth, sucking deeply, pulling the nipple between his teeth, the sensation almost more than she could bear. Behind them the night split in earnest as the storm hit in full fury, the windows rattling with the strength of the wind and thunder.

Hannah arched her back, closing her eyes, letting go of all logical thought. There was nothing but the storm and the man. And for tonight at least she wasn't going to fight it.

He'd bared her other breast, her camisole around her waist, his lips caressing first one nipple and then the other until she was literally throbbing with need, her legs still locked around him, his pulse pounding between her legs.

She reached for the buttons on his shirt, heedless of propriety, ripping it open, the sound of popping buttons only adding to the power she felt surging through her. He moved back to her mouth, his lips slanting over hers, the kiss reaching deep inside her. Touching her soul.

It was a fleeting thought. One that she'd have laughed at if someone else had said it. But here, in this moment, it was truth.

She wrapped her hands around his neck as the kiss deepened, his hands moving lower, slipping beneath the waistband of her sweats. She sucked in a breath, waiting—her body tightening in anticipation as she opened her legs for him. Rain pelted the window behind her, the cold glass a contrast to his fingers, hot as they slipped inside her.

For a moment, he was still, his lips moving slowly against hers, and she felt like a bow drawn tight—stretched to the breaking point. Needing release. And then he moved faster, two fingers thrusting inside her, the rhythm matching the motion of his tongue.

Faster and faster. Deeper and deeper. Until she felt as if she were going to explode. Physically shatter. She was on the edge of ecstasy.

And then he was gone. His fingers still.

She cried out, eyes wide. But he smiled, kneeling between her legs, making short work of her sweats and panties, and then she felt the heat of his mouth as he worked his way up the smooth skin of her inner thighs, his soft hair caressing her as he moved higher, and higher still.

The thunder crashed, the sill beneath her vibrating as he found home, his tongue moving inside her. Tasting and teasing. She arched her back, throwing back her head, threading her fingers through his hair, urging him on. Needing him now with an urgency that couldn't be stopped.

Hannah shuddered, the pressure building again, the precipice higher this time than before. For a moment she teetered, and then his mouth closed around her throbbing center, sucking deeply. And she was gone, the spasms racking through her bringing pleasure so great she thought she might die of it. Sweet, sweet pain.

The thunder crashed again, reverberating as the glass behind her shimmied in protest. Pushing to his feet, Harrison scooped her into his arms and carried her up the stairs. When they reached her bedroom, he released her, her half-dressed body sliding against his, the friction of skin against skin almost unbearable. In short work, they managed to undress each other, and then he kissed her again. Lightning flashed, and just for a moment, she could see the hunger in his eyes.

With a soft smile, she pulled away. Emboldened by the dark and the storm, she ran her hands down her own body, touching her breasts and her stomach, her gut tightening when she heard him groan, his need as palpable as her own.

"God, Hannah, I want you so badly," he breathed. His words coming out in fractured bursts.

She held out her hand, and when he took it, pulled him to her, the two of them falling back on the bed, the cool cotton of the sheets providing a counterpoint to the heat of their desire. Again the thunder crashed, the sound rolling through the room like a living, breathing thing, and Hannah shifted so that she was on top, straddling him.

Then with another smile, she lifted up, his hands guiding her as she impaled herself on him, sliding slowly downward until she was so full she thought she might burst. The sensation was exquisite. And slowly she began to move, following a dance older than time.

Up. Down. In. Out. Harrison moved with her. Their rhythms finding synchronicity until they essentially became one. Faster. Deeper. Harder. More.

She couldn't breathe. There was nothing but the two of them and the driving desire. His hands tightened on her hips, and she bent to kiss him, needing to feel his lips against hers as they reached higher and higher, the storm crescendoing as suddenly the world split into white light—her body convulsing around his. His spasms combined with hers in a climax beyond anything she'd ever experienced. It was as if she'd lost all control. And for a moment, she panicked. She'd gone too far. Given too much.

And then he was there, his fingers twining with hers.

And she knew she was safe. And so she let go. Giving over to sensation and feeling. Unafraid for the first time in her life. Understanding finally what it meant to know that someone—Harrison—would be there to catch her.

It should have frightened her even more. But somehow, against the sound of the dying storm, with the feel of him inside her—it didn't.

CHAPTER 16

Harrison lay in bed listening to the wind as it whistled outside the window, leaves rustling as they hit the pane. The storm had died, but he was still feeling the aftereffects. Hannah had been amazing. So much so that if he wasn't lying in her bed, he wouldn't have been sure it hadn't all been a dream.

He'd woken to an empty bed, but the sound of the shower coming from the bathroom had soothed any worry. He wasn't sure where they went from here. But he didn't regret anything. Truth was, he hadn't regretted the previous night either—it had just scared the shit out of him. He'd never felt like this before. And he wasn't sure what the hell he was supposed to do with it.

But he'd meant what he'd said. He wanted to stay. To figure out what it was that was happening between them. Beyond that, he couldn't make promises. But somehow, together, surely they could figure it out.

Easier said than done.

He considered joining her in the shower, the thought of taking her in there almost undoing him. But just as the thought blossomed, the water stopped. He shifted in the bed, suddenly feeling uneasy. This was new territory, and he had no idea what the rules were.

And then the bathroom door opened and she was standing there, wrapped in a towel, her hair slicked back, her skin still wet from the shower, and for the first time he realized, at least consciously, that she was drop-dead gorgeous. Without her spiky hair and glasses, her flawless skin was the star, her cheeks flushed from the shower, her lips still red from his kisses. And her eyes were the deepest blue he'd ever seen. This was Hannah unplugged. The real woman. And he wasn't sure he was ever going to breathe again.

"My God," he whispered, vaguely aware that he sounded like a besotted fan, "you're beautiful."

It was as if someone had shot her. The color drained from her face, and she reached for the wall to keep from falling. Ashen, she clutched her towel, her mouth moving, but no words emerging.

"What did you say?" she choked, as if the words were killing her.

"Just that you look beautiful," he said, jumping from the bed, heedless of his nakedness, certain that he'd hurt her, but not sure how. "I didn't mean to upset you."

"I'm not beautiful," she said, pushing him away. "Don't ever say that to me."

He wanted to pull back, but he knew instinctively that it was the wrong move. Whatever was happening, it wasn't about him. And he needed to be there—to fight through her fear. So he reached for her, ignoring the tension running through her. "But you are, Hannah, you're beautiful."

She went totally still, her body rigid. And then she erupted into a ball of fury. Fighting against him, clawing, tears streaming down her face. But her eyes were blind. Her anger not directed at him. Hell, she didn't even know he was there. She was fighting something else. A demon he couldn't see.

"Hannah, it's me. It's Harrison. Sweetheart, please. It's okay. I swear it."

For a moment he thought she hadn't heard him, and then with a strangled sigh, she buried her face in his chest, her breathing coming in gasps now, her tears burning his skin. And he swung her into his arms and carried her back to the bed, holding her close as they lay against the pillows, a part of him wanting to break something or hit something—someone—whoever it was that had hurt her so deeply.

When he felt her breathing slow, he dared words. "So you want to tell me what just happened?"

At first he thought she wasn't going to answer—and then he felt her draw on the strength that he'd come to expect from her.

She rolled onto her back, her fingers still twined with his, her gaze fixed on the ceiling above them. She chewed her lip for a moment, clearly considering her options, and then she spoke, her voice so soft he had to strain to hear.

"It was my foster father. He was the one who called me beautiful." She said the words as though they were a curse, and though he wanted to ask, he held his tongue—waiting.

"He...he molested me."

Rage rose so hot and black Harrison wasn't sure what exactly to do with it, but he was certain if the man were present he would kill him. No further questions asked. But again, he resisted the urge to sound off. Instead, he waited. Knowing that if she was going to tell him, she needed to take her time. Find the right words.

"I was ten. And I thought he'd hung the moon. I never had a real father. Mine died when I was little. And my mother couldn't handle a kid on her own."

"So she put you into the system."

Hannah nodded. "At first I thought it was a blessing. They bought me new clothes. And fed me. They even talked about adoption. Hal, my foster dad, he called me his beautiful girl. He was always stroking my hair or pulling me into his lap. I was just so glad to be somewhere I was wanted. And then one night he came into my bedroom. And he told me that he loved me...and that people who loved each other..." she trailed off, tears filling her eyes.

Harrison fisted his hands, his mind unable to even conceptualize such a betrayal.

She was silent for a moment, but he could still feel the tension in her body, and he was grateful that she didn't pull away.

Finally, she blew out a shuddering breath. "At first I didn't understand. I just wanted to make him happy. But it hurt. On so many levels, it hurt."

He pulled her closer, her heart pounding against his chest, and he was aware how much her admission was costing her. The memory clearly as painful now as it had been all those years ago.

"I wasn't old enough to fight. I didn't know what to do.

And so I didn't try to stop him." There was shame in her voice, and it cut him to the core.

"Hannah, you couldn't have known. You were a little kid." He wanted to kill a man he didn't even know. It was as simple as that.

"But I should have fought harder. As it progressed, I knew it was wrong. That I was too young and he was... but I was so afraid." She turned her head into his chest.

"Where was his wife? Couldn't you have told her?" His heart was breaking. The picture of ten-year-old Hannah filling his mind.

"She didn't believe me. She said I was lying."

Again there was silence. Hannah dealing with her memories. Harrison trying to control his anger. It wouldn't help Hannah now.

"I was almost eleven when the woman next door asked me if I was okay," she whispered, her fingers tightening on his with a vise grip. "At first I lied. And then I told her the truth."

Harrison felt the blood rushing to his head, rage mixing with anguish. "What happened?" he whispered, fighting to keep his voice gentle.

"She confronted Hillary, Hal's wife. But she said it was all in my imagination. That I was lonely and troubled. And then afterward she hit me. And Hal kept coming to my room, and... and asking for more."

"Did he..." Harrison asked, afraid to say the words.

"No. But he might as well have." She closed her eyes, her face tightening as she remembered.

"So how did it end?" He tightened his hold, wishing he could take the pain away, but knowing that he couldn't.

"The lady next door." He felt her shudder against him,

and tears filled his eyes. He hadn't cried since Bree had died. But then he hadn't cared about anyone this much since then either. "She didn't give up. And a few weeks later, a man from social services took me away." She turned over onto her back again. "I never got to say thank you."

"And so what happened to you?" Harrison asked, not sure that he wanted to hear the answer but still certain that he wanted to kill her foster parents.

"They took me to a doctor and a counselor, and then they put me right back into the system. By then I was a pretty angry kid, and so I never lasted anywhere very long. I figured it was safer that way. And the one thing I knew for certain was that being pretty was a horrible thing."

"And so you added the glasses and played up the intellect," he said, remembering Madison's words.

"It worked."

"So do you actually need the glasses to see?" he asked, fairly certain he already knew the answer.

"No," she said with a twisted smile. "They're just a prop. A shield of sorts, I guess. After I first started wearing them, no one seemed at all interested in me, and that suited me just fine. I think I would have totally faded into the background except that, when I got a scholarship to college, I realized it was a chance to start over. No background. Nothing to mark me as a victim. I actually thrived for the first time in my life."

"And then the CIA came calling."

"Not until after I'd gotten my Ph.D., actually. And then they approached me about coming to Sunderland. I was good at flying under the radar—and I'd learned early to read people. Skills they said they could use."

Again she sighed, and he pulled her closer, knowing

that he couldn't slay her demons, but nevertheless still wanting to.

"So does Avery know?"

There was silence for a moment as she considered the question. And then she shook her head. "I didn't want anyone to know. I'd killed the memory. As far as I was concerned that girl was dead."

"So no one at the CIA knows?" He wasn't sure why it mattered, but the idea that she'd trusted him above anyone else was important somehow. He felt humbled and honored and overwhelmed all at once.

"I'm sure they know something. It's in my records. But you're the first person I've confided in since I told my neighbor." She paused for a moment, turning her face away. "You believe me, right?"

"Of course, I do," he said, his voice overly loud, emotion getting the better of him. "I just can't imagine."

She lifted her hand to his face, a little smile playing across her lips. "It's all right. It was a long time ago. I'm sorry I took it out on you. It's just that those words..." she trailed off on a shuddering sigh.

"Remind you of something horrible," he finished for her. "I understand. And from now on, I promise to only compliment you on your brilliant mind."

He felt the gurgle of her laughter and for a moment felt like the king of the world, conquering the beasts.

"It's okay if you think I'm...I'm hot," she whispered, her nose still buried in his chest. "Just not...not beautiful. Okay?"

"Hot it is," he said, lifting her chin so that he could see her eyes. "And for the record, if I knew where to go, I'd kick some ass."

She was silent for a moment, but she didn't pull away. And then she sighed, her gaze still locked with his. "He's dead. Which means it should be over, but some part of me just can't let go."

"You trusted him. And it was the ultimate betrayal. That's not something you can just throw off. No matter how much you want to. But maybe it's time to put it in the past where it belongs."

"And how am I supposed to do that?" she asked, her gaze still holding his.

"I don't know," he admitted. "But I do know what it's like to have something horrible happen that affects your every waking thought. So maybe we can try to move on together? I've no idea what that means, so we'd be taking a huge risk, but I'd like to try."

She studied him for a moment, and then she nodded. "I think I would, too. As long as it's with you."

He wasn't sure that anyone had ever looked at him with that kind of trust. And he prayed that he wouldn't let her down.

She reached for him then, and he kissed her, a soft gentle covenant. She'd shared her most secret place and he was determined to honor that faith. Even though the idea still scared the holy shit out of him.

He wanted her. More than he remembered ever wanting anyone. It was as if she were a part of him, and he needed her to function. Hell, to survive. And suddenly he realized that he was falling for her.

The thought should have scared him—but it didn't.

He lifted his head, searching the dark blue of her eyes. "You're sure about this?"

She nodded. “Wherever it takes us. However it ends. I’m good.”

He was humbled again by the fact that she didn’t ask for anything. No promises. Nothing. She wasn’t like any woman he’d ever met. He pulled her close, resting his head against hers, feeling the rise and fall of her breathing.

And for the first time in his life, Harrison Blake considered that maybe he might be better off with someone by his side.

As long as it was Hannah.

CHAPTER 17

Hannah surfaced from sleep to the tantalizing aroma of coffee. She rolled onto her back, enjoying that blissful moment when her mind was clear—no clutter or baggage. Then someone cleared his throat and her eyes flew open.

Harrison.

He was standing by the bed, coffee cup in hand, dressed in jeans and a black T-shirt. With his tousled hair and multicolored eyes, he looked even more appealing than the caffeine he was holding.

In the light of day, she wasn't as certain that telling him had been the right thing. She'd held on to her secret for so long it felt strange to know that someone else knew. Especially when that person was Harrison. Still, it was done. And she wasn't one to spend time on regrets.

They'd made no promises last night. And she wasn't going to ask for them now. She'd just have to live in the moment. Which was easier said than done, but if it meant more time with Harrison, then it was worth the effort. She'd meant what she'd said. She was in it for the ride, no matter where it wound up taking them. She sighed, stretching as he sat down beside her, putting the cup on the bedside table.

"Morning, sunshine," he said, with a crooked smile, bending to drop a kiss on the end of her nose. "I thought you could use a shot of coffee. I just went with what was in the cabinet. I hope that's okay."

"It's fine," she said, pushing her hair out of her face as she sat up, pulling the sheet with her. "You been up long?"

"About four hours," he offered, his eyes dropping to her breasts. Desire blossomed, and their gazes locked, her breath catching as she let herself get lost in his eyes. "And as much as I regret saying it, there's not time for anything more than coffee."

Disappointment mingled with shock as she shot a look at the clock. "Oh, my God, it's almost noon. Why did you let me sleep when there's work to be done?"

"I figured you needed it," he said, reaching out to tuck a strand of hair behind her ear. "You went through some pretty heavy stuff last night."

She nodded, reaching for her glasses, not ready to talk about it again. "As I recall," she said, moving on to a better memory, "there were good bits, too."

"Just bits?" he probed, waggling his eyebrows. "I seem to remember hours and hours of—"

She hit him with a pillow, and he flipped her underneath him, his body hard against hers. He stared down at her for a moment, then dipped his head, slanting his mouth over hers, his kiss hard and possessive, but then he pushed away.

"Avery and the guys are on their way over here," he said, his expression regretful.

"Now?" she squeaked, grabbing the sheet as she jumped out of bed. "Why didn't you say so?"

"I was a bit distracted." He shrugged, his eyes tracing the lines of her body beneath the sheet.

"So why are they coming here?" she asked, sipping her coffee as she headed for the bathroom. "Did someone find something?"

"Me, actually," he said, still watching her. The color rose in her cheeks, and she tried to remember the last time she'd felt this much hope. "God, I wish I could come in there with you." He half rose from the edge of the bed, but the doorbell rang.

"I'd say I was saved by the bell," she sighed. "But I'm not sure I actually wanted saving. So what did you find?"

"A name. We've got a hit on the killer's DNA."

Hannah poured herself a second cup of coffee and swallowed a yawn. The team was gathered around her dining room table. Drake as usual was propped in the corner. Simon sat at one end, with Avery at the other. And Harrison was huddled over his computer, the scene somehow comforting in its normalcy. She sat down next to Drake and opened her laptop.

"So what have we got?" she asked, signing on to the computer to access her databases. "You said you had a name?"

"Yeah." Harrison nodded. "But it's not making any sense at all. The match came from Interpol."

"Someone international?" Her head jerked up, as she shot a glance first at Harrison and then at Avery.

"Seems so," Avery confirmed. "The hit was for a

Martin Vanderbeek. A Swede who was caught in the sweep of a suspected arms trafficking ring in Vienna. There wasn't enough to hold him. So he was released. Only reason they had his DNA was that he'd been drinking with other suspects at a local bar. The authorities took the samples as part of the investigation."

"So you're saying that a foreign national, one who may or may not have been involved with an arms deal, is our serial killer?" Hannah shook her head, wondering if maybe this was just a bad dream.

"Well, this is where it gets interesting," Harrison said. "Turns out his ID was fictitious. The real Vanderbeek was dead. So this guy just assumed the identity. No doubt covering a multitude of other sins. Only the local authorities didn't discover the fact until the man was long gone."

"Let me guess, after that he just fell off the map." Drake walked over to pour himself more coffee.

"Yeah, and even worse," Avery said, "the case files were lost when the evidence warehouse burned down a few years ago."

"So how'd we luck into the DNA?"

"As a matter of protocol, basic information on the case was passed on to Interpol. The operation crossed international boundaries, so they were involved in the takedown from the get go. Anyway, some tech there entered the pertinent details into their database."

"And there haven't been any other hits on the DNA?" Hannah asked. "Something that might give us this guy's real name? Or at least another alias?"

"Nothing so far." Harrison shook his head, his frustration evident. "We were kind of hoping you might be able to figure out another angle."

"Did they fingerprint him?" she asked, frowning as she typed the name into her computer.

"Hang on," Harrison said, scrolling through a document on his screen. "Yeah, got it right here, I'm sending it to you now."

The file downloaded, and Hannah transferred it to a program she'd created to cross-check fingerprints against various databases both locally and internationally. "I'll run the print and see if we can get a hit." She hit a key and the program started comparing prints in the databases to the one taken from the DNA match. "In the meantime, do we have a mug shot or a photograph? We can run facial recognition software as well. It might give us something more."

"Already on it." Harrison smiled, sending Hannah's stomach lurching in its wake. "I've got the program running now. I've linked it to Homeland Security and our database at Langley. But I figure it's a long shot. The only picture that survived is one Interpol has of the scene; the suspects are standing off to one side. One of the agents present at the time remembered Vanderbeek and identified him for us. But the picture is grainy at best."

"If this guy was smart enough to use an alias in the Viennese sting, he's probably too smart to have his photo readily available anyway."

"What I still don't understand," Hannah said, watching her computer as the fingerprints flashed across the screen, "is how some international thug wound up here at Sunderland murdering women and pretending to be a wanted American serial killer."

"I'll grant you it doesn't make any sense at all." Avery shrugged. "But then nothing about this has followed any real logic."

"When you worked the case for the cyber killer," Drake asked, his attention on Harrison, "was there any kind of international component? Something with the victims that might have pointed to a foreign connection?"

"No." Harrison shook his head. "In fact, we profiled that it was someone local. And I see no reason to believe we were wrong. But the case hit the airwaves big time. It's not unreasonable to believe that someone overseas could have heard about it. Either at the time or after the fact."

"Speaking of which," Avery said, "word on our killer here has gone national. The wire services picked it up after Jasmine's body was found."

"And it's traveling even faster on the Net," Hannah said. "I was just searching to see what was out there, and I came back with over a hundred thousand hits."

"Great, now the guy is headline news." Simon blew out a frustrated breath and drained the last of his coffee.

"It's definitely going to bring unwanted attention to the college, which means security threats for us," Avery said, "but so far I've managed to keep the campus closed. It's actually helpful that neither murder occurred on college ground. But the sooner we find this bastard, the better for all of us."

"Has anyone talked to Tina today?" Hannah asked, suddenly feeling guilty. She'd spent her night with Harrison while her TA had been cooped up in the admin building mourning her friend.

"I haven't talked to her, but I spoke with Reid this morning," Simon said. "He told me that she didn't sleep much, but she's coping better than expected. Reid's moved inside the apartment. Her request. So at least she's not alone."

"And her boyfriend is driving up from the city tomorrow." Avery leaned back, crossing his arms over his massive chest. "He'll take her back to New York, assuming nothing happens to warrant us keeping her here. Reid will go with them to make sure they get there safely and then continue to keep watch until this is over."

"Good," Hannah said, still feeling ashamed not to have at least called. "Her parents live in Brooklyn. She'll be better off with family."

"What about the videos?" Drake asked. "Don't we need her here for that?"

"No." Harrison shook his head. "I've tapped into all of her accounts. Phone, Internet, the works. I can monitor them from here. If she gets anything else from the unsub, I'll be able to see it here in real time."

"Talk about big brother watching," Simon said.

"It isn't ideal, but she understands the situation." Harrison shrugged. "And she has more reason than anyone to want us to catch Jasmine's and Sara's killer."

Hannah's computer emitted a soft beep and stopped scrolling, a flashing cursor indicating that it had found something. "Hang on, guys," she said. "I think maybe I've got a hit." She scrolled down, her eyes widening as she read. "Actually looks like we have more than one."

She took a minute to skim the data, frowning as she scrolled through the first two matches. "The first is a partial, taken from the scene of an assassination attempt in Bosnia a few years back. Some UN diplomat. Anyway, the print is unidentified. Just part of the evidence. Looks like they never found the shooter."

"What about the others?" Avery asked.

"The second one is a full-on match, but again it's an

unidentified print. This time from a bombing in Dubai. Sixteen people were killed. The print was found on a fragment."

"Great, so the guy's a ghost." Simon's words gave voice to everyone's frustration.

"Hang on," she said, "there's one more. From a recent police altercation." Hannah skimmed the pertinent details. "In Atlantic City. Looks like our guy—if it is him—got caught up in a vice sweep. He was booked but later released. And since he wasn't prosecuted, there wouldn't have been any reason for them to have checked him out with anyone higher up the food chain."

"Why? If he's a foreign national under arrest, wouldn't that have at least pulled in immigration?"

"Actually, according to this, he's not foreign. He's homegrown," Hannah said. "From right here in New York." She hit a button and a picture filled the large monitor Harrison had set up on the buffet beside the table. "Meet John M. Walker—aka Martin Vanderbeek."

"And Daniel Raiser," Harrison added, putting a second photo next to the first, the two photos unquestionably the same man, although the hairstyles and clothing worn were radically different. "A U.K. citizen, according to his passport. It came up through facial recognition. But like Vanderbeek, the ID's a fake. He was wanted for questioning in conjunction with one of the London subway bombings."

"So this guy gets around," Avery observed. "What have you got on Walker? Is it an alias as well?"

"So far, it seems to be checking out," Hannah said. "He was born upstate just outside of Syracuse. Went to college in Rochester. But there's nothing to show that he graduated. He pays taxes in Kingston. And he's listed as a freelance technical consultant. Self-employed. Travels quite a bit. There's not much information about where he goes or what he does once he's there. Basically, this guy is good at staying off the grid."

"Can you tie him to any of the locations where he used false ID?" Drake asked.

"Yes," Harrison answered, clearly doing his own online investigation. "I've got confirmation that he was in England at the time of the bombings. Supposedly in Manchester, but it would have been easy enough to slip down to London. And I've also got a record of trips to Vienna—although nothing that directly coincides with the arrest of Vanderbeek."

"Yeah, but I've got confirmation here," Hannah said. "An airline ticket in his name, flying into Geneva. The dates match. And he rebooked his return. Which would match up with his being detained by authorities in Vienna."

"But why use his real name if he was traveling under an alias once in Vienna?" Simon asked.

"Alibi," Drake said, taking a sip of coffee. "Dude, can't be in two places at once."

"So what are we talking about, here?" Hannah asked. "Some kind of mercenary? Three of the matches put him at the site of some kind of terrorist activity. Two bombings and an assassination attempt. You think he was the shooter?"

"It's possible," Avery said, studying the photograph. "Hannah, forward everything you've got to the brass at Langley. Maybe they'll have something more on this guy. And at the very least, they'll be able to shed some light on the various investigations he's been linked to. And in the meantime, if he is our killer, we need to run Mr. Walker to ground. Let's check rentals and hotels in the area to see if by some chance he's registered under his real name or one of the aliases we've found."

"I'm already on it," Hannah said. "And I'm also running the names we know he's used through several systems CIA analysts have created to analyze chatter. There's a possibility that the names we have are associated with other names. Which will broaden the list I can check against."

"Harrison, what about the FBI? Do they have anything on this guy?"

"They don't have any open files on him. And he's not in the serial killer or sexual predator database. But I'm not really surprised about that."

"What do you mean?" Simon frowned. "This son of a bitch has been hacking up girls for fun."

"That's just it. He hasn't been hacking them at all," Harrison said. "He's taken them and possibly roughed them up a bit in the process, but according to Tracy's forensic evidence, he killed them with one surgical slice. They were most likely dead before they had time to realize what happened."

"What about the stabbing?" Simon asked.

"Again, this guy isn't interested in torture," Harrison said. "For the most part, he inflicts the wounds postmortem. And there's no evidence of either hesitation or rage. It's surgical. As if he's—"

"Going through the motions," Drake finished for him. "We said that before. What if that's exactly what's been happening? What if he's been following a script?"

"The cyber killer's," Avery mused. "So using that line of thought, his attempts to get our attention wouldn't be about a power play, but about pulling us into his game."

"But for what reason?" Drake asked. "We have no connection with the raid in Vienna, the bombings in Dubai or London, and certainly nothing to do with his arrest in Atlantic City."

"And it doesn't seem likely that he would have been connected to any of my cases at the FBI," Harrison said. "Unless he really is a serial killer, and like you guys, I'm beginning to wonder if that's truly the case."

"So what the hell is really going on here?" Simon asked.

"No better way to find out than to take it to the source." Hannah turned her computer so that everyone could see. "There's a J. Melrose registered at the Twin Pines motel."

"Let me guess," Harrison said, his eyes on the screen. "John Walker's middle name is Melrose."

CHAPTER 18

How are you holding up?" Simon asked as they sat across from the Twin Pines.

The motel was T-shaped and set off the main highway at an angle. The pine trees that had inspired the name served as a backdrop, making the whole place look appealing from a distance. Unfortunately, close up, the Twin Pines had seen better days. The kind of motel popular half a century ago, it consisted of small attached units, each with its own front porch. Like little log cabins, they were meant to inspire feelings of warmth and comfort. But clearly that was no longer the case.

At the moment, they were waiting for the Camry parked outside the front office to pull away. A woman, dressed in a form-fitting red dress and four-inch, gold stilettos had emerged from a unit in the front about five minutes ago and pulled her car up to the office, conceivably to check out.

"I'm holding up fine," Hannah said answering Simon's question with a frown. "What makes you ask?"

"Nothing specific, just that it's your TA getting the videos. Plus Sara Lauter was a student of yours, and you were friends with Jasmine Washington. I can't imagine it was easy finding her or Sara like that."

"No." She shook her head. "It wasn't. And you're right, it did shake me up."

"Well, for the record, I didn't know either of them, and it threw me for a loop, too. I mean, I've seen men die in combat. Guys I lived and worked with, but this was different. You know?"

"Evil personified," Hannah agreed. "I don't see how Madison does it day in and day out. I don't think I'd ever sleep."

"I guess, if you're exposed to it enough, you develop defenses. Ways to cope," Simon said, his gaze moving somewhere far away. "Or you just go crazy."

"Was it bad—the war, I mean? You were with the SEALs, right?"

"Yeah. And the truth is that war seems almost civilized compared to all of this. But it was tough. I did three straight tours, and then I got caught in a firefight that took out three-quarters of my unit and effectively ended my military career. At least with the SEALs."

"Once a SEAL always a SEAL?"

"Something like that." He shrugged. "Anyway, let's just say I could read the writing on the wall. And so I got out before I wound up riding a desk until retiring."

"I can't imagine you doing that." She shook her head with a smile. "But you're here, so things have gotten better, right?"

"I'm young and healthy, if that's what you're asking." He grinned, his eyes not quite reflecting the sentiment. "But not enough to qualify for special forces."

"Their loss is our gain," she said, meaning every word of it. "I'm glad you're part of the team."

"Were you there when they found Jason?" Simon asked, his gaze still on the hotel in front of them.

She paused for a moment, surprised by the question, her emotions more on edge than she'd realized.

"I'm sorry, that probably came out of left field." His fingers tightened on the steering wheel. "I was thinking about losing team members, and so my thoughts just—"

"—moved to Jason. I understand. And it's never easy," she said, her voice catching in her throat. "But thankfully, no, I wasn't there. I'm not sure I could have handled that. It was hard enough to lose him. But at least I don't have that image branded in my brain."

They sat for a moment in silence, and then the woman emerged from the office and got into her car.

"Looks like she's on her way." Simon nodded as the Camry roared to life and the woman drove away. They waited a couple of minutes and then got out of the car, guns holstered, fake FBI credentials at the ready. The office was located in the center of the top of the T, a rusting sign out front indicating that there were vacancies.

With the departure of the Camry, the place was quiet. No sign of activity at all. Only a couple of cars were pulled up in front of rooms, and most of those were in the back.

"If it's a woman, I'll do the talking," Simon said, with a crooked smile as they headed for the door. "And if it's a guy, I'll leave it to you."

"Nothing like a little sexism to get us going."

"Hey," he protested. "I didn't mean anything by it. Just that it's usually easier to get cooperation from someone of the opposite sex."

"Especially when they look like you," Hannah said, laughing, as they walked into the office. "And you're right, it's a good strategy."

A bell tinkled behind them as they closed the door, the wooden floor creaking beneath their feet. Not exactly a stealthy arrival. But no one had answered the phone when they'd tried to call, so they still needed to find out which room John Melrose had been assigned to.

The front desk took up the length of the tiny room, a doorway behind it sporting rows of swinging beads.

"Looks like this place never left the sixties," Simon whispered as they waited. A minute passed, and then another one, and then the beads started to shimmy. Hannah reflexively closed her hand around her gun, but Simon shook his head in warning as a white-headed woman stepped into the room.

She was tiny, her face wrinkled with age, but her blue eyes shined with intelligence. "Can I help you?"

"Actually," Simon said, stepping up to the counter, "we're looking for a friend. And he told us he'd be staying here. John Melrose?"

The woman's eyes narrowed as she studied Simon, her gaze appreciative, but her expression resolute. "I keep my customers by keeping their confidence. People who stay with me like their privacy." She tilted her head, regarding them both now. "If you'd like a room, I can help you. Otherwise..." She let the words trail off.

Hannah reached into her pocket and produced the manufactured credentials, laying them on the counter in front of the old woman. "What we'd like is the key to Mr. Melrose's room. I'm sure you can understand our need for discretion."

She picked up the wallet and studied the information inside, then after shooting a look at the bulge beneath Simon's jacket she reached behind her for a key. "He's in number fourteen. It's in the back, almost at the end. You can't miss it."

Hannah took the key and the wallet, dropping the latter back in her pocket.

"See that you don't go wrecking my place," the woman warned, her tone just on the edge of ornery. "I ain't got the money to be fixing it up."

"No worries, all we want to do is talk to the man," Simon said, his words meant to soothe. "But if by chance you're thinking of giving him a heads-up—" he shot a telling glance at the telephone mounted on the wall "—well then I can't be held responsible for what might happen."

The old woman nodded once and then turned to disappear behind the undulating beads.

Hannah swallowed a smile. "Well played."

They walked outside, heading for the bottom end of the T. Most of the rooms had the curtains drawn, either the occupants not in residence or the rooms empty. About halfway along, a curtain twitched open but was quickly dropped again.

"Not exactly the cream of society staying here," Simon observed as they approached room fourteen.

"Yeah, I'm guessing she has a lot of hourly traffic."

Slowing, they drew their weapons, Simon crossing to the far side of the door, Hannah flanking him on the near side, both of them with their backs to the wall.

On his nod, Hannah reached out and knocked.

"Housekeeping."

She waited a second or two and then knocked again, repeating the identifier. No one answered.

Again with a nod from Simon, she slipped the key into the lock and turned it. And then on a silent count of three, she opened the door, Simon swinging through it, gun at the ready. Hannah followed close behind, ready to back him up, but the place was empty, the bed unmade, a pizza box on the bureau. Whoever had been staying in the room was long gone.

"The old bitch probably knew he'd left," Simon said, moving forward to check the bathroom. "She probably got a kick out of jerking our chain. There's definitely no one here."

Hannah holstered her gun, disappointment mixing with her abating adrenaline. "Well, at least we know that someone *was* here." She lifted the lid of the box. There was still a quarter of a pepperoni pie inside.

Simon pulled out his cellphone, heading outside for better reception. "I'll call in the techs. There's probably nothing to find, but we might as well be certain."

Hannah nodded, turning to survey the room again, and sighed. The SOB was still one step ahead of them, playing a game only he fully understood. She bent to pick up a piece of paper on the floor.

"This is the restaurant bill from last night," Hannah said, as Simon walked back into the room. "We should probably check with the delivery guy. At least we can get visual verification that the man staying here was actually John Walker."

"Good idea," Simon said. "You think he's finished?"

"No. I think he just moved locations. Either because he knew we were on to him or because he's being overly cautious."

"And so we're back to square one."

"Looks that way," she said, frowning as she noticed something sticking out of a Bible lying on the bedside table. She crossed the room, and using only her thumb and forefinger, carefully pulled out the envelope stuck inside the leather-bound book, her breath catching in her throat when she saw her name scribbled across the front.

"What kind of game is this bastard playing?" Harrison asked, as the team looked at the array of photographs the killer had left for Hannah. It was difficult to control his anger. The idea of a man out there playing God with their lives was untenable. And the fact that the killer now seemed to be focusing on Hannah set every nerve in his body on fire.

"I think that it's pretty clear he's sending a message," Avery responded to Harrison's question, "but unfortunately he's the only one who knows what it is."

They were back in the war room, Drake sitting on one side of the table, Hannah and Tracy on the other. Simon was in the back of the room on the phone, and Avery was at his customary place at the front of the room. Harrison paced beside the table in front of his computer console, fingers itching for something to do.

The envelope hadn't yielded anything that might identify the sender. No DNA or fingerprints. The handwriting was compact and upright, indicating someone with control issues (according to Tracy), but they'd already guessed as much. The photos inside were alarming but again offered little new insight.

There were pictures of Tina and Sara at various locales around campus. And four photos of the crime scenes—taken while the crimes were occurring. And perhaps most disturbing, at least from Harrison's point of view, were the pictures of Hannah.

There was one of her leaving the social sciences building. And another of her heading into the Aaron Thomas Academic Center. And worst of all, three of her outside her house, one of them showing her on the front porch—in Harrison's arms. The bastard was stalking her. He clenched his hands and forced himself to focus on the conversation. There was nothing to be gained by letting his emotions get the better of him.

"I just got off the phone with the pizza place," Simon said as he walked up to the table. "I faxed over a picture of Walker. The delivery guy said the guy barely opened the door. Just grabbed the box and shoved some money at him. But he was pretty sure it was Walker. So at least we're chasing the right guy. Although it seems surprising to me that someone with his background would risk the dude recognizing him."

"Maybe he wants us to know who he is," Hannah said, chewing on the side of her lip. She was handling all of this pretty damn well, considering, the nervous habit the only sign that she wasn't completely okay. "Maybe that's part of the game."

"It's definitely possible," Tracy agreed, her gaze on Hannah. "He obviously left the pictures for you to find."

"But nothing to give us a clue where he is now or what's next on the agenda," Drake said, a frown creasing his forehead.

"I think the pictures are part of it," Tracy offered. "He's clearly been watching Hannah. As well as Tina and Sara. It's interesting that there wasn't a picture of Jasmine except for at the scene."

"It supports the idea that maybe his taking her wasn't part of his initial plan," Avery said.

"You're thinking he was waiting for Tina," Hannah said, her eyes narrowing.

"Makes sense." Avery nodded, his expression grim. "He was in her house, after all. And I don't see how he'd have known Jasmine was going to be there."

"Yes, but he shouldn't have expected her to be there either," Drake said. "Not if he really had her under surveillance. He'd have known that we had her in our protection."

"Maybe he thought we'd let her go. Nothing this guy does follows solid rationale."

"Well, at least this time tomorrow, she'll be safely in Brooklyn," Hannah said. "Hopefully beyond this guy's reach."

"Yeah, except that with her gone, it's conceivable that the killer's focus will move to you." The words came out of their own accord, and Harrison wished them back the minute he'd spoken them. "I'm sorry, I wasn't saying that I wanted him to be fixated on Tina. Or to be able to get to her. I just don't like that Walker's been taking pictures of Hannah."

"None of us do," Avery said. "And you can bet your ass we're not going to let anything happen to her."

"Hey," Hannah protested. "I'm sitting right here, and it's not like I'm some helpless female." She lifted her weapon to underscore the statement. "Not that I mind having you guys watching my back." She tried for a smile but missed, sighing instead. "But isn't Walker's MO the video camera? So maybe this means something else. Maybe he's just trying to show us how close he can get to us without being seen?"

"Not exactly a positive factor," Drake said.

"True," Tracy agreed. "But Hannah may be right about the difference in the message of the medium. It's almost more like he's just trying to play a mind game with all of you. Make you jumpy. He'd know that you'd all be protective of Hannah—which might keep you off center."

"Keeping us from paying attention to the real target," Simon mused.

"I think it's a possibility," Tracy said.

"One we can circumvent by staying alert." Avery leaned forward, palms on the table. "But if Tracy is right—and he's using the photos of Hannah to screw with our heads, then I think we have a larger problem here."

"This asshole knows who we are," Drake said.

"But it could still be about Harrison, right?" Simon asked, picking up the picture of Harrison and Hannah. "I mean this is pretty damn telling." He shot Hannah an apologetic look. "What better way to get to you than to go through someone you care about?"

"Except that he didn't leave them for Harrison," Hannah said, her faint blush highlighted by the deep pink frames of her glasses. "He left them for me. And I don't mind saying that if he was trying to spook me, he did a damn good job."

Harrison wanted to reach out for her. To offer reassurance. Thanks to the killer, they'd been outed. So it wasn't as if he had to hide his feelings. But somehow, it just didn't feel right. The very fact that their relationship, or whatever the fuck it was, could be playing into this prick's fantasy made him feel as if he needed to use restraint. As if he might push too hard and send her running.

"But Harrison's got no connection to this dude," Drake

said. "At least not that we can find. Walker's much more likely to have run into one of us. I mean if he really has been involved in terrorist activities, that puts him in the middle of our ball field—not the FBI's."

"So you think he knows *me*?" Hannah asked. "That I'm the common denominator in all of this?"

"I'm not saying anything," Drake lifted his hands in apology, "except that I think Avery is right and that this is linked to us—to A-Tac. Either this guy has a score to settle or he wanted to get our attention when he took his leap over the psychological cliff."

"Is there any precedent for something like this?" Avery asked Tracy. "For a guy like Walker to cross the line into serial killing and target us in the process?"

"It actually fits the profile to some extent," she responded. "If he had bad dealings with the CIA, it's possible he'd choose something like A-Tac for his killing ground. But it makes a lot of suppositions about his ability to gather information, so I can't say with any certainty that this is about you guys. It could just be a happy circumstance—as far as Walker's concerned, I mean. Something he stumbled into after the fact."

"If he's who we think he is, he definitely has the skills to put it together." Harrison frowned.

"So the guy's mind fucking is either planned or a bonus round, and either way, we're on the damn firing line," Drake said. "If he's got a beef with us, he's also going to know that this is the kind of thing that could easily get us all burned. And if we're outed we can all kiss our careers good-bye. We'll be toast with the CIA and with academia. Hell, we'll be lucky to get jobs parking cars."

"As much as I want to protect A-Tac," Avery said, his tone a warning, "let's not forget that we've got two women dead, and nothing to make us believe that the bastard's finished. So until we can nail this guy, keeping the women of this campus safe has to be our paramount concern."

"But none of this reads like a normal serial killer, right?" Simon asked, his gaze moving over to Tracy.

"I'll admit, in some ways, the unsub seems to be all over the board. Organized, disorganized. Impulsive one moment, and almost anal retentive the next. But these guys don't always follow a pattern. Unfortunately, a profile is an educated guess. And some are more accurate than others."

"And it's also possible that someone with a knowledge of behavioral sciences could rig the game, right?" Drake leaned forward, eyes narrowed. "Make us believe he's something he's not."

"It's possible," Tracy acknowledged. "Although even in that case, there's a certain physiological pathology that must be present in order for him to pull it off. This guy is killing with the efficiency of someone who knows what he's doing. A pro. But judging by the videos, there's at least some evidence to support the idea that he derives a certain amount of pleasure from the killing. And while that combination can sometimes be suppressed, it can never be truly eliminated. And given the right set of circumstances, his true nature is going to rise to the surface."

"In other words," Avery said, "even if Walker didn't start out as a serial killer—he's most likely become one now."

CHAPTER 19

Tina Richards jerked awake with a start, blinking as she tried to adjust to the now darkened bedroom. It had been late afternoon when she'd opened the first pages of the book, hoping to erase the images that kept playing in her head. She glanced over at the clock, surprised to see how late it was. She hadn't expected to sleep at all. But maybe it was a blessing. Everyone was trying hard to make sure she was okay, but the truth was that she wasn't sure she'd ever be all right again.

Everything had changed.

She tipped back her head, blowing out a long breath as she walked to the window, looking out at the quiet campus. The lights in the trees shifted ominously with the movement of the branches, the whistle of the wind sending leaves swirling through the darkness. She'd always loved Sunderland at night. But now, the shadows only hid evil. Somewhere out there, he was watching. Stalking.

If not her, then people she cared about.

She wrapped her arms around her waist, shivering. Even with Reid outside her door, she still felt vulnerable. As if somehow the killer would be able to reach her no matter where she tried to hide. Hannah had said he got off on fear, and Tina had tried to keep hers at bay, but it was difficult. Especially now, in light of what had happened to Jasmine. Roger said that it would pass. But Roger wasn't here. He hadn't seen what she'd seen. He hadn't been targeted by a madman.

She shook her head, turning her back on the window—on Sunderland. Tomorrow she was going home. And from there, she'd work to find center again. Hannah had said it would take time. But maybe that had just been a platitude. Maybe some things were beyond recovery, their imprint changing a person forever.

Certainly whatever had been left of her childhood was gone. She'd been forced to grow up in an instant. Face a reality that most people never even imagined. And yet, at the end of the day, she was alive. Still standing. Surely that had to count for something.

She blew out another breath and moved toward the door connecting the bedroom to the living area. She was hungry. Reid hadn't woken her for dinner, the FBI agent no doubt choosing instead to let her sleep. Although the guy was predictably stoic, he'd been really great overall. Making her feel not only safe, but less alone.

Of course, Hannah had been with her every step of the way as well. Especially after Jasmine had been taken. Tina wasn't sure how she'd have managed without her mentor. She'd always admired Hannah's intelligence and self-assurance. But it was her compassion that had really impressed Tina. She genuinely cared about students, sometimes even putting their needs above her own.

Case in point.

And now Tina had experienced Hannah's caring first-hand, in a way she'd never have been able to anticipate. Murder was an ugly thing. And when it was personal... She shivered again, pushing the thoughts from her mind. Just a few more hours and Roger would be here, and all of this would be behind her.

She opened the door, surprised to find that the lights were out in the living room as well. Of course it was late. And although Reid had agreed to staying inside the apartment because she'd asked him to, he'd made it more than clear that he preferred to be outside in the hallway. Preferring to maintain a tactical advantage. Whatever the heck that was.

The fact that she was even using those words showed just how much her world had changed in the last few days.

Irrevocably.

The word echoed in her head as she stepped into the living room, torn between checking on Reid and getting something to eat. Her stomach grumbled, and she settled on the latter, reaching for the light switch as she moved into the tiny galley that served as a kitchen. She flipped the switch. And her stomach tightened when nothing happened, the room still dark. Fear filled her gut, acid churning up into her throat, but then she remembered that there were two switches, the first meant to attach to a lamp or appliance or something else connected to the electrical outlet on the wall behind the counter.

She hit the second switch, and the kitchen was flooded with fluorescent light, the accompanying buzz comforting in an almost tangible way. The living room looked ghostly as the light spilled through the doorway, but at least for the moment the shadows had retreated. She opened the refrigerator, the door momentarily blocking her view of the room, and as she studied the contents, she suddenly felt the hair on her arms raise.

Fighting for control, she slowly closed the door, turning to survey the room, her heart pounding. There was no one there. It was just her imagination on overdrive. But suddenly, she'd lost her appetite. Better to check in with Reid. He'd make her feel safer, if only because of the gun he carried. Again, she marveled at how much her life had changed in such a short span of time.

She closed her eyes, mustering strength from deep inside, the vitriol of everything that had happened threatening to overwhelm her. Hannah had said she had to be strong. For Sara. For Jasmine. And while she knew that Hannah was right, she wasn't so sure suddenly that she could actually pull it off.

Ashamed at her own weakness, she squared her shoulders and headed for the front door. It was a heck of a lot easier to be brave when you had company. She reached out to release the deadbolt on the door, surprised to find that it was already unlocked.

For a moment, caution reared its head, but as she paused indecisively, she realized that Reid wouldn't have locked the door if he was on the outside. She was just having a moment. A justifiable one, certainly, but that didn't mean she needed to invent problems where there were none. Shaking her head at her own foolishness, she turned the knob, surprised when the door didn't immediately open.

Frowning now, she put her weight into it, surprised when it suddenly gave, swinging inward just as the lights in the apartment went dark, something heavy hitting the floor—faint light from the corridor illuminating the entryway. Her voice froze in her throat, her stomach twisting into a knot as her brain telegraphed what lay across her foot.

A body—Reid's body.

Swallowing a scream, she ran forward but tripped, the momentum sending her sprawling across the floor. Something sticky coated her palms, and as she lifted her hand, the metallic smell of blood filled her nostrils. Her stomach threatened full revolt, and she choked back bile.

Self-preservation kicked in and she tried to scramble to her feet, but the floor was slick and it was difficult to find purchase. Heart threatening to break through her chest, Tina pushed up again, still fighting for balance, and this time she won. But she hesitated on the threshold of the front door, trying to decide the best course of action.

Behind her was a phone. In front of her freedom. Each option tantalizing in its potential reward. But in the end, freedom seemed the better course. Taking precious seconds, she bent to search the body with shaking fingers, her mind assuring her that Reid was long gone. She reached in his pockets and felt carefully under his body. There was no sign of his cellphone, but his gun was still in its holster, and she pulled it free, not certain that she could actually use it, but feeling stronger just holding it in her hand.

She stepped into the hallway, pressing herself against the wall, praying to be invisible as she strained in the dark for some sign of the intruder. She had no doubt he was out there somewhere—waiting for her to make the first move. Hunter and prey.

She swallowed and pushed away from the wall, taking the hallway on a sprint, focusing her attention on the stairs at the end of the corridor. They were lined with windows that opened out onto the front of the building. Just above where the men were stationed outside the door. If she could get the window open and scream—surely they'd hear her and come running. *If they were still alive*, the little voice in her head whispered, and she stumbled.

This time, however, she managed to keep her balance, to keep going. The head of the staircase was in sight now. Just a few more feet. She could actually see the light from the windows illuminating the stairs.

Then suddenly the light was gone, the door to the stairway slamming shut, the echo filling the corridor, the harsh ringing sounding a death knell.

Blood pounding in her ears, she whirled around, heading back the way she'd come, still gripping Reid's gun, praying for a miracle. The deserted building had seemed like a sanctuary with Reid alive and protecting her. But now, it seemed like a prison. A tomb. And she pushed herself faster, heading back to the apartment. If the killer was behind her and she could make it to the apartment and lock the door—

She fought the urge to turn and look, instead concentrating on the end of the hall. Three doors more. She passed the first and then the second, and then just as she reached the apartment, a shadow loomed out from the darkness behind her, a hand closing around her hair, yanking her backward. With panic driving, she jerked the other way, knowing that her hair was ripping away at the skull, the pain a price worth paying if it bought her freedom.

For a moment, she felt the pressure lessen, and she sprang forward, still intent on gaining the safety of the apartment, but he was faster, his hand closing on her arm. Desperate, she lifted the gun, her finger closing around the trigger, fear overriding any hesitation. And with a muffled curse, she fired, bracing herself for the recoil. But there was nothing. The gun was empty.

The killer had set her up. This was all part of the game.

Rage rose hot and bitter inside her, and she swung out, striking him with the gun. But the blow glanced off his shoulder, and with a roar of anger, he slammed her back against the wall, her head hitting the plaster so hard it cracked beneath the blow. Pinned there, she could feel his breath against her skin, his fingers digging into her shoulders as she struggled against him.

"It's no use," he whispered. "You belong to me now."

Her heart twisted, even as she continued to fight, knowing intuitively that he was right and the battle already lost. He covered her face with something cool and sweet smelling, and she tried to turn her head, to find some way to jerk free, but the chemical was already taking effect, her mind starting to swim, the edges of consciousness going fuzzy.

She thought about Roger. And Hannah. Feeling as though she'd somehow let them down. That if she'd only been a little bit faster or smarter, she'd have found a way to escape. But her thoughts were growing scrambled because suddenly it was Reid she'd failed. Reid and Jasmine.

She'd wondered how her friend had felt when facing certain death. And now, it looked as if she was about to find out.

* * *

"I feel like it's right here in front of us, and we're just missing it," Hannah said, pushing back from her dining room table and the computer screen she and Harrison had been studying.

They'd been at it for what seemed like hours. Studying the photos the killer had left for her, the footage from the videos, the crime scene evidence, the autopsy reports, and everything else they'd collected in the process of the investigation. But there was nothing new. Nothing to give them any idea where Walker had gone or where he might strike next.

"It's late," Harrison said, his eyes dark with worry. "You need to get some rest."

"There's no way I can possibly get any sleep. Not with that bastard out there taunting us. Besides, every time I close my eyes, I see Sara and Jasmine—and what he did to them." She shuddered, tilting back her head, fighting tears. "I just feel so helpless."

"I know. It's part of what gives him power. Knowing that we're always one step behind. But he's going to make a mistake, Hannah. We're going to catch him."

"I wish to hell I believed that," she said, shaking her head as she let the sound of Harrison's voice wash over her. Despite the severity of the situation, there was comfort in having him close. Just listening to the rhythm of his breathing made her feel calmer somehow. Helped her to keep focus.

She blew out a breath and pulled her chair back up to the table, her eyes back on the computer. "I just keep thinking that we'll find something. That he's left us a clue that we just haven't seen. I mean everything points to his wanting us to find him. Right?"

"I don't know," Harrison said, shaking his head. "I thought so in the beginning. But now, I just feel like he's toying with us. Getting off watching us chase our tails."

"Maybe," she conceded. "But if Tracy's right he's also letting himself fall into the fantasy. Letting the killings build into something more. A craving of some kind. Which means he's not going to stop. It's like an alcoholic taking just one drink—it's never enough."

"So do you want to go through all of this stuff again?" Harrison asked, frowning down at the scattered reports and photographs.

"No," Hannah said, pushing away from the table again, her mind made up. "I want to go see Tina. Maybe there's something else she's remembered. Something that we overlooked the first time. Besides, she's alone, and I'm guessing she'll be happy for the company."

"Are you sure?" he asked, not looking particularly pleased at the suggestion. "I wasn't kidding. It really is late. Surely she'll be asleep by now."

"Seriously? Jasmine was Tina's best friend. If I can't close my eyes, you can be damned certain that she isn't sleeping either."

He opened his mouth to protest, then clearly thought better of it. "All right. We'll go over there."

"You don't have to come."

"Hannah, I'm not letting you go out there on your own, even if you are armed to the teeth." He nodded to the gun she was slipping into her holster. "We're in this together—remember?"

A sliver of heat shot through her as their gazes collided, the little voice in her head reminding her that the connection was situational. That she shouldn't let herself come to count on him. Better to hold on to her heart. It was safer that way.

"Okay, fine," she said, turning her back, the effort costing her as she forced her attention back to the situation at hand. "We'll go together. But I think we should go now."

"All right then, let's go." He reached for his jacket and gun, and Hannah had the fleeting thought that Harrison Blake was the kind of man a woman would be a fool to throw away.

Fifteen minutes later, they were walking across the quad toward the administration building. The night sky was moonless, the stars burning pinpoints in the black-velvet sky. The trees moved in silent undulation as the cold wind whispered through the branches. The air was crisp, the smell of dying leaves punctuating the soft smell of wood smoke from somewhere nearby.

The upper floor of the building was dark, and for a moment, Hannah hesitated. Harrison had clearly been right. Tina was sleeping. And the idea of waking her to rehash the horror seemed unnecessarily cruel. But then a flicker of something against one of the upper-floor windows sent a shiver of dread coursing through her. Right or wrong, she needed to see Tina. Make certain that she was really safe.

If nothing else, she'd just talk to Reid. See for herself that everything was okay.

As they neared the front steps, a man stepped from the shadows of the portico that fronted the building. Harrison pulled his gun, moving in front of Hannah. But as the light revealed the man's features, she recognized one of the operatives assigned to protect the building. Casey James.

After trading identification, Hannah explained that she'd come to see Tina. "Is she asleep?"

"Far as I know." Casey nodded. "Reid's last check-in was at ten-thirty, and he said she'd been sleeping since late afternoon. And it's been quiet since then."

Hannah shot a look toward Harrison, unsure again what to do, but still fighting the feeling that something was wrong.

"Well, obviously we don't want to wake her," Harrison said to Casey, "but it's well past midnight now so I'm assuming you must be due to check in with Reid. Maybe we can kill two birds with one stone. You can verify everything's okay, and we can check on Tina."

"Suits me," Casey shrugged, and pulled out a radio. "It's a little early, but Reid won't mind. And I totally understand your wanting to check on your friend." He nodded in Hannah's direction, obviously having seen her coming and going over the past few days. "Echo two to Echo one. Come in, please."

CHAPTER 20

Casey waited a moment for a response and then with a frown, repeated the call. "Echo two to Echo one. Come in please."

"Is there something wrong?" Hannah asked, her worry ratcheting up a notch.

"He's probably just asleep," Casey said, still frowning. "But it's not like Reid not to answer." He spoke again into the radio's mic, the coordinates this time for the third man watching the building. The radio immediately crackled to life, the two operatives holding a brief conversation.

"Bill can't raise him either," Casey said after signing off. "So it's not my radio. But like I said, Reid's probably just asleep. We've been out here the whole time. Me on the door and Bill patrolling the perimeter. There's no way anyone's gotten by us."

The pronouncement should have made her feel better, but it didn't.

"I'm sure you're right," Harrison said, his eyes on the building as he drew his gun, "but with this guy, we can't be too careful. Better check it out."

"Sure," Casey said, also producing a weapon. "Do you want me to call it in?"

"Not yet." Harrison shook his head. "We don't actually know that there's anything to report."

Behind them, the bushes rattled, and all three of them spun around, weapons ready. A man emerged from the bushes, hands out. "It's just me."

Casey lowered his gun, and Hannah released a breath she hadn't realized she'd been holding as she recognized Bill—the third man.

"Jesus, Bill, we could have shot you," Casey said, his eyes shooting back to the still-darkened building.

"Sorry." The other man shook his head. "I should have radioed first. But I figured if there was trouble, you'd want help."

"You figured right," Harrison interjected. "There's definitely strength in numbers."

"So how do you want to proceed?" Casey asked, automatically deferring to Harrison, and Hannah wondered how much they'd been told about A-Tac.

"The three of us will head inside," Harrison said, tilting his head toward Casey and Hannah, "and Bill, you'll keep watch here in the front. I take it you've seen nothing to indicate that anyone has tried to get inside the building?"

"No. Everything's locked down tight. Most of the windows are too high to reach easily. And the ones that someone could access, we armed with motion detectors. If someone had tried to get inside, they'd have woken half the campus."

Harrison nodded. "All right then. We're probably looking at nothing more than Reid falling asleep and missing the call, or maybe some kind of radio malfunction. But either way, we need to check it out."

"Roger that," Casey said, checking the clip in his gun as Bill moved into place in the bushes near the front of the building.

On Harrison's signal, they headed past Bill and up onto the portico, stopping just short of the door, with Harrison flanking it on the right and Hannah and Casey on the left. Hannah's heart pounded in her ears as a swirl of dust and leaves skittered across the concrete floor.

Harrison's eyes met hers, and on a silent count of three, he swung out and pushed through the glass door, Casey following right behind him, with Hannah in the rear. After the tree-lit campus, the foyer was blindingly dark. The three of them moved automatically into a defensive circle, standing back to back, weapons drawn as they turned slowly, searching for any sign that something was amiss.

But the building was quiet, the only sound coming from the wind as it buffeted the windows. And as their eyes adjusted to the dark, it was clear that there was no welcoming committee. Still they remained on alert as they walked toward the stairs.

A grand mahogany affair hinting at the college's more opulent days, the staircase ascended to the second floor, where it turned and narrowed as it continued up to the fourth floor and the apartment where Tina was staying. With Casey now taking the rear position and Harrison in the lead, they climbed, passing the second- and third-floor landings without incident.

The windows that lined the upper-floor stairwells provided a small amount of light, and Hannah glanced at her watch, surprised to find that only a few minutes had passed. Somehow it felt like eons. She tried to tell herself that they were overreacting, that both Tina and Reid were fast asleep, but her gut refused to listen, her inner voice screaming that something was wrong.

They stepped out onto the fourth floor, the hallway dark. After they had waited a beat and nothing moved, Harrison flipped on his tac-light, the beam cutting along the corridor as they slowly moved forward, guns still at the ready.

"Reid?" Casey called as they approached the apartment, but there was no response.

An overturned chair lay in front of the door, the remains of the smashed radio scattered in front of it, but there was no sign of Reid. The door was closed, but when Harrison turned the knob it opened, swinging inward on silent hinges.

The apartment, like the hallway, was dark. And it took every ounce of willpower Hannah possessed not to push past Harrison calling for Tina. But protocol existed for a reason, so she held back as Casey and Harrison moved inside, checking the living room for signs of an intruder.

"We're clear, in here, but the power is out," Harrison said as Hannah pushed past him, calling Tina's name as she went—dreading what she was going to find. But the bedroom, like the rest of the apartment, was empty, and Hannah wasn't sure if she should be grateful or terrified. Probably both. She flicked on her tac-light, swinging it across the room. The bed was unmade, and just for a moment, Hannah could see Tina sitting there, bleary eyed, only half awake.

Hannah shook her head, the image vanishing. She turned to examine the rest of the room. Tina's phone sat on the bedside table, and her duffle was stashed in the corner, clothes spilling out of the top. Hannah fought a wave of desperation. Her friend was in trouble, and it wouldn't help if Hannah let her emotions get in the way.

"Any signs of a struggle in here?" Harrison asked as he walked into the room, his multi-colored eyes assessing.

"No. But her phone is here, so I'm..." She struggled to find the words, the image of Tina returning front and center. She clenched her fist, fighting for control. "So I'm thinking she didn't walk away willingly." She forced herself to breathe, running a shaking hand through her hair, her heart constricting at the thought of her friend in the clutches of a serial killer.

Harrison closed the distance between them, his hands covering her shoulders as he started to pull her into an embrace. But she jerked away, ignoring the flash of hurt in his eyes, certain that, if she let him touch her, she'd break into a million pieces.

"Hannah, I—" he started, reaching for her again, but she held up a hand, shaking her head.

"I can't. Not here. I shouldn't...we shouldn't...Look, maybe this thing between us is a mistake." She regretted the words the minute they came out, but she also knew there was truth in there somewhere. "Let's just let it go. Okay?" She blew out a long breath, waiting as his gaze probed hers, a little muscle in his jaw telegraphing his disappointment.

"Hey," Casey called, cutting through the tension stretched tight between them. "I've got blood in here."

Harrison searched her face for another long moment,

and then, apparently not seeing what he wanted to see, mumbled "whatever" and walked from the room, leaving Hannah feeling as if she'd lost her best friend. Then again, maybe she had. Clearly she was too messed up to ever be the kind of woman Harrison deserved.

Tears pricked the back of her eyes, but she rubbed them away, reminding herself that this wasn't about Harrison. It wasn't even about her. It was about Tina. And right now, that's all that mattered.

"So what have you got?" she asked as she walked back into the foyer where Harrison and Casey were kneeling on the floor.

"Blood," Casey said, shining his flashlight downward. "There's a pool of it here just inside the door. We missed it coming in because we were focused on looking for people. There's also a bloody print on the wall." He stopped, exchanging a glance with Harrison, who shrugged, then nodded his head. "It's too small to have been Reid's."

Hannah's gut clenched as she pictured her friend trying to flee the apartment—a madman in pursuit. "So we think the blood is hers?"

"There's no way to know for sure until Tracy has the chance to run some tests," Harrison said, his tone coolly professional. "But clearly something went down here."

"So where are the bodies?" Casey asked. "I'd swear on my life that no one could have gotten into or out of the building without our seeing them. Especially if they were dragging something."

"I guess that's what we've got to figure out," Harrison said. "In the meantime, we need to call it in. Casey, you touch base with Bill to see if he can do something about the lights and then call Avery. He'll take care of the rest."

The man nodded and walked back into the living room.

"Is there blood in the hall?" Hannah asked, pushing past Harrison to check for herself. There was nothing on the carpet, at least just outside the door, but the wall above it, to the left of the door, was smeared with blood—what looked like bits of skin sticking to the cracked plaster.

"Looks like someone was slammed into the wall," Harrison said, coming to stand beside her as she shown her light on the stained area. "Could be Reid."

"Not likely." Hannah frowned. "Reid's over six feet tall. This mark isn't more than sixty or so inches from the floor, and assuming the vic was shoved backward..." She trailed off, still studying the mark.

"You're thinking it's Tina?" he asked.

"It seems more probable. Which means that whatever happened here took place outside the apartment. That's why there's no sign of a struggle inside."

"So we've got an overturned chair. A pool of blood in the entry hall and signs of a struggle here in the hall—most likely not Reid. Ignoring the fact that the unsub managed to get into the building completely unnoticed, how does that play out?" He crossed his arms over his chest, waiting for her thoughts.

"I don't know." She frowned, trying to envision the series of events. "Maybe he surprises Reid out here. Tries to incapacitate him, maybe even kill him, but Reid manages to make it inside, and conceivably warn Tina."

"Yeah, but that doesn't explain the handprint," Harrison said. "Seems more likely that he made it inside, but collapsed, then Tina stumbles over Reid, he's either dead or dying so she—"

"—panics," Hannah interrupted, "and puts her hand on the wall, and then tries to make a break for it."

"Only she's intercepted by Walker when she heads out into the hallway," Harrison continued. "He grabs her there, and when she fights, he slams her into the wall."

"So where are they now?" she asked, her frustration evident. "And why wouldn't Walker just leave Reid? I mean I get why he'd take Tina, but Reid's just collateral damage. He's not part of the fantasy."

"Maybe he did leave him," Harrison suggested, the two of them working in tandem now. "It makes sense if he thought Reid was dead. But maybe he was just knocked out, and he came to and tried to follow Tina and/or the unsub."

"Except that there was no sign of anyone leaving the building," Casey insisted again, pocketing his phone as he stepped out into the hallway. "Bill's got school maintenance working on the lights. And the rest of your team's on the way. Avery said for you guys to stay on the scene until they arrive."

But Hannah wasn't really listening. "If you're right," she said, expanding on Harrison's earlier thought, "then there should be more blood. Somewhere here in the hallway, or maybe on the stairs. There was a lot of blood in the apartment's foyer. There's no way Reid could have moved without losing more." She waved her tac-light down the hall to emphasize her point.

And as if on cue, the hallway lights flickered on.

"Score one for Sunderland maintenance," Harrison said as he followed Hannah down the hall. "I'm not seeing anything."

"It's got to be here," she said, sweeping her gaze across

the floor and up the walls and then back again as she moved. "Wait." She dropped to her knees, bending to touch a wet spot on the carpet. "Here." She checked the surrounding area. "And here. I was right. There's more blood."

"It could be Tina's. Or even Walker's."

"Doesn't matter. It's a trail. And with any luck, it'll lead us right to them. But I'm still thinking it's Reid," she said, pushing back to her feet. "If it was Tina or even Walker, he'd have tried to stanch it, knowing that otherwise we'd do just what we're doing."

"Follow him," Harrison agreed. "But it's also possible that this is exactly what he wants us to do. That he's jerking our chain again."

"Only one way to find out." Hannah lifted an eyebrow, the gesture meant as a challenge. She and Harrison might not be able to work out their personal life, but professionally they meshed perfectly.

"Right behind you."

The next stain was on the stairwell, just before the third-floor landing. And there were four more spots on the flight heading down to floor two.

"You're right, this is like following breadcrumbs," Harrison said as they continued to move downward.

"Yes, but they're getting more frequent, which can't bode well for Reid, assuming it really is him." She quickened her pace, urgency pressing her onward. They rounded the second landing and headed down the main stairs, the droplets showing up on almost every stair now. In the dark, they'd been invisible, but with the lights back on, they shown like beacons, the increasing frequency only adding to Hannah's fears.

They reached the foot of the stairs, and for a moment, it seemed that the blood had disappeared.

"It's just gone," Hannah said, frustration cresting as she turned in circles, trying in vain to pick up the trail again.

"He didn't just vanish." Harrison walked around the end of the staircase toward the hall that led to the back of the building.

"But why wouldn't he head for the front door? If for no other reason than to call in reinforcements?"

"Maybe there wasn't time," Harrison said, gesturing for her to follow. "Hang on. I think I've picked up the trail." He touched a spot on the floor and lifted his finger to his nose. "Definitely blood."

"So where the hell is he going?" Hannah asked with a frown, bending down to check when she reached yet another spot.

"I don't know. But I'm not getting a good feeling about this. There's only one way out of here, right?"

"Yes," Hannah confirmed. "The door. I suppose they could have used a window, but I honestly don't see how Walker could have gotten Tina out that way with nobody noticing. Especially since Casey said that the bulk of them have motion sensors."

"So maybe he didn't take her out of the building."

She'd had the same thought, but was almost afraid to let it formulate. If Tina was still here, then she was most likely dead. The idea of her being taken was frightening, but the alternative was far worse. She sucked in a breath for courage. "So we keep following the trail."

Harrison nodded, his eyes already scanning the floor for more blood.

"Over here," Hannah said, frowning as she looked down. Instead of the spattered blood droplets they'd been following, there was a small pool. She stepped back to examine the wall, surprised to see the outline of a door in the wallpaper.

"What the hell?" Harrison asked, the question clearly rhetorical. He reached up, running his fingers along the lines in the paper until his thumb hit a crevice. "I think there's a latch here."

"It's a door to the basement," Avery said, as he and Simon came down the hall, halting beside Hannah. "It was hidden sometime in the fifties. When the building was remodeled. I guess they thought it was elegant to hide the back rooms of the building."

"Did you say a basement?" Harrison said, his face tightening with concern.

"Yeah—complete with boiler and washroom. Why?"

"Nothing," he said, still working along the edges of the doorway.

Hannah fisted her hands, her gut churning again. "He's thinking that both Sara and Jasmine were killed in cellars. And we've got blood here." Hannah waved at the stain on the floor.

"You think it's Tina's?" Simon asked.

"No." Harrison shook his head. "It's most likely Reid's. We think he tried to follow Walker when he took Tina. But we really don't have anything to substantiate the theory except the blood and the fact that both Tina and Reid are missing."

"It's a logical conclusion," Avery said as Harrison pulled the latch and slid open the door.

Steps stretched downward. Hannah pulled her gun and

flipped on the tac-light, shining the beam on the stairs as Harrison started down, Avery right behind him. Hannah followed, with Simon staying up top on the off chance that this was some kind of set-up. There were about fifteen steps and then they hit the concrete flooring of the basement.

At first, it seemed as if the room was empty, only the hulking shape of the boiler looming out of the shadows. Then Harrison hit the light switch, the flickering pall of fluorescent light filling the room. And in the corner they saw him.

Reid.

CHAPTER 21

He's dead," Harrison said, anger rising as he knelt to examine Reid's body. "Looks like his throat has been cut." Reid Kotchner might not have been A-Tac per se. But he was CIA, and as far as they were all concerned, he was one of the team.

"There's no way he could have made it all the way down here with a severed artery," Simon observed, his fists tightening as he dealt with his own rage.

"Looks like he was stabbed in the gut," Harrison said. "I'm guessing that's what brought him down to begin with. Walker must have left him for dead."

"But I was right," Hannah sighed. "Reid must have followed him downstairs."

"And the son of a bitch ambushed him," Simon said. "Then dumped him here."

"Except that it doesn't make sense that he'd leave the body upstairs when he first thought Reid was dead and then take the time to hide the body when he resurfaces downstairs." Avery knelt beside the corpse, staring down at it as if willing it to share its secrets.

"Judging from the spatter, I'd say he was killed down here," Harrison said, pointing at the wall in front of them.

"So maybe he was ambushed outside the doorway," Hannah postulated. "Which would explain why there's more blood at the door."

"And then Walker forced him down here for the kill," Harrison added. "But that still doesn't make sense, unless..." He trailed off, looking toward the small doorway that led to a second room, his stomach sinking.

He was closest, but Hannah was faster, stepping into the room on a sharp intake of breath. He followed behind, wanting to help, but knowing she wouldn't let him. She'd made her feelings more than clear back in the apartment.

"She's not here," Hannah said, her voice shaking. "I was so afraid that I'd see...that I'd..." She trailed off, and Harrison was transported to another house—another cellar—his sister strung from the rafters.

"There's more blood," Harrison said, pulling his thoughts away from the past. Maybe Hannah was right, maybe neither of them was capable of a lasting connection.

The rest of the team followed them into the room, shoving the two of them closer together. So close that Harrison could feel the warmth of her arm pressed against his, his body reacting even as his mind rejected the notion.

"So where the hell is she?" Simon asked, turning to examine the room.

"I think I might know," Avery said, his attention locked on the far side of the room. The wall there was constructed of bricks covered in part by old wooden planks. The masonry was crumbling, and on closer inspection, one of the planks appeared to be loose.

Harrison crossed over to it and yanked hard, half of the planks pulling free, the motion revealing hidden hinges.

"Son of a bitch," Simon whispered, as the improvised doorway swung open to reveal a cavernous hole. "What the hell is that?"

"Tunnels," Avery said. "All the original buildings at Sunderland were connected with them. Some people claim we were a stop on the Underground Railroad, but there's never been anything to support the notion. More likely they were built for storage and to help students move easily from building to building in the wintertime."

"Then why have we never heard of them?" Harrison asked, moving closer, shining his tac-light into the dank darkness.

"They were closed off in the seventies. The infrastructure was falling apart. It was getting more and more dangerous for students to use the tunnels. And despite an attempt to raise the money to repair them, it just proved to be too expensive. So they were sealed off, the entrances boarded shut."

"Except this one," Hannah said, the words a statement, not a question, as she nodded at the plank door.

"Looks that way," Avery agreed. "Although it's possible that someone else found it and reopened it. It's the sort of thing that would appeal to students."

"And serial killers." Harrison frowned. "But how the hell would he know this was here?"

"He'd have to have done his homework," Avery

shrugged. "But it's not impossible for him to have found it. The original blueprints are on file with the county."

"So Walker's got Tina down there somewhere?" Hannah whispered, her fear for her friend evident.

"Not likely," Avery said. "As I say, most of the tunnels are sealed off. I'm guessing he just used it as a means to get in and out of the building without anyone seeing him."

"Avery's right," Harrison said. "If this guy really wanted Tina, he'd have seen our sequestering her as a challenge. This is exactly the kind of thing he gets off on. Finding a way to make us look like fools."

"So where does this one go?" Simon asked, nodding toward the opening.

"It links to a structure that served as a vent on the far side of campus. Near the girls' dorms. Where the old infirmary was. If someone was determined enough, it wouldn't be that hard to get it open. Simon, you head for the vent, and if we're right, maybe you can pick up the trail from there. I'll coordinate with Drake and Tracy here. She's going to need to see Reid's body."

"Sounds like a plan," Harrison said. "And in the meantime, I'll check out the tunnel. You're probably right about his only using it for transport, but we need to be sure."

"I'm coming, too." Hannah's eyes dared him to argue with her, and he swallowed his protest. Challenging her wasn't the way to win points. And besides, he wasn't trying to curry favor anyway. Just get the job done.

"Fine." He nodded, gesturing to the opening, ignoring the little voice insisting that she stay here where she'd be safe. "You lead."

The passage was dank, the smell of mold pervading

every corner. The shiplap walls, originally plastered, were sagging from the pressure of the earth behind them. The beams that shored up the roof were rotting and slick with moss, the tin tiles that had once decorated the ceiling hanging drunkenly at angles that resembled some kind of macabre art installment.

The beams from their tac-lights glanced off the moisture-slick walls, highlighting the broken limestone flooring. What had once been a serviceable passage had now become a dangerous obstacle course, every movement threatening to bring the place down.

"I can see why they closed the tunnels," Harrison said, his voice echoing down the corridor. "This place is a death trap."

Hannah nodded but didn't answer, her eyes on the floor of the corridor as they walked, clearly looking for some sign that Tina had passed this way. They stopped once, what looked to be a handprint catching their attention. But in the light, the resemblance faded, and they had to accept that it was nothing more than a trick of the shadows.

Then as the passage turned sharply to the left, there was a wet spot that they thought might be blood, but again their eyes proved faulty, a sniff and a taste identifying the moisture as nothing more than rusty water. And still Hannah pored over every nook and cranny. About halfway along, a second passageway veered off to the left, but it dead-ended no more than twenty yards after they'd turned to follow it. There was the rotting frame of a doorway, firmly sealed with some kind of metal plating.

Hannah knelt, following the bottom edge of it with her light. "The dust is undisturbed," she said, her voice carrying her disappointment. "No one's been here before us." She pushed to her feet, using the light to trace the other edges, clearly unwilling to accept the obvious.

"Hannah, there's no way he could have gone this way," Harrison said, already turning to go. "At least not without a blowtorch."

"I just need to be sure," she pleaded. "He's fooled us before. And I owe it to Tina to be certain."

With a sigh, he turned back and helped her finish the search, testing the metal by pushing and pulling on it. Finally satisfied, she shot him a grateful look, and they headed back to the main corridor, their lights dancing off the floor and ceiling as they moved. He watched her, marveling at her strength, knowing from experience that there was nothing he could do or say that would help. She had to find her own way through this.

Harrison sucked in a shuddering breath, remembering. He'd survived his sister's death. But the cost had been immeasurable. It wouldn't be an easy road for Hannah if the worst happened.

And the thought that this guy could be connected to her through him was almost more than he could handle. But there was no doubt that Walker was fixated on Hannah. Harrison had seen the pictures. And the thought of the bastard getting his hands on her was more frightening than anything he'd ever experienced in his life. Just the idea of this guy touching her... Harrison swallowed an oath, pushing aside his troubled thoughts. It never did anyone any good to overthink things.

Maybe the asshole was just a crazy fuck who'd stumbled on to Sunderland by accident. It really didn't matter. Either way, Hannah was at risk. That much was clear.

And if she kept pushing him away, there wasn't a damn thing he was going to be able to do about it.

Caring about a woman was like diving headfirst into an abyss—forever falling, plummeting toward certain death, while waiting for that moment when you inevitably crash into the bottom anyway. It was worse than any nightmare.

With an exaggerated sigh, he pulled his thoughts back to the tunnel. The ground, which at first had been descending slightly, was rising sharply now. Ahead he could see a light and hear Simon calling them. They were almost to the end. But Hannah had stopped just ahead, her attention on one of the rotting beams, this one cracked and listing sharply to the left, a huge sliver extending into the corridor like a crooked lance.

"What is it?" he asked, coming to a stop behind her, instantly on alert.

She turned, holding out her hand, a tangle of red yarn on her palm. "It's from Tina's sweater. It's her favorite. She always said it was lucky." Hannah paused, staring down at the bit of wool as if she expected it to speak to her. To tell her where her friend was. Harrison's heart constricted. And he started to tell her it would be okay—but stopped, knowing that the words were a lie.

"He's got her," Hannah said, her voice softer than a whisper. "He's really got her."

Hannah stared at her computer screen, trying to focus. The team had gathered in the war room to regroup. Harrison at his computer showing something to Avery. Drake and Simon sitting across from each other at the conference table discussing what they'd found at the scene.

Tracy sat by Hannah, flipping through a stack of papers on the table in front of her. Medical reports. Jasmine and Sara reduced to chemical equations and statistics.

Hannah had seen a lot in her life. Both professionally and personally. She was a survivor. But she'd never felt so helpless. And to make things more complicated, she found herself actually needing another human being. Wanting him in a way that went far beyond physical desire. And it scared the hell out of her. She'd always dealt with life by running away. When she was a child, she'd found a safe place deep inside her. A place that no one could reach no matter what other parts of her they tried to possess.

She hadn't talked for almost a month after they'd removed her from her house, the words lost as she tried desperately to hang on to the sanctuary she'd built in her mind. And from then on when she'd found herself in a difficult position, she'd just retreated. Withdrawn until she could summon the strength to deal. And even after all these years, there was still a part of herself that she kept hidden.

Except that now…well, now she'd let Harrison in. And more than anything she wanted him out again. Or maybe she wanted him to stay forever. It was all so damned confusing.

"All right, people," Avery said, commanding everyone's attention. "I want to know where we are. We've got a ticking clock as far as Tina's concerned, and the more quickly we can distill the information we've gathered, the better our chances of finding her. Why don't we start with what we've got on Reid's death. Tracy?"

Tracy nodded, patting the papers into a neat stack as

she ordered her thoughts. And Hannah marveled at how calm she was, considering that only a short time ago, she'd been cutting into someone they'd all considered a friend.

"So it looks like you were right about Reid following Walker and presumably Tina to the basement," Tracy said. "The blood trail you guys were following definitely came from him. Most likely from the stab wound to the gut. My guess is that Walker thought he'd hit a major organ. A hit to the kidney or some part of the colon or stomach would have been consistent with the location of the wound, the end result being Reid bleeding out."

"But he missed?" Simon asked with a frown.

"He did." Tracy actually sounded surprised. "Considering this guy's finesse with a knife, I can't explain it. Maybe he was just in a hurry or maybe Tina interrupted him."

"That follows if Reid was attacked in the hall and tried to make it inside to warn her," Drake said. "If she walked into the middle of it all, Walker would have been forced to concentrate on her. After all, she was the prize."

"Maybe Reid played dead," Harrison suggested. "That would have given him the opportunity to go after Tina. And possibly gain the upper hand."

"Except that it didn't work," Hannah said, hating the fact that she sounded so condemning. But the truth was that no matter how hard he'd tried, Reid had failed to protect Tina.

"What about the print?" Avery asked, ignoring Hannah's outburst.

"The blood was Reid's, but the fingerprint was definitely Tina's. Which means we can place her at the scene after Reid was stabbed. In addition, we tested the blood and skin on the wall outside the apartment against a hair sample of Tina's. And it looks like it's a match. When we get the DNA back we'll know for sure."

"Son of a bitch hurt her, too," Drake said, the words clipped in anger.

"Slammed her pretty hard against the wall," Tracy agreed. "The cells from the skin were definitely from her scalp. Anyway, between the placement of the print and the blood in the hall, I'd say we've got pretty solid evidence to support the scenario the way you've laid it out."

"So we've established that Reid was stabbed either outside the door to the apartment or just inside in the foyer, and that Tina walked into the living room at some point after Reid had made his way inside. What about Walker?" Simon asked. "I suppose it's too much to hope that he left something behind as well."

"We've already established that the blood we found belonged to Reid and Tina," Tracy said. "And unfortunately we didn't find anything to link to Walker. Not that I'm surprised. For all the disorganization in his attacks, he's always been thorough at destroying anything that might definitively identify him."

"How about the knife he used on Reid?" Avery asked. "Did you find it?"

"No." Tracy shook her head. "Although I've got techs still looking for it. But I can verify that the width and thickness of the blade used to cut Reid's throat matches the one used on both Sara and Jasmine. Which at least ties the three murders together. There was also the same degree of expertise present. Reid died almost instantly. As I said before, this clearly wasn't the act of a sadist."

"Because there was no prolonging of pain," Simon prompted.

"Exactly. Unlike the original cyber killer, this guy is all about power. The thrill he derives from killing comes from his ability to best his prey."

"The main goal seemingly to stay one step ahead of us," Harrison said.

"I think you have to be careful about making this personal," Tracy cautioned. "Based on Walker's background, there's certainly some evidence to support the idea. But that could just be a spurious connection. In truth, it's just as likely that he's using us because we're here."

"Then how do you explain the pictures of Hannah?" Harrison asked.

"I'd say it's a fixation. Tied to either the college or Tina. Or maybe, if he's really trying to channel the cyber killer, to you."

"So you're totally dismissing the idea that this guy has some kind of issue with A-Tac?" Hannah asked, surfacing from her tumbling thoughts to try to shift the conversation away from talk about her and Harrison.

"I'm not dismissing anything at this point," Tracy said. "In fact, I'd feel a lot better if Madison was still here. She's the expert. Anyway, all I'm saying is that we want to avoid making any conclusion that isn't supported by facts. It's the easiest way for us to miss something else that might be important."

"I think your point is well taken," Avery agreed. "Assuming anything is always a mistake. We need to stick to what we know, not what we suspect. Even if in the end that turns out to be the truth. So what did we find at the tunnel's end?"

"Nothing conclusive," Simon said, his frustration echoing Hannah's. "The grate had been removed, and we found footprints. Two sets. Possibly male and female." He shot a look at Tracy and shrugged. "Definitely one smaller than the other. We also found some blood on the vent's frame at the opening."

Tracy sorted through her papers, pulling one sheet from the pile. "The blood has been identified as Tina's. So at least we know for sure she was there. And when you factor in the wool Hannah found, we can say with a fair degree of certainty that she was in the tunnels as well."

"The footprints petered out before they reached the parking lot by the girls' dorms," Simon continued. "We've got people canvassing the dorms now to see if anyone saw anything, but it was really late, and with so many people having left campus, particularly women, I'd be surprised to find a witness."

"I pulled the security footage from the parking lot," Harrison said. "And so far, I've got two vehicles that moved during the timeframe we've established. The first was a professor. And he's already verified that he didn't see anything."

"And the second?" Avery asked.

"A student. She was leaving to go home. Took me a while to reach her, but she also didn't see anything out of the ordinary. And I checked with both her parents and her roommate to make sure that she really was where she said she was."

"So where the hell did he go?" Drake slammed a hand on the table, giving a physical presence to all of their anger.

"Maybe across the street," Avery suggested. "The security cameras wouldn't have covered that. My guess is that if he knows about the tunnels, he's smart enough to have figured out how to avoid our security cameras. We've already checked everything we've got that shows the administration building, and except for catching the lights going out in the apartment, there's nothing."

"How about Tina's phone?" Tracy asked. "Every time Walker has taken someone, he's sent Tina an mpeg."

"I've been monitoring both her phone and her computer," Harrison said, tapping his keyboard for effect. "And so far there's nothing. I've also got passwords for her social media accounts, and there isn't anything there either. If this guy wants us to know where she is, he's not trying to contact us through Tina."

Hannah leaned back, rubbing her temples. She'd been multitasking, listening to the conversation while studying her notes, searching for something that maybe she'd missed the first time through. So far she hadn't found anything new. But it wouldn't hurt to go through it all again. She scrolled back to the top of the screen, paging backward to the beginning, and then just as she started to skim across the page, her computer beeped, the noise insistently repeating itself.

A small box at the bottom of the screen blinked in time with the beeping. And she frowned, trying to figure out what the hell it was.

Harrison materialized at her side, and she felt everyone's eyes on her as she moved the cursor down to the flashing box. She paused, finger hovering, suddenly certain that she didn't want to see what the box contained.

"It's okay," he said, moving his hands to her shoulders, and this time she didn't shake him off. "I'm right here with you."

"We all are," Avery said, and just for the moment, Hannah forgot that she was afraid.

Holding her breath, she concentrated on the warmth of Harrison's fingers against her skin as she depressed the mouse button. At first nothing happened, and then slowly the computer screen dissolved, the image forming both familiar and terrifying.

The footage was grainy, but there was no mistaking Tina tied to a bed, or the shadowy figure of the man with the knife.

CHAPTER 22

"I don't want you leaving her side, unless you get a direct order from me," Avery said, his tone grim as they stood in the hallway outside the computer room. "Is that understood?"

"Yes, but I'm not sure I'm the best person for the job," Harrison said, hating himself for his indecision. "She's... we're... ah, hell, it's so fucked up."

"Doesn't matter," Avery responded, waving aside his protests. "I've known Hannah a long time now. And she doesn't trust easily. But she trusts you. And believe me when I tell you what a rare gift that is. She needs you, Harrison. Whether she knows it or not. And I'm asking—no, I'm ordering you to watch over her."

"Not a problem," Harrison said, "I'd have done it anyway."

"Good. Right now our primary concern has to be finding Tina. But we can't ignore the fact that Hannah is clearly on this guy's radar. And I'll feel better knowing that you've got her back."

"So you really think he's after her?"

"I don't know. But even if there wasn't a threat to her personally, this is still going to be hard on her. Tina's part of her family. And if this son of a bitch kills her, it's going to hit Hannah really hard. And we know this guy doesn't play around. He killed Jasmine within eight hours of abducting her. The bottom line here is that Hannah is part of *my* family. And she's been through enough in her life already."

"I thought that..." Harrison broke off, not wanting to break her confidence.

"She's never really talked about it." Avery shook his head. "But the CIA does a pretty thorough background check on all applicants. And coming into A-Tac means even more scrutiny. I just never saw a reason to let her in on how much I know."

"But you're telling me."

"I'm not telling you anything," Avery said, his smile gentle for such a big man. "She did. I'm not blind, Harrison. And as I said, I've known her a long time. So you'll watch out for her? No matter how much she resents you for doing so?"

It was Harrison's turn to smile. "You do know her well."

"All right, then," Avery said, with a tight nod. "And for the record, this conversation never happened."

"What conversation?" Harrison shrugged as he watched the big man walking away, for the first time feeling as if he were really a part of the team. He'd been lucky in his life. He'd had the opportunity to work with a lot of really amazing people. But he wasn't sure that he'd really felt like he belonged. Not since Bree died. But maybe in A-Tac, he'd finally found a home.

The thought was comforting, and he wondered when he'd started letting emotion rule his life. But then he thought of Nash with his son, Adam. Or Drake and his excitement over Madeline's pregnancy. Maybe it was okay to need other people. Or maybe it was just about protecting family. And Hannah was family. Whether she liked it or not.

Shaking his head, he walked back into the computer room. Hannah was sitting at a console, staring up at the screen over her head, an image of Tina frozen on the screen.

"You're just torturing yourself," he said, moving over to sit beside her.

"I know," she sighed. "But the only way we're going to find her is if we study the video. It's the only lead we've got."

"So have you found anything?" They'd already been over the thing more times than he could count, but so far there was nothing to give them enough to identify a location.

"Nothing new. He's really been careful with his angles. The only thing we can see is the bed and the wall behind it. And that's just white plasterboard, which could be anywhere." She ran a hand through her hair. "Where've you been?" she asked with a frown.

"With Avery. He had some things he wanted to talk about."

"He asked you to watch over me," she said, swiveling her chair to face him.

He held back a smile. Hannah never missed a thing. "He's just worried about you. We all are."

"I know. I'd be lying if I said I wasn't worried, too.

It's just that as long as he's got Tina, I don't think I'm in any real danger." She paused, looking down at her hands, something she often did when she was nervous. "Anyway, I'm okay with you watching over me."

"Really? I actually thought you'd be pissed. I mean you were pretty clear back at the apartment."

"I was an idiot," she said, raising her gaze to his, her eyes apologetic. "I was upset and afraid. And I lashed out. I know you were just trying to be kind."

"Kind?" Harrison repeated. "Are you kidding me? It was a hell of a lot more than that, and you know it."

"Yeah, I do. And that's what scares me. I told you before I don't want to need you. I don't want to need anybody. But I..." She bit her lip, clearly struggling with the words. "...I can't seem to help myself." She smiled and shrugged, looking so uncomfortable and irresistible it was everything he could do not to pull her into his arms right then and there.

"Maybe you don't need help," Harrison said. "Maybe this is the way it's supposed to be."

"Scary?"

"No. Well, maybe." It was his turn to smile. "Look, I said it before, this is all new to me. We're in uncharted waters. And I'll admit that can be a little frightening. Especially for people like us."

"CIA operatives?"

"Well, I was actually thinking people with our kind of baggage, but you've got a point. I mean, we've spent our whole careers being told not to trust anything we can't quantify."

"So how are we supposed to know if what we feel is real?"

"I don't know. Maybe we're just supposed to trust it. Take a leap of faith. Hell, I'm the last person to be advising you about this. I don't know what the hell I'm doing. But I meant what I said before, I don't want to walk away. I want you in my life."

"Even if it turns out that we're just supposed to be friends?" she asked.

"Are you saying that's what you want?"

"No." She shook her head so quickly that he felt a rush of relief. "I just want to know that if things don't work out that we'll still have—"

"—our computers?" he quipped.

"You know what I mean," she said, her expression turning serious.

"I do. And as much as I want to promise you that nothing will change, I can't. It already has, Hannah. So the only thing we can do is plow forward."

"You make it sound so romantic."

"Yeah, well, we've already established that I'm not always good with words. What I'm trying to say is that I know this is scary. And I have no idea how things will turn out. But I want to give this a chance. And I want you to give it a chance, too."

"Okay," she said, eyes wide as if she'd just taken a leap into the deep end. "It's not as if I really have anything else to do anyway."

He laughed and pulled her chair closer, planting a kiss on her lips—feeling as if he'd won the fucking lottery. For a moment it was just the two of them, and then a computer alarm sounded and reality came crashing back in.

He held her gaze for a moment and then turned his

chair back to his console. Whatever the hell the future held for them, it wouldn't be good as long as Walker was out there and Hannah was a target.

He glanced up at the screen, searching for the source of the insistent beeping, but there was nothing on any of his computers. "It's not me," he said, swiveling back to look at her. "Were you running something?"

"Yeah." She nodded, staring down at the screen on her computer, shaking her head. "Walker's voiceprint. From Jasmine's mpeg. The computer found a match. And you're never going to believe where it came from."

"Okay, so what have you got?" Avery asked, striding into the war room followed by Drake and Simon.

"Something that's going to blow your mind," Harrison responded, exchanging a glance with Hannah.

"As you know," Hannah began, enjoying the moment, even though the news she had to impart was indeed a bombshell, "Harrison tried to find a match for the voiceprint we took off the mpeg from Jasmine's murder."

"Yeah, and he came up with bubkes," Simon said with a frown.

"Well, on the off chance of finding something, I took the print and ran it against wiretaps we had running on open investigations. I realize it was a long shot, but I figured it couldn't hurt."

"And you got a hit," Avery prompted.

"Three actually. All from the same source." She waited a beat, all four of her team members waiting—the anticipation building. "Turns out we've got Walker on tape talking to Alain DuBois. Twice in his office and once on his cellphone. He was using another alias. But there's no question it's him. I ran additional tests for verification and got a conclusive match."

"Son of a bitch," Drake said. "So Walker works for the Consortium."

"Looks that way. Or at least he has dealings with them," Harrison said. "After Hannah showed me what she'd found, I ran a couple of checks, and I can put DuBois in England and Geneva at the times Walker was there. It's not enough to tie DuBois into the bombing or the assassination attempt in Vienna, but it's definitely a red flag for possible Consortium involvement."

"What were the phone calls about?" Drake asked.

"On the surface, they were too vague to put any significance on," Hannah said. "But when you put them in context with everything that's happened here, they take on new meaning."

"In the first conversation, dated a month ago, DuBois is talking to Walker about a problem they need cleaned up," Harrison continued. "There's no reference to what the problem is. But DuBois specifically says that it's time to put an end to certain rivals. And when Walker asks how, DuBois says that he's working on it, but that the solution needs to be creative because previous attempts to eliminate the problem have met with failure."

"I'll admit that under the circumstances, it's pretty damn tempting to read something into that—like the attack on my wife and sister-in-law." Drake shook his head, looking skeptical. "But there's nothing there to corroborate the assumption."

"Not in the first conversation, no," Hannah said. "But listen to this." She hit a key and DuBois's voice filled the room.

"So I have a little proposition," DuBois said. *"And I think you'll find it's right up your alley. I've found an intersection between your problems and ours. In the process of researching personnel involved with the problem we discussed, I've uncovered a tragic incident I think we can use to our advantage. Tragedy always breeds fear. And fear has a way of undoing even the most strong-minded. Especially when it comes back to haunt you."*

"So how do I play into this tragedy?"

"You're going to recreate it."

There was a rustling sound and then Walker's voice replaced DuBois's. *"You're serious? What about collateral damage?"*

"There's a cost to everything. But what we stand to gain is far more important than a few casualties. And besides, I've known you a long time, my friend. And I'm more than aware of your particular talents as well as your predilections. I'm sure you won't find the task too onerous. And besides, as I said, there's a connection to you."

Again the sound of shuffling paper filled the hidden microphone.

"You're sure?" Walker asked.

"Positive. The proof is in the folder. This is your chance to even the score. For Timothy. So can I count on you?"

"Abso-fucking-lutely."

The tape stopped.

"It ends there." Hannah said. "The last conversation was taken off DuBois's cellphone. It's a verification that the project is on track and that Walker is en route. The call originated from a throwaway cell about seventy-five miles from here. Five days ago."

"Son of a bitch," Drake said again, clearly at a loss for words.

"So who's Timothy?" Avery asked. "And what connection does he have with us?"

"Not us," Harrison corrected. "Me. Timothy Allen was a suspect in a rape case I worked my first year out of Quantico. There'd been a series of rapes occurring in New Jersey and New York, and they seemed to be tied together, so the FBI was called in. The primary suspect was a seventeen-year-old kid. The evidence was circumstantial, but pretty damning. So we went in to make the arrest."

"In Kingston, I'm guessing," Avery interjected, as usual one step ahead of the game.

"Yeah. Anyway, we rushed the house, and in the commotion the kid, Timothy, tried to make a break for it. I cornered him and he drew a gun on me. I tried to talk him down, but he took a shot, and I was forced to take mine. He died in the hospital a few days later. He never admitted his guilt. But the rapes stopped."

"It took a little digging," Hannah added, her eyes on Harrison, "but it turns out that Timothy Allen was John Walker's half-brother."

"That's why he jumped at the opportunity to recreate Harrison's worst nightmare," Simon said.

"He wanted revenge." Hannah nodded. "But I'm guessing it was also about guilt. I read the rape reports, and there are some serious similarities to the murders here. The inability to perform leading to a stand-in for actual penetration. The cutting after the act. It's all there. The victims were even college girls. The only real difference is that those women are still alive."

"But if it was Walker, then why did the rapes stop?" Drake asked. "I thought these guys couldn't control the urge."

"Most of them can't," Harrison said. "But sometimes they find other outlets."

"Like killing for hire." Avery leaned back, his expression thoughtful. "I can see that there's a similar power rush in instigating a terrorist attack."

"And along the way, he'd have developed a taste for the kill," Hannah added. "Then along comes DuBois with an offer Walker probably thought too good to be true. The perfect storm, as it were."

"The ultimate target being to burn A-Tac," Drake said.

"Exactly. And the easiest way to get us off their backs is to force us out from undercover." Avery's expression was grim.

"And attacking the campus is the perfect way to do it," Hannah said, continuing the line of thought. "As the press coverage of the killings grows, there will be questions that could lead to an investigation into our role in all of this."

"Ultimately leading to our being exposed as CIA," Drake concluded, his anger barely contained. "Which puts an end not only to A-Tac, but to our careers as well."

"And on a bigger scale," Avery said, "our outing would throw the CIA into defensive mode as the political stratum starts to question the validity of using operatives to teach America's best and brightest. It would jam Langley up for years."

"A definite win/win for the Consortium. Turns out my idea wasn't so far-fetched after all." Drake leaned back, his gaze encompassing them all.

"Yeah, well, it's my past that brought this down on our heads," Harrison said.

"Nonsense." Avery shook his head. "If it hadn't been you, it would have been one of us. We've all got serious shit in our backyards. You just happened to have something that they could use."

"Yeah, but whatever's going through Walker's head, at least part of it is about avenging his brother. And there's no denying the fact that I killed the kid."

"You were defending yourself against a fleeing suspect," Hannah stated, unable to keep herself from jumping to Harrison's defense. "Any one of us would have done the same. This isn't about anything except a psychopathic killer hired by an organization bent on the destruction of everything A-Tac stands for. Clearly, destroying A-Tac has become a full-time occupation for the Consortium."

"Yeah well, this time it might just work," Drake said, his fist clenched in anger. "With DuBois dead, there's no one to rein this bastard in."

"Except A-Tac," Avery reminded them. "The one mistake the Consortium keeps making is to underestimate us."

"So we prove them wrong again," Simon said, determination coloring his voice. "We figure out where Walker has taken Tina Richards, and then we take him down."

CHAPTER 23

"Are you sure you're all right?" Hannah asked, walking into the dining room to hand Harrison a beer.

He took a sip, standing at the window, watching the seemingly pastoral scene outside. It could be any neighborhood in America. Suburbia at its best. But instead, it housed a group of trained operatives. It was a life he'd chosen willingly. But sometimes, like today, he wondered about the cost.

"I'm fine." He turned to face her, taking another sip of beer. In such a short time, she'd come to mean so much to him. Or maybe it had been that way from the beginning, and he just hadn't been willing to admit as much. Either way, she had become an important part of his life.

And in return he'd put her in the middle of a nightmare.

"I meant what I said earlier," she reminded him. "This isn't your fault. None of it. You did what you had to all those years ago, and you couldn't possibly have known that it would circle round like this. And even if you had, you couldn't have stopped it because you wouldn't have known when or where Walker was going to strike."

"But if I hadn't come here—"

"Then the Consortium would have found another way. And Walker would still be waiting for his opening with you. And sooner or later, he'd probably have found it. So it doesn't do any good to go through the 'what ifs.' Although that doesn't mean it's easy to stop either." She reached up to brush her hand against his cheek. "When Jason was killed, I kept thinking of all the things I could have done that might have kept him out of his study that day. Things that would have kept him alive. But no matter how many times I pictured things playing out differently—Jason was still dead."

"So how did you get past it?" he asked.

"Lara." Her smile was bittersweet. "She'd been blaming herself, too. And together we realized that it wasn't doing anyone any good. And it certainly wasn't honoring Jason's memory. The hard truth was that neither of us could change what happened. We just had to accept it for what it was and try to move on."

"And how's that working out for you?" he asked.

"Good days and bad days," she said with a shrug, her smile twisting ruefully. "At least I know that Lara's happy. She's found her calling, I think, working at the clinic in South America. And she's got Rafe now."

"And what about you?" he asked, his heart feeling lighter. Being around Hannah seemed to have that effect on him. "Have you found someone?"

"I don't know," she teased, her blue eyes alight behind the tortoiseshell frames of her glasses. "The jury is still out on that one."

"So maybe I need to give them something to think about," he said, putting his bottle on the windowsill before pulling her close, his mouth slanting over hers as he bent to kiss her. Her scent surrounded him as he took possession of her lips. What had started as an affirmation quickly shifted to passion, desire supplanting all conscious thought.

Heat rocketed through him with the power of fission. What was it about Hannah? He touched her, and everything else disintegrated in the path of his overwhelming desire for her.

He trailed kisses along the line of her jaw and the soft skin of her neck. She trembled at the touch, and he smiled, his fingers caressing her breast through her shirt. She moaned, and he swallowed the sound, drinking her in. She tasted like beer and toothpaste. And he wasn't certain he'd ever be able to get enough.

She pressed closer, the friction of their bodies moving together, ratcheting up both his need and his pleasure. Her hands slipped beneath his shirt, moving in circles against his back, his body tensing in anticipation as she pressed even closer.

Harrison marveled at the emotions rocketing through him. There was desire, certainly, more than he'd ever known, but there was so much more than that. There was a fierce possessiveness, a protective urge that he'd never felt before. And even more surprising, there was tenderness, the need to cherish and revere, his need almost unmanning him. He knew in that instant that he would give anything—do anything—if it would make her happy.

She arched against him, offering herself, and he

moved lower, his tongue circling one taut nipple beneath the thin material of her shirt, pulling it into his mouth and sucking, wanting nothing more than to take her here and now—thrusting deep into her heat.

Twining her fingers through his hair, she pulled his mouth back to hers, plunging her tongue deep inside. The motion both sensual and carnal. Then her hands slid lower and lower still, her fingers dipping beneath the waistband of his jeans, his stomach muscles contracting as she brushed against the swollen length of his penis.

Urgency built within him, the physical pull between them so strong now it had become essential. Like breathing. God, he wanted this woman. With desire shimmering between them, he framed her face, pulling back to look at her—eyes heavy with passion, lips swollen from his kisses.

"I want you, Hannah," he whispered, his voice hoarse with need.

"I want you, too," she answered, her breath caressing his cheek.

With a groan, he reached for her again, but somewhere in the kitchen behind them, something crashed to the floor.

In an instant, passion fled, and he grabbed the gun he'd laid on the dining room table, pushing her behind him, his only thought now to keep her safe. But Hannah, being Hannah, grabbed her own gun and was right behind him as he moved toward the kitchen door and the source of the noise.

He flanked the door, straining into the silence, listening for something to identify the source of the crash they'd heard. But the room was quiet, the only sound the hum of the computer array on the dining room table.

With a nod to Hannah, he swung into the kitchen. It was still swathed in shadows, the light from the dining room spilling out across the floor. He moved into the room, turning in a slow arc as he searched for something amiss.

Just as he started to relax, believing the coast to be clear, something launched itself at him, smashing against his shoulders, something sharp digging into his neck. He swung, connecting with whatever was attacking. Swearing, he pushed it away, all the while trying to align his gun for a shot, his neck stinging like crazy.

"Harrison, no," Hannah called, her voice breaking through his crescendoing adrenaline. "It's only the cat."

He spun around, still clutching his gun, his gaze falling to the spitting ball of white fur pressed against the bottom of the refrigerator.

"Son of a bitch," he said to no one in particular, pressing a hand to his neck, the raised welts there oozing blood. "Where the fuck did that come from?"

"It's Asha," Hannah explained, lifting her hands in apology. "Tina's cat. With so much going on, I forgot I asked one of the techs to bring him here. I think you scared him."

"Yeah, well, we're even," Harrison said, pulse still pounding. "He scared the hell out of me, too."

"I have to admit I was pretty freaked myself. I guess we're all walking on eggshells." She shivered as she reached down to pick up the still-terrified cat.

"Well, I'm glad it wasn't anything more threatening," Harrison said, reaching for a paper towel to blot the blood on his neck.

"You're hurt," she observed with a frown, still holding the now purring Asha.

"Cat's definitely got some claws," he agreed, feeling absurdly jealous as she stroked Asha. "And I get the definite feeling he's not all that fond of me."

"Sit down, let me clean you up." She set Asha on the counter. "You don't want to get an infection."

"I suppose you're right." He sat at the breakfast bar while she got a first aid kit, ignoring the cat, who was licking his paws. "I guess now I know how Walker felt when Asha attacked him."

"In that case, I wish the cat had done a lot worse, actually," Hannah said, as she dabbed antibiotic ointment on the scratches. "But like we said before, there's nothing to be gained by wishing things were different."

"The best we can do now is try to figure out where he's holding Tina," Harrison agreed as he involuntarily glanced down at his watch.

"I know," Hannah said, her face tightening as she put a Band-Aid on the worst of the scratches, "it's already been six hours. We're running out of time."

As if to echo the thought, one of Harrison's computers chirped to life in the dining room.

"That mean something?" she asked, shooting a look in the direction of the noise, her expression hopeful.

"Maybe," he said, pushing off the barstool. "I've been running the recognition software I used to identify the house on Sapphire Lake. It's a long shot, since there's nothing obvious to triangulate off of, but I figured it was worth a try."

He headed into the dining room, Hannah and the cat on his heels. He dropped down into the chair in front of the still-chirping computer, hitting a key to stop the noise.

"Damn it. It looks like it didn't find anything."

"Well, like you said, there wasn't much to work with. He pretty much limited the video to a close-up of the bed and the wall behind it."

"I know. No shadows, no identifying noises, no window. Nothing. It's like, this time around, he really doesn't want us to find him."

"Except that every time he's sent a video he's left a clue. So it's got to be there somewhere. We're just not seeing it."

"Maybe it's in the details," he said, queueing the video again as she took a seat next to him. "With Sara's murder it was all about the window. And with Jasmine's it was sound. So what the hell is it this time? What does he want us to find?"

He hit play, and Hannah reached for his hand, her eyes locked on the monitor. It wasn't any easier to watch this time, and he couldn't stop himself from checking on her every few minutes, but even when she flinched, her expression was resolute. This was the best way to find Tina, and she knew it as well as he did.

"You filtered for sound, right?" she asked as it came to an end.

"Yes, and like I said, nothing stood out. The was very little background noise."

"Which in and of itself should tell us something," she said, her mouth pursed as she considered the options. "We know there's screaming. Which means that there can't be another house close by or someone would hear her. And there's no highway noise or railroad traffic. Which rules out the busier areas of town. It's doubtful that he'd go back to the lake. We've got people watching."

"We know that he's partial to houses," Harrison

continued the train of thought, "and seems to prefer a cellar, even if he's just mimicking the cyber killer."

"Although he's fallen off the script, so maybe that's changed as well." Hannah frowned, still staring at the screen. "Can you start it again and then freeze it when the bed is in the center of the frame?"

He hit the button and fast-forwarded until it reached the point she'd requested.

"Good, now can you focus in on the wall behind the bed? The whole thing, only larger if you can do that."

He manipulated the image so that only the top of Tina's head was visible, the screen filled instead with the headboard and the wall behind it.

"It's just what you said before," Harrison shook his head, "white-painted wallboard."

"Yes, but there's something off about it. The perspective seems skewed."

He moved forward frame by frame, but there was nothing to see except white walls. "I don't know what you're seeing." He shook his head, fighting the feeling that time was running out.

"Wait a minute," Hannah said, leaning forward for a better view. "Can you pan out again?"

"Sure." He entered a command, and the entire picture appeared again, Tina unsuccessfully trying to move away from Walker as he threatened her with the knife.

"There," Hannah said, pointing to the far left of the picture. "And there." She pointed to the far right. "There's a shift in shading. A shadow, if you will."

"But I don't see—" he began, but she waved him silent.

"That's the whole point. There's nothing to see," she said, her voice filled with excitement. "No corners. The change in shading indicates a shift in perspective. A change of direction. And in a normal room, that'd be delineated by corners. But there aren't any. Even though the shading on both sides shows a shift in direction. The room is round, Harrison."

He frowned at the screen, moving it forward again frame by frame. "He's made it more difficult to see by not filming the ceiling or floor line, but I think you're right. I just don't know how it helps us."

"Well, to start with, it narrows things down a lot," Hannah said, typing something into her computer. "I mean, how many houses with round rooms can there be in the area?"

"Considering all the Victorian houses downtown, I'd say quite a few."

"According to city records, there are actually seventeen with towers," she said, studying the list of historical homes she'd pulled up on the computer. "But we've already established that there's not much background noise. Which means that he's either soundproofed or he's somewhere off the beaten path. And since I'm thinking there hasn't been time for remodeling, I'm going with off the beaten path, and that eliminates six houses right off the bat. All of them located on or near Main Street."

Harrison frowned up at the screen, still studying the picture. "I agree that Walker hasn't had time to change the room to suit his purposes," he said. "But the presence of painted wallboard indicates that someone else along the way remodeled. An original Victorian wouldn't have Sheetrock. The walls would be plastered or papered."

Hannah typed in the new parameter. "According to the tax records, seven of the remaining houses have been remodeled in the last twenty years. And of those, five are currently owner occupied. Two of them in areas where they're somewhat isolated, but it wouldn't be a sure thing."

"What about the other two?"

"They're listed as rentals, but they're both definitely in areas where there's high traffic. One on the highway, and the other practically fronting the new mall. And I've got nothing here to tell me if they're currently rented or empty."

"Well, it won't hurt to check on all of them," Harrison said, reaching for his cellphone, but Hannah leaned forward suddenly, her gaze locked on the frame he'd frozen on the screen.

"What's that?" she asked, pointing to something on the wall behind the bedframe.

Harrison moved closer, squinting. "It's just part of the headboard."

"I don't think so." Hannah leaned forward, eyes on the image. Can you enlarge it so that we can see it better?"

"Sure." He moved the cursor to the place she'd indicated and hit a key, enlarging so that the headboard was front and center. Larger now, and without the forward motion of the video, the spot took on more clarity, looking as if it might be separate from the headboard after all. "Okay, so maybe it's a shadow?" He shook his head, trying to make sense of the dark and light shadows that filled the spaces in the open frame of the headboard.

"I think it's the wall," Hannah said, typing furiously on her computer. "It looks like the Sheetrock has broken away to reveal the original structure. Can you make it any clearer?

He moved the cursor, highlighting the shadow, and

finessed the frame into sharper focus. "Good eyes," he said, the shape taking form. "It looks like—"

"Stones," Hannah finished for him. "It's stones. And I think I know where it is."

She turned her computer so that he could see, the screen filled with the image of a Gothic-inspired mansion complete with stone turret. He shook his head, not sure exactly what he was looking at.

"It's the castle," Hannah said. "It was built a couple hundred years ago. The family that owned it are founding members of the town. But more important, the last of them died about four months ago."

"So the place is empty?"

Hannah nodded. "And it's secluded. The grounds have got to be at least five acres."

Harrison felt the hairs on his arms rise as he looked from the picture on Hannah's computer to the image on the screen above them.

"I'll call Avery."

CHAPTER 24

The castle was located on the far west side of town amidst a forest of trees, the property surrounded by an old stone wall. What had once been a resplendent show of wealth had become run-down to the point of looking menacing. Like something out of a Hitchcock movie. And as Hannah joined Harrison and the rest of the team in the woods outside the house, she shuddered, thinking that the setting was fitting for the atrocities most likely occurring inside.

"All right, people," Avery said to the assembled team, which included not only A-Tac but Bill and Casey as well. The case had grown personal for them. Both because they'd been charged with watching Tina and because Reid had been their friend. "We don't have the luxury of time here. Walker's had Tina Richards for just under eight hours now. And we know that he killed Jasmine somewhere within that timeframe. So we need to move quickly while still maintaining some degree of stealth. We need the element of surprise, or we risk losing Tina."

"If we haven't already," Simon mumbled under his breath, giving voice to the sentiment they all shared.

"We'll split into two teams, Hannah, Harrison, and Simon—you take the back. Drake, Casey, and I will hit the front. And, Bill, you'll keep watch here—make sure there's not some other way for Walker to make an escape. Everybody ready?" Avery asked. "All right then, let's move out."

Harrison took the lead as they headed for the back of the mansion, with Hannah following behind and Simon in the rear. According to the house's blueprints, the turret had a separate staircase located in a small room off the kitchen. The idea was for the two teams to sweep the first floor, and after making sure it was clear, Avery's team would head for the cellar and Hannah's would check the turret.

As they rounded the back corner of the house, Harrison lifted a hand and slowed down, Hannah and Simon following suit. Pointing first at his eyes and then to a small covered porch surrounded by overgrown rhododendron, Harrison waited a beat and inched toward a grimy window for a quick look inside. Then, seemingly satisfied with what he saw, he motioned them forward.

Fighting the bushes, they climbed the steps and stopped on the landing, guns ready, while Harrison tried the door. It was locked. And without a second thought, he wrapped the bottom of his shirt around his fist and smashed the glass window, reaching through it to open the lock from the inside. Once there, they quickly searched the kitchen, pantry, and dining room, catching glimpses of Avery and company as they made quick work of the front of the house.

"We're clear," Harrison whispered into his comlink.

"Copy that," came Avery's reply. "We're clear, too. Heading now to secondary target."

Harrison nodded and waved Hannah and Harrison toward the tiny room that housed the turret staircase. Like a true medieval castle, the spiral staircase was made of stone surrounded by the turret walls, the pathway up narrow and claustrophobic.

For a moment, Hannah hesitated, fighting a wave of fear. She'd always hated enclosed spaces, probably because as a child, she'd spent many hours huddled in the closet beneath the stairs, hoping futilely to escape her foster father's attention.

"You all right?" Harrison asked, keeping his voice low, his eyes concerned. "Simon and I can handle this."

"No." She shook her head, determination fighting off her phobia. "I'll be fine. Let's move."

They started up the stairs, Harrison again in the lead with Hannah sandwiched between him and Simon. They moved as quickly as the narrow space allowed, trying to keep noise to a minimum. Finally, at the top, they stopped, the massive wooden door slightly ajar—the silence deafening.

Leading with his gun, Harrison moved into the room, Hannah and Simon following. Adrenaline crested as Hannah realized that the room was empty. Circular, with white walls, it was exactly like the one on the mpeg on Hannah's computer. Except that now the bed was empty, the wall behind it spattered with blood, a massive stain spreading across the mattress.

As with the other scenes before it, the metallic smell of blood permeated the air, and Hannah fought to keep from gagging, her heart twisting as her mind leaped to the obvious conclusion.

Tina was dead.

"Oh, God," she whispered, fighting her roiling gut. "We've got to get to the cellar." Without another word she turned, taking the twisting stairs at breathtaking speed, heedless of the danger, her only thought to try to reach her friend.

Harrison following close on her heels, Hannah hit the bottom landing and headed for the hallway and the stairs to the cellar. Again taking the stairs two and three at a time, she jumped down to the stone floor of the small room and skidded to a stop, only vaguely aware of Drake and Avery off to one side. Harrison stopped behind her, his hands reaching out to grip her shoulders.

Hannah blinked slowly, unable to make sense of the scene before her. Bile bubbled up in her throat even as relief rocketed through her. The man they'd known as Walker was strung up from the rafters, his hands stretched wide in supplication, his entrails spilling out across the floor. Blood stained the cellar's every surface. Walls, floor…ceiling. No part of the man was uncut. His hands were missing fingers. His torso eviscerated. His feet twisted and broken. His neck slit from ear to ear. Only his face was untouched. His eyes wide. His mouth slack and open.

"Jesus," Simon said, "what the hell happened here?"

Hannah swallowed, still trying to take in the enormity of the horror, one thought running through her head. "Tina," she pushed the name out on a strangled whisper. "Where's Tina?"

"I don't know," Avery said, his usually booming voice subdued. "She wasn't upstairs?"

"No." Hannah shook her head. "But there was blood all over the place there, too." She tried for additional words, but none came. She turned slowly, eyes searching the cellar for some sign of her friend.

Drake moved, too, evidently with the same idea. He edged past the body, careful to not disturb the scene, and then headed for the far side of the cellar, the corner shrouded in shadow. Hannah frowned and then leaped forward, her ears catching the same sounds Drake must have heard.

Something was moving, the resulting noise muffled but still audible.

Tina.

Heart pounding, she followed Drake, waiting as he pushed back a small crate to reveal a small door. Behind it, louder now, Hannah could hear someone banging against the wall. Drake wrenched the door open.

She was lying on the floor, naked, her hands and feet bound, a piece of duct tape over her mouth. Hannah pushed past Drake, already pulling off her jacket to cover her friend. After removing the duct tape, she cut through the ropes binding her hands, rubbing the skin to help bring back the circulation.

Tina burst into tears, burying her face against Hannah's shoulder. "I knew you'd find me," she sobbed, her shoulders shaking.

"The ambulance is on its way," Avery said, kneeling beside them, his eyes meeting Hannah's. "How badly is she hurt?"

"She's pretty banged up. Some bruises and cuts, but

most of it seems superficial. My guess is that the blood upstairs belonged to Walker."

"Tina," Avery said, his voice gentle, "can you tell us what happened?"

She lifted her head, eyes still wide with fear, and then swallowed, struggling to find her voice. "He...he was going to...rape...me." She swallowed again. "He had a bottle." Tears dripped down her nose. "I tried to fight him...but...he was strong..." She looked up at Hannah, who slipped a comforting arm around her shoulder.

"It wasn't your fault," she crooned, wishing with all her heart she could take away the fear in Tina's eyes. "It wasn't your fault."

"I closed my eyes," Tina said. "I just wanted to get away."

Hannah nodded, understanding completely. Sometimes the only way to escape was to hide inside yourself.

"What happened after that?" Avery prompted, his voice still full of compassion, and Hannah had never respected him more.

"I...I don't know," Tina whispered. "I felt a pinch. On my arm. And then the next thing I remember I woke up here. And someone was screaming." She flinched, pushing closer to Hannah. "Then after a while it got really quiet. And then I heard your voice." Her lips trembled as she tried to smile. "Is it really over?"

"Yes," Hannah said. "You're safe now. I promise."

She nodded, and Drake leaned into the closet. "The ambulance is outside."

"I can walk," Tina protested, trying to get to her feet.

"No way," Avery said, lifting her effortlessly into his

arms. "I've got you. But I need you to cover your eyes. All right."

Tina hesitated for a moment and then nodded, burying her face against Avery's chest as he headed for the stairs.

"She going to be okay?" Simon asked, his jaw tight with emotion.

"I think so," Hannah said, her eyes moving to Harrison, who was standing in front of Walker's body, looking at something tied around the man's wrist. "At least physically. Emotionally it's impossible to gauge how much damage he did."

"It's a good thing the bastard's dead," Drake said, his hand clenched in anger.

"Can't argue with that. But you've got to admit it does create a few questions. The principal one being who did this?" Simon frowned at the body.

"Someone with anger issues," Hannah said, the words coming of their own accord.

"Definitely not Tina," Drake offered. "She certainly had reason enough to want the guy dead, but she isn't strong enough to have pulled something like this off."

"Or mentally capable of it," Hannah was quick to add. "Not to mention the fact that we found her tied up in the closet."

"So who the hell did this?" Simon repeated.

"The cyber killer." Harrison turned, his eyes hard, a small gold chain draped across his fingers.

"No fucking way," Drake said.

But Hannah shivered. Harrison's pronouncement was clearly more than supposition. "How do you know?" she asked, her heart starting to pound.

"Because I recognize the handiwork," Harrison said.

"And because Walker was wearing this around his wrist." He held up the chain. It was a woman's necklace, a filigreed gold heart dangling from the chain. "My sister was wearing it the day he took her."

"But you can't know for sure—" Simon started and then stopped, as he saw the pain etched across Harrison's face.

"I gave it to her when we turned twelve," he said, his eyes on the necklace. Hannah bit into her bottom lip, her heart breaking. "See." Harrison carefully turned it over. "It's got our initials on it. Son of a bitch has had it all these years."

"So why would he show up now? And why kill Walker?" Drake asked.

"I don't know," Harrison said. "Maybe all the press coverage caught his attention, and he didn't like the idea of someone masquerading as him. Or maybe he figured out that I was involved. Either of those things could be considered a stressor. But whatever the reason, it's definitely him. He's back. And now that he's tasted blood again, I doubt he's going to stop."

"I can certainly see how that follows," Simon agreed, "but if he's got a bloodlust going, why didn't he kill Tina?"

Harrison stared down at the necklace for a moment longer and then looked up, the pain in his eyes laced with fear as his gaze met Hannah's. "It's simple really. He didn't kill her because she isn't his type."

"Hey," Hannah said, walking up to the ambulance where Tina was sitting in the open bay, wearing a pair of scrubs, with a blanket wrapped around her. "How are you holding up?"

"Better, now that I've got clothes again," Tina responded with a feeble smile. "They said that I was drugged." She lowered the blanket to reveal her upper arm. "You can actually see the injection site. That's why I don't remember what happened after..."

"Did he rape you?" Hannah asked, not certain she should be asking the question, but knowing that sometimes it helped to talk.

"No." Tina shook her head. "The EMT says not. Thank God. I don't know if I could have dealt with that on top of everything else."

"You'd have found a way," Hannah said, reaching out to squeeze Tina's hands. "But I'm glad it's not something you have to deal with. And if it's any help at all, he's dead."

"It is, actually. Although I'm not sure what kind of person that makes me. But I keep thinking of Jasmine and Sara. They weren't as lucky as me. You know?"

"I do. But you can't beat yourself up for being alive," Hannah said. "It just wasn't your time."

"That's what I keep telling myself. But there's a lot about all of this that doesn't seem fair."

"To any of you. I know. But it's over now."

"Is it?" she asked, her green eyes looking far too old. "I heard him screaming. The man who took me. And I saw his body."

Hannah felt sick. "Avery told you not to look. You shouldn't have to see something like that."

"Well, I did," Tina said, her expression resolute. "And I don't care that he's dead. But the way he was killed. It was like the papers said. Like the guy they called the cyber killer. Does that mean he's back?"

Hannah opened her mouth to lie and then changed her mind. Tina deserved the truth. "We don't know. It seems possible. But it doesn't change the fact that you're safe now. If he'd been interested in you—"

"—I wouldn't be sitting here talking to you. I know. It's not me I'm worried about." It was her turn to reach for Hannah's hands. "It's you. All the women he killed, they were like you. Single and successful and brunette."

"Don't worry about me. I can take care myself. And if not, I've got a lot of really tough friends."

"So I've seen," Tina said with a tiny smile. "They're pretty awesome. And they're not just professors, are they?"

Again Hannah considered a lie but settled for a half-truth instead. "Let's just say they have outside interests."

"You, too," Tina said, nodding at the holstered gun Hannah still wore.

"The only thing that matters right now is that you're all right. We'll talk about the rest of it when you're better. Okay?"

She nodded. "I didn't mean to push. It's just that if you hadn't found me..."

"But we did find you, Tina. And it's over now."

"And I'm not going to tell anyone what I saw. I mean, the part about you guys being...well, whatever it is you really are."

"We're professors, Tina. And we all care about you. That's what matters right now."

"Yeah," she sighed. "I know."

"So I'm sure they've already asked you, but you didn't get a look at the guy who drugged you?"

"No. Or if I did, I don't remember. The doctor said that

the drug he gave me was like a roofie. I was present, but the part of my brain that makes memories wasn't working. I'm sorry."

"It's okay. It's probably better that you don't remember."

"But I want to help. I need to feel like something good came out of all of this."

"Something good did happen, Tina," Hannah said, her smile gentle. "You're alive."

She looked down, studying her hands. "Yes, well, I'm not sure Jasmine's and Sara's parents would agree with that."

"Oh, honey, they'd be the first to tell you how happy they are that you made it. You can't take any of this on yourself. What you have to do now is try and let it go. Find a way to start living again."

"And you think that's possible? That I can really find a way to move on?" There was a note of desperation in her voice that Hannah recognized.

"Yes, I know it's possible. People come back from all kinds of things. It just takes time and healing. And a little faith."

"I know you're right," Tina said. "In here." She pointed to her head. "But when I close my eyes, I can still see him. Hear him. Smell him."

"It's going to take a while before that goes away. But it will go away. Or at least it'll stop haunting your dreams."

"How do you know?" she asked, a flicker of hope in her eyes.

Hannah felt tears sting her eyes. "Because I've been where you are. And I survived. It's not going to be easy. But you've got people around you who love you. And that's huge. Speaking of which..." She nodded toward

Roger Jameson, who was making his way toward the ambulance.

"Roger," Tina cried, and he broke into a sprint, pulling her into his arms when he reached her, holding her as if he never wanted to let her go.

Hannah smiled, thinking that when someone loved you anything was possible. She might have had to fight her demons by herself, but at least Tina wouldn't be alone.

Across the driveway, Harrison stood talking to Avery. As if he sensed her presence, he lifted his eyes, his gaze meeting hers, and Hannah's stomach did a little flip. And it occurred to her for the first time that maybe, if she was just willing to take the chance, she didn't have to be alone anymore either.

CHAPTER 25

"This whole thing is insane," Simon said, leaning back to prop his feet up on the table in the war room. "We start out thinking we're dealing with the cyber killer only to work out it's actually a copycat—some psycho connected to the Consortium bent on outing A-Tac. And now we find him dead, and it looks like he was murdered by the real cyber killer."

"Definitely one for stranger than fiction," Avery observed. "But even so, we've got to face the fact that we've got a seriously pissed-off serial killer out there."

"Which means we've got to find him before he strikes again," Drake said.

The team, including Tracy, had come back to the war room to regroup after processing the scene. Tina had been cleared by the hospital and gone with Roger to her parents', Casey going along for the ride just to be sure she was okay. Bill had remained behind at the site, still posing as FBI, to deal with the press and locals.

And although finding Tina alive had been a victory, Harrison couldn't help but think that there was worse to come. Involuntarily, his gaze went to Hannah, who was furiously typing something into her computer, and he felt a frisson of fear coursing through him. This bastard had already taken one person he loved...

"So what did you find at the scene?" Avery asked Tracy. "I don't suppose we got lucky."

"Not as far as trace is concerned," Tracy said. "There was no DNA and no fingerprints. Nothing at all to give us an ID. But the manner in which Walker was killed indicates that we're on target in thinking it's the original cyber killer. All the mutilation occurred before death. Which means that Walker was being purposely tortured, each cut designed to inflict maximum pain."

"Sadistic son of a bitch," Drake mumbled under his breath.

"You have no idea," Tracy said. "With this guy, killing is an afterthought. His primary goal is pain. Inflicting it provides stimulation."

"You're saying that he literally gets off on torture." Simon frowned, dropping his feet back to the floor.

"Yes," Harrison confirmed. "He's a psychopathic sexual sadist. Which means he likes seeing terror in his victims, and he'll do almost anything to keep ratcheting it higher. He feels no remorse. To him the victim is simply a means to an end."

"And the keepsakes?" Avery asked, referring to the necklace on the table.

"He took one from every victim. It's a way of reliving the event. Getting the high without actually having a victim present. He most likely pleasures himself while wearing the various articles. Over time, however, the thrill begins to wear off. Reliving it just isn't enough," Tracy said, "and he has to find another live victim."

"So once the memento loses its ability to recreate the moment, so to speak," Drake posited, "he wouldn't have any use for it anymore."

"No." Tracy shook her head. "Just the opposite, actually. Even if the object itself isn't enough for him to find satisfaction, he's still going to want to keep the collection as a whole. It'll be his most prized possession."

"So why was he able to give up Bree's necklace?" Hannah asked, looking up momentarily from her work at the computer. "Wouldn't he be breaking up the set?"

"He would," Tracy agreed. "Which tells us that his need to reach out to Harrison is more powerful than his need to maintain the collection."

"Because Harrison was involved both with the investigation here and with the one in Texas?" Drake asked.

"That's one possibility," Tracy said with a small shrug. "It could be that he simply wants to be sure that someone out there—in this case Harrison—knows for certain that Walker was an impostor and that he's the real deal."

"But he could also see me as part of what he perceives to be a conspiracy to steal his identity," Harrison added. "Even in today's share-your-life-online world, most people are still protective of their most personal data. Someone like the cyber killer would be even more likely to want to protect the persona he's created. And anyone he thinks is trying to take that way would be considered a threat."

"So when the original news broke that we believed the cyber killer was here at Sunderland," Avery leaned forward, palms on the table, "he could have seen you as the instigator."

"Or at least someone fanning the flames. As far as the cyber killer was concerned, we gave Walker a status he didn't deserve."

"And in his mind, 'we' could just as easily translate to 'Harrison.'"

"So, what? That means now he'll come after Harrison?" Simon shook his head in frustration.

"I don't think so," Tracy said. "It's highly unusual for someone like the cyber killer to break pattern. The fact that he killed Walker shows that he was experiencing extreme rage. The degree of brutalization reflects that as well. The evisceration in particular. So my guess is that torturing and then killing Walker went a long way toward releasing his fury."

"Which means he'll fall back into old patterns." Drake leaned back, crossing his arms over his chest.

"It seems reasonable," Tracy shrugged. "But as I've said before, it's not an exact science. One thing that concerns me is that the equipment Walker used to film his kills is missing."

"You think the cyber killer took it."

"I don't see who else," Tracy said. "He could just be curious. Maybe he wants to see the murder footage. Or maybe he's adopting that part of the MO. It wouldn't be unheard of. After all, he left emails for his victims. Using a digital camera and computer to stream information follows the same logic."

"But wouldn't that mean he's evolving?" Harrison asked.

"Absolutely. And considering he's been off the radar

for such a long time, not all that unusual. Additionally, the fact that he chose Bree's necklace to prove his authenticity indicates to me that this has become personal. Which means it's possible that his overall fantasy is now linked to you in some fashion."

"So it follows that his next victim could be someone that Harrison knows. Someone that fits the victimology," Avery said, his tone neutral, but his eyes cutting to Hannah, who was still typing on the computer, seemingly oblivious to this newest turn of conversation.

"So we just have to find this bastard and stop him before he can hurt anyone else," Simon concluded, his face tight with concern.

"And how do you propose we do that?" Drake asked. "We don't even know what this guy looks like."

"Well, if you're all finished predicting my imminent demise, I think I might be able to answer that," Hannah said, looking up from her computer with quiet resolution.

"We weren't..." Simon began and then trailed off. "It's just that..."

"I understand," Hannah said, her gaze moving to Harrison. "But predicting something doesn't mean it's actually going to happen. Especially not if we find him first."

"So what have you found?" Avery asked.

"A possible ID," Hannah said, typing again. "A man named Jeremy Draper. Corporal Draper, actually. U.S. Army." She hit a key, and a picture appeared on the screen above the table.

"And what makes you think this is our guy?" Drake narrowed his eyes, studying the photograph.

"The details fit," she said, turning her attention to Harrison. "Back at the castle you were talking about stressors. That something had to set this guy off. And it occurred to me that maybe there was an initial reaction—before he had the chance to come here and find Walker." She paused for a moment, hitting a key to change the photograph.

The picture was of a young woman. She'd clearly been stabbed to death.

"This is Eileen Draper. Jeremy's wife. She was murdered forty-eight hours ago. In Belton, Texas. Just about the same time the news about Jasmine's abduction and death went national."

"I see the potential for connection," Avery said. "She fits the victimology with her age and hair color, but you really don't have anything conclusive."

"Agreed. If this was as far as it went," Hannah said. "But it's not. First off, Belton is within the unsub's killing zone."

Harrison suppressed a smile at her use of the FBI terminology.

"And the stab wounds found on Eileen Draper," Hannah continued, "are similar in location, depth, and even pattern to those inflicted by the cyber killer. And like his other victims, her throat was cut."

"Could be another copycat," Simon suggested.

"Definitely a possibility, except that whoever killed her took her ring. And that part of the MO was never released publicly."

"So you think that in response to hearing the news about the killings here, he lost control and murdered his wife in Texas," Tracy repeated, her eyes on the photograph. "I assume he's missing?"

"He is," Hannah affirmed. "And for now, at least, he's

definitely the target of the investigation. The local police are looking for him."

"But that still doesn't mean he's the cyber killer," Tracy said. "There's no posing after the fact. And the way he's positioned the hands over her chest actually suggests remorse. That isn't something we'd expect to find in a psychopath."

"But there are exceptions to every rule. Right? Even psychopaths can be wired differently. Like you always say, profiling isn't an exact science."

"True, but what you've got here still isn't enough to be positive that Draper's the cyber killer."

"Agreed." Hannah nodded. "But if someone like the cyber killer did find love, or at least what he equated with the emotion, then that could explain why he stopped attacking other women."

"It's definitely possible," Tracy admitted. "But like I said it isn't conclusive."

"Right, but there's more," Hannah said. "When I talked with the local authorities and explained our situation, they agreed to send me their files, and additionally, they convinced the army to release theirs."

"What did you find?" Harrison asked, his gut telling him she was on to something.

"A time line," Hannah said. "Draper's unit was stationed in Fort Hood at the time of the original murders. That's about forty-five miles from Austin and dead center in the middle of the kill zone."

"But what about Eileen?"

"She wasn't in the picture then. Draper was single."

"So what else do we know about him?" Drake asked.

"According to army records, he was born in Georgetown, a small town near Austin. He comes from a broken home. Dad was a no-show from the get-go. And Mom didn't last much longer. I checked local records and apparently little Jeremy had some issues. And when he killed the family dog, Mom dumped him into the system and moved on."

"So we've got one part of McDonald's triad," Tracy said, frowning as she tried to process Hannah's information.

"Bedwetting, fire-starting, and torturing small animals," Simon offered.

"Exactly."

"Anyway," Hannah continued, "Draper lived in various foster homes until he graduated high school and landed in the army."

"And by then he was probably carrying around a whole lot of anger," Harrison suggested, gut still churning. "Most of it, no doubt, directed at his mother."

"I don't suppose you have a picture of her," Tracy asked.

"As a matter of fact," Hannah said, bringing up a new photograph, her expression grim, "I do."

The woman, dressed in a business suit, was smiling, long brown hair falling over her shoulder.

"She was a realtor," Hannah added. "Young, middle-class, brunette, and single."

"A perfect match for his victimology," Drake said to no one in particular. "But why would he have waited to act out? I mean, his mother left a long time before he was stationed at Fort Hood—so what was the stressor?"

"Well, I'm no expert. But according to the army's records, Draper was written up for attacking a woman in Dallas."

"His mother," Tracy said.

"Yes. Apparently, he'd run her to ground and was trying to reestablish contact."

"Only she rejected him." Tracy shook her head. "It's textbook. And I'm guessing there was a knife involved."

"Got it in one," Hannah said. "But the wounds were only superficial, and she refused to press charges. The army disciplined him, though."

"Which would have only made him more angry. He would have felt doubly wronged." Tracy leaned forward, her eyes on Hannah. "You said there was a time line."

"Right," Hannah said, consulting her monitor. "According to army records, Draper's attack on his mother happened about six months before the first of the cyber killer's attacks. But there was nothing at the time to link them. Anyway, Draper was stationed at Fort Hood the entire time the cyber killer was active. Then—and this is the important part—his unit was shipped out to Iraq three months after the last murder."

"Giving us a reason why he stopped." Harrison blew out a breath, everything falling together. "He was out of the country."

"And most likely releasing his rage in another way entirely," Tracy agreed.

"So how long was he gone?" Avery asked.

"Almost seven years—off and on. He did four tours of duty before being discharged at the end of last year." Hannah scrolled through the document on her computer screen. "He married Eileen about three years ago. Which I'm guessing worked mainly because he didn't see her very often."

"But her death was probably inevitable," Tracy said, "considering how much she looked like Draper's mother."

"The local police answered a couple of domestic violence calls, but Eileen never pressed charges. And there was never enough to merit an arrest."

"But the urges were building again," Tracy said, "and with his discharge he'd lost the only way he had to legitimately release his rage."

"And then when news about the fake cyber killer hit the airwaves," Simon continued, "he broke."

"It could conceivably have been the stressor that pushed him over the edge," Tracy agreed. "And he killed his wife. A woman who most likely represented his memory of a mother who loved him."

"And so he lost her all over again." Drake shook his head. "This guy is one sick dude."

"No shit," Harrison said. "And when faced with this kind of loss, he looked for someone to blame."

"The man impersonating him," Avery agreed.

"And the man who was part of the original investigation," Harrison sighed. "Which brings us full circle."

"Except that now we know who he is," Hannah said, switching the photograph back to the picture of Draper. "Which means we have a better shot at finding him. We can send this picture to the press and the police. Get everyone out there looking for him."

"Agreed," Avery said. "We'll just have to be careful how we release the information. We can use the FBI front to make sure no one knows we're the ones who put this all together. Hannah, I'm assuming you didn't identify yourself as CIA when you made the call to the locals in Texas?"

"Of course not," she assured him. "They think I'm an analyst with the FBI. And if anyone calls to verify, thanks to Langley pulling some strings, Quantico will back me up."

"Good." Avery nodded. "Then we'll continue to use the FBI to disseminate information about the killer. Bottom line here, we need to do whatever it takes to find this guy before he hurts someone new." This time everyone's eyes moved to Hannah.

"Look, guys," she said, her exasperation showing, "there's no reason to believe that Draper is going to come after me. I'll admit I fit the victimology, but so do a lot of other women in this town. Besides, for all we know, this was a one-off, and he's gone back to Texas."

"I don't think he's gone anywhere," Harrison countered. "He left me Bree's necklace for a reason, and he's not about to walk away now. I can feel it in my gut. This isn't over—not by a long shot."

"So what, I'm just supposed to hide in a closet until it's finished?"

"If I had my choice." Harrison nodded. "But I know you won't agree to that. So instead you're just going to have to deal with me watching your every move."

"I can live with that," Hannah agreed, her tone flip, but her eyes sending a different message.

"*Live* being the operative word," Harrison said, sucking in a breath, realizing that push come to shove, he'd die for her—hell, more realistically, he'd kill for her.

CHAPTER 26

Harrison stood by the window looking out at the night sky, and Hannah leaned against the kitchen doorway watching him. The dining room was lit with the eerie glow of the LED lights from the computer array, the narrow swath of light from the kitchen cutting across the room like a pathway to nowhere.

He hadn't said more than a few words all evening. And he'd hardly eaten anything. She knew he was angry and hurting, but she also knew that nothing she could say could possibly help. Some pain simply went too deep. Harrison opened his palm, looking down at his sister's necklace, the gold links reflecting the light as they draped across his fingers.

Hannah's heart constricted as she watched. She'd felt anger before. Even hatred. But nothing like what she was feeling now. Total and complete impotence. There was nothing to be done. They had identified the cyber killer, but they still couldn't find him. Everyone within a two-hundred-mile radius had been alerted to his presence. But there'd been nothing. No sign of him at all.

It was like waiting for the other shoe to drop. Or maybe searching for answers in the middle of a minefield. The best they could do was to shore up their defenses and wait. So Avery had sent everyone home. And the two of them had come here, ostensibly to dig into Draper's past. But the truth was there was nothing more to learn.

The man was a born killer, and nothing could ever truly assuage the fury that burned inside him. He was like a bomb waiting to be triggered. And Walker—with the help of the Consortium—had set the charge. And now there would be hell to pay.

"Can I get you anything?" she asked, pushing away from the door frame and walking over to the window to stand beside him.

He shook his head, his eyes still on the stars outside. "It all looks so normal," he said, his voice so quiet she almost couldn't hear him. "It looked a lot like this the night my sister died. I remember standing at a window a hell of a lot like this one, watching, waiting—unable to do anything else. God, I feel so fucking helpless."

"That's what he's counting on," she said. "He wants us to fall apart. He's just trying to get in your head."

"Well, it's working." Harrison blew out a breath and then carefully laid the necklace on the table. "I feel like he's taunting me. Making me relive it all over again."

"So what can I do?" she asked, reaching out to take his hand.

"Stay safe?" He gave her the ghost of a smile. "I honestly don't know what I'd do if anything happened to you."

"Nothing's going to happen," she said, shaking her head, willing him to believe, "not as long as I'm here with you."

With a groan, he pulled her into his arms, his eyes devouring her as he bent his head to kiss her. She opened her mouth beneath his lips, offering herself to him—wanting to become a part of him. To heal him. Even as he healed her. Two wounded souls coming together—forming a whole. If someone had said the words out loud, she would have dismissed them as romantic claptrap, but standing here in the half light, with the feel of his skin against hers, it seemed that anything was possible.

His tongue thrust deep, tangling with hers, the two of them taking and giving. Thrusting and parrying. It was like a dance. The movements already defined. The partnership the key.

He removed her glasses and kissed her eyelids, and her cheeks, his tongue tracing a line of heat that sent shivers of desire racing through her. His hand dipped beneath the simple camisole she wore, his fingers closing around her breast, his thumb moving across the nipple. The friction falling somewhere between pleasure and pain, the sensation arousing a fire deep within her.

She pressed against him, and he pushed the camisole off her shoulders, tracing the line of her shoulder with his tongue, then kneeling before her to take one of her breasts in his mouth, his hands hard against her bottom as he sucked, his tongue dancing over her overly sensitized skin until her entire body was throbbing in anticipation.

And then he moved to the other breast, rolling the nipple between his teeth, biting softly, shards of electricity dancing across nerve endings she hadn't even known she possessed. With gentle hands, he pulled off her pants and panties, his big hands closing around her bottom as he sank lower, kissing her abdomen and then the soft hair that curled between her thighs.

Hannah's legs turned to Jell-O and she would have fallen except that his hands held her firmly. With a smile, he lifted her leg, pulling it over his shoulder, the action opening her to the full ministrations of his mouth. She threaded her fingers through his hair as he parted the folds that guarded all her secrets. And then with a soft sucking kiss, he pushed his tongue deep inside her as he tasted and teased.

She writhed against him, swallowing a scream as he pulled her clit into his mouth, sucking deeply, building the rhythm as he flicked his tongue against it. The pressure was almost unbearable, and yet when he pulled free, she cried out in frustration.

But instead, he lifted her into his arms, his mouth finding hers again. And she tasted herself on his lips, the essence primordial, and she drank deeply—wanting him so badly she thought she might die from it.

With shaking fingers, she pulled his shirt free, working feverishly to remove it. He released her long enough to take off the rest of his clothes, and then he pulled her back into his arms, settling them onto one of the dining room chairs, his penis hard against her as she straddled him. She opened her mouth to protest, but he covered her lips with a finger, pulling her back so that her bottom was couched in the curve of his lap, her back against his chest, his hands circling her hips as he lifted her.

Opening her legs, he thrust into her, his hands moving to her breasts, fingers circling, kneading, pressing as he began to move, and she began to ride. Up and down. Up and down. He was so deep she felt as if he'd pierced her core. All the places that she kept hidden—secret. He was part of that now. Part of her.

Deeper and deeper still, he thrust. And she closed her eyes, letting the rapture of the movement and the accompanying sensations carry her away. It was like flying. She'd never felt so free.

Beneath her, she could feel his rising tension, feel his muscles contracting with his own desire. And she concentrated on the feel of him rising and falling—thrusting and retreating—matching his rhythm, determined to give him as much as he was giving her.

And then there was nothing but the feel of their bodies moving together, the strength of him moving inside her, and the powerful sensations rocketing through her as they climbed higher and higher, everything in the world disappearing but the two of them, riding a wave of pleasure so strong and pure she wasn't entirely sure she'd survive it.

But she didn't care. There was nothing more important than this moment with this man. He was everything. He was thrusting harder and faster now, and she met his challenge with movement of her own. Squeezing and releasing, the friction beyond incredible.

And then his hand slid down between her legs, slipping inside to pleasure her as she pushed downward, taking him deeper still, his lips moving against her neck, her body tightening as if she were a finely tuned bow. And with a spasm of pure joy, she let herself go, falling over the edge, her body shuddering around his as she splintered into shivering delight.

He pulled her close as he, too, found his release, his

breathing rasping against her ear, his fingers still stroking her body, his face buried in her hair. They stayed for a moment like that, and then he gathered her into his arms, carrying her up the stairs, but instead of heading for the bedroom, he took her into the bathroom.

Setting her on the soft warmth of the carpet, he ran a bath, the sound of the water sensual and soothing. Steam filled the air, swirling around them as he pulled her to her feet, and after a long languid kiss, helped her into the water.

It lapped around her breasts, teasing her as he took the soap and gently began to lather her body, starting with her back and then moving to her breasts. First one and then the other, his fingers moving tenderly, caressing each one, the soap sliding over her nipples. And then he moved the soap lower, sliding it across her stomach and back and then between her legs, the act more intimate somehow than anything they'd done before.

She shuddered, desire rising again, and with a smile, he moved to the front of the tub and slid into the water, pulling her soap-slick body onto his lap, her legs around him as he leaned in for a kiss, his tongue tracing the line of her lips before dipping inside.

The kiss was dreamlike. The steam and the water moving around them in slow undulation, enhancing the feel of his mouth moving against hers, and his penis growing hard again between her legs.

Buoyed by the water, she pushed closer, her heat surrounding his, her hips gyrating softly with the motion of the bath water. She felt him growing even harder, his pulse pounding against hers. And she pulled his tongue into her mouth, sucking as she opened her legs, lifting her hips to slide down onto his hard length, taking him deep inside her.

She felt him shudder, his passion laid bare, and she marveled at the fact that she had the power to give him pleasure. And then with a groan, he started to move again, his mouth taking possession of hers, the power shifting again as his hands circled her hips, urging her onward, setting the rhythm for their passion.

As the steam and water caressed them, they moved together, lost in each other's arms, their passion this time going deeper—the physical joining less important than the binding of their spirits. Hannah was aware enough to know that they were crossing into uncharted territory, and that there would be no going back, but as the power of their lovemaking swept her away, she was certain that she didn't care.

Wherever they ended up—the journey was going to be worth it. Something she could never regret. Harrison had said that it was important to have faith. But maybe the simple truth was that you just had to hold on to each other and take the leap.

She closed her eyes and let sensation take over. And there was nothing but the feel of their bodies moving together—their hearts beating in tandem. The two of them becoming one. And in that moment, Hannah knew that she was falling in love.

Harrison woke to a tangle of sheets, Hannah's body pressed against his, one leg thrown possessively across his thigh. For a moment, he simply lay listening to the sound of her breathing, content to be close to her. They had made love more times than he'd have thought himself capable of. Her nearness seemed to inspire him to greater and greater heights. The chair. The bathtub. The floor and the bed. So many surfaces, so little time.

The thought sobered him. And reflexively, he pulled her closer. She murmured something, and for a moment, he feared he'd awakened her, but then with a little sigh, she burrowed her nose into his neck, and her breathing grew even again. Her absolute trust was humbling. And he prayed that he would live up to it.

Loving was a scary thing. And yet, he couldn't imagine going back. Hannah was as much a part of him as breathing. There was no life without her. And the idea both elated and frightened him. He wasn't the kind of man to enter into anything halfheartedly. But he was also astute enough to know that there would be challenges ahead.

She was a strong-willed woman. And he suspected she'd never shared her life with anyone. At least not on this level. Hannah had found safety in solitude. And yet, clearly, she'd decided to let him in. His body reacted to the thought, her trust more of an aphrodisiac than any physical attribute.

He considered waking her, but decided against it. It had been a long night and she deserved to sleep, but just as he was pulling away, her eyes flickered open, and she smiled—reaching for him, her legs opening as she pulled him on top of her. And with his heart full to bursting, he entered her, feeling her contract around him in welcome.

It was like coming home. And Harrison wondered at the miracle that had brought him to A-Tac—to Hannah. And then, she started to move as instinct and passion took over, his hands moving over her body, memorizing every curve, every muscle.

He kissed her lips, her shoulders, her breasts, and her belly. And then when he would have moved to kiss the heat she carried between her legs, she broke free, sliding down between his legs instead, her mouth closing over the throbbing head of his penis, the sensation of her hot, wet mouth almost his undoing.

Grasping the base, she began to move her hand slowly as she sucked deeply, the warm embrace sending shards of fire piercing though him. At first she moved languidly, tasting him—savoring him. And then her fingers began to move faster, pulling up and then down, her mouth taking him deeper, her tongue moving in circles as she sucked, the rhythm growing stronger until he was so hard he thought he might burst.

Then she slid upward again, her body pressed against his, and he flipped them over as she opened her legs, and in one swift move, he was inside her again. And for a moment, they were both still, reveling in the heat of their connection. And then, impatient, she began to move, a mewling sound coming from deep in her throat as he thrust deeper and deeper still.

"God, Harrison, I didn't know it could be like this," she breathed, arching her back as she struggled to take even more of him. And he was lost. Everything about her was beyond anything he'd ever dreamed.

She was fierce and strong and loyal and utterly amazing.

He drove deep and then let go. The sensation of their movement overwhelming all other senses. Need combined with desire to ratchet his excitement higher—his body feeling as if it might burst at any moment. And he found himself praying for release. Wanting it. Craving it. Knowing that only Hannah could take him there.

As if sensing his need, Hannah moved faster, rising to meet his thrusts, her hand closing around the base of his penis, the rhythm of her hand matching the rise and fall of their bodies. For a moment, he was suspended in space, and then the world split into blinding particles of light, and he had the thought that this was it—that moment when everything came together.

When everything was perfect.

And suddenly—as he drifted back to earth—he was terrified.

But then she was there, her head on his chest, her fingers linked with his, her heart beating steadily against his side. And Harrison surrendered to her strength, knowing that for the moment at least, everything was right with his world.

Hannah awoke to the smell of bacon and an empty bed. The night came back in a rush, and despite the horror hanging over them, she smiled. Last night had been wonderful. And she intended to hold on to the feeling as long as possible. After a quick shower, she pulled on a pair of jeans and a T-shirt, reaching for her glasses and then ignoring them. It wasn't as if she needed them to see.

And maybe it was time to stop hiding.

Still smiling, she took the stairs two at a time, slowing only as she approached the kitchen, feeling a lot like a schoolgirl, her nerves fluttering in her stomach.

"Good morning," Harrison called, as he expertly flipped a pancake in the frying pan.

"I thought you said you ran to take-out menus," she said, shaking her head as he poured more batter into the pan.

"I'm not big on grocery shopping," he shrugged. "But as long as there's food in the larder, I'm actually a pretty good cook. A man's got to eat, after all."

"Apparently a lot." She laughed, her gaze moving to the enormous spread of food already on the breakfast bar. Scrambled eggs, bacon, fresh-squeezed orange juice, and a tower of pancakes. "Are we expecting company?"

He scooped the pancake from the pan, adding it to the stack. "What can I say? I'm a growing boy. And after last night, I've worked up quite an appetite. And I figured you might be hungry, too."

"I could eat." She slipped onto a barstool, picking up a piece of bacon. "But there's enough food here to last a couple of days at least."

"Have you seen me at the table?" he asked, the question rhetorical. It was true; Harrison could put away more food than anyone she'd ever known. It was a wonder he didn't weigh four hundred pounds. But after last night's intimacy, she was more than aware that wasn't the case.

Her body tightened at the memory, and she smiled.

"Thinking of me?" he asked, turning off the burner and dropping a kiss on the top of her head as he came to sit beside her.

"Yes, as a matter of fact, I was," she said, poking him in the ribs as she bit into the crispy bacon. "I was thinking that, based on what you eat, you should be a fat boy."

"But I'm not." He reached over to wipe a smear of bacon grease from the corner of her lips, his touch sending electricity sparking through her.

"I know." Her breathing was coming in little gasps now, and as he bent to kiss her, she had the thought that nothing in her life was ever going to be the same. Which, if it meant waking up to this every morning, was fine by her.

The kiss heated up, but the smell of pancakes was

tantalizing, and so with a satisfied sigh, she pulled away. "Nourishment first?"

He laughed, and after another quick kiss, reached for the pancakes. "A girl after my own heart."

"So how long have you been up?" she asked, sipping her orange juice, her breathing still not back to normal. The man had a definite effect on her.

"A while," he said, sobering. "I wanted to study the old case files for the cyber killer. I guess I was hoping that I'd find something that might lead us to finding Draper now."

"And did you have any luck?"

"No. He could be anywhere."

"So we just have to redouble our efforts," she said. "Maybe if I look at the files, I'll see something you didn't. Fresh eyes and all that."

"It's worth a try," he agreed, helping himself to more pancakes.

"These are really great," she said. "They don't even need syrup."

"Which is good, because I can think of all kinds of things to do with the leftover syrup." He waggled his eyebrows, and she actually blushed, her stomach back to quivering. The man made her crazy.

"Maybe for the moment we should stick to the pancakes?"

"All right—but only because I'm still hungry." He grinned.

"So where'd you learn to make them?"

"It's my mom's recipe," he said with a smile. "She always fixed them for us on Sundays."

"You've never mentioned your parents."

"It was just my mom. My dad passed away when we

were just kids. But she was great. Died a few years ago. Cancer."

"I'm sorry," she said, wishing she'd kept her mouth shut.

"Don't be. It was for the best. She was really sick. And besides, she was never the same after Bree was killed."

"All the more reason for us to find the bastard and make him pay." She pushed away her plate, draining the last of her orange juice. "I think we need to tackle the files first."

"Agreed," he said, looking resigned.

They walked into the dining room, Hannah heading over to the file folders spread across the table. But as she reached out to pick one up, the morning exploded, the walls literally shaking as the windows across the front of the house shattered. Harrison dove for her, pushing her to the floor, his body protecting hers as glass flew like shrapnel.

For a moment, they held position, her mind spinning as she tried to decipher what had happened. Then he rolled away, the roar subsiding as a wave of heat washed through the now open windows. "You okay?" he asked, his eyes searching for signs of injury.

"I think so." She nodded.

"You're sure?"

"Yes," she said, testing various limbs to be sure. "I'm fine. What the hell happened?"

"I don't know. An explosion of some kind." He pushed to his feet, grabbing his gun from the table, moving cautiously toward one of the windows.

She followed behind him, wishing she had her weapon, but not willing to leave him alone until they were sure what was happening. "Can you see anything?"

"Yeah," he said, moving aside so that she could see, too. "It's my car. Somebody blew up my fucking car." The burning remains of Harrison's Jeep sat on the street in front of the house, debris still raining down, a plume of black smoke belching up into the sky. "Stay here. I'm going to check it out." He started for the door, but she reached out to stop him.

"I'm coming, too," she insisted, still holding his arm. "I'm not letting you go out there on your own. We're in this together, remember?"

"I do. I swear. But if anything happened to you, I'd..." he trailed off, his eyes saying it all. "Look, I'll be fine. You can watch me from here. And as soon as I'm sure it's safe, I'll signal you. Okay?"

She nodded, knowing there was wisdom in his words. Besides, she could see Avery emerging from his house across the street. Drake right behind him. At least Harrison would have reinforcements. She watched as he moved out into the yard, still on alert, gun at the ready, but except for having to dodge charred pieces of the Jeep in the grass, there seemed to be no further threat.

Still, Hannah knew she'd feel better if she had her gun, so after watching a couple more minutes, she turned and walked into the kitchen where she'd left it last night in the lock box on the counter.

Harrison's empty pans sat on the stove, the breakfast bar still littered with dishes. Everything looked absurdly normal, considering the blast that had just occurred in her front yard. She ought to be freaked, but these days nothing was normal. Which was both good and bad. She crossed the floor, heading for the lock box, her mind drifting to Harrison and last night.

She knew that she should stay focused, but it was hard. Her body ached in the delicious way of a woman who'd been thoroughly and completely loved. She paused at the word. Neither of them had mentioned it. But it had stretched between them—unspoken. Or at least she'd wanted it to be so.

She shook her head, pulling her focus back to the bomb in the front yard. Better to stay in the present. The future would take care of itself. Walking around the counter, she reached for the box, but paused when she realized the back door was open. Her nerves went into overdrive, and she started to spin around, but before she could take a step, someone grabbed her from behind, a hard arm encircling her throat.

She shoved her elbows backward, kicking as she tried to scream, but the arm pressed harder, cutting off her voice. Panic warred with training, the latter winning as she twisted, trying to break the hold. Harrison and Avery were just outside; surely they'd hear her if she could just manage to make some noise.

She kicked out again, this time connecting with a barstool, sending it crashing to the floor. Her assailant swore softly and slammed his fist into the side of her head. The world went fuzzy, pain ripping through her brain. But she fought through it, determined not to give in.

Letting her body go slack, she pretended to have passed out, praying that he'd loosen his hold. For a moment, she thought it was working, his grip on her throat lessening. She opened her mouth to scream, striking out, trying to break free, but before she could make a sound, he'd regained his hold.

Frustrated, she kicked backward, hoping to throw

them off balance, but he held her steady, stabbing something into her arm, a line of heat working its way along her nerve endings. The son of a bitch had drugged her.

It felt as if her nerves were shutting down one by one, first her arms, and then her legs. Nothing seemed to be working right. Even her brain felt sluggish and heavy.

Across the kitchen, she could see Asha pressed against the wall, spitting with fury. And summoning all of her strength, she reached up and raked her nails against her assailant's face with the intention of drawing blood. It had worked for Asha, maybe it would work for her.

Cursing again, he pulled her toward the back door, and as he pulled her through, Hannah managed to slam her hand against the wall, satisfied to see a print. He jerked her onto the back porch, and she realized she could no longer feel her arms and legs at all. He swung her over his shoulder, and she struggled to hang on to consciousness, but the drug was winning the war.

And with a sigh she slipped into blackness, her last conscious thought that she should have told Harrison she loved him.

CHAPTER 27

"This is all my fault," Harrison said, fighting both fear and panic as he paced in front of the dining room table. Members of Tracy's team carefully combed over every inch of the kitchen, trying to find something that might tell them what had happened to Hannah. From his vantage point, he could see the remnants of their breakfast on the counter, reminding him again of how completely he had let Hannah down. "I shouldn't have left her on her own."

"You did exactly what any of us would have done," Avery responded, as he closed his phone. "There's no point in blaming yourself."

"Yeah, well that's not going to happen."

"Understood," his boss said, "but we haven't got time for you to melt down. I know how much you care about Hannah. We all do. But the only way we're going to find her and beat Draper at his own game is to focus. And you can't do that if you're busy blaming yourself."

"I know." He blew out a breath, pulling himself together. For Hannah. "So who was that on the phone?"

"Tyler. She and Nash are taking the first flight in from Montreal. If anyone can find something amidst the wreckage out there, it's her. And besides, they want to be here for you. And for Hannah. Annie's going to hold the fort in Montreal."

Harrison nodded, thinking how much all of these people had come to mean to him in such a short time. And it was because of him that this maniac had landed in their midst.

"Draper wouldn't be here if it weren't for the Consortium," Avery said, correctly reading his mind. "They're the ones who stirred the pot. Not you. And believe me, they're going to get theirs. But obviously our first priority is to get Hannah back alive."

The last word hovered in the room and Harrison felt as if he might explode. Emotions rocketed through him. Guilt. Anger. Fear. All of them threatening to eat him alive.

"So what about the handprint?" he asked. "Is it Hannah's?"

"The print is hers," Tracy said, walking into the room. "But not the blood."

"That was fast." Avery turned to face her, leaning back against the table, his eyebrows raised in surprise.

"I figured it was important—so I handled it myself. It was easy to rule out Hannah. You have her DNA on file here. And thanks to the U.S. Army, I've got a record of Draper's DNA as well. So I didn't have to run the complete panel, just a microscopic comparison. And the blood on the wall appears to be Draper's. I've sent it off for full DNA analysis."

"So the son of a bitch does have her," Drake said, walking into the room, glass crunching under his feet. "Simon's outside now with the local fire marshal. He doesn't think it was a bomb. All the signs seem to point to a simple accelerant. Probably paint thinner or some other solvent. Enough to start a fire and let the gasoline in the car do the rest. Tyler's team can run the tests when they get here. But the bottom line is that the explosion wasn't meant to do anything but create a hell of spectacle."

"And pull our attention away from Hannah," Avery agreed.

"Well, it worked." Harrison ran a hand through his hair, fighting to keep the frustration from his voice, but it was no use.

"What I don't understand," Tracy said, her forehead creasing, "is how he could have known you wouldn't bring Hannah outside with you."

"It was a calculated risk," Avery acknowledged. "But he's bound to know that we'd assume she was a target, and as such, take every precaution to protect her. Which in this case would mean keeping her away from what we perceived as a direct threat."

"The explosion," Tracy nodded.

"Exactly."

"So how the hell did he get into the house?" Drake asked.

"Through the back door," Tracy said. "There's no sign of forced entry, so either it was open or he picked the lock. We think he took her out through the back gate. There's access behind the fence for the grounds crew." One of the perks of Professor's Cove was having the college's landscape crew take care of their yards as well.

"Looks like she didn't go easily," Drake observed, standing in the kitchen door taking in the fallen barstool and bloody handprint.

"Hannah's a fighter," Harrison said between clenched teeth.

"You don't have to tell me," Drake turned, his cool gaze assessing. "I've worked with her a hell of a lot longer than you."

"Hey," Avery said, "there's nothing to be gained by fighting amongst ourselves. And trust me, Harrison doesn't need any help beating himself up over this."

"I'm sorry." Drake lifted a hand in apology. "This is just hard."

Harrison shook his head, feeling as if the world had somehow gone off kilter and he was reliving the worst days of his life. The night Bree had been taken, he'd been supposed to telephone—the weekly chat, she'd called it. But a case he'd been working detained him. And he hadn't even thought about it until nearly midnight. And by that point, it had been too late.

"I've got people checking the security cameras now," Avery said. "Although there's not a camera around back, and the one on the street has limited angles. But maybe we'll find something."

"And if he came in by vehicle," Harrison said, "he had to pass through one of the checkpoints, right?"

"Yeah," Avery agreed. "I've got them looking at that, too. And after Tina's abduction, I closed the dorms, so there's only essential personnel left on campus and no students."

"But?" Harrison prompted, hearing something else in the big man's answer.

"But as we know from previous experience, there's no such thing as airtight security. And on top of that, Draper had special forces training."

"Meaning he's good at subterfuge," Drake said.

"Right, and he's already proved he's determined."

"So she could be anywhere." Harrison blew out a breath, still fighting for control.

"What about Hannah's computer?" Tracy asked. "Maybe there's something there. If he follows pattern, he should have sent her an email. Maybe you can pull something from that."

"All right," Harrison said, already moving to sit in front of her laptop—typing in her password, grateful that he'd had the foresight to ask for it beforehand. He'd actually been honored when she'd surrendered it without any hesitation. At the time, he'd only thought to have it in case she was out of pocket and he needed to access her databases. But now…

The computer's operating system came to life, displaying her program files. And he scrolled down to the email program, clicking twice to open it. The list of emails were mostly routine. Answers from queries to Langley and Quantico, along with a couple from Tyler and one from Annie, which he didn't open, figuring she wouldn't want him perusing her private emails.

He scrolled further down, the messages in descending order, until he reached the newest ones. There were three that had arrived this morning. The first was from Annie. It simply read "You deserve to be happy. Go for it," and his heart twisted, no doubt at all as to what it was Hannah had been discussing with her friend.

The second message was from someone at Fort Hood

sending additional information on Draper. He sent it to the printer to read later.

He moved to the last one, the skin on the back of his neck crawling as he saw the title. "Gotcha." Drake swore as he read over Harrison's shoulder. And Avery and Tracy moved closer as he clicked the file to open it.

The picture was of Tina. Tied up and stuffed in the closet.

Hannah woke up with a start, something dripping on her head. She tried to wipe it away, but she couldn't move her hands. Memory came rushing back. The explosion, the man in her house. Draper. She had no recollection of his taking her from her kitchen to wherever the hell she was. Only of him jamming something in her arm, the drug ultimately knocking her out.

She tried again to move her arms, peering through the semidarkness to try to assess her situation. Best she could tell, she was lying on a single bed, the mattress sour smelling. Her arms were tied to each side of the headboard, a metal affair that seemed strangely familiar.

Her feet were tied together with some kind of narrow rope, then secured to something either at the end of the bed or on the floor. From this angle, it was impossible to see. A single bulb burned from a socket hanging from a wire on the ceiling. It was rusted and damn near burned out but it gave off enough light for her to see that there was a door. A huge metal affair. The walls were brick and old, bits of the masonry visible on the little bit of flooring she could see to her right. The bed was wedged into a corner, the length of it running along the back wall opposite the door.

She shivered as another droplet fell from the ceiling onto her neck. Please, God, let it be water. She tried to shift, the mattress ticking rough against her skin—the thought grinding home as she glanced down and realized she was naked.

A scream bubbled up inside her, memories from a lifetime ago surfacing to mingle with this new fear. But Hannah had survived then, and she'd survive now. She clamped down on the terror with the single-minded determination that had been the cornerstone not only of her career, but of her life.

This, too, would pass.

She closed her eyes and counted to ten, concentrating on her breathing. Then opened them again, this time examining the room with a more professional eye. It was impossible to see much detail, the light was simply too dim. But all four walls were brick, the floor made of cement, and the ceiling plaster of some kind.

None of it was new, and none of it had been maintained. Except the door, which seemed newer. And definitely impenetrable. Even if she could free herself, she doubted she'd be able to break through the door. At least not without some kind of help.

But high up on the wall to the right, there was a tiny window, too small to crawl through—and at the moment, not admitting any light—which made her wonder how long she'd been unconscious. Still, it was an opening. Although it might as well have been in Nigeria for all the chance she had of reaching it.

In the far corner to the left of the door, there was a stack of boxes. Several with writing. But she was too far away and the room was too dark for her to be able to read them. Something yellow stuck out of the top of one of them. But beyond the color, it was impossible to tell anything else about it.

Another drop fell, hitting her just above the eye, and she rolled her head trying to avoid a second one, the movement making her wince, sharp pain shooting through her head. Draper had hit her. Unable to check the wound, she rolled as far as her restraints would allow, checking the mattress for blood. A small spot close to where her left ear would have been indicated that she'd been bleeding, but the stain was almost dry—telling her that the cut wasn't serious and that she'd been here awhile. Long enough at least for her wound to clot and the stain to begin to dry.

An hour—maybe two. Jasmine had been killed in the first eight hours. The number rang through her head, threatening to swamp her grim determination, but she clamped down on it, concentrating instead on the restraints holding her arms. Maybe if she were lucky, she could find a way to pull herself free.

She twisted her wrists experimentally, frustrated to find that neither of the ropes binding her had much give. Clearly, Draper was good with knots. Still, if she closed her fingers tightly, it was possible to slide her left hand down a little bit, the nylon cording cutting into her skin as she pulled harder.

She managed about another inch or so, but when the rope reached the broadest point in her folded hand, it refused to move any farther, instead slicing into her hand, resulting in a stream of blood dripping down her arm. She slid her hand back up, waiting to make sure she hadn't cut into a major vessel. But the stream turned to a trickle, and in short order, stopped.

As much as she wanted to try again, she didn't dare push it any harder. While she didn't give a damn about her hand if it bought her freedom, she couldn't risk incapacitating herself. At least not until she'd examined her other options first. She tried lifting her feet, but there was no give there at all, and she only managed to get them an inch or so off the mattress.

But when she tried lifting her body, she was surprised to see that the rope on the right side of the headboard slid upward with her motion. Craning her neck, she realized that the headboard was solid metal with two large posts on each side. The cord was attached to the posts.

On the right, he'd also run a second line to the bottom of the headboard. But on the left, that line had come loose. Either from her thrashing around or because he'd never tied it in the first place. Never one to look a gift horse in the mouth, Hannah started to rock the small bed frame, using the momentum of her body to tip the entire thing as far to the left as she could manage. Each time the bed moved, her arm went slack, and she was able to slide the rope a tiny bit farther toward the end of the post and freedom.

She jerked harder, rolling to the left, the tension stretching her right arm, pain shooting from shoulder to fingertips. But like her hand, her shoulder was dispensable. And there was little threat of permanent injury. Worst case, if she pulled it out of the socket, she could probably jam in back into place herself. So with clenched teeth, she summoned all of her strength and began rocking harder, the bed frame actually pulling away from the floor on the right side.

The pain excruciating now, she sucked in a breath,

eyeing the rope. Almost there. Once more, and she ought to be able to obtain enough force to pull it free.

One. Two. Three.

She rocked back and forth several times to start the momentum and then jerked her entire body to the left, rolling into it, the bed frame coming with her. Like jumping rope, she had to move at the exact right time, with only seconds before gravity pulled the bed back into place again, so as the bed teetered on two legs, she ignored the pain and flung her arm upward, flicking her wrist, freeing her left hand.

It seemed to take forever to release her other hand, the rope tied so tightly that she broke her nails to the quick fighting to get it off. But finally, bruised and bloodied, she had both hands free, and, in short order, had loosened the rope around her feet.

At first she was afraid to move, certain that he was watching, but gradually she gained confidence and pushed to her feet, the room swaying around her, her stomach threatening revolt. But after a moment, and a hell of a lot of determination, everything stabilized, and she climbed up on the bed, reaching up for the little window. It was too high.

For a moment, defeat rushed through her, then she remembered the only one she could truly count on was herself. So she managed to climb onto the headboard, propping one foot on the adjacent wall to keep balance. Outside the window there was nothing but earth. It looked like some kind of museum exhibit. "See the way the ants live."

She dropped back to the mattress and then stepped off the bed, moving like a cat, keeping low, back arched as she moved forward. But still nothing moved, and slowly she straightened, heading to the door. Not surprisingly, it was locked from the outside. And as it was made of metal, there was nothing she could do to break it down. So she walked over to the boxes, thinking that maybe she'd find something there that could help her jimmy the hinges.

Most of the boxes were, unfortunately, empty, or their contents had long ago turned to rotting piles of mildew. There were two barrels, the sort often used as trash cans, and an old oar, stained at the bottom with something she wasn't certain she wanted to identify. Behind the rotting boxes and the barrels, there were remnants of an old yellow sign.

But the words had long faded, the letters G, H, and S the only thing remaining legible.

With a sigh, she reached into the muck in one of the boxes, praying for a screwdriver, but the only thing she found was a paint-stained stake of some kind, the sharp end blunted with age. Still, the wood was solid, and it was better than nothing. Using the handle of the oar as a mallet, she hit it against the stake, which she held beneath the bottom hinge.

After working for a good long while, she stopped, exhaustion threatening, to examine her progress. The hinge pin had only moved a fraction of an inch. Hannah's heart sank. But she tried again, knowing that doing something was better than letting her mind get the better of her.

When he came back, and she knew that he would, she'd be behind the door, which should give her a chance to hit him with the oar. So one way or another, she'd make it outside. Altogether, it seemed as good a plan as any, so she returned to work on the hinge. Avoiding the little voice in her head constantly reminding her that there were two more hinges after this one.

She'd managed to knock the first pin out almost three-quarters of the way when she heard something moving outside the doorway. Dropping the stake, she sprang to her feet and grabbed the oar. Taking a deep breath, she waited, arms shaking as the lock rattled and the door began to open. Adrenaline flowing, she sprang out, swinging the oar with all her might.

It connected with a thwack, but Draper managed to turn away in time, avoiding the brunt of the blow, one hand snagging the end of the oar as she tried to swing it again. In any other situation, it would have been comical. Draper was a huge man, and Hannah wasn't very hefty. He literally lifted her up along with the oar, his arm closing like a vise around her waist.

He threw her across the room, her head slamming into the concrete floor. She fought to clear her head, but before she could do so, he was on her, picking her up like a sack of potatoes, slapping her hard enough to send her mind scrambling again.

With swift moves, he retied her hands and then her feet, his glowering face filling her foggy vision. "Try that again, and I'll kill you," he said, his breath hot against her skin, his eyes burning into hers.

"You're going kill me anyway," she said, bucking up to slam a knee into his hip.

He hit her again, this time hard enough that her teeth cut into her upper lip, but she thrashed out again, knowing that she had to try.

Once again, he slammed his fist against the side of her head, white-hot pain robbing her of clear thought. The edges of her vision turned black, consciousness fading, but for a moment she could see Draper at the end of the bed. He was setting up a tripod next to a small table with a laptop attached to a camera, the bed broadcast front and center on the screen.

Bile filled her throat, as she realized with horror that like Walker, Draper intended to film his debauchery, which meant that Harrison would be forced to watch her die.

CHAPTER 28

I feel like I'm on a fucking first-name basis with Draper," Harrison said to Tracy as he paced in front of his computer. "But there's nothing here to tell us where he might have taken Hannah. We know he has a propensity for cellars. But that's after the fact. And the bedrooms in the houses he chose seem to have nothing in common. And the same goes for the houses themselves."

"And in all honesty," Tracy added, her face reflecting Harrison's fear and frustration, "we don't even know if he'll stick to that MO. He left his wife in the bedroom where he killed her. And Walker is hardly the right victimology and his death raised the degree of violence more than a couple of notches."

"So we're never going to find her."

"Of course we are." Nash Brennon strode into the room, his presence reassuring in a way Harrison hadn't expected. "We've just got to keep plugging away at what we know."

"He's right," Tyler Hanson said as she dropped a duffle by the door, "it's just a matter of putting ourselves into his head. Thinking the way he'd think."

Harrison introduced them both to Tracy. And the four of them took seats at the table he'd set up to examine all the documentation they had on Draper.

"I stopped by the explosion site on the way in," Tyler said. "And from what I can tell, the fire marshal was dead on. The point of origin seems to have been an old paint can stuffed with rags and filled with paint thinner. The whole thing was placed beneath the gas tank. It wouldn't have taken more than a couple of minutes from ignition to explosion. It's primitive, but it worked."

"But that means Draper was there to set it off, right?"

"Possibly," she shrugged. "But Avery said that he doesn't show up in the footage from the house, right?"

"Yeah," Harrison confirmed with a frown. "We've just been going over the report from security, and there was no sign of him. The angle isn't perfect, but they would have at least been able to recognize movement."

"Well, I found a bit of filament wire," Tyler said, pulling a Ziploc from her pocket and tossing it on the table. "I'll need to do some further testing, but it's possible he wired it so that he could spark the fire while out of range of the cameras."

"Okay, but he still would have had to put it there." Tracy shook her head. "And no one saw him."

"How far back on the tapes did the security team go?" Nash asked.

"It's on a continuous loop," Harrison said. "It resets every two hours or so. But they looked at the whole thing. And, at least according to the report, there wasn't anything to see."

"Except that, based on what the fire marshal said, they probably didn't even consider remote detonation. Which means they'd have only concentrated on the fifteen minutes or so leading up to the explosion. Which is probably exactly what Draper wanted."

"So we need to go over the footage again," Harrison said, already bringing up the proper recording. "This time focusing on the earlier parts."

The video feed appeared on a wall-mounted monitor behind the table. "Okay, so it was already dark when we got there." The footage showed the Jeep pulling up to the curb. Then Hannah got out, laughing at something Harrison said. His stomach tightened as he realized he might never see her laughing again.

"We're going to find her," Tyler said, her hand covering Harrison's, her word's echoing Nash's.

"Okay," Harrison said, pushing through the pain, "once we were inside we didn't come back out again. We worked for a while and then went to bed."

The video played on, the street quiet and heavily shadowed. They watched in silence, Harrison occasionally moving it forward at a faster speed. The night grew darker as some of the brighter stars set, and Harrison squinted to try to discern movement against the grainy black-and-white photography of the security footage.

"Wait a minute," Nash said. "Run it back. About two minutes."

Harrison hit rewind and then play, and they all leaned forward in anticipation, staring at the shadowy shape of the Jeep.

"There." Nash pointed to the screen, and Harrison froze the image. "By the bushes. See?"

Sure enough, there was a darker shadow. Taller than the surrounding shrubs by a foot or so. Harrison hit play again, and the shadow detached itself from the bushes.

"That's got to be Draper," Tracy said. "Is there any way to make it clearer?"

"I can try." Harrison nodded, centering on the shadow and hitting keys to try to pull the image into sharper focus.

The computer whirred to life, and the image enlarged, the shadow clearly becoming the figure of a man. He moved forward, then bent and placed something under the back of the Jeep, straightened, and after a quick look at the houses across the way, disappeared into the bushes again.

"Go back to where he looks up," Tyler said. "The light hits his face for like a second. See if you can freeze it and enlarge."

Harrison moved to the proper time setting and then ran the footage from there, freezing the frame just as the man looked out toward the street in front of him. The light hit his face, and as Harrison enlarged it, the face took on the shape and features they knew to be Jeremy Draper.

"Looks like we've got visual confirmation that he was behind the explosion," Tracy said, "which, tied with the microscopic evidence we have for the blood from the back kitchen wall, means we've got him dead to rights, if we can just find him."

"So what about the rest of the security cameras? Is

there anything in the report to give us an idea how he got on campus in the first place?" Nash asked, leaning back in his chair with a frown.

Harrison flipped through the pages of the report. "There was nothing on the tapes that suggested an unauthorized person trying to get in. In fact, they were able to visually verify everyone in the footage."

"Wait a minute," Tyler said, still staring at the enhanced image of Draper by the Jeep. "What's he wearing?"

"A jumpsuit?" Tracy shook her head, clearly not following Tyler's train of thought.

But Harrison followed it instantly. "A Sunderland jumpsuit." He typed in another command, zooming in on the breast pocket. At first the image was blurry, but with a little adjustment, Harrison cleared the focus and the Sunderland crest filled the screen. "He's been masquerading as one of us."

"That still doesn't explain how he got through the checkpoints," Nash said.

"He probably didn't," Tyler shrugged. "There are all kinds of ways to access campus on foot. And if you're paying attention, it isn't even that hard to avoid the cameras. But once on campus, especially with the lockdown, it would be harder to avoid detection."

"Unless he's hiding in plain sight," Nash said. "No one would think to question a maintenance man."

"So then he'd have used the same way to get her out?" Tracy queried. "Surely that would raise more suspicion. I mean people might overlook a guy in Sunderland garb, but if he's hauling a woman with him, I'd think that'd raise questions. I mean after all, it was broad daylight when this happened."

"So maybe he never left the campus," Avery said, striding into the room. "Good to see you guys made it." He nodded at Tyler and Nash. "I've just been having an interesting conversation with one of the cafeteria ladies. She'd forgotten her purse in the haste to evacuate yesterday. So she came back for it this morning, and on her way out of the building, she saw a man with a wheelbarrow walking away from the quad.

"It registered because she thought that the sack in the wheelbarrow was moving. She thought it odd, but wrote it off to her imagination, because when she shifted for a better view, the sack was perfectly still, and the guy was clearly staff. She didn't think anything else of it until she saw on the news that Hannah was missing. So she called the security office, and they sent her to me."

"So you're thinking he's holding her someplace on campus?"

"What better place than a warren of deserted buildings?" Avery posed. "And right under our noses to boot."

"So how do we go about searching?" Tracy asked. "If we aren't careful, he'll know we're on to him and kill her before we get the chance to rescue her."

"Well, I figure we have two things in our favor," Avery said. "First, he likes to take his time with his victims. If I remember correctly, you said the original murders took place a full twenty-four hours after the women were abducted. He's bound to know there's a ticking clock, but even if his MO is evolving, he's still going to need time to work up to fulfillment of the fantasy."

“You do realize,” Harrison said, his fingers tightening on the edge of the table, “that the fantasy you’re talking about involves torturing Hannah.”

“I do,” Avery acknowledged. “And I also realize that we can’t separate our personal feelings for her from the situation we’re dealing with. But we have to try. It’s her only chance.”

Harrison nodded, knowing that Avery was right. But it was so goddamned hard.

“You said there were two things,” Tracy prompted, offering Harrison a moment to pull himself together.

“Yes,” Avery said. “The second is that if this guy is truly interested in punishing Harrison, he isn’t going to play this out in a vacuum. He’s going to want to share the play-by-play.”

Hannah came to slowly, the plaster ceiling above her coming into focus only with great effort. She could feel blood dripping into her eye and down the line of her nose. But with her hands bound, there was nothing she could do about it. As the world stabilized, she took the chance and looked toward the end of the bed.

Draper was still there, adjusting the lens of the camera he’d set up on the tripod. His attention for the moment was centered on the photographic equipment, so Hannah took the opportunity to check her bonds. This time there was no give. He’d even tightened the rope holding her feet so that she could no longer raise her body.

Obviously, the man was quick on the uptake. She watched him through half-open eyes, looking for something—anything—she could turn to her favor. He was tall, and as she’d already witnessed, incredibly strong. His hair was cut short, military fashion, and he had a tattoo on his arm. A snake curling through some kind of shield, two M60 machine guns angled on either side.

This guy wasn't going to be easy to outwit, but she was determined to rise to the challenge. And his need to screw with Harrison might just buy her the time she needed to figure out where she was and, hopefully, convey that fact to Harrison. But to do that she had to survive whatever hellish things Draper had in store for her.

There was no way he was going to provide Harrison with video images unless there was something to show him. On the surface, the idea scared the shit out of her. But deep inside, she knew that, if necessary, she could survive almost anything. She'd done it before. And somehow she'd find the strength to do it now.

According to Madison and Tracy, this guy only got off when his victims showed their terror. And that was something Hannah had learned to compartmentalize a long, long time ago. It was going to take a lot for him to break her. And with any luck, Harrison would find her before that happened.

Draper finished futzing with the camera and walked over to the bed. "Good," he said, smiling as he bent over her. "I'd hate for you to miss anything."

She lifted her gaze to his and spat, hitting him on the chin, thankful that she'd had a foster brother who'd thought it a useful skill.

He hit her, backhanding her this time. But she took satisfaction in the fact that she could rile him. He stared down at her a moment, his eyes reflecting anger, not excitement, and despite the pain, she took joy in the fact that she'd managed to score a point. He moved back to the camera, adjusting something and then turning it on.

With a smirk, he picked up a hunting knife, the kind with a serrated edge. And as he walked back over to her, careful to leave the line of sight to the camera unobstructed, she had to fight against rising panic. She wouldn't give in. She couldn't.

Steeling herself, she watched as he lifted the knife and, with a self-satisfied smile, made an incision in the lower quadrant of her abdomen. The pain was instant and so intense it robbed her of breath. But she swallowed her scream—staring up at him defiantly.

But his smile only widened as he lifted the knife again, and this time she turned away, staring at the far wall, concentrating on the yellow sign and the letters GHS visible now in the light from the camera.

The cut this time was shallower than before, but the pain was just as intense. She sucked in a breath, still staring at the sign. G_ _H_ S, her mind, desperate for anything to take her away from the pain, suddenly recognizing the spacing and making sense of the letters. Good Things Are Happening At Sunderland. GTAHAS. It was an annual party at Sunderland, dating back to the founding days.

The barrel and the oar were for making hurricane punch.

Her heart started pounding as Draper ran the knife edge along the new incision, but she forced herself to ignore him. To concentrate on the sign.

She was somewhere on campus.

Another image filled her mind. The metal bed—from a dorm. She felt a flood of triumph. But almost as quickly she remembered the earth-filled window. She wasn't *in* a dorm. She was underneath it.

The color yellow danced before her eyes like a beacon. Her mind scrambled to make sense of the message, but her head was growing cloudy again, so she closed her eyes and let the pain carry her away.

CHAPTER 29

I'm not sure I can watch this anymore," Harrison said, gut churning and heart twisting as he watched Draper cutting into the woman he loved. "Goddamn it." He pushed away from the table in the computer room, shaking off both Tracy and Tyler, who'd been hovering since they'd discovered the mpeg on his computer.

The footage was amateurish and, thankfully, grainy, but he could still see Hannah and feel her pain as that bastard carved into her with a relish that physically made him sick. "Have we heard anything more from the rest of the team?" Harrison asked, forcing himself to concentrate.

"Not in the last two minutes." Tyler shook her head. "No." She was poring over blueprints of the college, which had always seemed small to Harrison, but now that they had to search every nook and cranny, seemed unbearably large.

"They've finished with the buildings by the quad,"

Tracy said. "So at least they're making progress. They just have to go carefully. You know that."

"I should be out there." He walked over to the table, looking up at the screen, the image of Hannah burned into his retina. "I should be looking for her."

"You need to be here, Harrison. If you can figure out where this came from, or if we can find something in the room that could identify where she is..." Tyler broke off.

"I know." He sighed, sitting back down in front of the computer. "But he's rigged the transmission so that it's an endless loop, it bounces from server to server and then lands smack dab here at my IP address again. If it were live, maybe I could tweak the feed, but this is like a static print. It's already past tense. So there's nothing more I can do."

"So what about the room?" Tracy asked. "Surely you guys can recognize something."

"I wish I could," Tyler said, "but there's nothing to see but a brick wall and a bed."

And Hannah, Harrison finished silently.

"They could be anywhere on campus. All the buildings are brick. We're searching blind, which means we're totally dependent on luck." Tyler sat back, exchanging a glance with Tracy, their faces grim.

"What?" Harrison asked, trying to interpret the look. "You think it's hopeless? That we're already too late?" He looked down at his watch. It had been almost ten hours. "We've still got time. He likes to toy with his victims. Hell, he likes to toy with me. We've got time."

"I'm sure you're right," Tyler said, her voice artificially cheery as she picked up the stills they'd printed from the video.

"What aren't you telling me?" he asked, panic rising as he turned to Tracy.

She hesitated, her dark eyes full of regret. "The first wound he inflicted. It was deep. Really deep. And in her abdomen."

The reality of her words hit hard, but Harrison managed to form the sentence. "She's bleeding out."

Tracy nodded.

"How much time?"

"I don't know. It varies depending on the person. The relative health, size, weight. And there's no way for me to judge the severity of the internal injury."

"How long," he pressed.

"Somewhere between three to five hours, if I had to call it," she said on a sigh. "Maybe a little more if the injury is primarily venous as opposed to arterial."

Harrison clenched his fists, fighting a wave of hopelessness. Hannah was a fighter. And this was A-Tac, for God's sake. They'd find her in time. They had to.

Avery walked into the room, shaking his head at Harrison's unspoken question. "They haven't found anything. There are just so many different places she could be."

Harrison nodded, and turned back to the computer.

"Has he sent anything new?" Avery asked, coming to sit at the table.

"Not yet," Tracy answered. "Although I'm surprised. He needs for Harrison to see this. It's become part of the fantasy. In his mind, he's exacting revenge for his wife."

"But he killed her, not me," Harrison said, his head spinning.

"In his mind, somehow, he equates his break with you."

"I can't believe any of this is happening," he said,

burying his face in his hands. "If she dies—it's my fault." He knew that self-pity wasn't going to do anyone any good, but he felt so damn helpless.

In front of him the computer chimed, a signal for incoming email. Harrison lifted his head, his eyes already scanning for the new missive. There was no title, just an attachment. With shaking hands, he activated the icon.

The screen above them sprang to life. Hannah was still tied to the bed, but she was covered with blood—her blood. Draper was tracing patterns in it with his knife, the angle such that Harrison couldn't tell if he was actually cutting her, but the image still sending shudders of revulsion and fury washing through him.

His fingers raced over the keyboard as he tried to trace the source of the video. At first the results were similar to the first time. His search bouncing from proxy server to proxy server, but then he noticed something new. A timestamp.

"Guys," he said, his gaze still on the trace, "this feed is live." His eyes jerked back to the screen, his heart threatening to break through his chest. He wasn't just watching this maniac hurt Hannah—he was doing it in real time.

Draper moved to sit on the side of the bed, stroking Hannah's hair. But she jerked away from him, her eyes flying open. Harrison's heart rejoiced. She was still alive. Draper bent low, whispering something in her ear. And she turned away. And he stabbed the knife deep into the skin between her shoulder and chest.

Hannah's eyes closed as she bit off a scream, her body tensing as the pain lanced through her. Harrison slammed his fist into the table, feeling like his nerves were going to jump out of his skin.

Draper's hand remained on the knife embedded in Hannah's shoulder, his eyes steely, focused. He was still talking, his voice muffled by the distance. Harrison forced himself to shut out the horror—to concentrate. He adjusted the feed for sound, focusing on the timbre of Draper's voice. The words became clearer.

"Talk to me, pretty Hannah," Draper was saying. "Or better yet, talk to your boyfriend." He nodded toward the camera. "Before it's time for you to say good-bye."

Hannah's eyes flashed open, and even with the distortion of the shadows, he could see her determination. She opened her mouth, but no sound emerged. He could see her fingers digging into the mattress as she struggled to find strength. He willed her to speak. His entire being focused on the screen above him.

"I...just..." she began, her voice barely a whisper.

He hit the sound button, pushing it all the way to the top, feverishly working to adjust the levels.

"I want to tell him that I'll..." she sucked in a strangled breath. "...that I'll always remember the night at GTAHAS...when he told me..." She faded and then roused herself with a small shake of her head. "...when he told me that he loved me..."

Her voice was growing stronger. "...in the gazebo..." she paused, this time seeming to gather her thoughts "with the girls...singing...I was beneath...beneath him...in a yellow...dress..." The words faded on a sigh, and Hannah closed her eyes again, whatever strength she'd summoned clearly deserting her.

Draper stared at the camera for a moment, then reached back to twist the knife. A shudder rippled through Hannah's body, but she didn't scream. And Draper turned back to the camera, leering into the screen. "An eye for an eye—" he said.

Then he hit a button on the console in his other hand, and the feed went dead.

For a brief moment, Hannah forgot where she was, her mind filled instead with the smell of bacon and pancakes. *Harrison.* She smiled at the memory. Their night together had been so wonderful. So magical. She started to stretch, and the pain superseded everything else—searing, unbearable agony. She struggled to hold on to the image of Harrison. Of his strength and his love. But another face filled her brain.

Draper's.

Her eyes flickered open, and her gaze darted around the room as she searched for him. But her prison was empty. Maybe he'd finished with her—leaving her to die. But even as she had the thought, she knew that it wasn't true. Madison had told them. Every cut, every slice, was part of a plan. A way to inflict the maximum amount of pain. There was no way he was finished with her.

It would be too easy.

He still wanted more. And he'd take it. She tried to remember the rest of what Tracy and Madison had said. The cyber killer tortured his victims for at least twenty-four hours. She had no idea how long it had been—but she also knew that, with A-Tac searching, he'd most likely speed up the timetable.

Maybe that should be a relief. The thought resonated in her head, and she rebelled against it. She wanted to live. She needed to live. Angry, she tried to raise her head, but the effort was simply too much, the pain spiking with the movement. She stopped moving, concentrating instead on breathing. She needed to keep her blood pressure down.

There was no question that she was dying, bleeding to death. Slowly, but inevitably, if she didn't get to a hospital. Time was running out. But he hadn't brought her here to leave her to die alone. Draper would definitely be back. He'd want to witness life slipping away from her. And he'd want to make it as painful as possible.

At least she had the satisfaction of knowing that she'd be leaving him frustrated. That she hadn't given in to her fear—depriving him of the terror he needed so desperately to get himself off. If she was going down, she sure as hell wasn't giving him the satisfaction he craved.

She swallowed, pushing thoughts of Draper aside. It was better to try to use the respite to build her strength. So instead she visualized Harrison. His oddly colored eyes, one brown, the other green. And his hair—the way it curled over his ears, and the way he ran his fingers through it when he was frustrated or tired. She pictured his smile—crooked and endearing.

God, she loved him so much. It had snuck up on her. Surprising her with its intensity and passion. But nevertheless, she'd never been more certain of anything in her life. She was in love with Harrison Blake.

She laughed at the irony, wincing at the pain. Typical that she'd realize how very much she cared only when it was too late.

But there was still an inkling of hope.

She turned her head so that she could see the yellow sign. She still hadn't figured out the significance of the color, but she knew that it mattered, so she'd included it in the clues she'd given Harrison. Of course, he could be dismissing everything she'd said as pain-induced rambling, but she prayed that he'd understand. Hear her words for what they really were. If they didn't come soon...

She closed her eyes, the pain overwhelming her now. In front of her, with her mind's eye, she could see an open door. And she longed to go there. It had saved her when she was a child. And now, she knew it offered an escape from the pain. But if she crossed the threshold, she knew that this time, she might not come back.

So as much as she longed for the solace it offered, she turned away, forcing herself to remain conscious. All she had to do was wait.

Harrison would come. He had to come.

"I'm telling you, she's trying to tell us something," Harrison said, turning away from the images projected onto the screen to the team assembled around the conference table. They'd moved to the war room. Everyone present, the enormity of figuring out Hannah's clues better served with all of them working together.

He knew they were working against time, the fact that Hannah was bleeding to death also playing into the schedule in Draper's twisted mind. The break in the feed had scared him at first, but Tracy was certain that it was because Draper wanted to stretch the moment—build the fear.

So they were frantically trying to figure out what Hannah had truly meant to say.

"How can you be sure," Tyler asked, her voice gentle. "She's in a great deal of pain. She could have just been talking nonsense."

"No." Harrison said. "I know her. She'd never waste the opportunity like that. Look at her eyes." He pointed to the frame frozen on the screen. "She's alert. She's thinking, for God's sake."

"All right then." Avery nodded. "Let's figure it out."

"I've made a transcript," Simon said. He was sitting in Hannah's place, using her computer console, the effect jarring, but under the circumstances, necessary. "I'll put it up on the screen."

Hannah's words looked even more bizarre on the screen, but Harrison forced himself to try to look at them rationally.

"So what do you see?" Drake asked.

"Well, first off, she's making it up," he said. "Because I haven't told her I love her yet. At least not in so many words..." He trailed off, knowing that he'd revealed too much, but then suddenly he realized he didn't care who the hell knew. He loved her. So fucking what?

"Which you think she said to get you to pay attention." Tracy stared up at the screen, frowning as she, too, tried to make sense of seeming nonsense.

"Exactly. And look at the way some words stand out," he said, pointing to the places where she'd paused, marked on the screen with ellipses. "Especially in the middle when her voice gets stronger."

"Okay. So we need to break it down." Drake was pacing in the back of the room, but he stopped now, studying the words on the screen. "Did you guys go to GTAHAS?"

"Is there even such a thing as GTAHAS?" Simon asked, his expression skeptical as he mangled the acronym.

"It's GA-TA-HAS," Tyler said, pronouncing it for him.

"It's a party we have every year here. The dorms all participate. It stands for Good Things Are Happening At Sunderland. There's a big basketball game and the dorms compete in contests. It's steeped in tradition."

"Okay..." Simon said, clearly still not quite understanding. "So did you guys go?"

"No. But see how she pauses when she says 'GTAHAS'?" Harrison asked. "I think it means she's emphasizing the word or the event."

"All right," Simon said, moving the cursor to highlight and underline the acronym. "Next she talks about you telling her you love her. Which we've talked about. So the next break is at gazebo." Again he looked at the group askance, clearly still too new to Sunderland to recognize all the landmarks.

"The gazebo sits between the girls' dorms. It's used a lot for various functions," Avery mused, "but not as far as I can remember for GTAHAS."

"The next break is after girls," Simon continued. "Do the girls sing at GTAHAS? Or at the gazebo?"

"No to both," Tyler said, shaking her head. "It's the boys who sing. For shirttail serenade. And it's not at GTAHAS, and they start out at the gazebo but they spend most of their time at each of the women's dorms individually."

"Okay." Simon frowned. "So far we've got an event that Harrison and Hannah never attended together and a gazebo that doesn't play into the party either. And we've got girls who don't actually sing. And next up we have Hannah beneath you in a yellow dress—emphasis on 'beneath' and possibly 'dress.'" He underlined both words along with "gazebo" and "girls."

"Well, that helped," Drake said, his frustration fueled by anger. "What the fuck are we doing in here? We need to be out there looking for her."

"I understand where you're coming from," Avery consoled, "but Harrison's right. Hannah wouldn't waste words. We have to believe she's trying to tell us where she is. So all of us need to focus."

Drake nodded, pulling out a chair and straddling it, his eyes on the screen again. "Well, there's no way Hannah would ever wear a dress unless she absolutely had to—yellow or otherwise."

"So yellow is probably the key," Tracy said, as Simon removed "dress" and underlined "yellow."

"Okay, let's start with the fact that there's no way Hannah could know that we know that she's somewhere on campus." Harrison frowned, his mind working to decipher the clues. "So she'd need to tell us."

"GTAHAS," Simon said, pronouncing it correctly this time.

"Exactly." Harrison felt a stirring of hope. "And by talking about the gazebo—particularly when it has nothing to do with GTAHAS, she's pointing us in a direction."

"The word 'girls' would seem to substantiate that as well," Tracy added. "You said the gazebo was between the girls' dorms, right? How many are there?"

"Three," Avery replied. "Varsley, Regan, and Gallant."

"Is any one of them closer to the gazebo than the others?" Tracy asked.

"No." Harrison shook his head, hope fading. "And there's still the words 'beneath' and 'yellow.'"

"Wait a minute," Tyler said, jumping up so quickly she knocked her chair over. "Varsley. It's got to be Varsley. I was their sponsor a couple of years back. For GTAHAS, actually. Anyway, the point is that all of the dorms have colors. They use them for intramural sports, for posters—basically, anytime they want something to signify who they are. And Varsley's primary color is yellow."

"So we're thinking she's being held in Varsley?" Simon asked. "But aren't there still people in residence?"

"No," Avery said. "When I closed the campus, the dorms were the first places we cleared."

"And she's not *in* the dorm," Harrison said, the last highlighted word suddenly making sense. "She's *beneath* it."

Drake pushed to his feet, but before anyone could move, the video feed sprang to life again.

"Son of a bitch," Harrison said, his heart constricting. Hannah was still bound, but Draper had retied her feet—each one now secured to the posts at the end of the bed. It could only mean one thing. He was planning to rape her. And rape was the last thing he did before killing his victims.

"Harrison, can you interrupt the feed?" Avery asked, pulling him away from the hellish image on the screen, the other team members already springing into action, Drake and Tyler heading for the door.

"If I can tap into the computer he's using to broadcast, then it's possible."

"And would he know it?"

"Yeah. He'll be monitoring to make sure we're actually getting live footage. If I interrupt the feed, it'll show up on his computer, too."

"Well, if you can interrupt it, then maybe Draper will stop to try to reconnect. After all, he wants you as a witness. That could buy us enough time to get to her."

"But I can't stay here," Harrison protested. "I have to be there—I have to go to her."

"You have to do whatever it takes to help her," Avery countered.

"I can do it," Simon said, his voice commanding attention. "I've done this kind of thing before. And Harrison's already handled the hard part. I just have to follow the path he left for me until I find the original IP address Draper's using." He was already typing. "From there, it's all about satellites. I promise I can do this. You guys go."

Harrison grabbed his gun, and after shooting Simon a grateful look, followed the rest of the team out the door.

CHAPTER 30

Hannah was losing control, the pain winning the day. It filled every part of her mind. Taunting her. Threatening her very existence. Draper had cut her again, this time the knife sliding just between her ribs. She could feel the life draining out of her, her blood soaking into the mattress beneath her. It wouldn't be long now.

He'd retied her legs, spreading them apart. His intentions obvious. After everything she'd been through as a child, the idea didn't particularly frighten her. What scared her was the fact that this would be her last memory. The very last thing she thought about.

He approached her slowly, his gaze moving from her head to her feet. His eyes were cold—lifeless. This wasn't about passion. It was about control. He hated everything she stood for. And now he was going to destroy her.

He hit her, waiting for her to respond, but she refused. There was no way she was giving in to him. No way she would show her fear.

Behind him, the computer beeped insistently, the sound oddly out of place in the shadow-filled room.

He spun around with a curse, moving to the machine.

Hannah closed her eyes—accepting the reprieve, but knowing it wouldn't be enough. Her time had run out. The door inside her mind beckoned her, the light spilling out from it warm and inviting. It would be so easy now to let go. To walk into the warmth. Accept the solace it offered.

She could hear Draper moving again. It wouldn't be long now before he came back. She had fought a good fight, but it hurt so badly. And there was only more to come. Better to surrender. To go where she knew she'd be safe. Her mind had protected her from the horrors of her childhood. Now it would protect her from the grisly reality of her death.

So she let go, falling through the door like Alice through the mirror—the white light warm and enveloping.

"It has to be here," Harrison said, consulting the blueprint he'd downloaded to his phone. They'd searched Varsley's basement twice, finding nothing except the remnants of Varsley's past—a lot of it tinted yellow—but nothing to point to where Hannah could be.

So now they were turning to the tunnels. Except that Varsley's had been sealed off years ago, and where the door was supposed to have been, there was nothing but wallboard covered with stacks of boxes and shelving—all of it coated with a thick layer of dust.

"Maybe he came in from another direction," Tyler suggested.

"There's got to be at least seven different ways one

could have accessed the building through the original tunnels, and no way to know which ones are passable and which have been completely sealed off." He scrolled through the pages again looking for something he might have missed.

"We're running out of time," Drake said to no one in particular.

"Simon, are you still jamming the feed?" Avery asked, speaking into his comlink.

"Yes." The bud in Harrison's ear crackled to life. "It's down. But I'm not going to be able to jam it much longer. I'd say only a couple more minutes. I'm bouncing off a satellite that's moving out of range."

"Copy that," Avery responded. "We need to keep moving, people."

"Well, there isn't time to explore every other access point to the tunnels," Nash said. "So I say we break through the wall."

"Won't be necessary," Tyler said, pointing to a free-standing shelf behind a stack of boxes. "That shelf is empty. And look, the wallboard behind it isn't attached. The kids must have figured out how to get in."

Harrison and Nash shoved the boxes aside, and then Tyler and Drake moved the shelving. It took only seconds to pull away the wallboard—it wasn't attached at all. Behind it, the framework of a metal door emerged. It was locked. But Avery made short work of it with three well-placed shots, the silencer on his gun keeping the action fairly quiet. Guns drawn, the team fell into place, flanking the door on either side. Avery reached out and pulled it open, Harrison moving into the tunnel, Drake and Nash right behind him.

The brick-lined corridor stretched out ahead of them, all but the first couple of feet shrouded in shadow. After Avery and Tyler had joined them, Harrison flipped on his tac-light, the beam cutting through the darkness. This part of the tunnel extended about twenty yards and then dead-ended into a wall of brick and earth. A cave-in. But just before the pile of rubble, there was a tiny slit of light. A door. Harrison's heart rate ratcheted up. They were close, he could feel it.

He killed the tac-light, and the team, on Avery's command, began to move forward. The tunnel was quiet, the only sound coming from water dripping from the ceiling, the floor slick with it.

"We're down to seconds, guys," Simon's voice crackled in his ear. "If you're going to make a move, do it now."

Avery nodded, motioning everyone into place.

"We're out in three... two... one," Simon warned.

There was another moment of silence as they inched forward, and then Hannah screamed. Everyone moved at once, Harrison and Avery bursting through the door, guns leveled. At first, all Harrison saw was the blood. It was everywhere. But then he saw Hannah, still tied to the bed, and still alive. Her eyes were closed, but she fought against Draper, who was holding a knife.

"If you take another step, I'll gut her like a pig," Draper threatened, not even bothering to turn to look at them.

"But if you kill her, then you lose your power," Avery said, his eyes signaling Harrison to shift to the left, blocking Draper's view of Nash, who was standing just outside the doorway. "As soon as she's dead, so are you."

"Maybe I don't care," Draper hissed.

"You don't want her," Harrison said, holstering his gun and raising his hands as he inched closer. "You want me. This is between us, Draper. Let her go."

The man looked at him then with a calculated smile, and it was everything that Harrison could do not to reach for his gun to shoot. Any move he made Draper would see. And he still had the knife to Hannah.

"Come on, Jeremy. Surely, we can settle this ourselves. We don't need her. Hell, we don't need anyone." Harrison had no idea what he was saying. He just needed to keep the man listening until he could move into place and give Nash a shot.

"I needed someone," Draper snapped. "I needed Eileen."

"But you killed her, Jeremy," Avery said, tilting his head slightly. Harrison moved a little to the left, Draper's attention now on Avery.

"I couldn't stop myself. It was his fault." He jerked his head toward Harrison. "He brought it all back."

Harrison moved into position, eyes on Draper, as he lowered his hand to signal Nash and then rolled to the left out of range as his friend fired. The bullet tore through Draper's chest, and he lifted both hands in surprise, dropping the knife to the floor. With a fluid motion, surprising in such a big man, Avery grabbed Draper before he could fall on Hannah, pushing him back against the wall.

Harrison rushed to her side, calling her name as he cut her bindings and Tyler searched for a pulse.

"I've got it," Tyler said, her voice triumphant. "But it's really thready. We need to get her out of here now. She's bleeding out."

"Draper?" Harrison asked, his eyes still locked on

Hannah as he ripped off his jacket, using it as a makeshift bandage to apply pressure to the worst of Hannah's wounds.

"Dead," Avery responded. "Good fucking riddance." He pulled off his coat, draping it over Hannah, the gesture filled with respect.

"I'm here, sweetheart," Harrison said. "And you're safe. Draper's dead. You've just got to hang on." He couldn't lose her. Not like this. Not again.

"Simon," Drake barked into the comlink. "We need an ambulance. Now. In front of Varsley."

"Already ahead of you," Simon replied. "They're on their way."

Without further discussion, Tyler, Nash, Drake, and Avery moved to the corners of the mattress. "On my count," Avery said. "One. Two. Three." They lifted the mattress, and Hannah moaned, but didn't open her eyes.

Harrison moved alongside her as they carried the mattress down the corridor back into the basement. By the time they'd reached the stairs, the EMTs were there, replacing Harrison's bandage with a pressure tourniquet and hanging a line to give her fluids. She was so pale. And her hands were so cold.

"We're ready," one of the EMTs said. And Harrison stepped back as they picked up the stretcher, Avery and Nash helping to carry her up the stairs. Once at the top, they shifted her to a gurney and rolled her outside to the ambulance. At the doors, Harrison hesitated, suddenly feeling unworthy. What if he'd been too late?

"Go," Tyler said, shoving him forward. "We'll meet you at the hospital. *Go.*"

He climbed into the ambulance, settling down beside

her, reaching for her hand—praying for the first time since his sister had died.

It looked like an A-Tac wing, what with all the people standing or sitting in the waiting room just outside the operating theater. Besides the team members who'd rescued Hannah, Annie had flown in from Montreal to be there. Along with Alexis, Tucker, and Madeline from California. And Owen, Tyler's husband, had arrived an hour or so ago, straight from some classified mission for Homeland Security. Lara had even called from South America. They all wanted to be there for Hannah.

And surprisingly, Harrison realized, for him.

He rose from his chair, too jumpy to sit still, pacing back and forth across the room. Hannah had been in surgery more than seven hours now, and Harrison was having trouble containing his anxiety. She'd lost a lot of blood, and the damage to her internal organs was significant. Draper's death had been too easy.

"Any word?" Annie asked, coming in with a cardboard container full of coffee cups.

"Nothing," Harrison said, shaking his head when she offered him a cup.

"You should eat something," Madeline said, her swelling stomach indicating that impending motherhood had magnified her natural tendency to nurture.

"Leave him alone," Drake cautioned. "The waiting's hard enough without the two of you hovering."

"I know," Madeline acknowledged, reaching over to pat her husband's hand. "It's just hard when there's nothing to do." Her words echoed what they all were feeling.

"It's not like we haven't been here before," Avery said,

his face etched with worry. “It seems like lately all we do is wait for the doctors to tell us someone is going to be okay.”

Tyler and Owen exchanged a look, Tyler reaching up to touch the scar just beneath her breast. She’d almost died during an attack in Colombia. As had Madeline.

“Yes, but we’re survivors,” Alexis said, with conviction, having made it through more than her fair share of danger. Most of it with Tucker and Harrison in tow. “And Hannah is one, too.”

He smiled over at her, grateful for her words, again feeling the bond of family.

Tucker came to stand behind his wife, his hands on her shoulders. “Alexis is right. As long as we have each other, we can deal with anything.”

“Even the Consortium.” Simon’s face hardened with the thought of the people that had started this whole episode rolling. “We’re going to find them. And then we’re going to destroy them.”

“For Hannah,” Annie said. “And Jason.”

“For all of us,” Avery added. “They have no idea the sleeping tiger they’ve awakened.”

“Well, believe me, it’ll be my pleasure to show them,” Nash said, fire flashing in his eyes. “Whatever it takes, we’ll run them to ground.”

“While I support the sentiment,” Annie said, her hand on Nash’s arm, “this isn’t the time.”

“Annie’s right,” Madeline agreed. “Enough with the plans for revenge. Right now we just need to concentrate on those doctors in there bringing Hannah back to us.”

Harrison sighed, his mind playing games with him. If only he’d never been involved with the cyber killer. If only he hadn't come to A-Tac. If only he'd taken Hannah with him when he went to check the explosion. If only he'd told her he loved her.

"She knows how much you care," Alexis said, covering his hand with hers. "Women are built like that. I guess God knew we'd need to be able to read the things you guys can't say."

He nodded, words deserting him. He could see Hannah in his mind's eye, her blue eyes challenging him as they argued about some piece of software or intel. A smile lurking at the corner of her mouth. Her hair going every which way, streaks of some color or another making her look more like a character from Harry Potter than a CIA agent.

He couldn't imagine her not being a part of his life.

"Harrison," Avery called, and he looked up to see a scrubs-clad doctor walking out of the double doors.

He stood up, swallowing, his throat dry, his hands clammy. *Please, God*, he prayed, knowing that he'd promise anything—do anything—if only she were okay.

"It was touch and go," the doctor said as they all gathered around. "As you know, there was a lot of damage. And she'd lost a lot of blood. But we managed to repair everything."

"So she'll have a full recovery?" Owen asked, putting Harrison's tumbling thoughts into words.

The doctor shook his head, his expression not giving anything away. "It's too early to say for sure. She's in a coma right now. And while we have every reason to believe she'll come out of it, her system has been through a hell of a shock. And sometimes," he said, not pulling any punches, "people just can't come back from that."

Harrison nodded, fists clenched as he tried to deal with his rising fear.

"The next twenty-four hours are key," the doctor offered.

"She's going to be okay," Nash said, his hand on Harrison's shoulder.

"When can I see her?" Harrison asked, his voice raspy with emotion.

"Right now, she needs rest," the doctor said. "We're restricting visitors to family only."

Harrison opened his mouth, but Avery was faster. "We're the only family she has." The big man didn't leave room for argument, and the doctor acquiesced.

"Fine, but we'll need to limit it to one at a time."

"You go," Avery said to Harrison. "She'll want to see you first. And don't worry, we'll be here when you come out."

Harrison sucked in a fortifying breath and followed the doctor down the hall into the recovery room. She looked so goddamned small. There were bandages and tubes and machines surrounding her. All of his life he'd been the one to solve the problems. Physical, technical, whatever. He was always the go-to guy. And now he just felt helpless.

He sat in the chair by her bed, taking her hand in his, tears filling his eyes. "I love you so much, Hannah," he whispered. "More than I could ever have believed. And I can't imagine my life without you. So you've got to fight. Do you hear me? You're the strongest woman I know. Fight for me, Hannah. Fight for us."

Hannah sat back, basking in the warmth of the light. The breeze carried the smell of flowers, the air carrying the soft music of a garden, the hum of a bee providing melody, the bass courtesy of a cricket. Tympani from a frog.

She couldn't remember how long she'd been here. Or even why she'd come. Just that she'd chosen this place. And that it was a sanctuary. There was no pain. There was no fear. There was only endless peace.

And yet somehow, somewhere, in the back of her mind, she had the feeling that there was something more. Something she was missing. It was a silly thought. What could be better than the endless beauty before her? This was where she belonged. Where no one could hurt her.

Or love her.

The words were jarring, and the music stopped, the light dimming. And she rose from the bench, the white walls fading as she took a step forward, remembering.

Harrison.

Harrison.

She loved him. And she was pretty damn certain he loved her, too. Hadn't he just told her so? The thought drew her up short. The memory fading. The light strengthening again. Harrison wasn't here. He couldn't have told her anything.

But he had. She could hear his voice. Hear the words. He'd asked her to fight. For him. For them. She could see the door now. And as before, she made her choice. Falling out of her sanctuary as easily as she'd fallen in.

The world faded to a fuzzy gray, and she could feel the distant thrumming of pain. Hear the mechanical beeps of a hospital monitor. And she could feel Harrison's hand wrapped around hers.

By sheer force of will, she opened her eyes. He was sleeping, his head slumped onto the edge of her bed. And she smiled, lifting her other hand to caress his cheek. His eyes flickered open, recognition dawning.

"Hannah," he said, his voice hoarse with emotion. "You're here. You're awake."

She nodded, feeling alive, as if everything was only just beginning, here and now, with him. "And, Harrison," she whispered, "I love you, too."

EPILOGUE

So are you happy?" Harrison asked, offering Hannah another beer from the bucket in the sand beside them. The breeze washed over them, the sun shining down on the azure water as the waves washed onto the shore. Above them, gulls circled, their cries plaintive as they waited for some sign of supper.

They'd been in Bali for almost three weeks. And it had been a magical trip. The two of them alone together in paradise. To everyone's delight, Hannah had come back full force, surprising even her doctors with the speed of her recovery. She credited it all to Harrison's ministrations, but he knew that it was her spirit that had prevailed.

"I can't remember ever feeling so contented," she replied, squeezing fresh lime into the bottle. "I've got beer. I've got shelter." She waved at their cabana behind them. "And I've got you." She sighed, her fingers twining with his. "The only fly in the ointment is that our time's almost up."

"We could stay," he suggested. "Or we can start a new adventure. I'm game for whatever you are." He waited, not sure what she'd say. She'd been through a horrible ordeal, and though outwardly she'd recovered, he wasn't as certain that she'd healed on the inside. The truth was that he wasn't sure she'd ever want to go back to their old life. And he was prepared to honor that. Although he wasn't as certain of the other team members. He knew that they were ready for her to come home. But it had to be Hannah's call.

"I mean it," he said, reaching over to push a strand of hair behind her ear. It had grown long over the past few months. And he kind of liked it that way, although sometimes he missed the streaks of fuchsia and purple. "We can go wherever you want. Do whatever you want."

"Anything?" She smiled provocatively.

"Well, that's a given," he said, leaning over to kiss her, her lips tasting of citrus and beer. "But we can't stay here forever."

"Just as well." She sighed. "I'd hate to think we'd be content growing soft." She took a sip of beer and he watched the movement of her throat, his body tightening with seemingly insatiable need.

"So..." he prompted, "where are we off to?"

She pulled off her sunglasses and turned to him with a smile. "Home. Where else? I'm feeling the need to kick some Consortium ass."

"Good answer," Drake Flynn said, walking across the sand carrying a cooler. Nash, Annie, and Adam were right behind them, Adam tossing a beach ball into the air. And beyond them, Harrison could see Avery and Owen walking with Tyler and the rest of the team. "You didn't think we were going to let you have all the fun, did you?"

Hannah just smiled, jumping up to take the ball from Adam. And Harrison sighed, relishing the moment. Hannah had been correct. He had everything he needed right here. Beer, shelter, his friends—and the woman he loved. His gaze locked on Hannah, his heart swelling with the magnitude of his feelings. Hell, it couldn't get any better than that.

CHAPTER 1

New York City, Hospital for Special Surgery

"So on a scale of one to ten, how would you rank the pain?" Dr. Weinman asked as he probed the deep scars running across Simon's thigh.

"Three," Simon said, fighting against a grimace, pain radiating up into his hip.

"So a six." The doctor released the leg and scribbled something on his chart.

Simon opened his mouth to argue, but Weinman smiled. "Look, I've been patching up people like you for most of my career. Which means I'm more than aware that in your world, a three would definitely be a six for the rest of us. God's honest truth, probably more like an eight or nine."

"Apples to oranges," Simon said, his smile bitter. "The rest of you wouldn't have a leg full of shrapnel. So am I cleared for duty?" The long hike through the Afghan mountains plus the stress of the firefight had aggravated his injury, his pronounced limp causing Avery to send him to the orthopedist for a look-see.

"Yeah." Weinman shrugged. "You're good to go. There's no new damage. But I'm afraid as long as you insist on engaging in the kind of *work* you do, there's always going to be risk. And sooner or later, there's going to be additional injury. So it's not a matter of if, but when."

"Nothing I didn't already know," Simon said, jumping off the table to get dressed.

"I assume you're still working with the PT?" the doctor asked, glancing up over the top of his glasses.

"Actually, I'm not. With the new job, there just isn't time to come all the way into the city. But Sunderland has a great gym. And I've memorized the moves by now. So it's easy enough for me to work out on my own."

"Well, I suppose that'll have to do," the doctor said, still scribbling in the chart. "Just be careful not to push too hard. Do you need something for the pain?"

"No, I'm good." Simon shook his head as he shrugged into his shirt. The pain meds only dulled his brain, slowing his reflexes. And in his line of work, that wasn't an option. Besides, he prided himself on being tough.

"There's nothing dishonorable about managing pain," Weinman said, correctly reading Simon's train of thought.

"Look, I said I'm fine." Simon blew out a breath, forcing a smile. The doc was only trying to help.

And if Simon were truly being honest, he'd have to admit that sometimes, in the middle of the night when the pain threatened to overwhelm him, the pills were his only ticket to oblivion. But he'd seen what had happened to men he'd fought with when the meds had taken control. And he wasn't about to let himself go there. No matter how fucking much it hurt.

"It's up to you." Weinman shrugged, closing the chart and rising to his feet. "But if you change your mind, I'm only a telephone call away."

"Good to know. But I'll be okay."

"All right then. We're done." Weinman paused, his gaze assessing. "Until next time." Leaving the words hanging, he turned and left the room, and Simon blew out a long breath.

The bottom line was that he knew he was on borrowed time. His injuries had been severe enough to force him out of the SEALs. And sooner or later, they were probably going to mean an end to his career with A-Tac, at least in the field.

But for now, he was determined to carry on. He was a soldier. Pure and simple. And just because he could no longer be a SEAL, he didn't have to settle for some piddly-ass desk job. A-Tac was as good as it got when it came to working counter-terrorism. And he was lucky to have found a home there.

And he sure as hell wasn't going to fuck it up by letting his injury get in the way. Anyway, all that mattered now was that he was good to go. Which meant he could get back to Sunderland—and the hunt for the Consortium.

He walked out of the exam room, striding down the hall, ignoring the twinge of pain shooting up his leg. Compared to a year ago, this was a cakewalk. And the way he figured, another year and it would hardly be noticeable. Everyone in his line of work lived with injury. It was part of the package. It just wasn't something most people could understand. Their idea of the fast lane was eating fried food on a Saturday night—his was perpetrating a raid on an Afghan terrorist encampment.

He waved at the receptionist as he walked through the waiting room and pushed through the doors to the clinic. Dr. Weinman's offices were on an upper floor of the hospital, the corridor leading to the elevator lined with windows looking out over the FDR and the East River. Outside, beyond the congestion of traffic, the river was flowing out toward the harbor. A tugboat, barge in tow, was making its laborious way upstream. Above the swiftly flowing water, the skyline of Long Island City stood illuminated against the bold blue sky.

It was the kind of day that made a kid want to skip school. And suddenly Simon was struck with the thought that everything was right with his world: the past firmly behind him and the future beckoning bright. It had been a long time since he'd felt hopeful about anything. Hell, with his past, who could blame him? But maybe it was time to move on. There wasn't much point in letting the past or the future hold too much sway. Better to live in the now.

He laughed at the philosophical turn of his thoughts. Had to be the hospital. All that life and death crap. He stopped for a moment at the door to a large waiting room. Inside, a small army of what looked like nurses were triaging patients, most of them non-ambulatory, with bleeding wounds and broken limbs.

Of course, the blood was fake, and the moaning and groaning more about theatrics than pain. A disaster drill. He'd seen a notice in the elevator on the way up. Judging from the chaos ensuing inside the room, he'd have to assume it wasn't going all that well. But if it had been the real thing, the hysteria would have been much worse.

But this was just play-acting, and, thankfully, he didn't have a role to play. With a rueful smile, he turned to go, then stopped, his brain conjuring the picture of a blue-eyed blonde in blue scrubs.

Frowning, he turned around again, certain that the image must be wrong. That his mind had merely superimposed a memory onto a stranger. He rubbed his leg absently as his gaze settled again on the woman. She had her back to him, her sun-streaked ponytail bobbing as she talked to another woman wearing scrubs. She was waving her hands, her slim fingers giving additional meaning to her words.

Even from behind, he knew that his instinct had been dead-on. It was in the way she stood, the way she moved. He'd have known her anywhere. And then she turned, as if somehow she'd felt his presence, her eyes widening in surprise and then shuttering as she recognized him.

His mind screamed retreat, but his feet moved forward, taking him across the room until they were standing inches apart. Behind her, out the window, he could still see the river, the blue of the sky almost the same color as her eyes.

"J.J.?" he queried, the words coming out a gruff whisper, his mind and body still on overdrive as he tried to make sense of her being here in New York.

"I go by 'Jillian' now," she said, her voice just as he'd remembered. Low and throaty. Sexy. "It's easier." There was a touch of bitterness in her words and a tightness around her mouth that he'd never seen before.

He paused, not exactly sure what to say. It had been a long time. And he hadn't thought he'd see her again. Memories flooded through him. The smell of her hair. The feel of her skin beneath his fingers. An image of her standing with Ryan in her wedding dress, eyes full of questions, Simon's heart shriveling as he chose loyalty over everything else.

J.J. was Ryan's girl. She'd always been his. Since they were practically kids. And one drunken night couldn't change that fact. Ryan was his best friend.

And he'd failed him twice. Once an eon ago on a hot summer night, and the second time, years later, in a compound in Somalia. He'd managed to avert disaster the first time, common sense and loyalty overriding his burgeoning libido. But in Somalia, he hadn't been so lucky, and because of his decisions, Ryan was dead. J.J. had lost her husband. And there was nothing Simon could do to make it right.

"I can't believe you're standing here," he said, shaking his head. "It's been a while since I saw you last."

"Five years," she replied, the words a recrimination.

"You look the same," he said, wishing to hell he'd never seen her. He didn't need this.

Again she laughed, but this time with humor. "You always were a flatterer."

"Yeah, well, I guess some things never change," he said, studying her face. There were faint lines at the corners of her eyes and mouth. And her hair was longer and slightly darker than before. But over all, she looked like the girl he remembered. Except for the smile.

J.J. had always been smiling, dimples flashing. Or at least that's the way he'd chosen to remember her. But the last time he'd seen her, she'd been anything but happy. He remembered the pain on her face as she'd accepted the flag that had been draped across Ryan's casket. Simon had promised to come by later that day. But instead he'd left town. And never looked back.

"You look good too," she said, her eyes moving across his face. "So what brings you to the hospital?"

"Checkup." He sighed, absently rubbing his injured

leg. "But it's all good. I'm healthy as a horse." *And babbling like a fucking idiot.* She'd always been able to reduce him to baser levels.

"I'm glad," she said. "I heard you left the team."

"Didn't have much of a choice." He shrugged. "But I landed on my feet, and I'm doing okay. What about you? You a nurse now?"

"Something like that." She nodded. "Speaking of which, I suppose I ought to be getting back to it."

"Right," he said, the silence that followed stretching awkwardly between them.

And then with an apologetic shrug, she turned back to her "patients," and Simon forced himself to walk away. Hell, the past was better left buried. Hadn't he just been having that exact thought?

He stepped back into the corridor and then, despite himself, turned for a last look. She was bending over a man with a rudimentary splint on his arm, her fingers gentle as she probed the imaginary wound.

Almost involuntarily, his gaze rose to the window, his senses sending out an alert. A high-pitched whine filled the room, the glass on the windows shaking. The sky disappeared as the window turned black. For a moment everything seemed to move in slow motion. And then all hell broke loose as the windows shattered and something rammed through the side of the building, the walls shredding like corrugated paper.

People screamed, and Simon called her name. "J.J.—*Jillian*."

One minute she was standing there, eyes wide with confusion and fear.

And the next, she was gone.

THE DISH

Where authors give you the inside scoop!

From the desk of Vicky Dreiling

Dear Reader,

HOW TO RAVISH A RAKE stars shy wallflower Amy Hardwick and charming rake William Darcett, better known as "the Devil." I thought it would be great fun to feature two characters who seem so wrong for one another on the surface but who would find love and happiness, despite their differences.

Miss Amy Hardwick is a shy belle who made her first appearance in my debut historical romance, *How to Marry a Duke*. When I first envisioned Amy, I realized that she was representative of so many young women who struggle to overcome low self-esteem. Amy doesn't fit the ideal image of the English rose in Regency Society, and, as a result, she's often overlooked by others. But as I thought back to my days in high school and college, I remembered how much it helped to have girlfriends who liked and supported you, even though you didn't have the flawless skin and perfect bodies airbrushed on the covers of teen magazines. That recollection convinced me that having friends would help Amy to grow into the woman I knew she was destined to become.

Now, during her sixth and quite possibly last London Season, Amy is determined to shed her wallflower image forever. A newfound interest in fashion leads Amy to draw designs for unique gowns that make her the fashion darling of the *ton*. All of her dreams seem to be coming true, but there's one man who could deter her from the road to transformation: Mr. William "the Devil" Darcett.

Ah, Will... *sigh*. I confess I had a penchant for charming bad boys when I was in high school and college. There's a certain mystique about them. And I'm certain that the first historical romance I ever read featured a charming bad boy. They really are my favorite type of heroes. So naturally, I decided to create the worst bad boy in the *ton* and throw him in sweet Amy's path.

William Darcett is a younger son with a passion for traveling. He's not one to put down roots—just the occupation for a bona fide rake. But Will's latest plans for another journey to the Continent go awry when he discovers his meddling family wants to curb his traveling days. Will refuses to let his family interfere with his carousing and rambling, but a chance encounter with Amy in a wine cellar leads the wallflower and the rake into more trouble than they're prepared to handle.

This very unlikely pair comes to realize that laughter, family, and honesty are the most important ingredients for everlasting love. I hope you will enjoy the adventures of Amy and Will on their journey to discover that even the unlikeliest of couples can fall madly, deeply in love.

My heartfelt thanks to all the readers who wrote to let me know they couldn't wait to read HOW TO RAVISH A RAKE. I hope you will enjoy the fun and games that finally lead to Happily Ever After for Amy and Will.

Cheers!

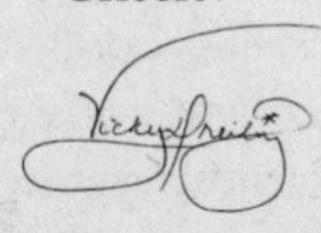

♥ ♥ ♥ ♥ ♥ ♥ ♥ ♥ ♥ ♥ ♥ ♥ ♥ ♥ ♥

From the desk of Amanda Scott

Dear Reader,

What happens when a freedom-loving Scotsman who's spent much of his life on the open sea meets an enticing heiress determined to make her home with a husband who will stay put and run her Highland estates? And what happens when something that they have just witnessed endangers the plans of a ruthless and powerful man who is fiercely determined to keep the details of that event secret?

HIGHLAND LOVER, the third title in my Scottish Knights trilogy, stars the fiercely independent Sir Jacob "Jake" Maxwell, who was a nine-year-old boy in *King of Storms*, the last of a six-book series beginning with *Highland Princess*. Lifting a fictional child from a series I wrote years ago to be a hero in a current trilogy is new for me.

However, the three heroes of Scottish Knights are friends who met as teenage students under Bishop Traill of St. Andrews and later accepted his invitation to join a brotherhood of highly skilled knights that he (fictionally) formed to help him protect the Scottish Crown. I realized straightaway that the grown-up Jake would be the right age in 1403 and would easily fit my requirements, for several reasons:

First, Jake has met the ruthless Duke of Albany, who was a villainous presence in Scotland for thirty-one years (in all) and is now second in line for the throne. Determined to become King of Scots, Albany habitually eliminates anyone who gets in his way. Second, Albany owes his life to Jake, a relationship that provides interesting twists in any tale. Third, Jake is captain of the *Sea Wolf*, a ship he owns because of Albany; and the initiating event in HIGHLAND LOVER takes place at sea. So Jake seemed to be a perfect choice. The cheeky youngster in *King of Storms* had stirred (and still stirs) letters from readers suggesting that an adult Jake Maxwell would make a great hero. Doubtless that also had something to do with it.

Jake's heroine in HIGHLAND LOVER is Lady Alyson MacGillivray of Perth, a beautiful cousin of Sir Ivor "Hawk" Mackintosh of *Highland Hero.* Alyson is blessed (or cursed) with a bevy of clinging relatives and the gift of Second Sight. The latter "gift" has caused as many problems for her as have her intrusive kinsmen.

Alyson also has another problem—a husband of just a few months whom she has scarcely seen and who so far seems more interested in his noble patron's affairs than in Alyson's Highland estates or Alyson herself. But Alyson is trapped in this wee wrinkle, is she not? It is, after all, 1403.

In any event, Jake sets out on a mission for the Bishop of St. Andrews, encounters a storm, and ends up plucking Alyson and an unknown lad from a ship sinking off the English coast two hundred miles from her home in Perth. The ship also happened to be carrying the young heir to Scotland's throne and Alyson's husband, who may or may not now be captive in England.

So, the fun begins. I hope you enjoy HIGHLAND LOVER.

Meantime, *Suas Alba!*

Amanda Scott

www.amandascottauthor.com

♥ ♥ ♥ ♥ ♥ ♥ ♥ ♥ ♥ ♥ ♥ ♥ ♥ ♥ ♥

From the desk of Dee Davis

Dear Reader,

I've been a storyteller all of my life. When I was a kid, my dad and I used to sit in the mall or a restaurant and make up stories about the people walking by or sitting around us. So it really wasn't much of a leap to find myself a novelist. But what was interesting to me was that no matter what kind of story I was telling, the characters all seemed to know each other.

Sometimes people from other novels were simply mentioned in another of my books in passing. Sometimes they actually had cameo appearances. And several times now, a character I had created to be a secondary figure in one story has demanded his or her own book. Such was the case with Harrison Blake of DEADLY DANCE. Harrison first showed up in my Last Chance series, working as that team's computer forensic expert. It even turned out he'd also worked for *Midnight Rain*'s John Brighton at his Phoenix organization, even though the company was created at the end of the book and never actually appeared on paper.

Interestingly enough, Harrison, although never a hero, has received more mail than any of my other characters. And almost all of those letters are from readers asking when he's going to have his day. So when A-Tac found itself in need of a technical guru, it was a no-brainer for me to bring Harrison into the fold. As he became an integral part of the team, I knew the time had come for him to have his own book.

And of course, as his story developed, he needed help from his old friends. So enter Madison Roarke and Tracy Braxton. Madison was the heroine of the first Last Chance book, *Endgame*. And like Harrison, Tracy had been placed in the role of supporting character, as a world-class forensic pathologist.

What can I say? It's a small world, and they all know and help each other. And finally, we add to the mix our heroine, Hannah Marshall. Hannah has been at the heart of all the A-Tac books. A long-time team member, she's always there with the answers when needed. And like Harrison, she made it more than clear to me that she deserved her own story. With her quirky way of expressing herself (eyeglasses and streaked hair) and her well-developed intellect, Hannah seemed perfect for Harrison. The two of them just didn't know it yet.

So I threw them together, and, as they say, the plot thickened, and DEADLY DANCE was born.

Hopefully you'll enjoy reading Harrison and Hannah's story as much as I did writing it.

For insight into both Harrison and Hannah, here are some songs I listened to while writing DEADLY DANCE:

Riverside, by Agnes Obel

Set Fire to the Rain, by Adele

Everlong, by Foo Fighters

And as always, check out www.deedavis.com for more inside info about my writing and my books.

Happy Reading!

♥ ♥ ♥ ♥ ♥ ♥ ♥ ♥ ♥ ♥ ♥ ♥ ♥ ♥ ♥

From the desk of Katie Lane

Dear Reader,

Before I plot out the storyline and flesh out my characters, my books start with one basic idea. Or maybe I should say they start with one nagging, persistent thought that won't leave me alone until I put it down on paper.

Going Cowboy Crazy started with the concept of long-lost twins and what would happen if one twin took over the other twin's life and no one—save the hot football coach—was the wiser.

Make Mine a Bad Boy was the other side of that premise: What would happen if your twin, whom you didn't even know you had, married your boyfriend and left you with a good-for-nothing, low-down bad boy?

And CATCH ME A COWBOY started with a melodrama. You know the kind I'm talking about, the story of a dastardly villain taking advantage of a poor, helpless woman by tying her to the railroad tracks, or placing her on a conveyor belt headed toward the jagged blade of a saw, or evicting her from her home when she has no money to pay the rent. Of course, before any of these things happen, the hero arrives to save the day with a smile so big and bright it rivals the sun.

For days, I couldn't get the melodrama out of my mind. But no matter how much the idea stuck with me, I just didn't see it fitting into my new book. My heroine had already been chosen: a favorite secondary character from the previous novels. Shirlene is a sassy, voluptuous west Texas gal who could no more play the damsel in distress than Mae West could play the Singing Nun. If someone tied Shirlene to the train tracks, she wouldn't scream, faint, or hold the back of her hand dramatically to her forehead. She'd just ask if she had enough time for a margarita.

The more I thought of my sassy heroine dealing with a Snidely Whiplash–type, the more I laughed. The more I laughed, the more I wrote. And suddenly I had my melodrama. Except a funny thing happened on the way to Shirlene's Happily Ever After: My villain and my hero got a little mixed up. And before I knew it, Shirlene had so charmed the would-be villain that he stopped the train. Shut off the saw. Paid the rent.

And how does the hero with the bright smile fit into all of this? you might ask.

Well, let's just say I don't think you'll be disappointed.

CATCH ME A COWBOY is available now.

Enjoy, y'all!

Katie Lane

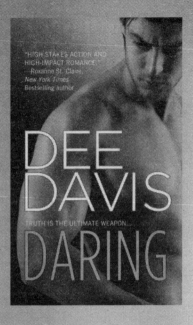